Praise for Alan Dean Foster's Founding of the Commonwealth

PHYLOGENESIS
Book One

"Foster does a fine job with his misfit heroes and even with his minor characters (such as the reptilian Aann). He shows his usual mastery of narrative pacing and slips in a great deal of wry wit. The novel will be a treat for those who have followed Foster's tales of the Humanx Commonwealth."
—*Publishers Weekly*

DIRGE
Book Two

"Fast-paced action and likable human and alien protagonists."
—*Library Journal*

DIUTURNITY'S DAWN
Book Three

"Unexpected players in this engrossing drama are the brothers, human and Thranx, of the anything but dogmatic United Church, which ministers both species with laughter and sensitivity."
—*Booklist*

By Alan Dean Foster
Published by Ballantine Books

THE BLACK HOLE
CACHALOT
DARK STAR
THE METROGNOME AND OTHER STORIES
MIDWORLD
NOR CRYSTAL TEARS
SENTENCED TO PRISM
SPLINTER OF THE MIND'S EYE
STAR TREK® LOGS ONE–TEN
VOYAGE TO THE CITY OF THE DEAD
. . . WHO NEEDS ENEMIES?
WITH FRIENDS LIKE THESE . . .
MAD AMOS
THE HOWLING STONES
PARALLELITIES
STAR WARS®: THE APPROACHING STORM
IMPOSSIBLE PLACES

The Icerigger Trilogy:
ICERIGGER
MISSION TO MOULOKIN
THE DELUGE DRIVERS

The Adventures of Flinx of the Commonwealth:
FOR LOVE OF MOTHER-NOT
THE TAR-AIYM-KRANG
ORPHAN STAR
THE END OF THE MATTER
BLOODHYPE
FLINX IN FLUX
MID-FLINX
REUNION

The Damned:
BOOK ONE: A CALL TO ARMS
BOOK TWO: THE FALSE MIRROR
BOOK THREE: THE SPOILS OF WAR

The Founding of the Commonwealth:
PHYLOGENESIS
DIRGE
DIUTURNITY'S DAWN

DIUTURNITY'S DAWN

BOOK THREE OF
THE FOUNDING OF THE COMMONWEALTH

ALAN DEAN FOSTER

BALLANTINE BOOKS • NEW YORK

Diuturnity's Dawn is a work of fiction. Names, places, and incidents either are products of the author's imagination or are used fictitiously.

This book contains an excerpt from *Drowning World* by Alan Dean Foster. This excerpt has been set for this edition only and may not reflect the final content of the book.

A Del Rey® Book
Published by The Ballantine Publishing Group

Copyright © 2002 by Thranx, Inc.

All rights reserved under International and Pan-American Copyright Conventions. Published in the United States by The Ballantine Publishing Group, a division of Random House, Inc., New York, and simultaneously in Canada by Random House of Canada Limited, Toronto.

Del Rey is a registered trademark and the Del Rey colophon is a trademark of Random House, Inc.

www.delreydigital.com

ISBN 0-345-41866-2

Manufactured in the United States of America

First Hardcover Edition: March 2002

First Mass Market Edition: February 2003

10 9 8 7 6 5 4 3

We shall not cease from exploration, and the end of all our
exploring will be to arrive where we started,
and know the place for the first time.
—T. S. Eliot, 1942

1

B~ugs~.

Hundreds of bugs. Thousands of them, many nearly as tall as she. All chittering and clicking and waving their feathery antennae at one another as they went about their daily business. Magnified by the heat and the more than 90 percent humidity they favored, the atmosphere in the teeming underground avenue was saturated with the natural perfume emitted by their massed bodies. Understandably, they stared at her, their gloriously red-and-gold compound eyes tracking her progress. When she felt it necessary, she would respond to their inquiring gazes with a *crr!lk* of acknowledgment. Astonished to hear a human speaking High Thranx, their multiple mouthparts would invariably twitch in startled response. Such moments made her smile—though she was careful not to expose her teeth. Through such small diplomacies were relations between species improved for the better.

They were not bugs, of course. Though commonly used to describe the highly intelligent insectoids, that word was typically insensitive human shorthand. The thranx were arthropods, insect*like* but internally very different from their primitive Terran look-alikes. Four-armed and four-legged, or two-armed and six-legged—depending on the needs of the moment—they had helped humankind finally defeat the invidious Pitar. That notable achievement was now more than thirty years in the past. Since then, relations between the two victorious species had improved considerably over the suspicions and uncertainty attendant upon First Contact.

Stagnated would be a more accurate description, she mused.

In certain specific instances, it could even be argued that they had decayed. As a second-level consul attached to the human embassy on Hivehom, it was the job of Fanielle Anjou and her colleagues to see that they did not worsen any further. Those who entertained higher hopes found themselves frustrated by the sluggish pace of diplomacy on both sides.

The electrostatic wicking of the shorts and shirt she wore reduced the effect of the oppressive humidity by more than half, and the electronic cooler integrated into her neatly cocked cap did much to mitigate the heat, but there was no way to pretend she was comfortable. It had been worse on the transport capsule that had brought her into the inner city, even though the commuting thranx had politely allotted her more space than they would have one of their own. As she wiped at her face, she reflected on the eternal low-tech usefulness of an absorbent handkerchief.

Diplomatic offices were on this level, but another half quadrant forward. She passed a nursery, where larval thranx were cared for and educated while awaiting metamorphosis; an eating establishment, with its rows of padded benches on which a tired thranx could stretch out on its abdomen, legs dangling comfortably on either side; and a large public information screen. The activities it proffered were utterly alien to her. Despite nearly ninety years of casual contact, and much closer interaction during the Humanx-Pitar War, humans still knew all too little about the enigmatic eight-limbed acquaintances with whom they shared the Orion Arm of the galaxy.

The public announcements that periodically echoed above the constant clacking of busy mandibles were all in Low Thranx. She had not mastered either language, but for a human, she was considered fluent—at least by her colleagues. What the thranx thought of her attempts to speak their complex language she did not know. No doubt they considered soft lips and a flexible tongue poor substitutes for hard mandibles.

At least, she thought, I can make myself understood. That was more than many of her click-challenged coworkers could claim.

An adult female with two adolescents in tow passed close

by. Unlike human postpubescents, the pair of youngsters were perfect downsized versions of the adult. They were in the premolt stage, preparing to shed their hard exoskeletons preparatory to growing into another size. Both had their antennae pointed rigidly and impolitely in the direction of the bizarre biped coming in toward them. As she strode past, Anjou overheard one chitter excitedly.

"But Birth Mother, it's so soft and pulpy! How can it stand upright like that? And on only *two* legs!"

Anjou did not hear the birth mother's answer. From what the diplomat knew of thranx culture, the reply was most likely in the form of some mild chastisement coupled with an attempt at explanation. What the latter would consist of would probably be highly imaginative. The average hive dweller knew as much about human physiology as a hydroengineer whose business it was to work on the venerable water system of London knew about a thranx's internal plumbing.

The particular burrow complex she was traversing was home to, among other segments, the Diplomatic Contact section. Its sub-burrow loomed just ahead. The main entrance, with its impressive portico of anodized metal and floating holoed worlds, presented no problem. Entering the lift and hallway that lay beyond, however, forced her to watch out for low-hanging appliances. Here her short stature was a positive advantage. Her male colleagues dreaded having to visit anything smaller than a main burrow corridor. If Jexter Henry, who stood a shade under two meters tall, wanted to spend some time in a city like Daret, his travels would be restricted to the main corridors. As a consequence, he was essentially confined to the human outpost at Azerick.

Thoughts of that establishment, of its comfortable surroundings on the temperate Mediterranea Plateau on the largest of Hivehom's four continents, did not improve her mood. At least, she reflected as she turned into a tertiary access tunnel, the Contact facilities were located in a brand-new section of the city. Being the capital not only of Hivehom but of the entire thranx expansion, Daret had been among the first burrows to transform itself from a traditional hive into a real city.

As a diplomatic representative, she had been allowed to visit the older, archeologically important sections of the metropolis, with their early nurseries, food storehouses, and primitive arsenals. She had maintained a smile—tight lipped, of course, so as not to expose her teeth—throughout, but had no desire to repeat the tour. Even to a nonclaustrophobe, the ancient quarter of the city was oppressive.

As she passed through the unobtrusive security scan, the male thranx of mid-age who had been following her ever since her arrival in Daret was at last compelled to abandon his pursuit and continue on past the entrance. He was not disappointed. Though he possessed within his backpack the means for evading the security system, now was not the time to employ it. That would come later, when the fractionated time-part was deemed right by himself and his compeers.

Even fanatics have a sense of timing.

Unaware that she had been followed, Anjou presented her thranx security chit to a series of scanners. It took her longer to gain entrance to the facility than thranx who ambled up from behind and passed her, since the automated security system had to not only verify that the pass she carried was indeed a match to her particular cerebral emissions, but that she was of the species claimed by the embedded photons. The eye scan that served to pass most thranx was of no use in identifying humans, with their oversized, single-lensed oculars.

Eventually she reached the corridor that led to Haflunormet's office. He greeted her with a cheerful click and whistle, to which she replied to the best of her increasing fluency in Low Thranx. He also inclined his head slightly forward, presenting his feathery antennae. Bowing in turn, she reached up and flicked them gently with the tips of her index fingers before allowing them to make contact with her forehead. Formalities concluded, he employed both a truhand and foothand to direct her to one of the three benches that fronted the free-form arc of his workstation. Composed of a wondrously light yet strong beryllium-titanium alloy, it was anodized with a flux that gave it the look of a dark, fine-grained wood.

There were no windows in the chamber because there was

nothing to look out upon. Dwellers within the ground throughout most of their history, the thranx were equally comfortable on the surface, but a complex assortment of reasons kept their communities underground. A human forced to work every day in such confinement would have found it suffocating, despite the excellent simscene of luxuriant jungle that filled one wall with color, depth, and a farrago of fragrance.

"I bid you good digging, Fanielle." The Terran diplomat and her thranx counterpart had been on a first-name basis for several months now. As he settled himself back on his elongated seat, she retired to one of the low visitors' benches. Instead of lying prone on her chest and stomach while straddling it head-forward in the thranx manner, she simply sat down on the soft artificial padding. It made for a perfectly comfortable perch, if one discounted the absence of any back support. It was certainly preferable to sitting on the floor.

She did not need to see Haflunormet to recognize him. Every individual thranx emitted a distinctive personal perfume, each more aromatic and sweet-scented than the next. A visit to a city the size of Daret could easily overpower the olfactory sensitive. To her, entering a thranx hive was like plunging into a sea of freshly plucked tropical flowers. Even those humans who disliked the appearance of the thranx were hard put to remain hostile in their astonishingly fragrant presence.

Unfortunately, she reflected, a way had yet to be found that could effectively transmit true smell via tridee. It was too bad. If every human could meet a thranx face-to-face, the continuing uncertain and unsettled state of relations between the two species might be at least partially alleviated.

The improvement in Haflunormet's Terranglo had kept pace with her growing fluency in both Low and the more difficult High Thranx. "I trust you had a pleasant journey from Azerick?"

"The flight was smooth enough, if that's what you mean." She shifted her rear on the near end of the long, narrow cushion, wishing for something to rest her spine against. "The tube transport from the port into Daret was a little slow."

"It's a busy time of year. Fourth cycle of the Dry Season here."

She chuckled softly. "You have a dry season?" It had rained hard and steady ever since the atmospheric shuttle had begun its descent into Daret Port East.

"Taste in atmospheric conditions is relative." Haflunormet gestured expressively with both truhands. "I don't see how you humans stand that high, cold desert you call the Med'ranna Plat'u."

Anjou tried not to think of the pleasant, temperate hillsides where the human outpost was situated. Despite the best efforts of her specialized attire, she was sweating profusely. Though she had grown personally fond of Haflunormet, she couldn't wait to get out of the chamber, with its low ceiling and windowless environment, and back onto the surface.

"I see that you are uncomfortable."

His observation startled her. "I didn't know you had become so adept at interpreting human expressions."

"It is difficult." He gestured casually. "It takes continuous effort for us to realize that those species equipped with flexible epidermi utilize them to convey the same kinds of meanings that we do with our hands. And your skin is more elastic than that of the AAnn, the sentient race you most closely resemble physically. I have had to work hard with my study visuals."

"You watch my face; I observe your limb movements." She gestured decorously. "By such studies do we learn from each other."

He rose from behind the workstation. "Enough to know that you would be more at ease outside the city." Approaching until he was standing next to her on all four trulegs, he reached up with a foothand and gently urged her in the direction of the portal.

"Let's take a riser to the surface, *keerkt*. It will be just as hot and humid, but I know that your kind respond with favor to the unrestricted flow of open air." He made a short gesture of curious indifference. "A peculiar affectation, but a harmless one."

She was more than tempted. "What about security?"

Compound eyes flashing golden beneath the overhead illumination, he indicated reassurance. "We can talk freely in the Park. There are many secure places."

She did not need further convincing. Together, they exited his work chamber and retraced her steps as far as the main corridor. Instead of continuing on past Security, they turned down another narrow passageway that terminated at a bank of oval gateways. Her head just did clear the entrance to the one he selected, but she had to bend slightly at the waist to avoid bumping it on the ceiling of the internal transport motile. Nearly all her male and most of her female colleagues would have been forced to sit on the floor.

Haflunormet coded in a destination, and in seconds they were ascending at a rapid rate of speed. When the riser halted and the portal reopened, she was greeted by a vista of tangled alien rain forest, wondrous aromas, and ferine screeching. The ostensible wildness was illusory. The bulk of the terrain that lay directly above the subterranean capital consisted of carefully tended parkland. The filtered water sources, holoed directions that appeared at the wave of a truhand, concealed emergency communication devices, artfully disguised food-procuring facilities, and other technologically inconspicuous paraphernalia scattered strategically along the path Haflunormet chose pointed to the highly domesticated nature of the "jungle track" down which they began strolling. In appearance, the forest they were entering was little different from those undomesticated tracts that survived elsewhere on Hivehom. But this one had been tamed.

Not only did the heat and humidity not assault her as they exited the riser, it was actually cooler and drier on the surface than in the vast hive conurbation below. Repressing a smile, she hoped it was not too chilly out for Haflunormet. Their divergent preferences in climatic conditions provided numerous opportunities for amusement. In contrast to their weather, the thranx sense of humor was noticeably drier than that of humans. The intent of traditional human slapstick, for example, escaped them completely. To a thranx, a pie in the face was food wasted; nothing more. In contrast, whistling thranx were often clearly amused by conflations that humans found nothing more than common coincidence.

We still, she reflected as she strolled down the path alongside the thranx diplomat, have so very much to learn about one another.

A quartet of *qinks* bobbled past over their heads, gyrating from one tree to another. Both mating pairs capered around each other, performing an intricate mating dance in the air. As she understood it from the Biology Department, qinks only mated in fours, the twofold coupling bolstering the chances of producing viable offspring instead of unsettling it. Like little helicopters, the multiwinged qinks whirled overhead in tiny, tight circles. This meant that at any one time, one or two of the participants was actually flying backward. Ordinarily, it would put that individual at risk from lurking predators. But since qinks only flew the mating dance in tetrads, two of them were always keeping an eye on the sky ahead.

She lengthened her stride, not wishing to be standing directly beneath the whirling aerialists when the time came for them to consummate their performance. Though his legs were markedly shorter than hers, Haflunormet had six of them at his disposal and had no trouble matching the pace. In a sprint, she knew, she could easily outrun him and most other thranx. With his three sets of legs and greater endurance, over a distance he would catch up to and surpass her.

Qinks and sprints, witticisms and woes, she reflected. All grist for the mill of diplomacy. Haflunormet felt similarly, though he was inherently more pessimistic than his human counterpart. Or maybe it was patience, she decided. Humans frequently mistook the immoderate patience of the intelligent arthropods for pessimism.

"How are you coming with arranging that meeting we spoke about?" she asked him. In presenting the question, she employed a combination of human words and thranx words, clicks, and whistles. This useful and informal shorthand manner of speaking was gaining increasing favor among not only the diplomatic but the scientific staff at Azerick. Combined with thranx gestures and the resident humans' best attempts to imitate these utilizing only two hands instead of four, it formed a kind of casual symbolic speech. This allowed thranx to practice their Terranglo and humans the opportunity to train their throats in the elaborate vocalizations of the thranx.

"*Krriik,* it is proceeding slowly. Discouragingly so. I think the physicists are not the only ones who are absorbed in the study of inertia." He glanced over and up at her to make sure she understood the last term correctly. As she did not immediately laugh in the human manner, he could not be certain she had understood his attempt at humor. Of all the humans he had met—admittedly this was not a large number—Anjou was the most consistently serious. Perhaps, he ruminated, this was why she got along so well with the thranx. To Haflunormet it appeared she sometimes acted in this manner to the detriment of her relationship with her fellow mammals.

Watching her step easily alongside him, he tried to admire the play of her muscles, obscenely visible beneath the semi-transparent epidermis. Diplomat or no, he found he could not do it. There was simply too much movement, too much visible play within the anatomical structure. In this it resembled that of the AAnn, but the reptiloids' internal composition was concealed by tough, reflective, leathery scales. If a person peered closely at a human, individual blood vessels could be seen not only beneath the skin but forming rills and ridges above it. Their entire corporeal structure was, inarguably, turned inside out.

He forced himself not to look away. It would be impolite. This female was his hive counterpart. Much as the sight unsettled his stomachs, he was determined to maintain visual contact. As to the sharp, distinctive, and wholly unpleasant smell that emanated from the biped, he steadfastly refused to dwell on it. No matter how their future relations evolved, he realized that there were some things that could not be changed through negotiation.

He worked to pay attention, realizing that the tottering upright stinking blob was speaking. No, he corrected himself resolutely: It was a graceful, fluid biped who was addressing him. Formal diplomacy aside, the thranx were exceedingly polite: a consequence of having evolved in surroundings so confined that humans could not even conceive of the social forces that had been at work. To the thranx, of course, they did not seem confined at all, but perfectly normal and natural. It was wide-open aboveground spaces that tended to occasionally make them nervous. Consequently, their conquest of space had been a more impressive feat than that of humans. Psychology was harder to engineer than spacecraft.

Anjou was deep in thought as they turned a bend in the trail. Eint Carwenduved was Haflunormet's superior. Because of the rigid thranx chain of diplomatic command, only she could properly accept a formal proposal from the Terran government and pass it on to the Grand Council for discussion and consideration. It had taken a select group of forward-thinking statespeople from half a dozen human settled worlds almost two years to finally hammer out a preliminary proposal for establishing closer ties between their respective species. This had not even been voted on by the Congress on Terra, yet the signatories felt that opening negotiations with their thranx counterparts at the same time as the details were being debated on the human homeworld would, if nothing else, serve to accelerate mutual consideration of the delicate issues involved.

It was an acknowledged diplomatic ploy, a means of forcing reluctant individuals on both sides to consider politically highly sensitive issues they might otherwise prefer to ignore. Easy enough for the executive director of the colony world of Kansastan to ignore the question of closer human-thranx relations—but not if he felt that his thranx counterpart on Humus was ready to vote on the matter. Merely having the proposals presented for contemplation forced those to whom they were delivered to deliberate their possible ramifications. A good deal of the work of real diplomacy consisted of engaging such individual uncertainties.

Just agreeing on what was technically a compilation of informal suggestions was a triumph for those thranx and hu-

mans involved. Others, they knew, were actively working to
discourage the implementation of even one of the proposals.
One way to do this was to persuade those in positions to actually make decisions to simply ignore anything relevant that
crossed their desks. Hence Anjou's intense desire to have a
face-to-face meeting with Eint Carwenduved. Haflunormet's
superincumbent could not only present proposals to the Grand
Council; she could go so far as to make recommendations.

Through Haflunormet, Anjou had been trying to arrange
such a meeting for more than six months. Patience or pessimism, whatever one chose to call it, the seemingly endless
procrastination was driving her crazy. She could not give vent
to her true feelings, however—not in front of Haflunormet.
The xenologists had been firm on that from the beginning.
She had yet to meet a thranx who would not recoil in distaste
at what was to them an often explosive human outburst of
emotion.

Anyway, she told herself, diplomats do not do that sort of
thing. So the fact that she wanted to stop right there and then
in the middle of the domesticated alien jungle and scream out
her frustration to curious qinks and any other exotics within
range of her voice had to remain nothing more than a passing
fancy. But the desire did not wane quickly, she realized.

The delay was not Haflunormet's fault. She knew that.
Thranx diplomacy made the human equivalent appear to progress at lightning speed. There was nothing to be done about
it but persist, stay polite, and keep her hopes up.

"Why the continuing reluctance?" She gazed over at glittering compound eyes that were more advanced than that of
any terrestrial insect. "It's just a meeting. It needn't even last
very long."

Haflunormet stepped, one set of legs at a time, over an artfully positioned *zell* root. "Eint Carwenduved continues to
study the proposals."

"I know that—she's been 'studying' them for the better part
of a year." At once, Anjou regretted her tone, even though it
was unlikely that Haflunormet was aware of its significance.
His knowledge of human gestures, facial expressions, and

linguistic peculiarities was improving rapidly, however, so she was more concerned than she would have been a few months ago.

He did not react as if he detected any bitterness, however. "You must understand, Fanielle, that such things take more time to be resolved among my kind than they seem to among yours. Carwenduved must be certain of herself before she commits to any course of action because she will inevitably be held responsible for relevant consequences."

Which was a fancy and not altogether alien way of saying that the eint was stalling, Anjou knew.

"The eint marvels at your earnestness," Haflunormet continued. "She sees no need for a 'face-to-face,' as you call it." As the thranx diplomat spoke, he absently employed a truhand to preen his left antenna.

"My people believe strongly that personal contact is an important component of diplomacy."

Haflunormet indicated understanding. "You do realize that not all my kind take pleasure from being in your physical presence." He hastened to qualify his comment. "I did not mean you personally, of course! I meant humans in general."

"I know what you meant." Anjou was not naïve. She was fully aware that most thranx, especially those who had experienced little or no contact with humans, found the presence of her kind physically unappealing. It was something she had worked hard to overcome, in everything from her attire to her manner of speaking. "But as a diplomat, I am entitled to certain accommodations." This time her tone was firm. "Eint Carwenduved realizes this as well."

"I know that she does." Haflunormet sighed, the air wheezing gently from the breathing spicules that lined his b-thorax. "Your patience gains you merit in her eyes as well as in mine, Fanielle."

What patience? she thought. I'm going crazy here, hanging around up at Azerick waiting for your mommy bug to deign to see me. She promptly shunted the undiplomatic and very unthranxlike thought aside.

Instead of thinking antithranx thoughts, what might she

make use of that the thranx themselves would react to? Perhaps she had been stalking the impasse from the wrong direction. Perhaps she had been thinking too many human thoughts.

How would a thranx diplomat gain speedier access to a counterpart? It would have to be something informal, she knew. The delicate intricacies and involved traditions of thranx hive government were still largely a mystery to the human researchers charged with interpreting them. More was known about thranx culture and society in general. Mightn't there be something there she could apply?

She halted so suddenly that Haflunormet was momentarily alarmed. Both antennae fluttered in her direction. "Is something the matter, Fanielle? If you are feeling stressed by the local conditions, we can find you a climate-controlled chamber in which to revitalize—though I personally find the weather outside today a bit on the cool side."

"Yes," she told him. "Yes, I am feeling a little—a little faint." She put the back of one hand to her forehead in a melodramatic gesture any human would have found amusing, but which the anxious thranx could only view as potentially alarming. "It happens to us—at such times."

He indicated confusion. "Of what 'times' are you speaking?"

"Oh, that's right. You don't know. I haven't told you before now, have I? An oversight on my part. You see—I'm pregnant, Haflunormet. With, um—" She thought of the dancing qinks. "—quadruplets." Unfamiliar with the nature or frequency of human birthing, the anxious diplomat ought to accept her admission at face value. He did.

"*Srr!lk!* You should have told me!" Setting aside his instinctive distaste for such contact, he took her free hand in both his foothands. "Do you want to lie down? Can I get you fluid? Do you wish an internal lubrication?"

"Uh, no thanks," she replied hastily, dropping the hand from her forehead even as she wondered what an on-the-spot internal lubrication meant to a thranx female.

In a determined gesture of interspecies concern, Haflunormet continued to hold her hand, doing his best to ignore

the unnatural warmth that radiated from the pulpy flesh. He
realized how much he had come to like this particular human.
If something were to happen to her while she was in his company, not only would it reflect on his individual and family
history, he would regret it personally.

"How are your eggs? Excuse me," he corrected himself,
"your live feti. Fetuses?" Despite his disquiet, he could not
bring himself to contemplate the wriggling, unshelled larvae
that must even now be jostling for room within her womb. He
tried to lighten the moment. "As you possess no ovipositors
that I could observe going into pre-laying spasm, I had no visual clue to your condition."

"It's all right. I'll be fine." Meeting his gaze, which she assumed reflected his concern even though his compound eyes
could not convey anything like such a complex emotion, she
announced firmly, "Tell Eint Carwenduved that the pregnant
human Fanielle Anjou is making a formal *Bryn'ja* request."

Haflunormet started, his antennae twitching. Then he simultaneously whistled his amusement and understanding.
"The news will place the eint in a difficult position."

That's the idea, she thought, wincing perceptibly for effect.
If she understood the pertinent aspect of thranx culture correctly, no adult could refuse a first Bryn'ja request from a female who was about to lay. Such a compunction applied
equally to ordinary citizens, respected poets, noted teachers,
and everyone within the hive irrespective of function. It even
applied to diplomats.

Of course, it was a blatant lie. Surely, she told herself, the
first time in history one had been employed in the service of
diplomacy. She would have to make sure her colleagues at
Azerick were informed of her "condition" lest the always
thorough thranx decided to check on it with a second source.
Once her rather abrupt pregnancy was verified, it would be
interesting to see how the thranx would react. Time would at
last become a factor. To refuse a first Bryn'ja request from a
gravid female until after she laid her eggs would earn the re-
fuser significant opprobrium. Her only real concern was
whether or not the custom would apply across species lines.

And if it did, would it be subject to the same onerous, lingering deliberation as every other communication she had asked Haflunormet to pass along to the chamber of the eint? Could any thranx authority move at more than a sluggard's pace, no matter the incidental circumstances?

The official response was as revealing as it was gratifying. So much of successful diplomacy was not about knowing how to do something, or when, but how to step just ever so slightly outside the boundaries of traditional, formal negotiation without falling into the pit of cultural transgression.

Within thirty-two hours, she received acknowledgment of her long-sought-after appointment.

2

The Bwyl were furious. They had been ever since the revelation of the presence on Willow-Wane of the covert human outpost there, with its clandestine attempts to bring humans and thranx closer together, had been divulged to an unknowing hive public more than eighty years earlier. It was bad enough, from the standpoint of the Bwyl, that humans and the thranx had cooperated in a war against the Pitar that was no hive's business. The disclosure that the soft-bodied, bipedal mammals had been allowed to establish what amounted to a de facto colony on a developed thranx world amounted to cultural sacrilege. The purity of the Great Hive had been defiled.

Worse still, the vast majority of thranx had reacted indecisively at best, indifferently at worst, to the announcement. Now that the war against the Pitar lay nearly in the receding past, where humans were concerned the average burrower seemed to hold little in the way of strong opinion. So long as the humans posed no overt threat to the Great Hive and did not ally themselves with the bellicose AAnn, the typical worker was content to ignore them. And if the respective life tunnels of the two species happened to intersect now and then, why, it would only be polite to pause and allow those traveling crosswise to pass without confrontation.

It was all very bewildering to the Bwyl. What about the sanctity of the hive? Where was traditional deference to poetic purity? Bad enough to allow these red-blood-pumping creatures access outside the usual restricted diplomatic missions. To allow ordinary citizens to mix with them at will,

16

without proper safeguards or preliminary acculturation, was
to invite cultural degradation and worse. What was a newly
metamorphosed adolescent to think when confronted with
sophisticated sentients who wore their skeletons on the *inside*
and peered at the universe out of single-lensed eyes?

It was not to be tolerated. But the Bwyl, though a multihive
fellowship, were few in number. They could not influence the
councils proportionately. They did have many who were sympathetic to their aims, but who were afraid to express their beliefs openly. The Bwyl base of support was large, but diffuse.

It did not matter. They could wait no longer. Already, there
was talk at significant hive levels of formalizing a much closer
alliance with the humans. True, such talk had been rampant
since the end of the Humanx-Pitar War. Lately, though, it had
taken on a certain urgency. Important eints who believed they
could make use of the humans as a bulwark against the ad-
venturism of the AAnn had been pressing for more than talk.
Regrettably, they found sympathetic hearing organs among
traitorous members of the lower councils. Now dialogue
threatened to become action, and action, decision. For the
sake of the Great Hive, this had to be prevented.

Which was why the Bwyl had called the meeting on Willow-
Wane. Its members were not alone in their stand. There were
two other interhival societies that had on more than one occasion expressed similar sentiments. Representatives of the S!k
and the Arba had arrived on Willow-Wane only days before to
participate in the critical discussion.

Now the twineight gathered on the shore of the River
Niivuodd, chattering amiably among themselves. To passersby they looked for all the world like a group of taskmates out
for a day's relaxation. They carried food and drink and humming amusements, and talked of inconsequentialities. But
their intentions were far more serious than an afternoon's casual distraction. They had not joined together beneath Willow-
Wane's searing sun for purposes of frolic.

When all had assembled by the river's shore and settled
themselves in a half circle facing the water and one another,

and when assurance came from posted sentries that no patrollers, first class or otherwise, were lingering in the vicinity, Tunborelarba of the Arba waved all four hands for quiet and proceeded to open the solemn convocation with a pugnacious, if not downright martial, paean to the virtues of the Great Hive. His fine words and whistles encompassed them all, from outworld visitors to their resolute Willow-Wane hosts.

Then Beskodnebwyl of the Bwyl rose on his four trulegs and declaimed what all of them were thinking. Overhead, a flock of silver *taiax* flew past, dipping and looping to snap in unison at the smaller arthropods that filled the steamy afternoon air. Their sedate *ke-uk, chitt-chitt, ke-uk-uk* did not interrupt the flow of the charismatic speaker's words.

"We are gathered here because we agree that anything deeper than the traditional, polite, formal relations that exist between sentients of different species is an abomination that is not to be tolerated." Attentive antennae and glittering compound eyes were focused in his direction. Near the back, the ovipositors of a young female S!k as fanatical as she was attractive contracted in response to the forcefulness of the Bwyl's words.

"There are those among the hives of several of the burrowed worlds who believe that a stronger relationship can be forged with these humans. These fools dwell in the nursery of delusion. The bipeds are too different—not only in appearance, but in culture, actions, psychohistory, and every other standard that is used to take the measure of another species. Our alliance with them for the duration of the latter part of the Pitarian War was superficial and designed to achieve maximum diplomatic benefit in a limited period of time."

"Principally to forestall the designs of the AAnn," an Abra could not refrain from pointing out.

Beskodnebwyl did not upbraid his impassioned listener for the discourteous interruption. All were allies in this place: supporters of a similar philosophy. He had no intention of alienating a collaborator over a point of etiquette.

"That is so. Yet despite what appears to us to be the obvious, there are among our own kind those who are sufficiently deluded to desire to place the security and sanctity of the Great Hive itself at risk. They intend to do this by forging ties with these humans of a nature so intimate I can scarcely bring myself to contemplate it. You will understand my feelings when you receive the detailed reports that will be provided to all of you at the close of this gathering. All I can say without going into further particulars is that there are varieties and types of corruption not even new larvae can dream of."

"They must be blind!" someone chirruped above a chorus of lesser clicking.

For a second time, Beskodnebwyl deferred his right to criticize an outburst. "There are all kinds of blindness, many of which have nothing to do with the sense of sight. It is these we must correct, even at the risk of carrying out bitter antisocial behavior. The very ancestral integrity of the Great Hive is at stake." Reaching back into a thorax pouch, he withdrew a compact projector and spurred it to life. Immediately, a semitransparent globe appeared before the body of thranx assembled by the river. It was a representation of an attractive world even the most galographically sophisticated among them did not recognize.

"The planet Dawn, as the humans have named it. A fetching place, by all description. Newly settled and growing rapidly. There is also, in this subversive spirit of specious cooperation that presently exists between our respective species, a sizable burrow located beneath the swamps and savannas of the minor southern continent."

"What has this to do with us and our avowed purpose?" a female S!k inquired reasonably.

Manipulating the projector, Beskodnebwyl increased the magnification substantially, until they found themselves eying one of the distorted, sprawling aboveground conurbations that had become more and more familiar recently in the information media. Frivolously tall, slim edifices, not only unaesthetic but impractical, thrust absurdly all the way up into the weather. Extensive agricultural facilities bumped up against a surprising amount of undeveloped green space. Free-standing bodies of water were spotted with fishing craft. Clearly visible were all the mysterious accouterments of a characteristic aboveground human hive.

"There is to be a fair held on Dawn, to be situated not far outside the capital city of Aurora." Beskodnebwyl continued to manipulate the details of the holo as he explained. "A cultural fair, exhibiting the best and newest of human music and arts."

"Is that not a contradiction in terms?" someone ventured. Amused whistling spilled from the assembled to drift across the river.

"Obviously, not to humans, it isn't," Beskodnebwyl observed when the laughter had died down. "This gathering will also present contributions from the local thranx of the southern continent." He leaned forward, stretching his b-thorax, his antennae quivering with barely concealed passion. "It is to be a wholly cross-cultural, cross-species event—the first of its kind on Dawn. In addition to presentations by the locals, a number of important artists from nearby settled worlds, both human and thranx, are also to participate. For so young a colony, it promises to be a most prestigious and important convocation, a watershed in the settlement's evolution." He drew himself back, pausing and gesturing for emphasis.

"We of the Bwyl also intend that it shall be so, and in a manner that will leave a deep and lasting impression on perceptive sentients everywhere. We hope that you of the S!k and the Abra will join us in making our own presentation at this fair."

"Which will consist of?" The senior Abra present waved an antenna inquiringly.

Beskodnebwyl did not hesitate, nor did his tone change. "We hope to disrupt the fair, and in doing so push the course of human-thranx relations back onto a proper level, by killing as many of the participants as possible. Operating under the guise of the ancient Protectors, we hope to make our case so irresistibly to all citizens of the Greater Hive that they will have no choice but to see the correctness of our doctrine." He indicated first-degree confidence.

"The humans will respond immediately to our actions, of course. Once word of our involvement and efforts is disseminated, they will enter the fair and kill us as quickly as they can. With luck, some of us will escape to carry on the necessary work. Those of us who do not will be recycled knowing that they gave their essence to preserve the Great Hive, much as our ancestors did in the course of thousands of ancient battles. This cause is nobler than any of those, because it is carried out on behalf of the entire Great Hive itself." He switched deliberately to the rougher but more straightforward Low Thranx.

"Males and females of the S!k and the Abra: Will you join with your hive mates the Bwyl in this great and noble undertaking?"

Animated discussion followed, lively but by no means uniform. Clearly, there remained among the disputants considerable difference of opinion. Having chosen directness over diplomacy, Beskodnebwyl had no leeway for hesitation. Nor had he intended to leave any.

"How would you intend to do this thing?" Velhurmeabra of the Abra was clearly taken aback by the proposal and not afraid to say so. "Will the humans have in place no precautions against such an eventuality, no guards?"

"Why should they?" Beskodnebwyl replied expansively. "It is a cultural fair, not a military caucus. As to the actual methods to be employed in the carrying out of our intentions, we have already spent much time refining our options."

"What about introducing into the atmosphere of the gathering a powerful cyanotoxin?" one of the more enthusiastic S!k proposed.

"For the same reason that we cannot spread a lethal hemolument." This time the images generated by Beskodnebwyl's handheld projector were more detailed, full of charts and sketches that floated in midair before the assemblage. "Human blood binds oxygen through the use of iron, not the usual copper. I am assured that given enough time and resources, suitable poisons could be engineered for use against them. We have neither. By the same token, biological agents that would devastate us are just as likely to pass harmlessly through their systems. For example, the *gin!gas* wasting disease for which no cure has yet been discovered degrades chitin. I am told that malignant as it is, it might at most cause the hair and fingernails of some humans to fall out. That is hardly the bold statement we wish to make."

"Then what do you propose to do?" Uhlenfirs!k of the S!k asked, then waited quietly.

Beskodnebwyl underlined his response with deliberate movements of antennae and truhands. Behind him, an aquatic *hermot* splashed in the river, pursuing a school of hard-shelled *couvine*, predator and prey alike oblivious to the convocation on the nearby bank vigorously contemplating mass murder.

"Explosives have the advantage of not discriminating between species. Volunteers have already been chosen. They will infiltrate this detestable fair and wreak such havoc as cannot be imagined. The fact that individuals will be free to do their work independent of any central control ensures that even if one or more are detected and forced to abort their mission, the others will be able to proceed unimpaired. Additionally, every operative will enter adequately armed for their personal defense."

The nominal leaders of the S!k and the Abra conferred, supported by their most able aides. When they were through, Velhurmeabra of the Abra faced his expectant counterparts across the semicircle.

"While we of the Abra and the S!k feel much as you do with regard to this too rapid and too intimate mixing of species, we have decided not to participate in your plans to disrupt the cultural fair on the world of Dawn. While we are not entirely opposed to the use of violent means of dissuasion, indiscriminate bombing of so large a gathering will inevitably slay or injure numerous artists as well as ordinary visitors."

One of the S!k spoke up. "The killing of an artist is an abomination unto itself. The stifling of any fount of creativity, however modest, diminishes us all."

Beskodnebwyl gestured understanding. He had expected this line of objection. "Humans feel otherwise. They make no such sharp distinctions between, say, composers of music and purifiers of water. It is further proof of their degraded culture."

"But you cannot guarantee," Velhurmeabra continued inexorably, "that only human artists will die."

"Unfortunately," Beskodnebwyl responded, "explosives are notoriously undiscriminating. It is conceded that thranx will also perish in the making of our statement. It is unavoidable."

"Then we cannot participate actively," the Abra concluded.

Beskodnebwyl pounced on an inflection. " 'Actively'?"

The leader of the S!k spoke up. "We have no legs to provide you, no antennae to aid you, no eyes to share. But—" He hesitated only for emphasis. "—we wish you well in the enterprise, which seems almost certain to accomplish the goals you have set out for it. While not participating directly, we can perhaps provide some small encouragement."

"In any event, we will do nothing to discourage you from burrowing in this chosen direction," the Abra concluded.

It was not all that Beskodnebwyl had hoped for. But logistical support would be useful and would free up the dedicated members of the Bwyl to carry out the more active components of the scheme. The Abra and the S!k could not overcome the deep-seated cultural prejudice against the killing of artists. Only the Bwyl had progressed far enough to do that. But the support of the others would be welcomed. They wished to share in the credit for the ultimate disruption of human-thranx integration, but not in the ultimate risk.

It was better than outright dissension, Beskodnebwyl knew. The Abra and the S!k had access to materials and contacts and useful facilities that were denied the Bwyl. When the deed was done, the truth would come out. Credit would be apportioned where due. Beskodnebwyl was not concerned with the refining of such matters. He cared nothing for credit. He wanted only to put a halt to this abhorrent, noisome mixing of species.

If the Burrow Master was with them, they would do precisely that—once and for all time.

Elkannah Skettle stepped off the shuttle and examined the world spread out before him with great interest. Ahead, he saw Lawlor and Martine passing rapidly through Customs. Pierrot, Botha, Nevisrighne, and the others were somewhere in the crowd behind him that was still filing off the transport vehicle. They had grown used to traveling together yet keeping their distance from one another.

The port facilities were efficient, the port's equipment spotless, the smiles on the faces of the local officials almost painfully welcoming. And why shouldn't they be? he mused. Dawn was a new world, bursting with opportunity, unclaimed lands, fortunes yet to be made. The climate was salubrious, the terrain inviting, the local flora and fauna reasonably pacific. A fine place to live and an enchanting place to visit.

Provided, he knew as he smiled pleasantly at the young woman who passed him through the body scanner, it could be kept free of bugs.

Not that there was anything inherently wrong with the bugs, he reflected as he presented himself to Customs. Or with the Quillp, or the AAnn, or any of the diverse other intelligent races with whom humankind shared this corner of the Orion Arm. He had reason of his own to be grateful to the bugs. Without the aid they had rendered to humankind in the Pitarian War, a favorite grandniece of his might not have survived the fighting. Military assistance in the midst of conflict was always welcome.

But the idea that relations should proceed beyond *that* was simply intolerable to one who loved his kind. The thranx might be all twirling antennae and sweet smells on the surface, but they were as alien as any sentient species humanity had yet encountered. The revelation that they had an actual colony in the Amazon Basin had been enough to trigger simmering outrage not only in men like himself, but in many who previously had given little thought to the problem.

And it *was* a problem. How could humankind ever be certain of its safety, of its very future, if empty-headed authorities allowed aliens to expand beyond the customary, restricted diplomatic and commercial sites where they were allowed? The notion that such growth should not only be permitted but encouraged and codified was sufficient to prod Skettle and those of like mind to move beyond protest to action. Negotiations, he knew, were presently at a delicate stage and could go either forward or back. A well-timed statement might be enough to put a stop to foolishness that bordered on the seditious.

Unlike others who felt similarly, Skettle did not think those humans who blindly advocated intimate ties with the thranx were traitors. They were simply ignorant. The bugs had deceived them. They were very clever, the thranx. Polite to a fault, ever conscious of the feelings of others, they had lulled supposedly astute people into a false sense of security the likes of which humankind had never before experienced.

But not all of us, he thought resolutely as he presented his travel case for inspection.

He waited while it passed beneath the Customs scanner. His corpus had already been cleared. Now it remained only for his luggage to do the same. Lawlor was the only potential weak link in the group, he knew. The man tended to exhibit unease even when no threat was apparent. That was why Skettle had chosen to carry this particular case. Old men were not usually the first to be suspected of smuggling.

With a tip of his cap and a practiced smile, the earnest young inspector passed him through. Picking up his case on the other side of the scanner, Skettle resumed his trek through the terminal, staying in the middle of the stream of disembarking passengers. Compared to those on major worlds like Terra or Amropolus, the terminal was not large. The scanner had detected nothing inside his case beyond the expected: clothing, vacation gear, personal communicator—the usual unremarkable assortment of travel goods.

It had not, however, performed a detailed analysis of the luggage itself. Even had it undergone that thorough an examination, the local authorities would still have been hard pressed to prove anything. Had they noted the composition of Lawlor's case, and Martine's, and subjected them to observation by a trained physical chemist, however, they would no doubt have been persuaded to investigate further.

Each of the three cases was composed of a different set of materials. When certain specific sections of the trio were cut up and then layered together in the appropriate proportions, then treated with a commonly available binding fluid, the result was neat little squares of an extraordinarily dynamic explosive. Utilizing this product, Elkannah Skettle and his colleagues intended for the widely advertised Dawn Intercultural Fair to give off even more heat than its organizers intended.

Everything had been carefully prepared in advance. It was meant for the deadly consequences to be blamed on unknown provocateurs working together with renegade thranx elements, but the apportionment of blame was not really crucial. What mattered was the disruption, and preferably the destruction, of the fair itself. If nothing else, it would put an end to what was supposed to be an exchange of "culture" among the races. What nonsense! Skettle chuckled to himself. The idea that humans and bugs should create art in common, that thranx culture should be allowed to contaminate human painting, music, song, or sculpture, would have been laughable if it was not so dangerous. Such aesthetic degradation could not be allowed. Were no one but Skettle and his associates thinking of the children as yet unborn? He thought, as he had so very many times, of the brave forebears of his own organization who had given their lives in the attempt years before to wipe out the foul thranx colony located in the Reserva Amazonia. Their sacrifice would not go unavenged.

The Preservers took separate transport to the small hotel they had booked. Located on the outskirts of Aurora, capital of the semitropical colony, the establishment overlooked a small natural lake and was within easy commuting distance of the fair. Following a suitable pause after checking in, they assembled by ones and twos in a prereserved commons room. There they bantered trivialities while Botha checked for hidden sensors and erected an industrial-strength sound envelope. There was no reason to suspect the presence of the former and no demonstrated need for the latter, but they were taking no chances—especially when the hand weapons they had contracted for were due to arrive with their local contact later in the day.

Feeling secure, they activated the tridee and waited the necessary few seconds for the room unit to warm up. As soon as the menu appeared in the air on the far side of the room, Pierrot directed it to provide them with as much local background on the fair as was available for viewing, commencing with material recorded as recently as ten days prior to their arrival.

The site was expanding impressively. Portable structures had been raised on the far side of the main lake, facilities for transport vehicles had been prepared underground, a high-speed transport link with the city continuing on to the shuttleport had been constructed and tested, and the usual virtually invisible molegel had been suspended in place above the entire site to shield it from any adverse weather, since Dawn did not yet possess the advanced climate-moderating facilities of more technologically mature worlds. Most of the larger exhibits were already in place and undergoing final checkout.

"Show us the thranx pavilions," Skettle ordered the tridee. Obediently, it supplied perfectly formed floating images on one side with a running printed commentary, in addition to the accompanying audio, on the other. Cerebral plug-ins were available, as was to be expected in any decent hostelry. Skettle disdained their use in favor of group observation.

"Look at that grotesquerie." Pierrot called for magnification, and the tridee unit complied. "What can that abomination possibly be?" She was shaking her head disdainfully.

"Some kind of organic sculpture, I would guess." Botha possessed more imagination than most of them, Skettle included. "It's not so bad, if you ignore the color scheme."

"Remember," Skettle announced, "it's not the content of the fair that we're here to terminate. We're not art critics." A few laughs rose above the ongoing commentary from the tridee.

"It's the possibility that such content may lead to a freedom for thranx on human worlds that will let them infiltrate and eventually dominate our very lives, from the way we create to the way we live." This time his words were greeted not with laughter, but with grim muttering.

They watched for more than an hour, until Nevisrighne could take it no more. Rising, he walked over to the room's food service bay and ordered a chilled alcoholic fruit drink. "I'm sorry, but I can't watch anymore. Too many bugs for one morning."

"Time we finalized more than observations, anyway." Botha looked expectantly to Skettle.

The old man nodded, his fine gray beard bobbing prominently. "All right. I know you're all anxious to begin the actual work, but we must be careful not to rush matters. Now that the time for action is so near, it is all the more imperative that we exercise restraint and caution. The last thing we need is to attract the attention of local authorities."

Pierrot made a rude noise. "Security here is primitive compared to even New Riviera."

"General security, most likely," Skettle agreed. "But because of the sensitive nature of the fair, more than local government is involved. As a consequence, there will be extra precautions in place. Not only those of Earth, but from Hivehom as well."

No one followed Skettle's observation with any abrupt, disparaging comments. They had a healthy respect for thranx technology. But technology only added to the challenge. As to the eventual success of their mission, none among them had the slightest doubt. They were each of them well and truly dedicated to their avowed cause.

From his luggage Botha produced a purpose-built three-dimensional diagram of the fair site. It was exceptionally thorough. As well it ought to be, Skettle reflected, since he and half a dozen sympathetic associates of the Preservers had worked at refining and improving it almost constantly ever since the idea of the fair had been proposed and acted upon. It was safe to say that even the fair organizations themselves did not possess a schematic any more detailed than the one that presently floated before the oddly hushed crowd in the commons room.

Everything from food service to sewerage to controlling electronics to items as simple and straightforward as disposal bins were reflected in the diagram. There was nothing that could not be expanded and rotated so that the finest detail of construction and integration could be analyzed. Though not of a technical mien himself, Skettle could admire the artistry that had gone into the compilation of the schematic. It was a most beautiful diagram of destruction.

Fanning out to preselected locations throughout the fair, at the height of general festivities, he and his companions would install and try to simultaneously detonate the blended explosives. An impartial, emotionless beholder might have observed that among the myriad devices intended to be planted throughout the fair, not one was designed to impact upon the integrated fire-control facilities. With a cutting-edge emergency plant designed to cope instantly with even a minor blaze, the destruction of such facilities would seem to an outside observer to be a priority for a group of terrorists planning wholesale destruction. That such a contingency was nowhere in evidence was a tribute not to oversight or ignorance, but to the skill of Botha and the team he had worked with back on Earth.

It was astonishing, Skettle mused as he admired the schematic, how few people ever gave a thought to the fact that the time-proven, complex, fire-fighting chemicals used to put out unwanted blazes were composed of a precise chemical mixture that could also, in combination with certain laboriously engineered additional elements, stimulate instead of suffocate the very flames they were designed to extinguish. The anticipated, indeed hoped-for, attempt of the local emergency command to fight the blazes to be fomented by the Preservers would result not in a smothering of those conflagrations, but in their enhancement. Skettle smiled inwardly. The resulting chaos and confusion should contribute nicely to the blossoming cataclysm.

Botha assured him that upon contact with the materials to

be spread by the multiple explosions, foams and liquids intended for combating out-of-control blazes would themselves be turned into a substance suitable for supplementing the very conflagrations they were designed to quench. By the time a sufficiency of nonreactive chemical retardants and suppressants could be brought from Aurora City, much of the glorious but debauched fair should be reduced to wind-blown cinders among which would drift the carbonized components of as many baked bugs as possible.

The consequent reaction among the human populace of this portion of the galaxy upon learning that the destruction had been cosponsored by thranx opposed to any deeper alliance among their respective species ought to put a clamp on any enthusiastic treaty making for some time to come, Skettle knew. Which thranx? Skettle's associates back on Earth had spent much time devising a complete bug terrorist hierarchy, the veracity of which *might* eventually be disproved. But by that time, the delay in negotiations that would result would give him and the rest of the Preservers ample time to spread their message to a more alerted population. Relations between human and thranx would progress no further than humankind's relations with any other intelligent species.

That was as things should be, he mused. But education required time. This they would gain from the chaos that would be bought by the destruction of the fair. It would have the added beneficial effect of destroying the viability of any further such profane convocations. The Humanx Intercultural Fair on Dawn would be the first and last of its kind.

The fire in his eyes and those of his companions was a precursor to the greater conflagration that within a few days would engulf thousands of unsuspecting visitors.

It was not a blaze that was amenable to reason.

3

Cullen Karasi stood on the edge of the spectacular escarpment that overlooked the Mountain of the Mourners and reflected that he was a very long way from home. Comagrave lay on the rim of the bubble of human exploration, more parsecs from Earth than was comfortable to think about. If not for the well-established colony in the nearby system of Repler and the discovery of valuable mineral deposits on Burley, it was doubtful humankind would have pushed so far so quickly into this section of the Arm. By KK drive, the capital of the AAnn Empire, Blassussar, was closer than Terra.

This latter fact was not lost upon the AAnn, who freely coveted Comagrave. A semidesert planet whose ecological parameters all fell near the center of their habitable paradigms, it was ideally suited to their kind. To survive on its surface, humans had to exercise caution. In this regard, however, it was no worse than many desertified parts of Earth itself and was more accommodating than others. Survey after survey revealed a wealth of mineral and biological potentiality—not to mention additional archaeological treasures yet to be unearthed. With proper preparation and development, humans would do well enough here.

Humankind's claim was clear, indisputable, and grudgingly recognized by the AAnn. In return for permission to establish a limited number of observational outposts, strictly for purposes of study and education, the reluctant reptiloids had offered to put their knowledge and expertise at the service of the colonists. Despite certain reservations within the

Terran government, it was an offer that could not be denied. The AAnn had forgotten more about surviving on desert-type worlds than humans had ever known, and the government on Earth was far, far away.

Certainly, Cullen reflected, the assistance his team had so far received from the AAnn had been a great help. It was they who had provided material aid when funds from his supporting foundation had been temporarily reduced. It was they who had saved thousands of credits by knowing the best places to establish safe camps. AAnn geologists invariably knew where to locate the deep wells that were necessary to tap Comagrave's elusive aquifers, which made settlement expansion as well as long-term scientific work in the field possible. And it was his AAnn peer, the scientist Riimadu CRRYNN, who had been the first to descry the secret of the Mourners.

That was why a base camp had been set up near the edge of the great escarpment. Below him, the sheer sandstone wall fell away more than a thousand meters to the flat valley floor below. Only the narrow and intermittent River Failings meandered through this desiccated vale, an echo of the immense watercourse that had once dominated this part of the continent. Already, field teams had gathered ample evidence that Comagrave had once enjoyed a much wetter and greener past. Whether this was the reason, or one of the reasons, for the demise of the Comagravian civilization and the highly advanced people who had called themselves the Sauun had yet to be determined.

Already, human exoarcheologists had accomplished much. Ruins of sizable cities were to be found on every continent. There was evidence of extensive agriculture, mining, and manufacturing—all the detritus of an advanced culture. And yet, tens of thousands of years ago, it had all perished. Nor was there any proof that the Sauun had achieved more than rudimentary space travel. Preliminary surveys of the planet's three moons revealed the ruins of only automatic stations, with no provision for habitation or development.

This did not jibe with the level of scientific achievement visible in their abandoned cities. There were gaps in technological evolvement where none ought to exist. It was the presence of such gaps in the Comagravian historical record and the desire to fill them in that drew researchers like Cullen to a world so distant.

Behind him, portative digging equipment hummed softly as fellow team members and advanced students strove to bring to light the answers that hopefully lay buried beneath the hard, rocky surface of the escarpment. A vanager cried as it dipped and soared above the valley floor. With a leathery wingspan equal to that of a small aircraft, the indigenous scavenger could stay aloft indefinitely, carrying its two offspring in a pouch beneath its neck. Vanagers lived in the clouds, mated while aloft, and raised their progeny without ever touching the ground. To feed, they dove and plucked what they could from the surface or snatched it out of the air. Long ago they had lost all but rudimentary evidence of legs and feet. A vanager caught on the ground could only flop about clumsily, its great wings useless until a gust of wind sent it aloft once more. Or so the biologists insisted.

Far across the valley, the Mountain of the Mourners stared back at him. Literally. Hewn from the solid green-black diorite of the mountain from which they seemed to be emerging, the Twelve Mourners were at eye level with the top of the escarpment. Counting elaborate headdresses whose significance had yet to be interpreted, they averaged some fifteen hundred meters in height. How they had been carved, when and with what tools, was another of the many mysteries that Comagrave proffered in abundance.

With such gigantic representations of their kind available for study, there was no wondering what the Sauun had looked like. Tall and slim, with long, humanoid faces and horizontally slitted eyes, the colossal carvings were clad in flowing robes embellished with elaborate decorations and intricate designs. Despite their immense size, the Twelve had been depicted with extraordinary care and detail. Who they had been, no one yet knew. Knowing that the Sauun had progressed beyond kingdoms to a modern, planetwide government, all manner of possibilities had been proposed. The Twelve could be famous artists, or scientists, or the carvers themselves. Or politicians, or criminals, or individuals chosen at random, or composites of a theoretical species ideal. Cullen and his colleagues did not know, and they burned to find out. On one verity they were pretty much agreed: It seemed unlikely any civilization would go to the trouble of chiseling fifteen-hundred-meter-high images out of solid rock, finishing and polishing them with extraordinary care, to perpetuate the memory of a dozen nonentities. Whoever the Twelve were, they represented personages of some importance in the history of Comagrave.

It was the AAnn Riimadu who had first noticed that the enormous, solemn eyes of the graven icons were aligned on a level with the top of the escarpment. It was he who had theorized that the pupilless orbs were each and every pair subtly positioned so that they all focused on approximately the same spot—the one where Cullen's crew was presently engaged in exploration. Cullen owed the AAnn a debt that would be hard to repay. At the very least, they would share in the subsequent fame and profit of any discovery.

Riimadu was the only AAnn attached to the project. When he was not on site, Cullen missed the alien's expertise. Like all his kind, the AAnn exoarcheologist displayed an instinctive feel for the makeup of the ground. Adopting his suggestions had already saved the team days of hard work. With most of the busy crew untroubled by the AAnn scientist's presence from the start, one concern of Cullen's had been removed early in the process of excavation.

He did have to be careful to keep Riimadu and Pilwondepat apart. Though diplomacy was not a province of his expertise, Cullen knew enough of the traditional enmity that existed between AAnn and thranx to see to it that the two resident alien researchers encountered one another as infrequently as possible. Unlike the AAnn, who took an active part in the excavation, Pilwondepat was present as an observer only, on behalf of several thranx institutes. They had as much interest in ancient races as did humankind, but Comagrave was not to their liking. Though humans could survive and even prosper on a desert world, to the thranx it was an exceedingly uncomfortable place to be.

While humans had to worry only about sunburn because of Comagrave's comparatively thin atmosphere and take an occasional slug from a bottle of supplemental oxygen, and while Riimadu strolled around in perfect comfort, poor Pilwondepat lumbered about burdened by all manner of gear designed to supply him with the extra oxygen thranx required, as well as special equipment to keep his body properly moist. To a creature who thrived in high heat and even higher humidity, the climate of Comagrave was withering. Unprotected and unequipped, a thranx like Pilwondepat would perish within a few days, shriveled like an old apple. That was assuming it could keep warm at night, when surface temperatures dropped to a level tolerable to both humans and AAnn but positively deadly to a thranx.

So Pilwondepat was not comfortable with his assignment. He kept to his specially equipped portable dome as much as possible and only emerged to take recordings and make notes. When he spoke, it was with difficulty, through a special unit that covered his mandibles and moistened the air that flowed down his throat. Cullen felt sorry for him. The eight-limbed exoarcheologist must have done something unpopular to have come to a world so disagreeable to his kind.

As he turned to head back to camp, Cullen could feel the immense green-black bulges of the eyes of the Twelve drilling into the back of his neck. If only they could speak, he thought. If only they were not made of stone. And if only the Sauun had left some surviving record of what had happened to their civilization. It was such riddles that drove curious men and women to willingly endure harsh conditions on isolated outpost worlds. It was what had driven Cullen Karasi from a successful family business to the study of ancient alien civilizations.

The resolution to all the great unanswered questions lay somewhere on Comagrave, he was certain: buried in an abandoned city, secreted within a protected metal vesicle, locked in the overlying lines of incredibly complex Sauun code that Cullen's colleagues working elsewhere on the planet had not been able to fully decipher. The first requirement of a good archeologist was curiosity, but the second was patience. Just as one could not hurry history, so too could the unveiling of its mysteries not be rushed.

But waiting for the key was hell.

Meanwhile, each individual science team hoped theirs would be the one to bring to light the Rosetta that would unlock the enigma of the Sauun. While Cullen's hopes were as high as those of any of his colleagues, realistically he knew he was not likely to be the one to make the meaningful breakthrough. As others labored to interpret the riddles of the abandoned Sauun cities, he was stuck on a distant plateau whose isolation was notable even for an empty world like Comagrave. More than he cared to admit, he was relying for direction on the unofficial counsel and expertise of a visiting alien.

"I would not sstep there." As he spoke, Riimadu underscored his words with a second-degree gesture of admonition.

The AAnn's Terranglo was remarkably proficient. Seeing nothing but a few bumps in the ground ahead of him, Cullen nonetheless eased to his left before resuming his advance. He had come to trust the alien's instincts.

"I don't see anything," he commented as soon as he had drawn alongside the other biped. Unlike the insectoid thranx, the anatomy of the scaled, sharp-eyed AAnn was fairly similar to that of humans. The AAnn had evolved from a reptile-like ancestor, and they shared with humans the same upright bisymmetrical build and the same large single-lensed eyes, though their hands and feet each boasted one less digit than their human equivalents. They had no external ears, vertical pupils like cats, and highly flexible, prominent tails that they used to supplement their serpentine, courtly language of gestures. But for these details of design, and the bright, iridescent scales that covered their bodies, they might pass at a distance for wandering bald primates. In build they were slim, slightly shorter on average than humans, and muscular. Sexual dimorphism was more subtle than in primates, so that Cullen had to be certain who he was talking to before addressing individuals of the species as male or female.

Riimadu had established himself as male from the day he had first been allowed to visit and conduct observations of the human archeological team. Now he unslung a small, painstakingly embossed leather pouch from around his neck and right shoulder. Despite the dry heat that radiated from the rocks atop the plateau, he was not panting, and AAnn did not sweat. While Cullen and his coworkers perspired profusely, Riimadu was very much at home in the hot, arid climate.

"Look and learn," the alien hissed softly as he tossed the pouch.

It landed atop one of the slight bumps in the ground. Soundlessly, it was jolted half a dozen centimeters into the air, fell to the ground nearby, and lay motionless. Striding forward, his limber tail flicking from side to side, Riimadu recovered the pouch. Cullen noted that this time the AAnn handled it with extra care.

Bringing it back, he held it out for the human to inspect. Three small brown spines had pierced the bottom of the pouch. One went all the way through the fine leather to emerge from the other side.

"Defenssive mechanissm for an endemic ssoil-browsser. Not a predator." Using his clawed fingers, Riimadu slowly extracted one of the spines from the pouch. Its tip was so sharp it seemed to narrow down to nothingness.

"Poisonous?" Cullen examined the needlelike implement respectfully.

"Analyssiss will be required. With your permission." Removing the other pair of spines one by one, the AAnn carefully placed them within the pouch's padded interior.

"I wonder if they would have gone through the sole of my boot." Turning away from the no-longer-innocuous, quiescent mounds, Cullen continued back toward the site.

"While I am a firm believer in dynamic experimentation in

the field," Riimadu responded, "I did not feel it would be entirely ethical to utilize you for ssuch a purposse without firsst sseeking your conssent." He hissed softly, an exhalation that Cullen had come to recognize as AAnn laughter. While the reptiloids were by nature more solemn than the thranx, and positively wooden alongside the Quillp, that they possessed and displayed a sense of humor could not be denied. It was the subject matter that was occasionally off-putting.

"I appreciate the consideration," he told the alien dryly. "My feet hurt plenty as it is." The AAnn did not react, taking the comment at face value. Well, Cullen mused, one couldn't expect every witticism to make the whimsical jump between species.

The ability to espy hazardous camouflaged fauna was something he had come to expect from Riimadu. He told the AAnn so as he thanked him more directly.

"You humanss are alwayss looking up, or ahead," the exo-archeologist commented. "Anywhere but where you sshould. On a world like Vussussica you need to keep your attention focussed much more often on the ground in front of you."

Vussussica was the name the AAnn had given to Comagrave. It was rumored that certain elements among the Imperial survey services had never fully relinquished their claim to the distant world humans had begun to explore long before the first AAnn ships had arrived in orbit around its sun. Subsequent to the conclusive imprinting by both sides of the formal agreements regarding Comagrave's future status, it was presumed that these dissident elements had been suppressed. Certainly no one had mentioned them to Cullen or to any of his staff. To Riimadu they were of no consequence. "A hisstorical footnote," he had called them when asked to expound his own feelings on the matter.

On an entirely practical level, Cullen did not know what he would have done without the AAnn's help. It was Riimadu who had suspected that the eyes of the Mourners held a secret, and it was he who had triangulated the gazes of the twelve monoliths and chosen this site for excavation. That

they had so far failed to find evidence of anything more significant than local subsurface life-forms like the spine shooter
did not mean the site was barren of potential discovery, only
that they had more work to do and deeper to dig. Certainly the
preliminary subterranean scan had generated some interesting anomalies highly suggestive of the presence of unnatural
stratification. Digging proceeded by hand only to protect the
topmost layer of whatever they might uncover. Thereafter,
once they knew what they were dealing with, more advanced
excavation tools could be brought into play according to the
fragility of the site. They knew they were onto *something*.
They just did not, as yet, know what.

Patience, he reminded himself.

A thickly bundled figure was lurching clumsily along the
western edge of the main excavation. Setting his hopes of discovery aside, Cullen spared a brief rush of sympathy for the
awkwardly garbed Pilwondepat.

Despite making use of all six legs for locomotion, the thranx
scientist was still tottering. The humidifier that was wrapped
around his b-thorax covered his breathing spicules completely. It was not quite silent and made him sound like he
was wheezing even though the source of the sound was entirely mechanical. Though the device drew moisture from the
air, there was not enough in the atmosphere of Comagrave to
satisfy even the hardiest thranx. The humidifier's draw had
to be supplemented by the contents of a lightweight bottle
that rode on the scientist's back. Coupled with leg and body
wraps that helped to retain body moisture, Pilwondepat resembled a child's toy engaged in a clumsy and ineffectual
attempt to break free of its packaging.

Only the scientist's head was completely unprotected, allowing him to observe without obstruction. The chafing of
his chitin from the dryness of the air was plain to see, even
though Cullen knew the exoarcheologist employed several
specially formulated creams to maintain his exoskeleton's
shine and character. The site administrator had often wondered what awful blunder the thranx had committed to get

himself assigned to Comagrave. He had been shocked to eventually learn that Pilwondepat had actually requested the assignment.

"What are you?" he had asked in an unguarded moment. "Some kind of masochist?"

Pilwondepat had clicked to the contrary. "The love of self-suffering is a human trait. I simply felt the opportunities here too intriguing to eschew. Like you, I want to know what happened to these people—to their cities, and to their dream of space travel that was never fulfilled despite their having apparently achieved an equivalent level of technology in all other aspects of science."

"But to volunteer for duty on a world so blatantly inhospitable to your kind . . . ," Cullen had continued.

The visiting scientist had responded with a cryptic gesture the human had been unable to access in his pictionary of thranx gestures. "This is the world where the Sauun lived. As a field researcher, you must know yourself that recordings and records are no substitute for working on site."

Cullen recalled the brief but instructive conversation as he watched the thranx totter to the edge of the excavation. If the eight-limbed academic's dedication did not exceed his own, it certainly matched it. Despite the appalling conditions, his hard-shelled counterpart rarely complained. As he put it, the fascination of the Sauun enigma helped to moisten more than his curiosity.

Advancing in front of Cullen, Riimadu approached the thranx from behind and addressed the scientist in his own language. "*Srr!iik*, you musst be careful here, or you will fall in."

Pilwondepat looked back and up at the AAnn, who loomed over him, though not by as much as would the average human. "I have six legs. Have a care for your own footing, and don't worry about mine."

"I worry about everyone'ss footing on thiss world." Leaning forward, Riimadu peered into the excavation. Neatly partitioned with cubing beams of light, the hole was now some thirty meters in diameter and seven deep. At the bottom, humans labored in thin, lightweight clothing, exuding salt-

laden body water as they worked. Their skins, in a variety of
colors, rippled unsettlingly in the light of Vussussica's midday sun. Unlike AAnn or thranx, their epidermal layers were
incredibly fragile. Why, even a feeble thranx could split them
from neck to ankle with a single sharpened claw!

They were very quick, though. Agility was their compen-
sation for lack of external toughness. To an AAnn or thranx,
the human body seemed composed of lumps of malleable
material, stretching and squashing unpleasantly in response
to the slightest muscular twitch. Their anatomy had no gravity,
no deliberation. The AAnn would have found them amusing,
had they not been both gifted and prolific. And dangerous.
The Pitarian War had revealed their true capabilities. To the
AAnn, who had remained neutral throughout the conflict, the
war had been exceedingly instructive.

Lurching forward, he leaned his body weight against the
thranx's right side. Pilwondepat's foothands slid over the edge
of the excavation, dirt and gravel sliding away beneath them
as he scrambled to retain a foothold. Under such pressure, a
biped would have taken a serious tumble into the open excavation. The thranx's four trulegs kept him from falling.

Turning his head sharply, the thranx's compound eyes
glared up at the AAnn. "That was deliberate!"

"I kiss the ssand beneath your feet if it wass sso." Gesturing apologetically, the AAnn exoarcheologist stepped back.
Sharp teeth flashed between powerful, scaly jaws. "Why would
I do ssuch a thing? Esspecially to a fellow sstudent of the unknown."

"Why do the AAnn strike and retreat, hit and retire?" As
he regained his composure, Pilwondepat held his ground,
determined not to give the AAnn the satisfaction of seeing
him flee. "Always testing, your kind. Always probing for
weaknesses—not only of individuals, but of worlds and alliances." The thranx gestured with a truhand. "I don't even
blame you, Riimadu. You can't help yourself—it's your nature. But don't push me again. I may not be as strong, but I
have better leverage than you."

The AAnn was visibly amused. "Colleague, are you challenging me to a fight?"

"Don't be absurd. We are both here as guests and on sufferance of the human establishment, *crrllk*. They are not fond of either of us, and must regard our presence here as an imposition and distraction from their work."

"Not the human Cullen." With the tip of his highly flexible tail, the AAnn gestured to where the human in charge was descending the earthen steps that had been cut into the side of the excavation. "He knowss that it wass I who found thiss ssite, and I can assure you that he iss properly grateful."

Pilwondepat turned away. He knew the AAnn was right. The human Cullen Karasi owed the AAnn his gratitude. Pilwondepat possessed no such leverage with the human, or with any of his coworkers. Stumbling to and fro among them, weighed down by the humidifying equipment that kept him alive if not entirely comfortable, he noted their sideways stares and heard their murmurings of disapproval. The archeological team represented a cross section of humanity, though a well-educated one. There were among them some who actively espoused closer ties with the thranx. They were opposed by those who fervently desired that the two dissimilar species keep their distance from one another. The majority listened to the diverse arguments of their fellows and tried to make up their as-yet-undecided minds. Pilwondepat feared that his personal comportment under trying circumstances was insufficient to elevate the status of his people in the humans' eyes. At every opportunity, he did his best to counteract the sorry image he was certain he was presenting.

If only he could get rid of the awkward, encumbering survival gear! Within his private dome he could do so, and actually relax. But those few humans curious enough to pay him a visit did not linger. Coupled with the temperature on the plateau, the 96 percent humidity Pilwondepat favored within his living quarters soon drove them out. There was nothing he could do about it. If he lowered the humidity in the dome to a level humans would find comfortable, that would leave him miserable all of the time, instead of just when he was working outside.

So he tried to learn their language, a form of communication as slippery and fluid as their bodies, and make friends where he could. Meanwhile he was forced to watch as Riimadu strolled freely about the site, interacting effortlessly with the humans, sharing the same basic body structure and single-lensed eyes, and positively luxuriating in what for the AAnn was an ideal climate.

Had the reptiloid deliberately nudged him in an attempt to send him tumbling over the edge into the excavation, or had it been an accident? One could never be sure of anything except their innate cunning where the AAnn were concerned. They would gesture first-degree humor while cutting the ground out from beneath you. Yet he could not complain. The humans, who had far less experience of the AAnn than did the thranx, continued to remain ambivalent in their attitude toward them. Humans, Pilwondepat had noted in the course of his studies, had a tendency to react against assertions they themselves had not proven. Accuse the AAnn, insult them, insist on their intrinsic perfidy, and well-meaning humans were likely to leap to their defense.

It was infuriating. The thranx knew the AAnn, knew what they were capable of. Humans did not want to hear it. So the insectoids had to proceed discreetly in all matters involving the scaled ones, whether in personal relationships or at the diplomatic level. Humans would have to learn the truth about the AAnn by themselves. Like others of his kind, Pilwondepat only hoped this education would not prove too painful.

For their part, the AAnn were being more patient and proceeding more slowly in their developing relations with humankind than the thranx had ever known them to do with any newly contacted species. This knowledge allowed Pilwondepat to smile internally. Having to proceed with such unaccustomed caution must be causing the AAnn Imperial hierarchy a great deal of discomfort. He certainly hoped so.

Meanwhile, he was but one representative of his family,

clan, and hive, isolated on a world of great mysteries, dependent on the unpredictable humans for continued permission to work among them and, indeed, for his very survival. That many of them viewed his presence among them with suspicion and xenophobia he could not help. He could only do his work and try, when the opportunity presented itself, to make friends. For some reason he enjoyed greater sympathy from human females than from the males. This, he had been told before embarking on his assignment, was a likely possibility, and he should be prepared to take advantage of it.

It had to do, he had been informed, with the thranx body odor, which nearly all primates found exceedingly pleasant. More than once, human workers had commented upon it, and he had been forced to resort to his translator to ascertain the meaning of strangely emollient words like *jasmine* and *frangipani*.

With a sigh, he started around the edge of the excavation. It was time to do some work among the human field staff. That meant making his way to the bottom of the excavation. In the absence of a familiar ramp, he would have to cope with human-fashioned "steps." It was uncivilized and awkward, but he dared not ask for help. Special treatment was the one thing he was determined not to request. Many humans did not realize that thranx, built low to the ground, were terrible climbers despite boasting the use of eight limbs.

A young worker named Kwase saw the scientist struggling at the top of the first step. Putting down his soil evaporator, the young man turned and vaulted up the earthen staircase to confront the alien. Smiling encouragingly, he made a cup of both hands in front of his own legs. Quickly discerning the sturdy biped's intent, Pilwondepat gratefully dipped both antennae in the mammal's direction before carefully placing one foothand in the proffered fleshy stirrup and resuming his descent.

Brr!!asc—we make progress! he told himself with satisfaction. The annoyed look on Riimadu's glistening face as he observed the human voluntarily assisting the thranx was even worth a few deep breaths of inadequate, desiccated air.

The bottom of the excavation was no familiar homeworld burrow, he mused when he finally hopped down off the last step, but it was far more calming than the wind-blown, lonely surface.

4

Fanielle watched the Hysingrausen Wall slide past beneath the aircar's wings. Running east to west across this portion of the central continent, the immense, forest-fringed limestone rampart was interrupted only by a succession of enormous waterfalls that spilled over the three-thousand-meter rim. Despite the heavy flow, most evaporated before they reached the ground. Only a very few, the offspring of mighty rivers that arose in the northern mountains beyond the Mediterranea Plateau, thundered against rocks at the base of the wall.

The majestic geologic feature had kept the thranx from making anything more than cursory explorations of the high tableland. Humans were delighted to be allowed to establish themselves in a sizable region the thranx had ignored, and many thranx were pleased to see humans making use of an uplifted portion of their planet that was to them the perfect picture of a half-frozen hell.

She sealed her field jacket as the aircar, once clear of the strong downdrafts that raked the wall, commenced a gradual descent. The afternoon temperature at Azerick Station was sixteen degrees C. Bracing to a human, unbearably frigid and dry to a thranx. Azerick did not receive many visitors from the heavily populated lowlands. Most of the thranx who were assigned to help facilitate the station's development stayed down in Chitteranx, in the rain forest, where the humidity and heat were pleasantly overpowering. A few unlucky souls were assigned permanently to the human outpost. Being thranx, they rarely gave voice to their displeasure. Only someone like

Anjou, who had learned to interpret many of their gestures, could tell how unhappy they were.

In less than two weeks she would have her meeting with the eint. She intended to be forceful but congenial. There were years worth of particulars that needed to be discussed, lists of individual items that needed to be addressed in detail. She would have to pick and choose carefully so as not to offend, or bore, or isolate her estimable audience. Haflunormet was a good soul, but during the time they had worked with each other he had been able to offer little more than sympathetic encouragement on issues of real import. Working at last with someone who could actually make decisions promised to be enlightening as well as effective.

There was so much to prepare. She worried about overwhelming the eint with minutiae before paradigms could be agreed upon.

The aircar set down gently amid the quasi-coniferous forest that covered the plateau. While the trees resembled nothing arboreal on Earth, at least they were green. Jeremy was waiting for her. They embraced decorously. Other moves would have to wait for greater privacy.

He took her bag as they walked through the terminal. "I hear you finally got your meeting with a higher-up. Some of us were beginning to wonder if any of the diplomatic staff here ever would."

"You know the thranx." They turned a corner, squeezing past chattering travelers outbound on the aircar that had just arrived. "Caution in everything."

He made a rude noise. "It's more than that. It's deliberate. They're trying to stay friends, close friends, without committing themselves to anything definite. The Pitarian War was an exception, brought on by exceptional circumstances. Now they've reverted to the hive norm." Outside, he placed her bag in the transport capsule. In seconds, they were racing along a grassy trail split by the glistening metallic strip of a powerguide.

"I don't think that's the case at all, Jeremy." Leaning back in the seat, she watched the forest whiz past. At this speed, details vanished in a green blur, and travelers could almost imagine they were speeding through the far more familiar woods of Canada or Siberia.

He shrugged diffidently. "Well, if anybody should know, it's you, Fannie. You've spent more time among them than anyone else on staff. Personally, I don't see how you stand the climate and the crowding inside their hives." Reaching out, he took one of her hands in his and with a fingertip began to trace abstract designs on the back. "I'd rather have you spend more time here, you know. It's not real great for my ego to think that you prefer a bug's company to mine."

She smiled and let him toy with her hand and fingers. Little sparks seemed to materialize with each contact. "Unfortunately, while humankind has conquered deep space, cured the most serious primitive diseases, and spread itself across a small portion of one galactic arm, we have yet to solve the unfathomable complexities of the male ego."

His fingers jetéed up her arm. "Chaos theory. That's the ticket."

The darkened capsule arrived at Azerick with both passengers considerably relaxed in mind and body. Jeremy bid her a reluctant farewell, leaving her to compose the report she would present in person to the ambassador. Upgrading the embassy here to full settlement status was one item on the crowded agenda. The humans wanted it—for one thing, it would mean promotions all around—but the thranx were reluctant. Granting such status implied recognition of a condition existing between the two species that they were not sure they were prepared to acknowledge.

She showered and redressed, leaving off the field jacket since the station was heated to an Earth-ideal standard of twenty-two degrees, with humidity to match. Ambassador Toroni was anxious to hear her preliminary report. Details could come later.

Smiles and congratulations awaited her in the main conference room. Outside, the forest of the Mediterranea Plateau, as the resident humans had come to call it, marched away toward distant high mountains. A smattering of applause greeted her rising. She did not blush, was not uncomfortable. The acclaim had been earned.

Spreading a brace of viewers out before her, she folded her hands and waited as the ambassador rose. There were eight other people in the room, most of whom she knew well. Living in an outpost on an alien world left little room for people to be strangers.

"First," he said, "I want to extend my personal congratulations to Fanielle Anjou for securing what we had come to believe might never come to pass: an appointment to discuss, and to present, multiple items of diplomatic importance on which we have all been working for years. While the method of finally obtaining this long-sought-after meeting may have been unorthodox, I think I can say safely that no strenuous objections will be raised at higher levels."

"Especially since 'higher levels' have no idea what a Bryn'ja request is," Gail Hwang observed tartly.

"Funny, you don't look pregnant." From his seat next to the ambassador, Jorge Sertoa grinned down at her. "Who's the father?"

"Probably that thranx she's been seeing so much of," someone else put in quickly. Laughter rolled the length of the table.

"I don't think so." Aram Mieleski pursed his lips as he rested his chin thoughtfully on the tips of his fingers. "The delivery mechanism involved is so different that . . ."

"Oh, shut up, Aram," Gail chided him. "I swear, if ever anybody needed a humor transplant . . ."

"Emotional conditions cannot be transferred between individuals," an unruffled Mieleski calmly observed, by his words confirming the necessity of her observation.

"What will you do," Enrique Thorvald asked seriously, "if the thranx continue to inquire as to your condition?"

"They'll be informed that I lost the multiple larvae prior to giving birth." Anjou held one of her readers before her. "I've worked it all out. If anything, that should gain me even more sympathy. And it doesn't hurt that Eint Carwenduved, with whom I am to meet, is female."

"Yeah," Sertoa muttered. "You can compare the glaze on your ovipositors." While basically a good guy, Jorge Sertoa was among several outspoken members of the outpost staff who were less than enthusiastic about cementing deeper relations with their hosts.

"And I bet you'd like to be there to see that." Her rejoinder prompted more laughter and defused what could have been an awkward moment. Putting the jovial banter to rest, she hefted the reader and commenced delivering her formal report. They would all receive copies in due course, but this way questions could be asked as soon as they were formulated. Ambassador Toroni was a firm believer in encouraging staff interaction.

When she concluded, less than an hour later, there were fewer queries than she had anticipated. Her accomplishment in securing the official meeting was duly applauded once again, but most of the questions thrown her way concerned maintaining the security of the ruse she had invented to gain the appointment rather than what she was actually going to discuss when it finally came to fruition.

"It all depends," she commented by way of summation, "on how much authority I'm given going into the meeting."

All eyes shifted to Toroni. Running a hand through his shock of white hair, he leaned back in his chair and considered. For an ambassador appointed to what was arguably the most important nonhuman populated world known, he was casual in manner and laid-back in his work habits. It was an attitude much appreciated by those who labored under him. Azerick was a lonely enough place to be stationed without being forced to toil for some inflexible martinet.

"If it were up to me, Fanielle, I'd give you permission to vet and sign treaties. But you know I can't do that. I don't have that capability myself. As soon as we adjourn here, I'll get on the deep-space communicator and find out just how far the authorities on Earth are prepared to let you go. One thing you can be sure of: You won't be allowed to negotiate anything controversial."

"I already know that," she responded.

"But we might be able to procure more authority for you than you think, by trumpeting the importance of this meeting, how it's likely not to be repeated for some time, the sensitive nature of relations between you and this Eint Carwenduved—I intend to call in every favor and promise I've been stockpiling." He leaned forward. "I want you to have as much autonomy going in as we can manage. This is the first real breakthrough we've had in months, and I don't want to squander it."

"Even so, sir," Sertoa began, "we don't want Fanielle to agree to anything hasty." He smiled deferentially at her. "Careful perusal and dissection of any potential covenant is demanded before the authority to sign can be conferred."

"Loosen up, Jorge," she told him. "No matter what I manage to get the eint to agree to, I don't think you have to worry about some thranx sharing your bathroom anytime soon."

It was an exceedingly mild put-down, but whether for that reason or one unknown, Sertoa said nothing more for the duration of the meeting.

"I've been working on proceeding to the next step in securing a stronger alliance among our respective species." Holding up her reader, she touched a contact and waited the couple of seconds necessary to transfer the relevant documentation to everyone else's handheld. "If the eint doesn't dismiss it out of hand, I intend to at least broach a number of possibilities for future discussion."

"Such as what?" Hwang asked with obvious interest.

"A lasting, permanent alliance. Nothing held back. Military presence on one another's worlds, mutual command of tactics and weaponry, joint colonization of which this plateau and the Amazon Basin are only the most preliminary sorties." Someone whistled.

"You don't want much, do you, Fanielle?" Genna Erlich observed.

"You're talking about the kind of treaty that would require

not only a vote of the full Terran Congress, but approval by majorities on all the settled worlds." Mieleski's tone was somber. "It's a very adventurous program."

"What are we here for, if not to press for closer relations?" Toroni smiled paternally. "Though you've certainly chosen an ambitious agenda for yourself, Fanielle."

"Everything depends on the eint's reaction to my prefatory suggestions," she replied a bit defensively. "Depending on how things go, I might not even have the chance to make known my more elaborate proposals."

"Quite right." Rising, Toroni indicated that the conference was at an end. "I look forward to reading all the details of your report, Fanielle. With luck, we should within a couple of days have some guidelines from Earth detailing how you will be allowed to proceed. I myself am optimistic, and intend to frame the request for those guidelines in the most anxious manner possible.

"In the meantime, we all of us have much to study, and to digest. I take it you are amenable to criticisms and suggestions, Ms. Anjou?"

"Always," she replied, at the same time hoping there would not be too many. Putting what had previously been an informal succession of guidelines into presentation format was going to take most of the time she had remaining until her meeting with the eint. The last thing she needed was a flood of well meaning but essentially superfluous advice.

Only when word came back from Earth that she was to have essentially a free hand in making proposals—though she could not commit to anything more significant than, for example, the Intercultural Fair about to get under way on the colony world of Dawn—did she realize how truly important the encounter would be. Though usually an island of calm amid her often frazzled colleagues, she finally had to take some minor medication to still her nerves.

I am going to go in there, she told herself, as the chosen representative of my entire species, knowing that I have gained that access on the back of a lie. But while the burden was making her increasingly uneasy, she would not have turned the meeting over to one of her colleagues for all the suor melt on Barrabas.

As the time for her to return to Daret drew near, she found herself relying more than ever on Jeremy's strong, self-assured presence. A microbiologist, he had no diplomatic ax to grind, nothing of a professional nature to gain from her success or failure. He was interested only in her and their future together; not in her mission. It was a gratifying change from the characteristic infighting and arguing that took place within the highly competitive diplomatic hierarchy.

When the day scheduled for departure finally did arrive and she had little to take with her but her hopes and anxieties, he took time off from his lab work to join her for the brief journey in the transport capsule that would convey her to the settlement airport.

Once more, the great green forest of the Mediterranea Plateau was rushing past outside the transport's port. To the thranx, it was their deepest jungle, the most biologically mysterious region left on their homeworld. Visiting human researchers, strolling about comfortably in pants and shirts, were making valuable reports and passing on the results of their research to their thranx counterparts, who would have required special gear and attire simply to survive in the temperate-cool lower oxygen environment humans found perfectly amenable. Similar revelations were being made by thranx researchers stationed in the deep Amazon and Congo Basins on Earth. By such serendipitous exchanges of data and knowledge were scientific alliances, if not diplomatic ones, strengthened.

During the high-speed commute they held hands and talked. Jeremy's research was going exceptionally well, and everyone at the outpost was talking about Fanielle's breakthrough in securing a meeting with a thranx who ranked high enough to actually make decisions as well as recommendations.

"I'm not going to be able to get near you when you get back," he told her teasingly. "You'll be blanketed by representatives of the media."

"If this visit is a success," she reminded him.

"There are no *ifs* where you're concerned, lady-mine."

"Maybe not where I'm concerned, but diplomacy is something else again." Why, she wondered, did someone who was perfectly comfortable trolling the corridors of interstellar power suddenly and so frequently in this man's presence devolve to the maturity level of a sixteen-year-old? She had long ago become convinced it was due to a recessive gene on the Y chromosome.

"Just like you're something else again." Leaning forward, he kissed her as passionately as the time remaining to the airport conveniently allowed, then rose. "I could use something to drink. Do you want anything before—?"

She became aware of the pain as vision returned. It seemed to increase in proportion to the intensity of the light that splashed across her retinas. Memory loaded in increasingly large chunks: who she was, where she ought to be, what she was supposed to be doing. Too much of it failed to jibe with what she was feeling and seeing. Though the first words she heard were in themselves entirely innocent, their import was uncompromisingly ominous.

"She's awake."

She recognized the voice. Ambassador Toroni had a distinctive, measured way of speaking, slightly nasal but memorable. It matched his face, which moments later was smiling down into her own. There was relief in his countenance, but no humor.

A voice she did not recognize said, "I'll leave you alone with her for a while. Her vitals are fine, but she's liable to be less than completely coherent until the comprehensive neural block has fully worn off. The aerogels will keep her comfortable. If anything untoward occurs, or something doesn't look right, just hit the alert."

"Thank you, nurse."

Nurse. Anjou liked the sound of that even less than the absence of humor in her superior's expression. She struggled to sit up. Reading the relevant cerebral commands from the patch fastened to the back of her skull and ascertaining that rising did not contradict her medical profile, the bed complied.

Sitting up, she found that the light did not hurt as much. In addition to Toroni, Sertoa was also present. He did not even try to fake a smile. "Hello, Fanielle. How—how are you feeling?"

"Sleepy. Confused. Something hurts. No," she corrected herself, "everything hurts, but something is muting it." Looking past them, searching the hospital room, she did not see a third face. Especially not the one she sought. "I've been in an accident."

Toroni nodded, very slowly. "What's the last thing you remember, my dear?"

"Packing to go to Daret. No," she corrected herself quickly, inspired perhaps by their stricken looks. "I was already on my way there. On the transport to the airport. With—" She looked past them again. "—Jeremy Hyguens."

"He was a good friend of yours," Sertoa commented softly.

"Yes. We are—" She broke off as Toroni threw the other man a look of quiet exasperation.

He was. That was what Sertoa had said. *He was.* She sank back into the cushioning aerogel, wishing it was solid enough to smother her. When she had finished crying, when the tears had subsided enough for her to form words again, she believed that she heard herself whispering, "What . . . happened?"

Bernard Toroni sat down on the edge of the bed, the transparent aerogel dimpling under his extra weight. He wanted to take this exceptional young woman's hand, to hold it tightly, to make things better. But that was not a procedure allowed for in the diplomatic syllabus, and circumstances dictated that he keep a certain distance. He did not want to keep his distance, though. He wanted to hold her the way he had once held his own children back on Earth, before he had begun to receive assignments to other worlds.

"You were on a transport capsule in line for the airport. There was an empty cargo carrier on the strip ahead of you.

No one knows exactly how it happened, but there was a program failure. The cargo unit's drive field reversed. The two capsules hit very hard."

"The kinetic energy released—" Sertoa started to say before a look from Toroni silenced him.

"Once engaged, transport capsule fields don't 'reverse.' The programs are designed to be fail-safe. At worst, onboard in-line safeties should have cut its drive. Had that happened, your capsule's onboard sensors would have had time to detect the failure ahead and bring it to a stop prior to impact." He paused for reflection. "There were a total of twelve people on board the capsule you were traveling in. You and a fellow named Muu Nulofa from Engineering were the only survivors."

"Jeremy—" She did not swallow particularly hard, but her throat was on fire.

Toroni shifted his position on the edge of the bed. No one else had been willing to pay this first visit. "The lifesavers who extricated you from what was left of the capsule found his body sprawled across yours. They theorize that the extra . . . padding . . . is what saved your chest from being crushed when the front wall of your cubicle caved in. There was nothing they could do for him. Cerebral and internal hemorrhaging." He hesitated. "I did not know the man, but I have since spoken to some of his colleagues. They all describe him as a fine human being who was dedicated to his work. And to . . . other things."

Her eyes rose to meet his. He did not enjoy the experience, but he respected the woman in the bed far too much to look away. "Did they also tell you we had been discussing marriage?"

"No." The ambassador's lips tightened. "No, nobody mentioned that to me."

She relieved him by turning her head to one side, letting the warm aerogel supply the support her muscles no longer cared to provide. "We didn't talk about it much except among ourselves. There were too many other distractions. Professional—" She choked softly on the word.

It was quiet in the room. No one spoke for many minutes: the two men remaining silent out of respect, the woman because she no longer had anything to say. Behind her eyes, something had gone away.

"It's very interesting," Toroni finally murmured. When she failed to react, he added, "Unprecedented, certainly."

Moving with a slowness that had as its source something deeper and more profound than medication, she rolled her head back in his direction. "What is?"

"The expression of concern. On a personal level. From our hosts."

She frowned ever so slightly. "I don't understand."

"Some of the recently communicated terminology is unique to our translator's experience. I am told there are nuances involved they have never before seen expressed." He mustered a fatherly smile. "There are several from your contact Haflunormet, as well as from other contacts you have made among the locals. Of particular note is the one from Eint Carwenduved. Not only are deepest regrets expressed, but she wishes to assure us that as soon as you are able to resume work, she looks forward now more than ever to making your acquaintance."

"Your meeting is still on." Sertoa looked pleased. "You'll carry into it with you the extra benefit of added sympathy."

Her mind stirred, roiled, thoughts and emotions crashing into one another before slipping away in opposing directions. "No I won't," she responded tersely.

Toroni blinked. "I'm sorry, my dear?"

The look in her eyes was very different from the one that had commanded her countenance only moments earlier. "I won't be carrying sympathy or anything else into that meeting because I'm not going to be in attendance. I'm not going, Bernard. I'm finished here. Finished with Hivehom, finished with the bu—with the thranx, finished with everything." She turned away, until all she could see was the aerogel support. The portion in front of her face opaqued when she closed her eyes. "I want—I need to go home."

The ambassador considered. In the course of his distinguished career he had been faced with similar situations before. Some had even been inflected with highly emotional overtones. But never before anything like this. Never. That did not keep him from pressing forward as he knew he must.

"Fanielle," he told her as tenderly as he could, "you *have* to do this. No one else here at the mission has managed to achieve as intimate a rapport with our hosts. No one else is as facilely comfortable with their ways, with their habits or mannerisms. *You are the best qualified to take this meeting.* That's why you were given the assignment of trying to secure it in the first place. It's your moment of triumph. You have to take it."

From the vicinity of the aerogel came the agonizingly still-born response. "I don't want it anymore."

Hating himself, Toroni refused to let it, or her, go. Both were too important. "It's not a question of you wanting or not wanting it. You have to do it because no one else can do it as well. This is a highly sensitive moment in the development of relations between our species and the thranx. Perhaps even a milestone. We won't know until we see the fruits of our labors begin to blossom. The fruits of your labors, Fanielle. Do you really want to cast aside everything you've worked for here?"

"I've already cast it, Bernard. Find somebody else to go. Find somebody else to take my place."

Swallowing determinedly, he leaned toward her, careful not to initiate a significant disturbance within the highly responsive aerogel. "Don't you think, Fanielle, that if I felt someone, anyone else, was sufficiently qualified I would have assigned them to the task already? Before coming here to see you?"

Deep within, a certain component of her shattered self was pleased by the sincere words of a man she greatly respected. But like so much else that was Fanielle Anjou, that part of her was hiding now, isolated and shunted aside by the nightmare that had overwhelmed her life.

"I told you, Bernard. I don't care. It's not important anymore."

He nodded slowly, even though she was not looking at him. Or at anything else. The ensuing silence lasted longer than its predecessor. Once again, it was the ambassador who broke it.

"Program failure. Transport capsule drive fields just don't go into reverse. The system is replete with fail-safes—every one of which failed. The engineers are working on it, working hard. They're good people, but they're baffled. They cannot afford to be, because we must know what caused the accident. If we don't know, then we cannot with any certainty prevent a repetition. Of the accident. If," he concluded concisely, "it was an accident."

It was enough to turn her head. "Bernard?"

Sertoa took his turn. "Fanielle, you know as well as any of us that there are elements, some of them with substantial backing, both among the thranx and our own kind who will do anything to prevent the kind of union between our species that the enlightened among us seek. I'm not talking about the great mass of undecideds on both sides. I'm talking about the kind of blatant, old-fashioned fanaticism we thought we had evolved beyond."

Slowly, she digested what her colleague was saying. Contemplated it from an assortment of viewpoints. In the end, every one of them was equally ugly.

"You think someone deliberately reprogrammed that cargo capsule to reverse and smash into the one that was taking me to the airport?"

"We don't know that." Toroni was relieved to see some small flicker of alertness return to his junior colleague's expression, even if it was thus far focused entirely on concern for something unconnected to professional interests. "At this point it is only speculation. But I am not the only one to have considered it. Azerick Authority is pondering the possibility with utmost seriousness. If, and I caution if, the hypothesis should turn out to have any basis in fact, it would mean that our entire modus here will have to undergo the most strict review. We will continue to press forward with our work, of course. More fiercely than ever. But we will have to do many things differently."

She heard everything he said, but in manner muted. Her own thoughts were churning. "Somebody would kill a dozen innocent people just to get to me, to keep me from a stupid meeting?"

"Not stupid." The strength of her response allowed the ambassador to employ a stronger tone of his own. "Highly important. Possible milestone."

"And maybe it wasn't someone," Sertoa added. "Maybe it was some thing." He eyed her sternly. "The thranx have their own fanatics, remember."

"But to resort to killing a diplomat . . ." Her voice trailed away into disbelief.

"Why not?" Turning, Sertoa began pacing slowly, waving his hands to emphasize his words. "If successful, they set back our efforts until we can find someone else capable of achieving your kind of personal rapport with their kind. If discovered, word reaches Earth that thranx have carried out a mass killing of humans here on Hivehom. Either way, they achieve at least one of their ends."

"Which is why," Toroni went on, "no word of our suspicions is being allowed to go beyond Azerick. Officially, there was a programming failure. A transport accident. Nothing more. Unofficially, desperate unease is being bounced between worlds at high speed and without regard to the cost."

She was silent for a moment, wrapped in a cocoon of conflicting concerns. "What will you do if the investigating authorities determine that the crash was no accident, and that thranx were responsible?"

Bernard Toroni had been in the service all his professional life, had ridden the currents of diplomatic ebb and flow until all the rough edges had been knocked off him long ago, leaving him polished and smooth. Nothing surprised him; nothing could crack his learned demeanor; nothing could get a grip on his emotions. For the first time since he could remember, maybe for the first time ever, he was shaken.

"I don't know, Fanielle. I don't think anybody does. The reaction on Earth, among the colonies . . ." He swallowed hard. "It would result in . . . a setback."

She nodded, the movement a barely perceptible stirring against the aerogel. "If it's true, then someone—" She glared disapprovingly at Sertoa. "—some*one*, will go to any length to keep me from meeting with Eint Carwenduved."

Toroni's face betrayed nothing. "To keep you from doing so, yes. You specifically, Fanielle."

She gazed back at him evenly, more awake now than at any time since the two men had first entered the room. "You're a very cunning man, Bernard Toroni."

He shrugged, his face a perfect blank. "I'm a professional in the diplomatic service, Fanielle. Nothing more."

She turned her gaze to the ceiling. It displayed a soundless, peaceful holo of drifting clouds. In the distance was a small rainbow. She did not see it, just as she no longer saw peace. That had been taken from her. Forever? She chose not to think about it. Forever was a very long time.

"How soon will they let me out of here?"

The ambassador's tone was glib, controlled. "In a day or two, if you like. Then there will need to be a period of rest. You are one bipedal contusion from head to toe. But nothing significant was damaged. Nothing was broken."

"I wouldn't say that," she whispered wearily. "So . . . I will follow through with the lie, and make the meeting. You must be pleased, Bernard." Seeing the look on his face finally gave her the means to again consider the feelings of others. "I'm sorry. That wasn't fair."

"It doesn't matter." He rose from the side of the bed. "I'm used to it. It's part of my job." He hesitated briefly before continuing. Noting his superior's expression, Sertoa nodded solemnly and left the room. "There is one other thing. At least you will no longer have to worry about lying when you refer to the Bryn'ja request."

She did not reply: just stared up at him.

"The staff here knows nothing is broken or damaged because when you were brought in from the wreck you underwent the most thorough medical scan the facilities here are capable of rendering. I am more sorry than I can ever say,

Fanielle, but there is no point in keeping it from you. Truth always seems to emerge before it is convenient for us to have it do so. When you meet with Eint Carwenduved you will be able to do so as someone who has not obtained an encounter on the basis of a prevarication."

She examined the implications of his words from a distance. It only made her that much more determined to confound those who might have done this to her. To her, and to one other, and to a future that now would never have the chance to be.

Her voice as taut as duralloy stressed to the point of destruction, she gazed up from the bed out of damp eyes and asked him softly, "Do they know how long I've been pregnant?"

5

It certainly was a lovely world, Elkannah Skettle reflected as he and Botha took their ease along the shore of City Lake. New pathways had been laid to accommodate the anticipated tide of guests. Transparent lobes thrust out over the lake's surface so that visiting children could experience the illusion of walking on water while delighting in the play of native and introduced aquatics swimming just beneath their feet. A multitude of chromatic-winged flyers swooped and darted above the shimmering splay of water, making fearless dives to pluck small, wriggling creatures from the depths. They filled the air with an unexpectedly sonorous honking, surprisingly tolerant of the increasing numbers of visitors who had begun to throng the lakeshore prior to the official opening of the fair.

Too bad it all had to be marred by the presence of thranx.

For all that he had devoted much of the previous decades to decrying humankind's intensifying relationship with the insectoids and then taking his philosophy and intentions underground, Skettle had seen very few thranx in person. Observing them on the tridee was no longer a problem. The disgusting creatures were all over the media. You could hardly find one delivery source out of the thousands available where they were not eventually to be encountered; all bulging compound eyes, wriggly antennae, and obscene multiple mouthparts. If anything, meeting them in person was even worse.

He could sense the same robust revulsion in the shorter, darker man who matched him stride for stride. Botha was not especially talkative, ill at ease in get-togethers even of his own kind. But there was nothing subdued about his dislike of

63

the bugs. Equipped with poor social skills, he had to be
watched over constantly lest his deeply felt feelings manifest
themselves in ways that could be dangerous to his friends as
well as to himself. Skettle had taken it upon himself to do
this, which was why he had insisted that the engineer be
paired off with him today. Hatred is healthy, he had assured
Botha on more than one occasion. But it must be moderated
by wisdom. To be effective, ruthlessness must be appropri-
ately timed.

So when they passed a mated pair of the creatures, all suffocating scents and pearly aquamarine exoskeletons, he
shifted his weight just enough to nudge Botha off stride.
Wearing a hurt look, the stumpy engineer blinked up at him in
confusion.

"What was that about, Elkannah?"

"Keep walking. Keep looking at the wildlife on the lake.
That's better." When he was certain they were well out of
earshot of any other visitor, and after checking to make sure
that his individual privacy field was at full strength, Skettle
absently placed an open palm in front of his face to confound
any possible distant lip-readers and proceeded to explain.

"How often must I remind you, friend Botha, to conceal
your true feelings toward the bugs?"

The smaller man's expression changed to one of honest
surprise. "I wasn't! . . . Was I?"

"Your face is pure plastic, Piet." The older man stroked his
beard. "I at least can rely on these long gray whiskers to hide
emotions that might otherwise escape. If you will persist in
using a biannual depilatory, you must be prepared to monitor
every wrinkle of your lips, every arch of your brow, every
twitch of your cheek muscles."

Botha replied while considering something on the ground—
which also allowed him to conceal his lip movements from
potential far-seeing viewers. "I'm sorry. You're right—I need
to be more aware. Especially now, when we are so close to
accomplishing something really important. But is it really
necessary to be so careful, every minute? We've both seen

non-Preservers who obviously feel as we do yet aren't afraid to express themselves visually."

"That's because it doesn't matter if somebody confronts them, or questions them." Raising a hand, Skettle waved at a passing couple. Charming little girls they had with them, too. "Without appearing effusive, we must seem to be among those in favor of closer, not more distant, ties to these bug beings. We must not merely deflect suspicion; we must embrace it, engulf it. Then it can be safely disposed of, the way targeted eukocytes kill cancer cells."

Botha nodded understandingly. Except for the thranx presence, which would not begin to become truly onerous for another day or two until the full panoply of the fair was thrown open to the public, he was quite pleased with how things had been going. The weather, the freshness of the unspoiled atmosphere, the subtle tingling tastes and aromas of a new world: all were meant to be enjoyed.

Several times that day they tarried to eat something, or sit and have a drink. These many pauses allowed time for reflection. They also allowed Botha, through the sophisticated instrumentation woven into his attire, to coordinate the actual final layout of the fairgrounds with the multiple schematics he had spent nearly a year preparing. The inconspicuous display that occasionally flashed onto the organic readout that floated atop his left pupil would have gone utterly unnoticed by anyone but a very attentive lover.

By late afternoon they had covered a good deal of ground. Having studied stolen diagrams of the grounds for months prior to actually arriving on Dawn, they were able to avoid dead ends and cover only those areas it was absolutely necessary for them to visit and confirm in person.

"We could do another quadrant." Botha had perfected the art of reading the optical display without squinting. "They won't close for another hour yet." When the fair opened officially, they both knew, the grounds would remain accessible to visitors around the clock. This was very convenient for their own purposes, which did not include nocturnal sight-seeing.

"No need to rush things." Skettle was sitting in a chair

floating above a small pond. Trained leeshkats, local amphib-
ians, popped up in cleverly choreographed rhyme-time to spit
sparkling fountains into the air. Despite the seeming random-
ness of their alien exertions, not a drop of water fell on giggling, appreciative patrons of the small snack bar. Flowers
flush with streaks of pink and vermilion swayed atop flexible
aqueous roots. "We'll come back and finish up tomorrow."

"Fine with me. Everything matches up with the charts
we've been using. I haven't seen anything yet that will com-
plicate our planting of charges." Frowning abruptly, Botha
spun in his seat. His chair rocked playfully with the sharp
movement. "What is that awful screeching?"

"Poetry reading." As he pointed with one hand, Skettle
took a sip from the self-chilling glass of his tall, teal fruit
drink. "Watch your expression, Piet."

From atop a rotating mobile platform drawn by picture-
perfect simulacra of eight-legged *covuk!k* from Willow-Wane,
an ornately attired thranx was declaiming melodiously. Enchanted by his exotic appearance, quaint mode of transportation, silvery clicks and whistles, and a wafting fragrance
redolent of crushed orchids, a sizable crowd trailed behind.
They hung on the poet's every gesture and sound. Though the
majority of the entranced entourage was human and could
understand little of the actual meaning of what was being
said, they were fascinated nonetheless. The few thranx tourists
in the procession endeavored to translate as best they could,
and to convey some sense of the trenchant artistry that un-
derlay the courtly performance.

"Look at those people, slavishly hanging on that filthy
bug's wretched croakings!" Botha had to turn away from the
noisome spectacle, so repellent did he find it. "What's wrong
with them?"

"They have not been educated." Far more in control of
himself than his companion was, Skettle took a longer swallow
of his drink, then eyed the nearly empty glass appreciatively.
"This is very good. We will have to try and take some concentrate back with us. It is the task of such as ourselves, Piet, to
educate them. That is why we are here." He listened for an-

other moment as the procession wandered out of earshot. "Desvendapur."

"What?" Botha blinked at him.

"That was the thranx poet who escaped from their treacherous outpost in the western Amazon. Before your time, really—but I remember it quite well. I spent more time than it was worth trying to see what even a few disoriented, misguided humans found in his so-called poetic random barks and gargles. None of it ever made the least sense to me. Absolutely worthless drivel."

"Apparently not to a bug," Botha commented.

Skettle emancipated his empty glass, watched as it carefully negotiated a path between diners and drinkers on its way back to the kitchen. "Who knows what a bug thinks? Who cares? Let's get back to the hotel and find out how the others did."

Botha slipped out of his chair. It rocked briefly in his absence, then steadied to await the next set of perambulating buttocks. "Hopefully, Pierrot hasn't blown up anything prematurely."

"If she has, she better have included herself." Skettle did not look in Botha's direction, for which the smaller man was grateful. He admired, even revered, Elkannah Skettle as much as any member of the cause. But the old man could scare you sometimes, without even intending to. Something in his manner, in his mental makeup, was skewed: a powerful ego skimming swiftly across the ice of the mind on skates fashioned of parallel psychoses.

That did not make him any less of a leader in Botha's eyes. You just had to be wary of his occasional . . . moods.

Like his companions, Beskodnebwyl found Dawn unappealing. Had the authorities in charge not decided to hold this misconceived melange of a fair in the middle of the hottest month on the northern continent of the colony, he did not think he could have stood being outside for very long without proper survival gear. The idea of spending a winter on such a world . . .

As it was, it was near noon and he was still chilly. Afternoon would be better. The local temperature tended to reach its most intense just before sunset. Nothing could be done about the dryness of the atmosphere, however. Like the temperature, the local humidity fell just within the limits of what was tolerable. He felt some sympathy for the thranx who were actually participating in the fair. They did not have his flexibility, could not always come and go when the weather suited them best.

It was not enough sympathy to keep him from watching them die, however.

Flanked by Sijnilarget, Meuvonpehif, and Tioparquevekk, he wandered in apparently incessant spirals that in fact were designed to carry him and his square of four to a specific destination. Not one of the many clever amusements that had been constructed by the resident humans, nor any of the engagingly familiar displays that had been erected by the invited thranx, distracted the Bwyl from their chosen course. The four resisted all such blandishments, ignoring lights and music, recitations and performances, disdaining to sample even the finest examples of thranx foodstuffs imported by invitees from Hivehom, Willow-Wane, Eurmet, and elsewhere. They had no time to partake of such diversions. The truly dedicated are not easily swayed from their intendment.

The closer they got to their destination, the more edgy they became. It was not necessary to conceal the emotions running through them, however, because certain movements of limbs and antennae that would have been highly suggestive to another thranx meant nothing to the humans among whom they passed, and all other thranx were busy operating exhibits. The fair infrastructure had been designed, laid out, and was being run solely by the hosting humans of Dawn.

Even if they were confronted at the wrong time or in the wrong place, Beskodnebwyl knew, they could easily plead ignorance.

No one challenged them as they reached the building that had been constructed on the shore. A large portion of it extended out over the lake. This bulky apparatus was to be expected, since the building's task was to integrate communications within the fairgrounds, both private and public. Concessions, restaurants, exhibits, and most of all, Security—all depended on the gleaming new transmission and relay system to supply their needs. This it did admirably, in manner mostly automated.

Working with data extracted from restricted reports, a mated pair of renegade scientists sympathetic to the Bwyl cause had developed a wonderful set of miniaturized explosives easily deliverable by hand. At their chamber in the temporary hivelike structure the humans and their thranx advisors had built to provide comfortable climate-controlled lodgings for thranx visitors to and workers at the fair, the Bwyl had left a small packing case containing an assortment of favorite drinks. One drink container held enough of the explosives to kill a significant number of people.

Utilized throughout the fair, they would quickly cause widespread havoc. When the source of the havoc was identified as thranx, it should not be enough to start a war, but should prove more than sufficient to place a freeze on the upgrading of diplomatic relations that would last for years at a minimum.

They located and memorized several entrances to the structure, which was to be one of their principal targets. All were secured, as Beskodnebwyl and his companions knew they would be. Beskodnebwyl and Tioparquevekk kept watch while Sijnilarget and Meuvonpehif inspected the security arrangements.

"Difficulties?" Beskodnebwyl asked as soon as they returned. Few humans had passed their way. Those that glanced in the direction of the four thranx had assumed they were part of the fair maintenance staff. A reasonable, if totally incorrect, assumption.

"Not many." Sijnilarget was peering through a device that no human would have recognized. "Though important to the smooth functioning of the fair, this is not a military installation. I would estimate less than ten time-parts to gain entry without setting off any alarms. Admittedly, I have not had as much time as I would like to study human designs of this nature, but I see nothing insurmountable. Regardless of the sentient species that designs them, security systems for oxygen breathers adhere to certain fundamental patterns."

Beskodnebwyl gestured his understanding. "Gaining entrance is the difficult part. Once inside, it becomes a simple matter of setting and timing a couple of containers. In the absence of communications, the chaos we will create will only be magnified."

"There may be human guards inside," Tioparquevekk cautioned. "Or at least maintenance workers we may have to deal with."

Meuvonpehif flicked her truhands sharply forward, producing a small cracking sound as chitin snapped against chitin. "You concern yourself with getting us in. The rest of us will handle matters should any unfortunate humans decide to try and intercede."

"Anyone observing our activities must be silenced." Sijnilarget deliberately spoke in Low Thranx to emphasize the crudity of his response. "They must not be allowed to raise the alarm."

"We don't even know if there will be any humans to be encountered in what must surely be a largely automatic operation." Beskodnebwyl continued to shield Tioparquevekk's instrumentation with his body. "No one enters a strange burrow looking for trouble. How are you coming?"

"Almost finished." Tioparquevekk hovered over his equipment. "I have analyzed and ascertained the requisite patterns. All that remains is to record them and then run a phantom, to ensure that everything will work on the day we choose to act." He went silent, busy with all four hands and sixteen digits.

"Hey!"

Beskodnebwyl, whose knowledge of human speech forms verged on fluency, recognized the word as an exclamation of accusation. What mattered, he knew from his painstaking studies, was the intensity with which it was delivered, and whether querulousness was implied. It struck him that in this instance all the relevant ingredients were involved.

"What are you doing there?" The human who had spoken now adopted a tone more belligerent than curious. Beskodnebwyl did not panic. There were only two of the bipeds, and they were not clad in the attire of the several maintenance teams that serviced the fair. That meant they were only casual fair-goers, not unlike himself and his three companions. Behind him, he could sense Tioparquevekk concluding his work and hastily downpacking his equipment. Despite a rising sense of anxiety, the other three thranx worked smoothly and efficiently. With four hands, they were not prone to fumbling.

If this human did not occupy an official position, what right did it have to bark accusingly at Beskodnebwyl and his companions? Assuming a defensive stance, he moved forward to confront the human. It was rangy, even for its kind. Standing tall on his four trulegs, Beskodnebwyl could not have raised his head to the level of the biped's chest. Nonetheless, he was not intimidated. Proximity to the lumbering, lurching mammal brought on feelings of disgust and mild nausea, not fear.

"I will tell you as soon as you have shown me your license."

Looking bemused, the two men halted. The taller one continued to do all the talking. "What license?"

"The one that gives you the authority to challenge peaceful visitors to this fair." Behind him, Beskodnebwyl sensed his companions shifting their stances to form the rest of a traditional defensive four-headed square. Whatever happened now must be resolved quietly, he knew, lest the confrontation draw unwanted attention.

The smaller of the pair spoke up, speaking to his friend. "Not only talkative bugs, but sarcastic ones." His hand, Beskodnebwyl noted, was hovering over a slight bulge in the garment that covered his lower body. The Bwyl was not worried. If the human flourished a weapon, Sijnilarget, Meuvonpehif, and Tioparquevekk would be ready to respond with firepower of their own. Though differing greatly from thranx in their physical makeup, human bodies reacted similarly to an encounter with high-velocity explosive pellets.

The taller one's tone became slightly less combative. "I

asked you what you were doing here." His head bobbed in
a gesture Beskodnebwyl knew was meant to indicate the building behind them. "This isn't part of the fair exhibit. There's
nothing here for the public to see."

"We know," Meuvonpehif commented readily in her
heavily accented Terranglo. "It's the central communications
facility."

Beskodnebwyl was furious enough to reach back and snap
one of the female's antennae. By her physical reaction, he
could see that she recognized her error almost as soon as she
made it. Perhaps, he hoped agitatedly, the humans would find
the comment innocuous.

They did not.

The tall man chose to continue to direct his words to Beskodnebwyl. "Is it really? That's interesting. How do you know
that? It isn't marked as such on the outside."

"Its function is quite obvious," Beskodnebwyl replied a bit
too quickly. "The necessary apparatus for the transmission of
information dominates the roofline."

The human nodded again. Beskodnebwyl thought his expression now indicated thoughtfulness, but it was difficult to
tell. Mastering the range of human facial expressions took
time and patience. "So you've been studying the communications center from other vantage points besides this one. That's
even more interesting. I wonder what the Dawn police would
make of your interest?"

The biped was preternaturally perceptive, Beskodnebwyl
thought tightly. This was threatening to get out of hand. He
could feel his companions shifting their stances behind him,
preparatory to . . .

He was contemplating how best to dispose of the humans'
bodies when the short human appeared to lose control of himself. Drawing the bulge from his shirt, he aimed a device that
was as lethal-looking as it was compact directly at Beskodnebwyl's head.

"Goddamn dirty bugs want to get their filthy claws on
everything!"

Reacting almost instantaneously, the trio of thranx behind

Beskodnebwyl extracted from their thorax pouches weapons of their own. Confronted unexpectedly by thrice his number, the stocky biped hesitated, unsure now how to proceed, his initial bravado much reduced by the revelation that his intended victims were armed. He stared at them, glanced up at his companion, then back at the thranx. Like the rest of him, the muzzle of his weapon wavered.

Admirably calm, the tall human stepped between his friend and the armed defensive square. "Now, this I would not have expected. Piet is quite right: It is unthinkable to have disgusting, germ-ridden quasi-insects such as yourselves stumbling about this close to a vital human installation. It inevitably raises the question of why you would want to do so. The presence of concealed weapons at a peaceable venue like this fair greatly enhances those questions. As does the undeniable skill and readiness with which they have just now been deployed. Yet you are not members of an officially recognized organization."

"I dispute nothing you say, but what does it prove save that thranx are always ready to defend themselves from reasonless attack?" Beskodnebwyl was watching the tall human carefully. The man's stocky companion he had already dismissed as unimportant, despite the fact that he was the one holding the weapon.

"It may prove a very odd thing indeed." The human smiled, fully exposing his teeth. Beskodnebwyl had to force himself not to turn away from the distasteful sight. "It suggests that you and I may be here for the same purpose."

Beskodnebwyl had nothing to frown with, and the human could not understand the thranx's gestures. It was left to inadequate words to convey subtleties of meaning. "And what purpose could that possibly be?"

"Elkannah?" the shorter man murmured uneasily. "Are you sure about this?"

"I always trust my instincts, Piet. If there's another explanation, we'll divine it in short order." Turning his attention back to Beskodnebwyl, he continued as calmly as if requesting a change of shuttle seat assignment. "You and your dirt-dwelling friends are here to disrupt this fair, aren't you? You're planning to do something to, or with, local communications. You are here to cause trouble."

This was it, Beskodnebwyl reflected. They would have to kill both bipeds, and kill them quickly. All it would take would be a gesture from him. The humans would not recognize it, and so the one holding the gun would not have time to react. But . . . he was curious.

"That's the kind of observation that could get an individual killed. Why shouldn't it?"

"Because my friends and I are here for the same reason. From civility, we plan to bring forth chaos. We don't like your kind, you see. Among us are many, too many I fear, misguided people who think we should cuddle up to you bugs, make you part of our cultural and political lives, let you set up your teeming, odious colonies on our own worlds. That sort of thing is reprehensible, unnatural, and must be prevented at all costs." He stopped, waiting while the bugs digested his words.

"How very astonishing." At a gesture, the trio behind him lowered, but did not put up, their weapons. Somewhat reluctantly, the shorter human did likewise. "Your speech is admirable, except that for sake of veracity the word phrase for *stinking soft flesh* should be substituted for the derogatory term *bugs*."

The biped smiled again. Beskodnebwyl found he was better able to tolerate it this time. "I think we may be able to come to an understanding. If we do not cooperate, our natural antipathies will surely undo our respective plans. Ours do not especially involve the communications facility. Your plan is just to destroy it?"

"Yes," Meuvonpehif replied before Beskodnebwyl could silence her.

The biped looked in her direction. "You are lying. Such as you would not come all this way, smuggling in weapons as well as intentions, just to render the visitors to and promoters of this abomination of a fair unable to communicate with one another. You must have something more extensive planned." He returned his gaze to Beskodnebwyl. "I will reiterate: If we do not cooperate, we will end up at cross-purposes, when what we both want is the same result."

Beskodnebwyl nodded, an absurdly easy human gesture to imitate. "We intend to set off explosives not only here but throughout the length and breadth of the depravity." Behind him, he heard Tioparquevekk and Sijnilarget inhale sharply in disbelief. "The more fair-goers—human and thranx alike—that we can kill or incapacitate, the stronger will be the reaction among your kind."

Again the human nodded—approvingly, Beskodnebwyl thought. "We plan to make use of some custom-built explosive devices. As I understand it, the more creative types we execute, the angrier will be the response from your infernal hives."

"Quite correct." Beskodnebwyl found himself staring up at the human. Used to dwelling underground, the human's greater physical stature did not intimidate him. That sort of psychological positioning was for open-air dwellers only. "You confirm what we already believe: that your kind are inherently violent and murderous, and must be kept as far away as possible from a truly civilized society such as our own."

"We want nothing less. Back on Earth, you know, we step on bugs all the time. Have been doing so since the beginning of our recorded history."

"What more can be expected," Beskodnebwyl responded, "from a species that flops about like ambulatory sacks of iron-based blood and loose meat?"

Skettle's smile faded slightly. "We understand each other, then. We will not interfere with whatever it is you intend to do, and you will not interfere with us. Working separately but with the same goal in mind, we will with our endeavors here succeed in putting relations between our species where they belong: at a distance sufficient to ensure that we have to do no more than tolerate your presence in the same galactic arm as ourselves."

"I could have put it better," Beskodnebwyl replied, "but your words will do. It may even be that we will, over the next several days, find reason to cooperate more closely in carrying out our respective efforts, and might even try to synchronize our operations in hopes of achieving maximum outcome."

"That's a fine idea." Skettle started to retrace his steps. At no time did he turn his back on the bugs. "We should arrange for some of us to meet daily to continue this exchange of information. How about at the Syxbex Restaurant, on the lakeshore?"

"That location will be eminently satisfactory." Beskod-nebwyl maintained the defensive square, watching as the pair of bipeds retreated. "We want to be sure to avoid any misunderstandings."

When we have done what we came for, he mused, we will also find a way to kill you. Loose antennae could not be allowed to flutter about. Besides, it would give him pleasure to preside over the demise of so forthrightly antagonistic a human. He raised a foothand in the human gesture of farewell.

Skettle waved back, thinking as he and Botha turned the first available sheltering corner that he was going to delight in seeing this particular bug's skull cracked and its brains oozing out over the colorful pavement that had been laid down for the fair.

There is nothing in art, in philosophy, or in politics to match the fervor of mutual cooperation among discordant bands of fanatics.

6

The supply station had a spectacular setting. Located on a low rise overlooking a vast salt pan smoking with geysers, mud pools, and hot lakes, it doubled as a geothermal research station for the score of scientists and their support teams studying the wonderfully bewildering variety of silicate and sulfuric minerals that gushed forth from the bowels of the planet. These often differed markedly from their terrestrial analogs. Every week of exploration, sometimes every day, elicited new cries of discovery from delighted geologists.

In addition to being crammed full of mineralogical revelations, the thermal wilderness was awash in beauty. While yellow and its variations were the predominant colors, there were also rich varieties of blue, green, and red thanks to the presence of the tough, active, endemic bacteria that thrived in the thermal pools. Occasionally, a brisk south wind would sweep through the valley, brushing away the clouds of steam to expose kilometer after kilometer of roaring geysers, gurgling hot springs, plopping mud holes, and steaming rivers. A certain species of thermotropic eel-like creature nearly two meters long had biologists almost coming to blows over its taxonomy. Was it a highly advanced worm or an exceedingly primitive fish? Or something entirely new to science?

On the rare occasions when it rained, the combination of steam, fog, and drizzle made it impossible to see more than a meter in front of one's face even at high noon. At such times fieldwork was restricted. Unseen, the tentative network of hastily laid prefab pathways could not be negotiated in safety, and even aircar work was halted. The resident scientists would cluster in frustrated, argumentative knots inside the air-conditioned labs and living quarters, anxious to be released from regulations even though they knew these had been drawn up with their own safety in mind. But when was there ever a scientist who paid proper attention to personal safety when a host of new discoveries lay close at hand?

Brockton was working on a robot probe designed to take samples from the hottest vents when he felt the first vibration. It was accompanied by a muted rumble, as if one of the back doors had been opened. A glance showed that both of the big service bay barriers were still shut. With a shrug, he returned to his work. He was alone in the shop except for the automatics, Norquist and Oppervan having decided to take a long lunch. They did not have many opportunities to interact with the scientific staff and took every chance to do so. To improve their education, both men insisted. To try to put the make on one of several attractive unattached ladies among the staff, Brockton knew.

Nothing more than casual flirting for him. He had a wife and two kids on Tharce IV. He was here because he didn't mind the desert, and because in a year on Comagrave he could make the equivalent of three years' salary back home. His family understood. When his contract was up, he would be able to take a whole year off doing nothing but watching his kids grow.

Though considered a party-killer, he got along well with his workmates. His skills, honed through fifteen years of experience, were greatly appreciated by both his colleagues and his employers, and he did not try to play the disapproving father figure to his predominantly younger coworkers. Removing his hands from the interior of the probe, he shut the access panel, picked up the nearby magnetic welder, and began to reverse the polarity on the interior latches. Once flopped, they would hold the panel shut as securely as if it had been melted into place.

There it was again. A second tremor, stronger than the first. He had picked up enough geology from hanging around the station's scientists to know that where geysers and thermal pools are present, stronger seismic activity was to be expected. But this didn't feel like one of the numerous minor temblors he had experienced many times during the preceding months. It had a different feel to it—more of a bump than a rumble.

The station was constructed on a flexor foundation that was designed to distribute any shock evenly across its base. Anything short of a tectonic convulsion would be dissipated by the integrated flexors before it could cause any damage. The contractors had known what they were doing. Though he had not worked in construction, Brockton had seen enough to know good work from bad. Upon arriving, he had taken an off day to make his own inspection of the station and its outlying structures. Everything had looked reassuringly solid.

That was when the ground fell away and the roof started to come down on top of him.

The roar that accompanied the collapse was frightful, a caustic clamor in the ears that masked the screams of those crowded into the central dining area for lunch. Feeling the floor fall away beneath him, he grabbed wildly for the probe. It was plunging downward as well, until he managed to hit the open programming panel. Bluish light emerging from its flat underside, the probe rose and steadied on its tiny repulsion field. Brockton's terrifyingly rapid descent slowed. Kicking the field up to full power, he found that the probe could muster just enough lift to keep them both aloft. For how long he did not know.

Then the rest of the roof came down.

Guiding the probe, he made a mad dash for the nearest crumpled doorway. He just did manage to slip through a rip in the crumpling, warping fabric. Outside in the glare and steam of the day, he turned his head to look back in the direction of the station. Keeping both arms and legs wrapped tightly around the laboring device, he tried to make some sense of what he was seeing.

The entire station—central hub, communications tower, living quarters, lab modules, service departments, hygienics plant—was collapsing in upon itself. No, not upon itself, he saw through the rising, swirling mists. Into a gaping cauldron. A roaring river of boiling water had suddenly manifested itself directly beneath the station. With nothing to support it, the advanced flexor foundation was no more useful than a row of wooden pilings.

Despite the damp heat, he was having chills. Rising above the groans and grindings of imploding buildings were the screams of those trapped inside. A few who had been near the front exits had tried to escape that way, only to find there was no place to escape to. Like those they had left behind, they died before they could reach solid ground, crushed beneath the subsiding structures or boiled alive in the torrent that had burst forth beneath their feet.

In less than an hour there was nothing left of the supply station. It had been swept away, down the steaming cataract that now gushed from the side of the rise and into the nearest expanse of hot lake. A couple who had been out all morning studying cyanotic bacteria returned in their aircar and pried his cramped arms and legs off the probe that had saved his life. Another researcher returned later that evening. He was accompanied by the resident AAnn advisor. Decamping on a mound of solid, well-vegetated ground half a kilometer away, the numbed survivors tried to make sense of what had happened.

Brockton knew what had happened. He had survived to feel his wife next to him once more, and to hold his children. As soon as rescue teams arrived, he was putting in for a pysch dismissal. He doubted he would have any trouble getting one. Not after what he had seen.

Norquist, Oppervan, all those other fine men and women— all gone. If the rescue teams were really lucky, they might be able to recover some bones. Sitting on the ground beneath an orgthic bush, he hardly heard what the others were saying. It was starting to get dark, and he was cold. Surrounded by hell, he was cold. Of everything his fellow survivors said prior to the angelic arrival of the first rescue craft, only a few words of the AAnn, speaking in clumsy Terranglo, remained forever stuck in his memory.

"*Ssstt,* we told your engineerss not to build on that ssite!"

The stitcher's harpoon struck the underside of the aircar with a familiar shrill *thwack*. Leaning cautiously over the side, Elrosa saw it wriggle out from under the sand, all three of its protruding, bulbous eyes triangulating on him, their intended prey. He wondered what, if anything, the voracious alien mind behind them was thinking. As he thrust his scanner over the side of the vehicle, he watched as the meter-long harpoon was slowly retracted. The stitchers learned quickly: It would not expend its killing mechanism on the armored underbelly of the aircar again.

So powerful was the expelled harpoon of a stitcher that it could penetrate the underside of a normal vehicle. Elrosa and Lu's aircar was not normal. It had been given a ventral sheathing of glistening golden percote that would have been more appropriate to a military transport. Nothing merely organic could penetrate that layer of sprayed-on armor. It reduced the aircar's speed and range, but not significantly. And it allowed the two biologists to proceed in comparative safety with their study of several varieties of desert-dwelling predator.

Another hopeful *thwack*. Another subsurface hunter disappointed. This was turning out to be an excellent study area.

The stitchers were one of several unique carnivores that lived and hunted beneath Dawn's scattered sand seas. They impaled their prey on long, sharp harpoons built up of concentric layers of hardened calcium carbonate. It was as if a human had learned how to sharpen a femur, spear it into prey, and reel the resultant kill back in by means of the ligaments still attached to the bone. Since no one had yet dissected a stitcher, the means by which their harpoons were propelled at such remarkable velocity remained open to explication. Elrosa favored compressed air as a nontoxic and readily renewable means of propulsion. Lu came down on behalf of those who postulated the existence of multiple knots of rapid-twitch muscle fibers.

They were not out today to catch and dismember—only to take measurements. Elrosa was duly excited by the work they had accomplished over the past several days. There were more stitchers per cubic kilometer of sand sea in this area than anyone had previously encountered anywhere else. Lu thought it might be a mating territory. Stitchers mating—now that would be a ripe subject for a monograph!

Another lackluster *thunk* sounded as a harpoon struck the impenetrable underside of the aircar. He smiled to himself. It would be useful to know if the stitchers considered the low-flying intruder a threat or a possible meal. Perhaps both, he mused. Previous fieldwork indicated that the predators sometimes appeared to hunt in tandem, or even in small groups. He and Lu had seen no evidence of pack hunting thus far, but like everything else on Comagrave, organic or otherwise, very little was known with assurance.

Behind him, his partner shouted a verbal command to the aircar console. It complied, and they found themselves jetting silently forward, leaving frustrated stitchers goggling in their wake. Only the predators' eyes and expended harpoons were visible above the surface of the dune.

Another sand-filled depression beckoned. With luck, they might find a line or two of migrating geulons, or a new species. So recently arrived were humans on Comagrave's surface that it was the unfortunate biologist indeed who did not return from a field trip without at least several new species to record. Taxonomy was almost as exciting as actually encountering the creatures in question.

Leaning over the open side of the car, careful to keep himself as small a target as possible for anything inimical that might be lying camouflaged under the sand, he directed Lu to shift them another ten meters northward.

"That's good!" He gestured with his upraised right hand. "This looks like a promising spot."

His assumption was correct. Every day, they grew more skilled at predicting the movements of the planet's endemic wildlife. No sooner had the aircar hummed to a halt than not one but three loud *thwack*s, one after another like shots from a gun, rapped on the underside of the vehicle.

Lu joined his friend at the edge. The air suspension craft hovered effortlessly some three meters above the sand. "There!" Lu pointed to where a brace of eyeballs, like pale white melons, protruded from the sand. Recorders were brought into play.

As they clicked away, Elrosa heard a decidedly different kind of *thunk*. It was higher in pitch, more immediate, and sharper of sonic detail. Turning, his eyes widened slightly as he saw the meter-long calcareous lance quivering upright in the deck. It had penetrated the plastic sheeting to a depth of a fifth of a meter. As he stared, a soft whistling sound drew his gaze upward.

"Look out!" Throwing himself to the side, he just did avoid the descending tip of the stitcher harpoon. It slammed into the deck centimeters from his scrambling right foot.

Rolling over, Lu stared in astonishment at the impressive weapon. "They know that there's food up here—us—that they can't get at from below. So they've started firing into the air, hoping to impale us on the way down. Amazing!"

The aircar was equipped with a retractable cover, but one designed to offer protection only from the weather. A harpoon would go through it like a vibrablade through gelatin. As Elrosa climbed to his feet and took a step toward the control console, a vast whistling suddenly filled the air, as of an approaching dustdevil. Lu let out an inarticulate cry and dove for the open hatch that led to the tiny, enclosed head.

He didn't make it.

Assembling silently beneath the sand, the pack of stitchers must have fired at least fifty harpoons.

Though its power pack was approaching empty, the aircar was still hovering in place when one of the several search teams sent out to look for the two biologists finally found it. Of the two biologists who had been aboard, there remained only bloodstains on the deck, and on the side where their harpoon-impaled bodies had been dragged from within by the hungry stitchers. Studying the scene of quiet butchery, the newcomers conversed in subdued whispers interrupted only by the occasional *thwack*s of harpoons striking their craft's underside and armored roof.

When the sole AAnn aboard suggested that perhaps she and her kind should take over field study of the stitchers, or at least supervise the work, the human in charge readily agreed. If the AAnn wanted to deal with such cunning carnivores until such time as enough was known about them to work their territories in comparative safety, he saw no reason to argue. Let the reptiloids be the ones to put their lives at risk.

"There will be less rissk for uss," the AAnn assured him sympathetically. "We are ussed to living in the ssandss, among thosse kindss of creaturess that make their homes thussly. You will, of coursse, receive copiess of all reportss as they are prepared, and will be kept fully up to date on all our progress."

"Fieldwork is usually better carried out by the many than by the few," the dejected human supervisor concluded. Another time, under different circumstances, he might have felt otherwise, but he was distraught over the unexpected loss of two of his colleagues. Besides, where was the harm in sharing field assignments with the willing AAnn? They were more at home in this kind of country than any human, and their willingness to share data had already been demonstrated. Let them do some of the hard work. With an entire new world to study, catalog, analyze, and report on, his staff was already stretched thin. They could find plenty to occupy themselves besides stitchers.

"I don't understand." Hibbing stood by the side of the glassine tower and stared dubiously at the readouts embedded in its smooth, curving side. "Everything was fine as of this time yesterday." Nearby, Tyree and Sauvingnon were examining the contents of the relay box that hugged the side of the tower close to the ground.

Tyree glanced up. "Everything's working, sir. The extractors just aren't pulling any water."

Turning, Hibbing saw his eyewrap darken as he gazed east-

ward. The site that had been chosen for the main settlement
on Comagrave commanded a sweeping view of the spectacular Carmine Cliffs, a geologic upthrust averaging a thousand meters in height that ran for hundreds of kilometers
from north to south. Below and to the west were the Berge-
mon Salt Flats, a perfectly flat pan devoid of vegetation, subsurface liquids, or tectonic instabilities. To the north lay the
maze of narrow canyons known as the Fingerlings. One of the
most biologically rich areas on the planet, it was but a short
journey from the outskirts of Comabraeth community.

Beneath the settlement site, hydrologists had located a sizable prehistoric aquifer big enough to provide a six-hundred-
year supply for a city of half a million. A better place to
establish the colonial capital of Comagrave could not be
found on the planet. There was water in abundance, more
than ample landing space for shuttles and aircraft out on the
pan, biological and geological riches practically within walking distance. Months had passed without a hint of trouble,
during which time the village had grown into a thriving small
town of more than ten thousand. There was talk of formalizing it as the capital of the incipient colony.

And now the water, every million acre-feet of it, was gone.
Or so his hydrotechs were telling him.

Reluctantly, he lowered his gaze from the glorious, multihued vista spread out before him. Comagrave was not yet developed enough to be able to accommodate tourists, and his
position never allowed him longer than a minute or two to be
one himself. "How could this happen?"

Sauvignon rose to confront the administrator. At his feet,
Tyree continued to fiddle with instrumentation, as if by so
doing he could somehow will the water to return. "There are
possibilities. Since the original discovery dated the top layer
of water to several hundreds of thousands of T-standard years
ago, it seems pretty clear to me that the only way it would
suddenly vanish is if some radical new regional development
did something to affect the underground geology."

Hibbing nodded slowly. "And the only new regional development is us."

Sauvingnon gestured in the direction of the extraction tower and the attached processing and filtration plant. "Everything above ground is working perfectly. So we have to assume that the problem is subterranean in nature. Personally, I've never heard of an aquifer that big disappearing this fast. But this is a new world. Geology isn't even a perfect science on Earth." He turned thoughtful. "This region might not be as seismically stable as the original surveyors first assumed. There might have been a catastrophic collapse in the shale strata underlying the aquiferic sands. It could have been set off by the continual vibrations of shuttlecraft landing and, especially, taking off."

"That doesn't sound very reasonable."

Sauvingnon sighed. "Since we don't have a reasonable explanation for what's happening, I'm starting a search for unreasonable ones. The aquifer is broad, but not deep. Realistically, a subterranean collapse on such a scale is unlikely. Theoretically, it's possible."

"What can we do?" Hibbing turned back in the direction of the town. "I've already activated emergency rationing procedures. I'm responsible for the health and well-being of nearly fifteen thousand people, Sauvingnon, every one of whom needs to drink and occasionally to wash. We don't have a waste problem—the solid-waste decomposing system needs no water—but I'm going to have to start having supplies tanked in from the Broughlach River. That's three hundred k's from here. A couple of months of that will bankrupt our municipal operating budget. As you know, initial planetary R and D stopped supplementing that over a year ago."

And I'll be replaced, he thought to himself. They'll send me somewhere quiet and out of the way to decompose, just like the town's solid waste. Hibbing did not want to be replaced. He liked his job, liked the beauty and solitude that Comagrave could boast in plenty. It was why he had applied for the position of colonial administrator in the first place.

"We can drill elsewhere." Souvingnon pointed across the valley, to the colorful crimson rampart. "Maybe at the base of the cliffs."

"Maybe." Hibbing was dubious. "But the initial hydro surveys chose this spot because there was water in plenty here. And if the shuttle landings are responsible for what has happened, who's to say the underground water table hasn't been collapsed everywhere in the vicinity?"

Tyree finally rose from his inspection, brushing dust from his hands. "We could ask the AAnn."

The AAnn had a very small deeded scientific outpost to the west of the town, near the edge of the salt pan. They had no view of multihued cliffs, no easy access to the valleys of the Fingerlings. As Hibbing understood it, there were no more than forty individuals working at the reptiloids' outpost at any one time. Insofar as he knew, they had their own water supply. An emergency line could be laid across the pancake-flat edge of the pan from the alien outpost to the town in a fraction of the time and cost it would take to build one to the Broughlach River.

If the AAnn had water to spare, and if they were so inclined.

Hibbing considered. Town storage was at 80 percent of capacity. Within a few days, like it or not, they would be tanking in water from the distant Broughlach.

"Let's pay our scaly neighbors a visit," he told his engineers softly.

Coblaath SSCDDG met them outside. Standing at the entrance to the AAnn outpost, it was difficult to tell that there was any kind of installation at the edge of the pan at all. That was because, in keeping with AAnn preference and design, the great majority of it was located underground.

"Very hot insside for humanss," the outpost commander informed them. "You like it warm. We like it hot."

That was an understatement, Hibbing knew. Vacationing AAnn would have no compunctions at setting up sand baths and scale scratchers inside a working oven. And they liked even less moisture in the air than did humans.

"I appreciate your concern for our welfare." Hibbing was new to this. He was an administrator, not a diplomat. But having explained the dire situation to his superiors via deep-space beam, he had been given emergency leave to do whatever he thought necessary and best to alleviate the situation.

"You heard what has happened to our water supply?"

The AAnn executed a gesture of third-degree commiseration coupled with fourth-degree understanding, all of which looked like nothing more than gratuitous hand waving to Hibbing. "A terrible missfortune. Who can explain ssuch a thing? We have never encountered ssuch a phenomenon ours-selves, and we have ssettled many worldss very ssimilar to Vussussica."

Hibbing ignored the use of the AAnn cognomen. He was not here to argue the fine points of diplomatic terminology. He had come for help.

"You heard what my engineers have theorized."

Coblaath gestured, then nodded. "Thiss head movement iss the correct one, yess?"

Hibbing smiled broadly. "That's correct, yes."

The AAnn commander drew himself up proudly. "I have been practissing. My people perussed your hydrology report. Your engineerss appear to have analyzed the ssituation mosst thoroughly. We ssurmise that there iss at leasst one, perhapss sseveral vertical upthrusstss of impermeable rock between here and your sstation. Thiss accident of geology keepss our aquifer sseparate from yourss."

"And you still have plenty of water?" Hibbing tried not to show too much interest, wondering in the midst of his caution if the vertical-pupiled, lizardlike alien would recognize such concern even if it was manifested.

"Truly ample. The equal of what ussed to lie beneath your own esstablishment, I am told." As the pointed tongue flicked in Hibbing's direction, the administrator tried not to flinch. "Enough to sspare whatever you need, perhapss even on a permanent bassiss." He gestured reassurance. "After all, we have only a tiny outposst here, and require very little water for our own needss. Why sshould you, our friendss, not make good usse of it?"

Hibbing was taken aback. The period of difficult, extended negotiations he had been prepared to embark upon in order to

secure the minimal amount necessary to keep the station
going had not only not materialized, but here was the AAnn
commander offering him all the water he needed—and for an
unlimited, or at least unspecified, time into the future. The
money alone that would be saved . . .

"I hardly know what to say, Commander Coblaath. I had
not expected such a generous offer."

The AAnn's tail switched sideways in yet another gesture
of significance Hibbing was unable to interpret. "While it
ssleepss underground, the water doess no one any good. We
can help you with the engineering. If we begin a pumping
sstation here while your people lay pipe from your end, it will
sshorten the time until you can receive our water."

"Yes, of course it would." Hibbing had gone from being
apprehensive to feeling positively buoyant. But while he had
seemingly achieved all he had come for, and much more, the
negotiations were not yet completed. "What would you require in the way of payment? My staff and I don't expect you
to give us access to this water out of the goodness of your
hearts."

"But that iss why we are doing thiss." Coblaath managed to
sound, if not look, surprised. "We would not let our good
friendss want for water. We assk only one thing."

Hibbing waited, trying to hide his unease. "What might
that be, Commander?"

"We wissh only to be accorded equal sstatuss in thiss region. To be free to go where we wissh, to do our own sscien-
tific work without having firsst to ssubmit it for approval to
your ressearch authority, to move about as we require. A little
freedom of action, that iss all. Iss not too much to assk in return for ssaving your largesst community on Vussussica—
your pardon, on Comagrave. Iss it?"

Hibbing hesitated. Did he have that kind of authority? The
AAnn wasn't asking for equal colony status, or control over
anything. Simply the ability to cut out the red tape that ham-
pered the free movement of his own staff. What harm could
there be in acceding? It wasn't as if Comagrave was home to

military secrets that needed to be protected. The money this
would save . . .

And he had been given the authority to deal with the emergency as best he saw fit, hadn't he? If the authorities back on
Earth didn't like it, they could deal with the agreement after
the fact. Meanwhile, the station would have all the water it
needed, and the AAnn would have a reason to continue to
maintain cordial relations with the staff and inhabitants. If
anything, Hibbing felt, in agreeing he was doing something
to promote better interspecies relations.

"I think I can safely say there will be no problem in getting
my people to agree to such a simple and straightforward request. That's really all you want in return?"

"That iss all." The commander extended a hand in imita-
tion of the human gesture. "Thiss is the proper indication, iss
it not?"

Hibbing took the proffered hand. The three fingers and op-
posable thumb were tipped with sharp claws that had been
painted with colorful whorls. He felt hard scales slide against
his own soft flesh. The sensation was not unpleasant. He was
charmed by the AAnn's effort to mimic human ways.

"Indeed it is. I extend my thanks and that of my entire staff,
not to mention those of everyone resident in the town."

"Tell them on behalf of myself and the Imperial Board of
Intersspeciess Relationss that I am mosst delighted we were
able to help. Truly."

Like everyone else on Comagrave, Pilwondepat kept abreast—
or more properly, *athorax*—of weekly happenings through
reports that were freely available via the planetary net. Not
only did it help him to stay well informed and aid him in
his own research, but it was an excellent way to practice his
Terranglo. The only information available in Low or High
Thranx came via sealed communiqués or direct orders from
the tiny thranx complement living on sufferance at Comabraeth community. During the past months he had become
used not only to speaking in Terranglo, but to thinking in it. It
made him less thranx, but not necessarily more human.

Presently, he was perusing a seemingly minor account about a poisoning that had occurred in the Talathropic Pond ecosystem. The Talathropics lay nearly a thousand miles from Comabraeth. A human resources-analysis team had been following up a stock satellite report, prospecting on the ground for possible ore bodies of certain metals, when one of their number had been bitten by a local arthropod. The man's circulatory system had reacted severely—so much so that he had not been expected to live. The site was too far from Comabraeth for help to reach the afflicted in time.

Only the presence in the same area of an AAnn troika that was taking mineral samples made the difference, as the AAnn possessed on their craft a small lab for synthesizing regenerative proteins. Ratiocination of the toxin's molecular structure allowed them to concoct a crude antidote that saved the man's life. As the report detailed, his friends were effusively grateful for the reptiloids' swift and efficacious intervention.

By itself, the article was a mere annoyance. While happy that the human who had been bitten had survived, Pilwondepat was irritated that it was the AAnn who had received gratitude for the deed. Then he began to think. Probably, he decided, the only problem was that, isolated in his self-contained chamber on the edge of the escarpment, he had too much time to think. But . . .

Wasn't it odd that a human should be bitten by a viperous indigene far from any human assistance, only to encounter AAnn working the same vicinity who just happened to have among their mineralogical gear a fully equipped portable lab for doing organic chemical synthesis that included among its research files sufficient data and material for calibrating human as well as AAnn biologenes? Was it more than odd, or did he need to turn the chamber's humidifier up yet another notch?

Something else pricked at his mind. Resetting the viewer, he began searching for similar articles, or even dissimilar ones that might involve human-AAnn interactions. Anything so long as it smacked of oddness.

Gradually, as the night wore on and everyone else in the

camp slowly slipped into deep, relaxing sleep, what he began to find were examples of something more than apparently unrelated oddities, the least of which smelled even stronger than the most odoriferous of his human associates.

And much more ominous.

7

It was a part of Daret she had never seen before, that no human had seen before, and it was spectacular. Accustomed to the crowded warrens of the capital hive, the last thing Anjou had expected to find was open space underground.

She felt as if she were walking in a park lifted from some elegant imperial past on Earth. To be sure, the scattered furnishings and artwork were utterly alien, and the botanical decor was unfamiliar; but the sense of luxury and good taste was apparent everywhere, even to a visiting human. Small waterfalls cascaded down slopes that had been sculpted from the raw rock out of which the high-domed chamber had been hollowed, their flow vanishing into the myriad conduits that were the lifeblood of the hive. The arching ceiling glowed with yellow-and-blue light supplied not by artificial lights but by hundreds of transplanted fungi. Mist swirled gracefully, only to be caught and borne away by concealed fans to be recycled through hidden ducts.

A small *myrk* peeped out from beneath spatulate, blue-veined leaves. Crouching, Fanielle extended a hand, and the palm-sized creature crept hesitantly over to her, ambulating on four legs nearly hidden by its dense coat of black-and-blue fur. It had the huge eyes and sensitive nostrils of an animal accustomed to living underground. As it sniffed cautiously of her open hand and then moved close so she could scratch it, she reflected that these were the kinds of furred creatures the thranx were used to dealing with: tiny, harmless, mewling things that had shared their hives and tunnels for millennia. It cooed delightedly and pressed up against her caressing fingertips.

In another part of the Arm, the tiny balls of fluff had stood up, shed most of their fur, and achieved a level of technology equal to that of any other space-traversing species. This was difficult for many thranx to accept. One shooed furry creatures out of the way, or paused to observe their strange behavior. One did not converse with or enter into treaties with them. One especially did not sign agreements that could be construed as even a partial surrendering of sovereignty.

Yet that was the ultimate end to which Anjou and those of like mind within the diplomatic corps strove. It was proving an uphill battle on both sides, against superstition, fear, prejudice, uncertainty, and inertia. She thought of Jeremy and imagined him waiting for her back in Azerick. Jeremy, with his quiet, confident smile and the way his face would light up at the news that another new kind of spore had been discovered. Jeremy, with his enveloping, comforting arms, and soft lips. Jeremy, with . . .

Jeremy was no more, and there was to be no more of him. She shuddered violently, uncontrollably, and angrily shoved the back of a hand against her moistening right eye.

"Are you feeling unwell, *crr!!kk*?"

Whirling, she found herself gazing into the face of the oldest thranx she had ever seen. Even the venerable female's ovipositors had turned a dark purple. Her chitin was the color of raw amethyst, the glow of her great golden compound eyes was significantly dimmed, and her antennae hung forward in limp arcs. At least two trulegs gleamed more brightly than their counterparts, showing that they had undergone forced regeneration, and one truhand was purple composite, suggestive of injury so severe it could not be regrown and had been replaced with a prosthesis. But the voice, though muted, was strong, and the concern it reflected genuine.

"I'm all right, thanks." Though she stood straighter, she still found herself at eye level with the sage. Most humans towered over the arthropods: not Fanielle. Whether they appreciated having a diplomat to deal with who came down to their level physically she did not know. Haflunormet had never commented on her height.

"You are the attaché who sought this appointment, are you not?" The valentine-shaped head cocked slightly to one side.

"I am Fanielle Anjou, yes. You are Eint Carwenduved?" A simple gesture on the part of the elderly thranx was confirmation enough. "I very badly want to talk to you about—"

The venerable eint interrupted, pointing with the artificial truhand. "Let us go and sit by the *prolerea*, and listen to the music of the waters singing. We can talk there."

The thranx moved slowly and with deliberation, picking her steps as if each one might be her last. She did not appear to be that feeble, Anjou reflected. Ancient, to be sure, but still capable of flexibility and movement. The human hoped her host's mind had the same capacity.

They paused at a little alcove close by one of the many small waterfalls. This one tumbled and tinkled over a succession of metal leaves, each droplet generating a musical tone. Looming above was a bush with a thick trunk that threw out great splays of bright pink-and-black flowers. The fragrance from so many blossoms reeking of cinnamon and honey was almost overpowering.

Reaching up, the eint plucked one and pressed it to her face. Anjou could see the multiple mouthparts working as the thranx devoured the center of the bloom. When it was half consumed, she extended the remainder to Anjou.

"I am told that your people can safely ingest this. Would you care to try it?"

Anjou did not, but diplomats are often called upon to extend themselves in peculiar ways on behalf of their profession. Accepting the remnant, she saw several centimeter-long structures protruding from its underside. Plucking one, she showed it to the thranx, who gestured encouragingly. Popping the alien pistil into her mouth, she bit down tentatively.

Flavor and a sugary sensation exploded across her suspicious taste buds. The pulp was so sweet it almost hurt her teeth. As she passed the blossom back, she needed no encouragement to finish what she had been given. It was superb.

"Very nutritious." Finishing off the remaining pistils, the eint set the bloom casually aside. In a subterranean garden as immaculate and ornate as this, Anjou doubted the debris would remain unattended to for very long.

"About the proposed treaty details," she began, the lingering sweetness still effervescing throughout the inside of her mouth, "have you had time to scrutinize the details?"

"*Sssllcci,* I have done little else these past major timeparts." Reaching out with a longer foothand, the eint put four hard-shelled fingers against the human's belly. "I cannot imagine what it must feel like to give live birth. I am told it is painful, and can well imagine it."

"It's not comfortable." Anjou was not pleased by the rapid change of subject, but did not try to force the conversation. "In ancient times, I'm told it was often fatal."

The eint gestured restrained disbelief. "Eggs are better. They do not kick. Now then, about this treaty of yours. It's very substantial. Mere translation took a goodly amount of time."

"A treaty is not a poem," Anjou admitted. "Nothing must be left open to misinterpretation."

"I assure you it was not. The entire series of documents was vetted most thoroughly."

"I know that you are in a position to make real decisions." Anjou leaned forward, trying to suppress her excitement. "That you can recommend directly to the Grand Council. What do you think of the proposals?"

The distinguished female caressed a blossom bud with truand foothand, bending the petals back ever so gently. "I love these flowers. I love the look of them, and the smell, and especially the taste." Dimmed but far from dead eyes regarded the watching human. "If you bring the plant into your sleeping chamber, it fills it with perfume—but only for a few days. Then it withers and dies. I would hate to see the very good relationship that presently exists between our species perish from too much contiguity."

Anjou was not put off. "That won't happen."

"Is that so?" The distinguished female set the barren bloom

aside. "So in addition to giving birth to this document, you can also predict the future?"

"No, no, of course not. I'm just saying that safeguards will be put in place to ensure that we don't intrude on each other. Close friends don't have to live together under the same roof."

Antennae bobbed and dipped. "That is what the council will say. I can tell you right now what the response will be if I propose your treaties for ratification. I don't have to tell you, of course, but I rather like you, Fanielle Anjou. And not simply because you are eggfull." A truhand reached out to stroke the woman's forearm. The superannuated chitin was still smooth and cool to the touch.

"You obviously believe deeply in these proposals on a personal as well as a professional level."

"I am not alone," she responded. "There are many who believe as strongly in the interdependent future of our two species as do I."

"And it is not to be denied that there are those in the hives who feel similarly, and who are not hesitant to express themselves in the strongest terms." The matriarch's essence filled the air, stronger even than the surrounding, lovingly tended flowers. "But they are not a majority. Nor are those who angrily oppose any contact with your kind beyond that which is absolutely necessary. The bulk of the Greater Hive remains undecided. The words in your proposal are reassuring, and well thought out, but they are not wholly convincing. Furthermore, they are only words." Reaching back, she removed a small tube from the embroidered pack on her thorax and sniffed deeply of one end by holding it flush against first one set of breathing spicules, then the other.

"We have to start with words." Anjou shifted her seat. "When we have agreed on certain words, then relevant deeds can be implemented. But treaties must come before action." Am I getting through to this ancient? she wondered. What was the eint thinking? Unlike face-to-face negotiations with another human, there was no way to tell from simply looking at the eint what was going through her mind. The chitinous countenance was inflexible.

"You speak well for your proposals, you and those who side with you. As for myself, I belong to that great, surging, heaving mass of egg-layers and tenders that has not yet made up its mind." A truhand wagged in Anjou's direction, and she did not need a visual guide to interpret its significance. "Push us too hard, young female, and we will wall up our tunnels away from you. You will not be able to reach us."

Anjou struggled to remain confident. It wasn't easy; the eint was offering little in the way of encouragement. "Then as they are written, you disagree with the basic tenets of the covenants?"

"I did not say that." Plucking a smaller, darker branch from the nearby foliage, the eint munched contentedly on azure petals. Her mouthparts made fastidious grinding noises as they masticated the succulent herbage. "What I think, what the majority of those I represent and those I deal with daily in council think, is that your kind and mine have a perfectly good relationship right now. There is no need to extend it further, except insofar as concerns the AAnn."

Anjou watched something small and metallic flit through the surrounding undergrowth. "We have no quarrel with the AAnn. Therefore we can't promise you any more assistance as regards them than what already exists. If they were to make some kind of serious frontal attack on a thranx world, that would be different. We would be bound, even in the absence of a formal military treaty, to render aid because of the help you gave us during the Pitarian War."

"Would you, my dear?" Carwenduved studied the human closely, wishing she understood the meaning of those remarkable twists and contortions that flowed through the biped's flexible epidermis. "There is no formal reciprocation. You are not obligated to assist us, just as we were not obligated to help you against the Pitar. There is no treaty, no pact that requires you to provide such military assistance. We helped you against the Pitar because we thought it was the right thing to do. In the event we are assaulted by the AAnn, will your people believe similarly?"

Diplomat though she was, it was too big a lie for Anjou to countenance. Besides, the eint probably knew in detail whereof she spoke. "I can't answer that, Carwenduved. It would depend on the circumstances. I can tell you that humans have always stood up against injustice, no matter where it has occurred."

"That is good to know. Is it so even among those of you who refer to us as 'bugs,' and would like to squash us underfoot like our tiny namesakes that occupy your worlds?"

"Shapeism is conspicuous among the thranx as well as among my people. It is a primitive animosity that will eventually die out."

"As it must also among my kind." The eint sighed, her b-thorax expanding and contracting sharply. "But for now, it exists, and must be dealt with." She stirred on her bench. "Although I admit there are those on the council who would like to forge a tighter relationship with your kind, they are outnumbered by the many who believe that the present situation is perfectly satisfactory. They see no need to dig the two burrows closer together. You have your worlds; we have ours. While we can share the same environments, we have different preferences. We like hot, humid worlds with a higher oxygen content than yourselves. From our point of view, you like to live in dry, cold places where no thranx would be comfortable for very long, and where depending on the relevant extremes we need special equipment to survive. There is no direct competition. Therefore, there is no need to modify the formalities that presently exist between us. The galaxy is a big place, and our explorations and exploitations need never overlap."

Anjou could not hide her disappointment. She had worked so hard to secure this meeting, and except for some casual, albeit friendly, chitchat, it was going nowhere. The eint was polite, but firm. "It could be so much more. The way our species worked together during the Pitarian War showed that."

"More than what, *yrriik*? What more could we wish for than what we already have? Trade proceeds as trade always does, according to the benefits that accrue to those participating. There is mutual respect, and even a certain degree of sometimes grudging mutual admiration for each other's unique qualities. There is even beginning to be appreciation on a deeper level, as witness occasional events like this intercultural fair on your new colony world of Pawn."

" 'Dawn,' " Anjou politely corrected her. "But it's not the same. It's not what it could be." Held in check since she had arrived, excitement finally overcame her professional equivocation. "We've never encountered anyone like the thranx. Physically, socially, you're completely different from us. Yet we enjoy so many of the same things. Not only art, but even humor. I don't know anyone who has spent time among you who has not made a permanent friendship or two."

She was waving her arms about now. Instead of alarming the elderly eint, it relaxed the alien. Speaking frequently as they did with their four arms, it was a pleasure for a thranx to see a human similarly utilizing her limbs. Carwenduved studied the movements with interest, wondering at the meaning of each individual gesture. She would have been disappointed to learn that nearly all served only to emphasize and did not carry specific meanings of their own.

"Friendship is a fine thing," the eint declared when Anjou finally ran down. "But you speak as one who has spent more time among us than most of your kind. Others are not so sanguine. What is to say that a closer, tighter association might not harm rather than help relations between our kinds? In the absence of proof, continued caution would seem to be the best course."

Here, at least, was a line of objection Anjou had anticipated and prepared for. "There are the outposts here, at Azerick, and in the Amazon Basin on Earth. In both places, humans and thranx have developed a working relationship that goes beyond the formal. Everyone gets along. There have been just one or two reported incidents of violent conflict between settlers, scientists, and locals. The more time our people spend in one another's company, the closer grows the bond between them. We have seen this happen over and over again. There is occasionally some mutual distaste involving appearance, but this soon passes as everyone gets to know everyone else." She nodded at the eint. "Your own reports, I am sure, show similar maturation."

"No one disputes that our species can get along, or that individuals can become fond of one another." Reaching out with a foothand, she ran the two center fingers down Anjou's arm. "*I* am growing fond of *you*. Your persistence gains you merit. And I must confess that I myself . . ." She looked away—or at least, Anjou thought that she did. With those compound eyes, it was hard to tell. "I am inclined to think that the proposals you set forth in these documents should be given serious consideration."

Anjou contained herself. Out of the cool, calm resistance of the conversation had come the first glimmer of hope. "It would be," she replied with as much gravity as her small voice could muster, "the greatest thing to happen to our two species since each of us independently detected the presence of intelligent life beyond our respective homeworlds. Think of it! An alliance between two different intelligences that for the first time in this part of the galaxy advanced beyond the usual agreements on trade and culture. Thranx would be able to visit any human world they wished, at any time. Humans would gain reciprocity of movement with the Greater Hive. We would share government, thus reducing many large expenses. And no potentially antagonistic species would dare to threaten so powerful a regional alliance. You would be safe forever from possible depredations on the part of the AAnn."

"Don't underestimate the determination and capability of the AAnn." The eint gestured first-degree vigilance. "They are afraid of nothing. Cautious, yes. Deliberate and calculating, yes. But afraid, no. You are right, of course. Such an all-encompassing alliance would give them considerable pause, and would therefore be to our great advantage. But it goes beyond the military commitment the Great Hive seeks."

Anjou sat back. "I don't see you ever acquiring the one

without the other." It was time for bluntness, no matter how unpleasant. "Despite what I said earlier, I personally don't see the great mass of humankind going to war to save the thranx. To save a human-thranx society, or humanx as some of us have taken to calling it, that would happen without debate."

"And I don't see the council moving in the direction of sharing government and dissolving at one dig all the usual barriers that stand between us."

Anjou wished there was another representative she could caucus with, someone else she could turn to for advice on how to proceed. But there was not. She was alone. The eint had agreed to see her, and only her, because of the Bryn'ja. There were at present no other diplomats serving at Azerick who happened to be pregnant.

"Will you at least present the formal proposal to the other members of the council?"

"They have much to occupy their time, and are very busy. Not only are they responsible for the stable operation of government here on Hivehom; they must consider progress and development on our own colony worlds."

"And wouldn't those functions be easier if they could be shared?"

The eint whistled quiet amusement. "You are righteously dedicated in this matter, I see."

"I, and those who think like me, dearly desire what we believe to be best for both our peoples."

"Well, the Pitarian War certainly gave a boost to your aspirations. There are those among the thranx who would sign such a treaty tomorrow. Unfortunately, they do not lie in council. But yes, I will present the relevant documents for consideration."

Anjou's heart leaped. It was not everything she had hoped for, but it was realistically as much as she could have expected from the visit.

"And now, enough of interstellar diplomacy, of debating the fate of worlds." Rising from her supportive bench, the rickety eint clasped Anjou's right hand in a foothand. "Such softness! One cannot only feel the warmth, but see blood vessels beneath the skin. I marvel that it does not tear as easily as a leaf."

Anjou let her hand lie freely in the hard chitinous grasp. It was like holding hands with a crab. "Amazing stuff, human skin. I'm afraid we don't take care of it the way we should."

"Yet if torn, it bleeds more slowly than do we." Antennae dipped forward, stroking the human's exposed arm. "And this business of exuding salt water through your epidermal layer. Most bizarre."

"No less strange than breathing through one's neck," Anjou responded. "Or employing a set of limbs alternately as hands or feet. Or smelling through feathers that stick out of one's head."

"You speak querulously of normal things." Tugging gently, the eint drew Anjou away from the bower where they had been talking to lead her down another garden path. "Not being a biologist, I take it you have never seen a nursery, or visited a pupation station."

"No," Anjou admitted. At the eint's words, images swam in her mind of glistening larvae and newly matured adult thranx bursting forth from swollen body cases.

"*Srr!!lpp,* if you're going to speak of merging our civilizations, our cultures, you need to know more than what they show you at formal briefings." The two fingers and two thumbs that had been holding Anjou's hand moved around to her lower back and pressed, urging her forward.

"You will come with me now, Fanielle Anjou. It's time you met the kids."

8

"Maman, look at the funny-looking man walking the big bug!"

The well-dressed woman leaned over and whispered urgently to the little girl, who looked to be about seven. "Hush now, Iolette. It's not polite to call someone funny-looking. It's only his clothes that are different. And he's not walking the big bug; they're walking together. That's a thranx, sweetheart. They're not really bugs. They just look a lot like bugs."

From the other side of the seven-year-old, her father bent over to speak. "A bug is an insect, sweetheart. The thranx are not insects. They're people, just like you and me, and they're supposed to be very smart."

The little girl's black ringlets hovered about her forehead as she looked sharply up at her father. "Can we go meet them, Dadan? Can we say hello?"

Mother and father exchanged a glance. "I don't know, sweetheart," the mother murmured. "Are you sure you really want to? I thought you told me that bugs were yucky."

The girl was insistent. Perhaps it was the play of color of the thranx's iridescent blue-green exoskeleton, or the flash of light from the red-banded golden compound eyes. Something drew her in its direction. "But Dadan says thranx are not bugs. Please, Maman, please!"

The woman hesitated, but her husband was encouraging. "This is supposed to be an intercultural fair, Peal. It would give her something to talk about in her next age-group mixer back home. I'll bet none of her friends have ever met a thranx in person."

"They haven't, Dadan." Ringlets and wide blue eyes swung around on the reluctant mother. "Please, Maman!"

"What can it hurt, Peal?" the husband wondered aloud. "Actually, I wouldn't mind face-to-facing one of the things myself. And if that guy at its side isn't walking it, maybe he's some kind of handler or something. See, they're wearing similar symbols. I'm sure it's safe." A sudden thought made him smile. "I know! It's some kind of wandering exhibit, as opposed to all the static displays we've been seeing on stages and in tubes."

Under assault from two sources, the woman finally relented. "Well, if you're certain it's safe . . ." Making sure her daughter's fingers were grasped firmly within her own, she glanced down one last time. "You stay close to Maman, Iolette."

"That larva has been staring at me for some time." Twikan-rozex gestured with antennae and truhand in the direction of the dark-haired little girl who was eagerly leading her parents toward him and his companion.

"Girl," Briann corrected his friend. "It's a little girl, not a larva. I know that for you they amount to the same thing, but I promise you no human parent wants its offspring, however cute, referred to as a larva. The word brings up unpleasant atavistic racial memories."

"*Little girl.* I will remember. But I think *larva* is a better description. Compact."

"I won't argue with you." Glancing down at himself, Briann made sure his robe was straight. As always, he wanted to make a good impression. Good impressions first, they had been told. Conversions later.

The approaching adults looked uncomfortable. The woman, Briann noted, studiously avoided looking directly at Twikan-rozex. "Hello," the man began, "I hope you don't mind, but my daughter expressed a desire to . . ."

"Can I touch it, Dadan? Can I touch it?" Wide-eyed, the little girl was bouncing up and down with barely repressed energy and excitement.

"You have to excuse our daughter," the woman began apologetically. "She's never seen a thranx before. We come from

New Riviera, and we've only seen thranx there on the tridee. So you can understand that—" She broke off abruptly, clearly distracted by something unexpected. "What is that *exquisite* fragrance?"

Briann repressed a smile. It was always the women who noticed it first. "I think you're probably referring to the body odor of my companion." He indicated Twikanrozex, who stood patiently. The sensitivity of humans to thranx body scent was no mystery to him. One had only to breathe in that of humans to understand the attraction.

"Really?" The woman had come unglued. Her eyelids were fluttering as she inhaled deeply. "I've heard about it, read about it, but it's not the same. Words just don't—they don't . . ."

"Peal, control yourself." The man breathed in and did smile. "I can't quite place it myself. Attar of plumeria? Essence of protea?"

"Everyone responds a little differently because of subtle variations in the neural connection between their olfactory nerve endings and the brain. And no two thranx seem to smell exactly alike." Briann was always gratified when the hesitant and sometimes openly hostile drew near enough to get a whiff of his friend. Twikanrozex's personal perfume was a better introduction to his species than any carefully scripted salutation.

As her mother stood swaying slightly, her eyes half closed in a private ecstasy of olfaction, the little girl broke free of the woman's diminished grip and rushed forward. Twikanrozex recoiled ever so slightly. Remembering the eighty-fourth maxim propounded by the founders Shanvordesep and Cirey Pyreau allowed him to relax and accept the assault. Human offspring, he had been told, were by nature far more physically forward and demonstrative than their thranx counterparts, not least because they already had arms and legs since they did not experience pupation. So when the girl reached out to lightly touch his thorax, he did not flinch.

"Iolette." The woman was coming out of her fragrance-suffused haze. "Maybe you shouldn't—"

"It's all right," Briann was quick to reassure her. "This is what the fair is about, really. Not rides and exhibits and food." He nodded to where the wide-eyed girl was enthusiastically exploring his companion. "This." When the woman looked uncertain, her husband put a reassuring arm around her.

Dropping to all sixes to bring himself closer to the young biped's level, Twikanrozex dipped his head in her direction. "Would you like to feel my antennae? That's what we smell with."

Reaching out and up, the girl gently let the feathery projections slide through her small fingers. "They're soft! Like feathers." She looked the alien directly in the eyes, utterly unafraid of its proximity. "You people smell really nice, but you sure are funny-looking!"

"And you are funny-looking to us, child," Twikanrozex replied without hesitation. The young one had said "people" instead of "bugs." Of such tiny steps were enduring relationships forged. "We can't imagine smelling the world through holes in the middle of our faces."

Giggling, the girl put a finger to the tip of her nose and pushed it first to one side, then the other. In response, Twikanrozex wriggled his antennae. This led to further giggling and brought forth a smile on the woman's face that was wondrous to behold. For the first time since her daughter had insisted on the confrontation, the mother looked relaxed.

"How about," Twikanrozex suggested, "a buggy-back ride?"

"Oh yes, ohyesohyes!" The angelic countenance whirled on her parents. "Maman?"

"I don't know . . ." The broad smile faded slightly, but did not disappear.

"It's perfectly safe, madam," Briann assured her. "Twikanrozex is quite used to humans. He's done this before. He enjoys it." That was only partially true, Briann knew, but Twikanrozex had offered. It was part of their calling. Briann was only sorry that he could not reciprocate, because thranx larvae had no arms or legs with which to hold on.

His reassurance was good enough for the girl. Without

waiting for formal consent—or further objection—from her mother, the girl scrambled around to the back of the alien. Kneeling, Twikanrozex instructed her to climb up onto the upper part of his abdomen. Once she was seated comfortably on his upper wing cases, he told her to hold on by putting her arms around his thorax, but to be careful not to cover any of the eight breathing spicules located there. That led to a discussion of whether it was better to breathe through holes in one's face or at the base of one's neck. Confident the girl was secure, the thranx started off, utilizing all six legs to support her properly. Once, he stood back on his four trulegs only, rising a little higher and making her shriek with delight as she was forced to hang on to keep from sliding off his smooth back and wing cases. Twikanrozex's aquamarine backpack, b-thorax muffler, and leg warmers did not get tangled in her limbs.

Looking on, the husband murmured to Briann. "They really are remarkable creatures. I mean, once you get past their unsettling physical appearance, they're quite likeable."

"It depends on how badly you're afraid of insects." Briann stood watching with arms crossed. Choosing not to chat, the woman had eyes only for her daughter. The longer the interaction went on, the louder her daughter screamed with delight, the more she mellowed. "Some humans have no trouble with it at all. Others are . . . Well, there are xenophobes among most intelligent species. The important thing to always keep in mind is that the thranx are not Terran insects. They're not related to the much smaller arthropods that we've been battling since we came down out of the trees. Appearance-wise, it's a pure case of convergent evolution."

The husband nodded slowly. "Not to mention that they helped save our butts at Pitar."

"There is that, too. But they would rather be known for their art and philosophy than their military prowess. As would we. At least, as most of us would."

They were silent for a while, watching and delighting in the sight of human child and thranx adult gamboling freely in one corner of the expansive fairgrounds. Then the father indicated Briann's garb.

"Interesting raiment you're wearing. I notice that it's the same color and shows the same symbols as that decorating your many-limbed companion. Is it significant of something more than friendship?"

The moment had arrived. As was proper, it was the attendee who had brought it up. As acolytes, Briann and Twikanrozex were discouraged from broaching the subject directly. "The United Church settled on aquamarine as its color designate because it is the predominant coloration among adult thranx as well as representing the bountiful and prominent oceans of Earth."

The man frowned. "United Church? Never heard of it." His expression mutated. "You're not going to ask me for money, are you?"

"No. We're not allowed to do that. One of the basic tenets of the church is that it never asks for donations. From the beginning, the idea was that it was to be entirely self-supporting."

The man relaxed, albeit not completely. "By charging for buggy-back rides?"

It was Briann's turn to smile. Not everyone he and Twikanrozex had encountered since arriving to work the fair had shown a sense of humor. "There is a set schedule of fees for services. You must request them. Nothing is proffered."

"Glad to hear it. If you're looking for converts, I'm afraid you're out of luck. I'm Catholic, and my wife is Fifth-Term Shiite Zoroastrian."

"We never look for converts. Though you could remain as you are and still enjoy the fruits of the Church."

The man was intrigued in spite of himself. "How can you belong to your church without converting?"

"It's simpler than you might think. The Church extends itself to everyone: other believers, atheists, agnostics, aliens. Everyone. One of the first things you learn is that to belong, you don't have to believe in anything. No deity, no special books, nothing. We minister to that part of sapience that is not entirely satisfied by logic and reason. It exists. We don't try to deny it."

"Sounds like a pretty weird outfit to me." When Briann did not reply or comment, the man continued. "Well? Aren't you going to offer me some free literature or something?"

The padre shook his head. "Reams of printout tend to intimidate people, or make them feel uncomfortable. The Church wants people to feel comfortable in its presence. We have a small display here—one among hundreds. If you're interested in learning more, or asking additional questions, you can find it on your fairgrounds readout. The display is unstaffed. Everything is automated. No one will try to talk your ear off."

"Even weirder. Not that Peal and I need anything like this. We're both perfectly happy the way we are. So is Iolette."

Briann nodded. "She seems a wonderfully well-adjusted child, with equally well-adjusted parents. I think you're right: You probably don't need any of the Church's services. But you might want to read more about it, just to satisfy the curiosity I see written on your face. You can have a good laugh about it with your friends when you get home. Another amusing anecdote from the fair on distant Dawn."

The husband eyed Briann uncertainly. "Are you serious about this Church business? This isn't some sort of wandering comedy routine sanctioned by the fair programmers? You're not a performer?"

"I am a true acolyte of the United Church. I can recite to you its founding principles as well as all the One Hundred and Five Maxims of Indifferent Contentment. I am qualified to minister in a number of specialties. But why should I bore you with that which you have not requested? Go and have a read about it if you're curious, or pull up the general literature on your personal communicator. Code MT-DF-186. You don't have to visit the display. You can also access the same information when you get home."

"So you're already on New Riviera, too?" The man was quietly impressed.

"The Church suffers from increasing popularity. We try to keep a low profile. Here comes your daughter."

"I hope she didn't wear your friend out." The man hesitated. "I've never heard of a Church that extends to all species. How do you manage it?"

Briann leaned close and whispered. "We proceed from the notion that good ideas know no shape. Then we're careful not to take any of it too seriously."

Uncertain whether to smile or not, the man settled on a half grin. Then he walked over to join his wife in assisting their daughter in her dismount.

"Careful of my spicules—that's it, there." As soon as the girl was off his back, Twikanrozex turned and preened an antenna. "Did you have fun, little one?"

"Ohyesohyesohyes! Let's do it again!"

Her mother bent to place a hand on the girl's shoulder. "Don't you think Mr. Twikel . . . Mr. Twiken . . ."

"Twikanrozex," the thranx said, enunciating it slowly for her.

She smiled gratefully at him. "Don't you think Mr. Twikanrozex might be a little tired? Maybe he needs to rest."

"For a little while, *crr!!ckk*." Briann could see that Twikanrozex was breathing hard but was far from exhausted. Clearly, the little girl would have been happy to bounce along on his back all day.

"Say thank you to Mr. Twikanrozex," her father ordered.

Walking up to the thranx, the girl extended a hand. Instead of proffering one of his own, Twikanrozex leaned forward and brushed her open palm with the tips of both antennae. She clutched at her hand, giggling.

"That tickles!"

"A last smile." The thranx stepped back. "Perhaps I'll see you again before the fair is over, little one."

"I hope so, Mr. Twikanrozex. Thank you for the buggy ride." Turning, she placed her right hand in her mother's and looked up. "Can we get ice cream now? I'm hungry!"

"I'm sure you are, after all that hopping around." The woman looked back at Twikanrozex and beamed. There was no trace of the uncertainty and hesitation that had marked her initial approach. It was utterly gone. "Thank you."

"You're welcome." Raising a truhand and a foothand, Twikanrozex imitated the simplistic human gesture of farewelling. "Another time." As soon as the couple and their daughter were out of earshot, he turned to his companion.

"How did it go?"

"The seed is well planted. Like most, he tried to affect disinterest. And like most who take the time to ask questions and to listen, he's interested. Maybe not today, or tomorrow, or even until he's back home months from now, but he'll definitely research the Church." Briann chuckled. "Nothing like telling them you don't want their money to pique their interest."

"That's good. The larv—the little girl was fun. Human children are so full of energy."

"That's a difference between us. Thranx larvae think before they act. Human children act before they think. Of course, being hatched with functional limbs has a lot to do with it."

"Yes." Twikanrozex sighed softly. "Many's the time I remember lying in the nursery longing for the day when I would be able to pupate and emerge with arms and legs. Your kind is fortunate in that fashion."

"It does make us more impulsive, though." Together, they resumed their walk. Briann badly wanted to see the demonstration of thranx acrobatic music, while Twikanrozex was fascinated by everything around them. Simply being on a human-colonized world was entertainment enough for him.

They had come prepared to deal with all manner of possible problems, of protests and objections. But the last thing they expected to have to deal with was competition.

They did not think of it that way, of course, but the cluster of well-dressed young humans who surrounded them in front of one of the numerous water sculptures contributed by the thranx hydrosculptors of Willow-Wane felt otherwise.

"We've been hearing about you." The young man who spoke was tall, slim, handsome, and syrupy of voice.

"Already?" Briann glanced at Twikanrozex, who could not

disguise his apprehension at being surrounded by so many exceedingly intent, larger humans.

"And we decided we had to do something about it." The woman wore her hair cropped short, like her syllables. "Before it got out of hand."

Briann was not yet ready to begin looking for fair security personnel, but the idea that he might have to do so had crept rapidly to the forefront of his thoughts. "That sounds ominous. Who are you, and what do you want?"

Members of the enclosing circle looked at one another in apparent disbelief before their spokesman turned back to Briann. "You don't recognize our garments? The white suits and dresses, the decorations of virtuous gold?"

"I'm afraid we don't."

It was the woman's turn. "We represent the Unity of Traditional Religions, Dawn branch. We were informed that an odd pair, consisting of human and thranx, were proselytizing here at the fair on behalf of some new cult. As representatives of the old beliefs carried out from Earth, we felt it incumbent on us to seek you out, and to appraise your message."

Another woman spoke up. "You understand, there are a lot of children here."

"The United Church makes no distinction between children and adults," Briann explained. "Only between intelligence and nonintelligence. The two do not always evolve in parallel." It would have been an excellent moment to eye the young leader of the white-clad group meaningfully, but Church protocol strictly forbade the application of sarcasm at the personal level.

"Or between humans and aliens?" another woman wondered aloud.

Briann nodded in Twikanrozex's direction. "My thranx friend is not an alien; he is only nonhuman. Again, we clearly differ in some of our definitions."

"There's no provision in terrestrial theology for sentients that are not created in God's image," another man declared with complete conviction.

"Many of us feel similarly," Twikanrozex replied calmly.

That put a momentary halt to the questioning as the assembled devoted murmured among themselves. The two representatives of the United Church waited patiently. Patience was among the first qualities they were taught. It was becoming clear that these young folk meant no physical harm. They wanted only to assure themselves that the eccentric couple were not bent on seducing human children to the ways of evil. Briann and Twikanrozex could deal with that. The United Church had firm ideas of its own about evil: It was against it.

"How can you offer to minister to something that looks like that?" The woman who had first spoken stared unashamedly at Twikanrozex. "That aroma, though . . ."

"Shapeism is to be abhorred in all things," Briann pointed out. "Intelligence marked by understanding and compassion are the hallmarks of a spiritual being. We don't go into specifics. Every species seeks the answers to the ultimate questions in its own way. The Church doesn't attempt to define them, or to restrict them."

"Then how," another man wondered, "can you offer solace?" His friend tried to interrupt, but the younger man, now curious, shrugged him off.

Twikanrozex gestured with all four hands, wondering if any of the humans would respond in kind. They did not, but neither were they visibly repulsed. He was encouraged. "Sympathy does not demand to be underwritten by dogma. Pain is a universal constant that may be assuaged by any concern irrespective of source."

"We don't feel the need to speak a lot of mumbo jumbo to help someone feel better," Briann added.

Several among the white-clad looked upset. "You speak blasphemy," one insisted.

"Fluently," Briann assured her. "Our organization has no truck with archaic attempts to help people by filling them up with guilt. Ample guilt is acquired soon enough, through the mere process of living. The last thing any sentient needs is the unrequested addition of external culpability. How many of you feel guilty about something?"

The several expressions of concern that appeared in reaction to Briann's question were drowned out by the loud words of the young spokesman. "Look here, we're the ones asking the questions! We're the ones who'll determine whether you'll be allowed to continue to work this fair or not."

"Firstly, *ci!!llp,*" Twikanrozex began, "we are not 'working' this fair. We confront no one, pressure no one, seek out neither individuals nor families nor groups. We only respond to questions freely directed at us. The UC does not seek converts. There is nothing to convert people to. We have nothing like official membership. The Church and its services are freely available to anyone who is interested."

"What happens," another woman demanded to know as she pushed her way forward, "if someone chooses to participate in your church? What happens to their former religion?"

"Annamarie," the man next to her began warningly. She ignored him.

"Whatever you wish to happen." Briann was warming to the discussion, now that it had turned into a discussion and away from unfounded accusations. "You may continue to practice as you did before encountering our organization. There are participants in the United Church who practice many religions, and participants who espouse none at all. We are very undemanding."

"How can someone belong to two churches and champion two different beliefs?" the woman persisted.

"Beliefs?" Twikanrozex waved his truhands in her direction. "We don't require that you believe in anything."

The spokesman's brows drew together. "What kind of a church is it that doesn't require belief?"

Briann smiled invitingly. "A new kind. Try it and see. You'll find it remarkably liberating. Most who come to us do."

The young man drew himself up. "I'm already liberated— by the knowledge that I am following the one true path."

"Of course you are!" Briann responded exuberantly. "All of you are, no matter what your particular individual belief. Realizing that allows you to participate freely in the UC."

One heavyset fellow on the edge of the group was nodding

knowingly. "I understand now." He smiled at his associates. "We have nothing to fear from these people, or from their establishment—because they're crazy. They argue in circles."

"That is it!" Twikanrozex gestured vigorously. "We argue in circles, just like the universe. In the same fashion as a gravitational lens bends light so that you can see behind large stellar objects, the United Church bends reason so that you can see the truths that hide behind reality."

"We're wasting our time here." The spokesman, now satisfied that the two robed preachers, or whatever they were, represented no threat to the established theological order, turned away. "The girot mimes from Coolangatta are starting their show soon. We still have time to hop a transport and get there before the opening."

The white-clad gathering began to fall away—but not quite all of them. A pair lingered: the woman Annamarie and a male friend. Ignoring the admonishments of their companions, they remained behind. They were curious, which is the first step toward enlightenment. Briann and Twikanrozex were delighted to accommodate their many questions. The man went so far as to buy Briann a cup of mochoka and Twikanrozex a helix of *cherel!l* tea. The four of them sat sipping and chatting for several hours. When the conversation was finally brought to an end by the woman named Annamarie, the two priestly acolytes watched the young humans depart still deep in conversation.

"There are good folk here." Twikanrozex sucked the last liquid from the bottom of his nearly empty turbinate. "People willing to listen."

"Yes." Briann scanned the milling crowds. "I would have wished for more thranx, though."

"The larger contingents will not be arriving for a day or two yet," Twikanrozex pointed out. "All have to come from offworld, and only the boldest will consider attending a function on a human-settled colony. But they will come, rest assured. My people are irresistibly drawn to the neoteric."

"I hope I can meet some and convince them of the kindly nature of my species," Briann murmured. "I've lost weight specifically for that purpose."

"It was a good thing for you to do," Twikanrozex told him. "Too much jiggling of loose human flesh can nauseate even the most courteous and well-disposed thranx. It is a reaction as unfortunate as it is involuntary."

"Not to mention one that's likely to put a damper on casual conversation," Briann noted dryly.

From time to time they would wander back to the automated display that had been set up and activated on the first day of the fair, both to ensure that it was functioning properly and to deal with individuals and sometimes small groups that had gathered there. Accustomed after the first couple of days to all manner of reactions, they encountered an entirely new one when, on the third morning, they confronted a well-dressed man in his early forties who was viewing one of the tridee hover messages while chuckling constantly.

"Usually," Briann offered by way of greeting, "our presentation meets with skepticism, or open hostility, or indifference, or interest. You're the first person we've met whose primary reaction has been laughter."

"Oh, hello." Turning, the man grinned at Briann, eyed Twikanrozex with more than casual interest, and reached up to dab at his face with an absorptive pad. "I didn't mean any disrespect."

"None taken," Twikanrozex clicked. His response intrigued the man even more.

"So you're a thranx. I've seen a number wandering about the fair, but mostly they're working displays and performances. It's nice to finally meet one of you in person."

"The touch be mine." Twikanrozex extended a truhand, which gesture humans found less alien than the caress of feathery antennae. The man took it, was surprised to find his own gently shaken, and withdrew his fingers thoughtfully.

"The actual contact is warmer than I thought it would be. Not crustaceanlike at all. Do you see multiple images of me out of those compound eyes?"

"While multiple images are perceived," Twikanrozex replied, "they are linked in my mind to create a single image.

Our eyes are more advanced than those of the terrestrial insects whom you are utilizing for reference."

"Not from Earth, myself." The man shrugged. "New Paris, actually." He indicated the lively display. "Your church sounds interesting. Complete waste of time, of course."

"In what way?" Briann was silently disconcerted by the casual dismissal from so obviously intelligent and interested an observer.

"Too many religions already. Humankind's got a house full of 'em. Always has. Every year, every month, it seems like a new fad pops up, attracts a horde of eager adherents, and then just as quickly fades away. At best, that's what you're looking at." He smiled approvingly at Twikanrozex. "Although with the thranx involved you certainly have real novelty value going for you."

Briann could tell from the man's tone and attitude that he was in no way trying to be offensive. He was simply stating his mind.

"We who believe think that you're wrong." Twikanrozex added a whistle of conviction.

"Well, without a doubt you would." The man's good nature continued to shine through his disparaging words. "But I've spent some years in the business of fads, done pretty well out of it, and I know whereof I speak. Just a friendly warning: Make sure you have some kind of professional position to fall back on when it all goes flat. How are you doing here, by the way?" Briann mentioned a number. The man was suitably impressed.

"You've been quiet about it, anyway."

"We don't believe in trumpeting our accomplishments."

Their visitor chuckled anew. "Believers in word-of-mouth, eh? Can't say as I blame you. It's the best advertising no matter what you're selling."

"We are not 'selling' anything," Twikanrozex corrected him. The thranx was growing irritated with this self-assured human.

"Sure, sure." The visitor spoke as if humoring a child. "That's the baseline every religion has used since the beginning of time. Well, how do I join?"

Briann frowned. They had finally encountered someone for whom their training had not prepared them. "You mean, after all that cynicism you're still interested in joining the Church?"

"Why not? I'm always in need of fresh amusement. In my work I have access to the latest stimsims, tridee plays, prose, you name it. So I'm highly cultured but easily bored. Your church will be a diversion, a lark, a fashionable fancy. My friends are very big on one-upmanship, but I don't know a single one who can claim to have worshiped alongside a bug. Your pardon, sir or whatever—a thranx. When I'm bored again, I'll move on to something else." He spread his arms wide. "Meanwhile, your organization will have gained another new, albeit transient, neophyte."

Recovering nicely, Briann extended a hand. Shaking it, the other man seemed to lose just a hint of his astonishing self-assurance. "You're going to accept me in spite of my avowed lack of expectation?"

"The United Church turns no one down. There is room within for all," Briann affirmed. "Even the incredulous."

"Well, that's mighty obliging of you! I look forward to reading your source materials, and to having a good laugh at their expense."

Twikanrozex saw to it that the visitor's communicator accepted the information transfer before congratulating him in turn. "If you gain a few days' amusement from all that we have given you, that will be reward enough. An amused species is a contented species."

"Glad to know that you bu—thranx have a sense of humor."

"You will learn more about us from the Church materials," Twikanrozex informed him. "The UC was formed by a human and a thranx working in concert. It is an entirely new idea in interspecies relations."

"And one that neatly sidesteps the current controversies raging between our respective governments." Exaggerating the gesture, the man put a finger to his lips. "You're very clever, you people are, but it won't make any difference in the end."

"We think it will," Briann replied. "Enjoy your literature."

"So I will; so I will. It'll give me something to wade through in space-plus, on the way back to New Paris." With that he departed, tucking his communicator back into his shirt pocket.

"What do you make of our chances with that one?" Twikanrozex tracked the human's progress across the strip of fairgrounds pavement, which looked and felt exactly like grass except that it was impervious to both footwear and the elements and needed neither light nor water to maintain its springiness and color.

"He's intelligent." Briann turned back to their display, wondering if he ought to switch the order of presentation to present a new field of images to first-time viewers who happened to be passing by. "But I have yet to meet the individual who was so smart they could keep from fooling themselves. If he reads, and doesn't just delete the load you gave him, I think he very well might choose to partake. I'd much rather try to convince an intelligent cynic than a willing ignoramus."

"Maxim forty-seven." Twikanrozex shuffled around to the back of the display tower. "Let's put the site selection first for a while. Looking at your equatorial lands helps to take the chill out of this air for me. Mentally, at least."

"Sorry you're cold. As soon as we're done here, we'll go spend some time in the Willow-Wane pavilion."

"*Srr!rrt*—ah, for the feel of real air in my lungs! You'll be all right there, Brother Briann?"

The human nodded. "I don't mind sweating in the service of the Church—or for my friends."

9

The more Pilwondepat thought about it in the days that followed, the more the affair nagged at him. Probably he was obsessing on nothing, haunted by matters of no real consequence, simply because he was personally irritated at what was happening on Comagrave. It detracted from his work, and he knew it. But he could not stop himself. He had always been afflicted with something of a suspicious nature, and as an exoarcheologist he was trained to draw substantiative conclusions from dozens, often hundreds, of minuscule, seemingly unrelated sources.

It wasn't just the circumstance of the unfortunate human who had been bitten by a native arthropod only to be saved by the extraordinarily fortuitous proximity of an AAnn mineralogical sampling team. That was what had sparked his imagination, true, but reports of other incidents had been festering in his mind for many weeks now. Festering, until the occasion of the arthropod bite had caused all of it to burst forth in the full flower of anxiety.

Too many bad things were happening. Surely, Comagrave was a dangerous place, newly discovered and barely explored. Trouble was to be expected, even the occasional disaster, but there were no hostile native sentients to fear, no overwhelming profligacy of inimical life-forms. Either the humans who had come to study and explore were an exceedingly inept bunch, or else too many of them had been born in the hive of the unlucky. From personal experience, Pilwondepat knew the former to be untrue, and he did not believe in the latter.

Therefore, something else was going on.

He was circumspect in his investigation. It was not his province to ask personal questions of individuals from various camps and outposts, though he had the means to do so. Drawing together individual recollections of seemingly unrelated incidents might have enabled him to come to a conclusion more swiftly. But it would also have drawn attention to him. He did not fear such attention from the humans themselves. It was the presence of so many AAnn "observers" on the planet that induced him to keep a low profile.

While he could only exchange communications with the occasional human, there was nothing to prevent him from examining the contents of every unrestricted report that was being filed or sent offworld. These were available to all at the touch of the right button. Electronic translation supplemented his growing knowledge of Terranglo, enabling him to inspect the relevant correspondence as rapidly as any other potential reader. And the more he read, the more convinced he became of the correctness of his suppositions.

They were very clever. Not every catastrophe was on the order of the complete destruction of the thermal supply depot and research station. The multitude of incidents varied in degree between that and the bite that had nearly killed a single researcher. Some of the details were almost amusing in their resourcefulness. A case of food poisoning at one paleontological camp, for example, resulted in not a single fatality. But once again, it was the AAnn who were conveniently positioned to provide the fresh fruit that cured the humans' digestive upsets. Studying the information, Pilwondepat stridulated involuntarily. Though they shared the omnivorous appetites of most intelligent species, AAnn appetites fell decidedly on the carnivorous side of the food spectrum. How convenient of them to have fresh fruit at their disposal! How implausible. And just the right sort of fruit to cure a digestive disorder within the human system, too.

An aircar carrying a quartet of avian researchers went down in a deep canyon. With human help already on the way, an AAnn craft in the vicinity arrived first to render assistance and effect the needed repairs. A lone prospector—half geologist, half entrepreneur—was found dead in the wildly eroded territory human cartographers had named the Bacunin Badlands. Cause of death: a bad fall. No AAnn available to recover the body, Pilwondepat read. He made a mental note to suggest that a larger, better equipped expedition explore the region. If the AAnn were responsible, as he was beginning to suspect they were in the majority of such unexplained incidences, it was because they wanted to prevent the humans, or in this case one solitary adventurer, from finding something. Pilwondepat was willing to bet a case of goldel *surr!onyy* from Trix that the Bacunin Badlands hid mineral deposits of some value.

Considered individually, the incidents he waded through would not have drawn more than passing commiserations from those who scrutinized them. Assessed together, they comprised a litany of AAnn involvement in human misery and misfortune on Comagrave that could hardly count as coincidence. But who could he lay his case before? The few other thranx on the planet were wholly immersed in their own activities. Sending his conclusions offworld might eventually bring a response, but without any hive authority on the human colony world, he would be left to implement any decision all by himself. And he was a scientist, not a soldier.

He was left to ponder who best among the human population to present with his findings. He knew none of the planetary authority personnel individually. Handing the information to a skeptical official might have any number of consequences, many of which could be bad. They might laugh at him or dismiss his allegations out of hand. Swamped by the difficulties of supervising the exploration and development of a complex new world, the authorities were likely to have little time to spare for the complaints of their own kind, much less for the wild inferences of a visiting alien. Worse yet, the AAnn might be monitoring, officially or otherwise, all such planetary transmissions. If he did not proceed with care and caution, he might well find himself the victim of still another of the inexplicable accidents that up to now had plagued only the resident humans.

Who could he talk to? Who could he converse with who would not treat him as a bug afflicted with paranoia? If it could not be an outsider, then it would have to be a colleague, and one with enough authority to make recommendations that would be listened to. His choices were very limited.

The following morning was bright and clear. The desiccating wind that perpetually scoured the crest of the escarpment was blissfully subdued, and there were even a few dark clouds marring the cerulean blue of the sky. His lungs sucked at the distant suggestions of humidity like a drowning man gasping for any hint of oxygen. Busy, energetic humans crawled over the excavation site, resembling more than they knew the terrestrial insects they professed to loathe.

He was pleased to find Cullen in his portable, prefab living chamber. Confronting him outside, where someone else might overhear, was best avoided. Not that Pilwondepat worried about the energetic bipeds who were laboring on the site, but there was always the possibility that anything said out in the open might get back to Riimadu. That was the one consequence Pilwondepat knew had to be avoided.

As soon as he descried his visitor, Cullen immediately shut off the chamber's air-conditioning. No thranx could take more than a few minutes of the dry, refrigerated air without passing out. Setting aside the viewer and spheres he was working with, he greeted the insectoid with a nod.

"Morning, Pilwondepat. You look tired."

"You've grown perceptive in my company." Unable to use any of the furniture in the chamber, Pilwondepat sagged into a six-legged stance opposite the desk. Thus positioned, he could barely see over it. "Most humans would not have noticed."

Putting his hands behind his head, Cullen leaned back in the chair. "I do occasionally look up instead of down." He gestured past his guest. "Work's going well. The clouds will cut the heat today."

"I welcome the clouds for the moisture they contain, but

lament the lowering of the temperature. As your kind are wont to say, in this place I am climatologically damned if it does and damned if it doesn't." Edging forward, he reached up to grasp the edge of the lightweight desk with both truhands. His blue-green exoskeleton gleamed in the filtered light that poured through the integrated skylight. "If something isn't done, I think the human presence on Comagrave is damned as well."

Blinking, Cullen sat forward. "I thought you seemed awfully preoccupied these past couple of weeks, but I couldn't be sure." Reaching up, he tugged playfully at the corners of his mouth with both index fingers. "Your people are the original poker faces."

Pilwondepat gestured with a truhand. "I am not familiar with the reference."

"It means someone can't tell what you're thinking just by looking at your expression."

"Because we have no expressions, due to the inflexible nature of our countenances. Now I understand. A good joke. As I said before, you are perceptive. And correct. I have been very much preoccupied, to the detriment of my work here, I fear. But what I have learned is of far greater importance."

Cullen checked the chamber's climate control one more time to make certain the air-conditioning was off. "And what have you learned, my friend?"

Pilwondepat wished for a greater mastery of Terranglo: for the ability to speak smoothly as if burbling, for the talent to convey overtones of meaning without the use of moving limbs. "That the AAnn are working to actively eradicate the human presence on Vussussica, as they so indifferently call it."

"Everyone knows they'd like to have this world." Cullen was rocking gently back and forth in his chair. The silent floating support conformed to and tried to anticipate the twitching of his muscles. "It suits them perfectly. But it does just fine for us, too, and we were here first. As they have acknowledged—rather gracefully, some of my colleagues feel."

"AAnn 'grace' is a cover for their natural cunning. They are very shrewd, are the AAnn. They want you off this world, and they mean to have it." Pilwondepat was gesturing with all four hands now; he couldn't help it. "They are not so foolish as to challenge you openly, or to attempt to take Comagrave by force. Though they could do so easily, ever since the war with the Pitar they have a healthy respect for human military power. Overrunning this world with ships and soldiers would only bring inevitable retribution down upon them."

"Damn right it would." Cullen had work to do, but the thranx's energy was infectious, even if his message was non-sensical.

"So they work slowly, with great subtlety. Instead of attempting to throw you off this world, or negotiate you off, they are working hard to see to it that you choose to depart voluntarily. They don't want you to surrender Comagrave to them. They hope to induce you to cede it gladly." Reaching back into a thorax pouch, the exoarcheologist withdrew a small mollysphere.

"This is one of your storage devices. In the time I have spent among your kind, I have learned how to manipulate and make use of many such moderately ingenious devices. I used one of your own recording appliances instead of mine so that copies could be easily made, transshipped, or otherwise passed along." He laid the molly on Karasi's desk. "It contains exhaustive documentation of the kinds of incidents I have been examining."

For the first time, Cullen's curiosity surpassed his sense of courtesy. "What incidents?"

"Almost from the day humans claimed Comagrave and began to establish a presence here, there have been a disturbing number of fatal accidents and confrontations."

Cullen was solemn, but not particularly impressed. "Exploration and development of a new world invariably entails sacrifices. And Comagrave is no New Paris or New Riviera—or Willow-Wane, for that matter. If not unreservedly hostile, the environment here can be difficult. So can the flora and fauna."

Pilwondepat gestured impatiently, not even bothering to wonder if the human exoarchaeologist understood any of the elaborate hand movements. "All that is true, but it does not explain the consistency of catastrophe you have been experiencing." He indicated the molly. "I have taken the liberty of putting together several mathematical models based on my studies that I think your people will find interesting."

"Why?" Cullen challenged him politely. "Because they'll show that Comagrave is a little more dangerous than most? We know that already."

Pilwondepat's frustration continued to grow. By now, his antennae were bobbing and weaving wildly. "It's not that! Far too many times, when misfortune has struck, the AAnn have been right there, either with assistance or advice."

Cullen pursed his lips. "Some people might think that was good of them."

"There is on Hivehom a class of scavengers who invariably materialize at the scene of a catastrophe, as if they can smell death. Unchallenged, they will immediately start to consume the dead. No one thinks that is especially good of them." He thrust the tips of both antennae in the human's direction. "The AAnn are too often present at the finish of assorted tragedies, like unsought punctuation at the end of a statement." A chitinous blue-green finger nudged the molly. "Go on, Cullen. See for yourself. Nearly every 'accident' reported therein coincides with a concurrent episode of AAnn 'helpfulness.'"

"I'm still not sure what you're trying to say," the exoarcheologist replied softly.

The thranx sat back on four trulegs. "That almost without exception, whenever some tragedy has befallen your people on this world, AAnn have followed close, too close, behind. That in these matters they are being proactive and not reactive."

Cullen's attention was now fully engaged. "You're trying to tell me that they're not responding to these mishaps, but that they're causing them?"

Taking no chances, Pilwondepat did not rely on strong gesticulations to convey his response. "That is exactly what I am saying."

"But . . . why?"

"To convince you that Comagrave is not worth the grief it

can cause you. To persuade your government, or at the very least your public opinion, that human interests in this part of the Arm would be better served by turning administration and development of this particular planet over to the Empire. And they will accomplish this, I fear, if your people are not enlightened as to what is taking place under their very olfactory organs, and do not become alert to the scaled ones' calculating machinations."

The chief scientist was silent for a long moment. Rising from his contemplation, he regarded the gleaming being who waited patiently on the other side of the desk.

"That's quite an accusation, Pilwondepat."

"I assure you, my friend, that it is not made lightly."

Cullen nodded, more to himself than to the thranx. "I hardly know what to say. I'm an exoarcheologist. I'm someone who's at home below ground level, not in the rarified atmosphere of interstellar intrigue."

"Say that you'll study the recording device, and consider its contents." To his satisfaction, Pilwondepat saw that the biped was doing that already. "And you must not discuss this meeting with Riimadu, or let on in any way that we have talked about such things."

"I won't. I promise. Just for the sake of discussion, though—why not? You don't think he'd do anything, do you? He's an exoarcheologist, just like you and me. He's completely absorbed in the excavation we're undertaking here atop this escarpment."

"Riimadu is AAnn. He is absorbed in promoting himself foremost, yes, but he is also part of the web that his kind are attempting to weave around this world. Step lightly in his presence, and have a care you are not unwittingly caught in that snare." One more time, Pilwondepat indicated the sphere. "There are already enough unpleasant statistics recorded on that device. I would hate to see you, my friend, become another."

"Now you're being overly dramatic."

"Am I, *chirritt*? Peruse the molly. Then decide."

Cullen looked unhappy. "I'm not saying you're wrong,

Pilwondepat. Not without having a look at that molly. But a conspiracy on that scale is hard to envision."

"The AAnn would not say conspiracy. They would say 'diplomacy.' Their definitions are somewhat rougher than yours or ours."

The exoarcheologist rose from behind his desk and began pacing parallel to the back wall of the room. "For the sake of discussion, let's say there's something to your assertions. What am I supposed to do with Riimadu? I can't just kick him off the dig. His government expects him to be here, recording and observing. He has authorization."

Pilwondepat gestured with both truhands. "You are in charge of the project. Exercise that authority. Find an excuse. Say that it's for his own benefit. Or propose that he enjoy the break from work that his hard labor has earned him. There are ways."

"I know; I know." Cullen's discomfort level was rising with every moment. "But it's going to be difficult. If not for his suggestions, we wouldn't even be digging here." He halted suddenly to stare down at the thranx. "How about that, Pilwondepat? If there's some widespread intrigue on the part of the AAnn, why would one of them point out what could prove to be an important archeological site? Why not direct us elsewhere and keep the site discovery quiet until they can excavate on their own?"

Air whistled softly through Pilwondepat's spicules. It was important to be patient with this human, he reminded himself. Sometimes they failed to make out certain aspects of the world around them until it landed on their heads. And they had experienced only a comparatively few years of contact with the AAnn, as opposed to the hundreds the thranx had been compelled to endure. They could not be expected to understand right away.

But somehow, he had to make at least one of them in a position of some importance learn to *see*. For a number of reasons, not least that he knew and worked with him, he had chosen the one called Cullen Karasi.

"Why not let you provide the muscle power and equipment

and do the work for them? If their ultimate aim is to ease you off the planet, what you do here will not matter. It's not as if you are attempting to ascertain the existence of an enormous body of valuable ore. It's only pure science. From my studies, I believe that pure science does not command many votes on your world council."

"You're quite the cynic, Pilwondepat."

Antennae bobbed. "All thranx are realists, Cullen. When you come from a society where in primitive times every individual knew their entire life's work from birth, you have no choices."

The human nodded slowly, another gesture Pilwondepat recognized. Humans preferred broad, easy-to-read gestures that rarely displayed the subtlety of the AAnn. There was not much there to admire, but it made for ready understanding.

Ceasing his pacing, Cullen resumed his seat behind the field desk. "All right. Let's have a look at this accumulated 'evidence' of yours." Picking up the molly, he dropped it into the appropriate receptacle on top of his desk reader. Images appeared in the air in front of him.

Though he wanted to comment on every picture, every article, Pilwondepat forced himself to hold his peace. Interrupting the already skeptical Cullen would break the human's concentration and prevent him from absorbing the full impact of the thranx's research. It was important that the man not blindly accept Pilwondepat's accusations, but that he draw his own conclusions directly from the available evidence. So Pilwondepat sat in silence, not moving except for the familiar involuntary weaving of his antennae, and tried not to stare.

Half an hour later, Cullen switched off the viewer and sat back in his chair. "It's disturbing. I'll give you that. Some of it is unsettling, even. But it's not conclusive."

"Will you at least agree that it is worthy of further examination?"

Cullen might be skeptical, but he was not stupid. A trained scientist, he could not ignore evidence when it was laid out before him. "Yes, I'm afraid that it is. I just don't think I'm the one to pursue it." He indicated the viewer. "This sort of thing needs to be distributed to the supervising colonial authority, not somebody involved in research, like myself. Why did you show it to me instead of taking it directly to them?" he finished curiously.

"Because it will have more force coming from you," Pilwondepat explained. "Too many of your people shy away from contact with my kind. Others are instinctively suspicious, and there are also those who are openly hostile. Had I been the one to lay this evidence directly before the most relevant human authority, I might well have been dismissed without a hearing. Or I might have been received politely, only to have the data tossed into the nearest disposal as soon as I departed. But if you, a recognized figure of some stature within your chosen specialty, make a presentation on its behalf, you will be listened to; and the documentation, if not instantly acknowledged, will at least be discussed." He dropped to all sixes again. "You will make such a presentation, Cullen? I did not invent the collusions you just viewed. They are as real as the rock we are standing upon. As are the intentions of the AAnn."

The human scratched at the back of his head. "You're putting me in a very awkward position, Pilwondepat. Especially as regards Riimadu's continued presence on the site. There are a lot more AAnn on Comagrave than there are thranx."

"A consequence of an unfortunate climate, but I sympathize with your circumstances. Consider that being dead would put you in a much more difficult position."

"Regardless of what his Imperial brethren may be up to, I'm not sure I can accept your portrait of Riimadu. He's been nothing but helpful ever since he was attached to the project. We talk science all the time, and I really do see him as a kindred spirit, albeit one covered with scales. It's very hard for me to envision him participating in some kind of hostile activity, much less one that might prove antiscientific."

Pilwondepat executed a complicated gesture that Cullen did not understand, which was probably just as well. "Whatever you think, whatever occurs in his presence, all I ask is that you never forget that he is AAnn. *Yi!mt,* he is a scientist. *Yi!mt,* he has been helpful. But if the appropriate situation presents itself, I can assure you from the bottom of my individual and racial hearts that he will put a weapon to the side of your skull and without a second thought, blow your brains out through your opposite ear."

He'd gone a little too far, Pilwondepat saw. In his anxiety to persuade his friend of the danger he had uncovered, he had stepped beyond the bounds of courtesy and diplomacy that Cullen was willing to accept. It was as visible in the human's rubbery face as if it had been written there with an antique stylus.

"Do this, then," he added quickly. "Leave Riimadu alone. Let him do his work. I'll watch him myself. I do it anyway, out of a historical sense of self-preservation. But convey my findings to the appropriate planetary authority. Relate what I have concluded, give your own opinion, and let them view the facts that are known. If you will do that much, I will be able to sleep a little easier knowing that something is being done."

Cullen willingly agreed. "I'll send off a copy of the information together with my personal comments right away. Tonight, if you think it that important."

"No, no!" Four hands waved frantically at the taller human. "Nothing can be sent via the planetary communications net. I would bet my antennae that the AAnn have been intercepting and monitoring all such transmissions ever since their presence on the planet was allowed. I would not feel secure forwarding the data under anything less than military-level encryption."

Cullen shrugged apologetically. "This is only a scientific outpost. I don't have access to anything that hard."

"I understand. Therefore, in order to ensure not only the security of the findings but of your own self, you will have to deliver the information in person."

Cullen hesitated. For an awful moment Pilwondepat felt as if the human was going to dismiss the entire matter. Then the senior scientist nodded once, slowly. "All right, we'll do it your way. The next regular supply flight will be in nine days. I have a few things I'd like to do in town, and I'm overdue for a scheduled break. In addition to making the necessary rounds, and enjoying a little rest and relaxation, I'll make an appointment with the highest-level enforcement official who has time to spare, and I'll present your report. I'll also relay your conclusions. Myself, I'm not quite ready to draw any. No final ones, at least."

Pilwondepat would have heaved a sigh of relief, except that thranx do not heave. He did, however, exhale softly. "That will be most satisfactory, Cullen. Meanwhile, I will keep track of the activities, both formal and otherwise, of our mutual acquaintance Riimadu. The critical thing is not that action is taken immediately, but that your authorities are made aware of what the AAnn are doing. Alerted, they will be able to draw their own conclusions. Especially when further incidents of the type I have compiled continue to recur. Your people will then be able to view them with a different eye. I am satisfied."

Cullen was relieved. "Then we can get back to the business of science?"

The thranx gestured straightforward agreement. "It will be a comfort to me, though I will not be able to entirely relax until the last AAnn is expelled from this world. Politely and diplomatically, or otherwise."

Cullen tried to explain without dismissing. "You have to understand, Pilwondepat, that in the absence of direct evidence of wrongdoing, human authorities have a tendency to move with caution. Nothing's likely to happen right away."

"It will come." Pilwondepat was confident now. "The more unfortunate coincidences involving the AAnn that occur, the more likely your people will be to see that they are not coincidences at all. There will be an acceleration of awareness."

"Nine days." Cullen came around from behind the desk to place a reassuring hand on the thranx's b-thorax. "Think you can stand working in Riimadu's company that long?"

"As long as should prove necessary." The thranx swiveled his head almost 180 degrees. "It's easier for me to watch my back than it is for you to guard yours."

At that point Therese Holoness burst into the chamber, nearly beating the doorway's announcing buzz. Her face was flushed and her eyes wide open and alert. She glanced uncertainly at the thranx before settling her gaze on Cullen.

"Come quick, Mr. Karasi!"

Cullen's eyes flicked in Pilwondepat's direction before returning to the young woman. "What is it, Therese? What's wrong?"

She blinked in confusion. "Wrong? Nothing's wrong, sir. Please, come with me. You're not going to believe what we've found."

10

The humidity at Chitteranx Port hit Baron Preed NNXV like a grit-heavy sandstorm. Gasping, he hastened to activate the dehumidifier strapped to his snout. Immediately, air from which virtually every trace of moisture had been removed flowed down his nasal passages and into his lungs. Relieved, he stepped out into the otherwise amenable climate that filled the terminal. What he really needed, he reflected, was the visual equivalent of a dehumidifier for his eyes. Or more properly, a debugger.

The place was full of thranx. The insectoids were everywhere: operating greeting stations, food and drink facilities, rushing to and fro in hideous numbers. That was not surprising, since Chitteranx was a major port of arrival and embarkation on this continent, and Hivehom was their homeworld. That did not make the place any easier to tolerate. Like all his kind, Preed loathed the multilimbed, hard-shelled creatures. What he wanted to do was wade into the seething mass and start pulling off arms and legs and heads. Aside from the fact that he was more than slightly outnumbered and such action would result in his own expeditious demise, it would reflect badly on his mission.

Diplomats, he reminded himself, were to be discouraged from dismembering their hosts.

It was not the thranx he had come to see, however. Had that been the case, he would have landed at Daret and checked in with the official Imperial Embassy there. His mission was rather more circumspect. The thranx had been reluctant to allow it. But since no state of active hostilities existed between the Great Hive and the Empire, they were unable to find a good reason to refuse the official request. It was to be an informal visit, the AAnn officials in charge of making the arrangements had insisted. Nothing conclusive was on order. As a major power friendly to both sides, the AAnn simply wished to see how the humans who had located on Hivehom were doing. The thranx didn't like it, but could not find a legitimate way to refuse without giving unnecessary offense.

Preed had been chosen because of his mastery of the humans' language and a tolerance for difficult conditions. He was flattered by the endorsement and could not in any event have gracefully refused. So here he was, surrounded by bugs, on his way to see spongy, soft-skinned mammals. The familiar comforts of Blassussar seemed a very long way off indeed.

The heavy protective clothing he would need to tolerate the visit to the human outpost was packed securely in the satchel he carried slung over his right shoulder. Striding forward, the dehumidifier across his snout distorting his otherwise courtly profile, he searched in vain for the tube that would take him to the shuttle that would convey him to the Mediterranea Plateau, where the humans had their settlement. His flight connection was deliberately scheduled tight, so that he would not have to spend any more time in lowland Chitteranx than was absolutely necessary. A check of his chronometer showed that he had no time to linger. Growling deep in his throat, he realized that he was going to have to ask directions.

Steeling himself, he used the general terminal guide to locate an information kiosk. At least he would be spared direct contact with one of the bugs. The kiosk was designed to be utilized by offworlders. As such, its instrumentation was intuitive, and though it could not communicate in the Imperial Tongue, he soon had his directions. Striding off in the indicated direction, he had to struggle not to kick crowding thranx aside. Bipedal and as tall as the average human, he towered over the milling natives. With their compound eyes, you could not even tell if they were looking in your direction, but he knew that they were staring. The presence of an AAnn on Hivehom, outside the diplomatic mission located in the capital, was highly unusual. He fancied he could smell hatred and fear emanating from them. A good feeling, it made him smile inside.

The aircraft that would carry him to the high plateau was specially retrofitted to accommodate humans as well as thranx but was virtually empty. The few insectoids aboard crowded as far forward as they could, maintaining as much space as was practical between themselves and the unusual passenger. This suited Preed well. As for his own perch, the AAnn found that while his legs bent in places different from those of humans, he could still fit his backside into one of the flight chairs that had been designed for them. The only difficulty lay with his tail. While flexible, it still had to go somewhere. As there was no proper slot in the rear of the seat, he was reduced to thrusting it off to one side and over the rim of the chair for the duration of the flight. The resulting contortion was uncomfortable, but not impossible. At least, he reflected, he was not reduced to being strapped down like a piece of cargo.

The flight on the superswift craft carried him high above the clouds that swathed the jungles, rain forest, plantations, and conurbations below. Once they passed over the edge of the Hysingrausen Wall, the weather cleared above the plateau. It would be refreshingly drier in the human settlement, he knew, but also much colder. He would be compelled to swap the uncomfortable dehumidifier on his snout for a bulky set of cold-wear gear. Such were the travails a multispecies ambassador was expected to endure.

There were compensations. Preed's ability to deal with an assortment of sentients, plus his unusual linguistic gifts, had elevated him to rarified status. Actually, his rank should have guaranteed him a home posting in a comfortable villa, with perhaps a view of the Sandronds on Blassussar's southern-most continent. But his skills made him too valuable to keep at home. So he had become a rover in the service of the Empire. The lifestyle suited his temperament if not his liver.

From the air Azerick was unimpressive. He had not expected much. The human outpost was still of comparatively recent vintage, both physically and politically. It could not be allowed to grow rapidly for fear of unsettling the locals. This was too bad. There was nothing Preed, or any other AAnn, enjoyed more than seeing the multilimbed thranx unsettled.

Hence his visit.

His principal purpose was not to unnerve the thranx. That was only a side benefit. He was here to talk with the resident humans, to ascertain a number of possibilities, to formulate appraisals, and with luck to make more than mischief. His hopes were high. Despite all the lies the thranx had told humans about the AAnn, despite their unprecedented and unrepeated cooperation during the course of the Pitarian War, relations between the two powerful entities were still in a state of uneasy flux. Relations could evolve, or devolve, on the basis of very small developments. It was these that Preed was on Hivehom to influence. His energetic, mischief-making colleagues, he knew, were busy elsewhere.

The dryness of the air that assailed his nostrils when he emerged from the aircraft into the local terminal was a huge relief after trying to breathe the damp mud that passed for atmosphere in Chitteranx. He immediately removed the clumsy dehumidifier and stored it in his baggage. Finding a personal hygiene chamber, he attended to necessary ablutions while donning the lightweight but still unwieldy special garb that would keep the air next to his scales fifteen degrees warmer than the ambient temperature outside. Only his head, tail, and hands remained exposed to the chill air. When he emerged from the chamber, he felt refreshed and ready to begin work.

A voice in halting Imperial hailed him as soon as he stepped outside. "Envoy Preed! Over here, sir."

Espying the only human who was both staring and gesticulating in his direction, Preed approached the individual and replied in near-perfect Terranglo. The language was easier on his larynx than either High or Low Thranx. Something else, he mused, his people and these mammals had in common. Extending a hand, he noted the human's obvious surprise as the clawed fingers enveloped the mammal's soft skin and shook gently.

"You ssee?" the envoy informed his greeter. "No brushing of antennae. Your kind have one digit too many, and your clawss are exceedingly inadequate, but otherwisse there iss virtually no difference."

Pleased by the flattering comparison, the human stepped back. "I'll be your principal contact during your visit to Az-erick, Envoy Preed. Members of our guest support staff will look after your daily needs. Whenever you are ready for formal talks, just let me know. I can say that I personally have been looking forward to them for some time."

"A chance to sspeak with ssomething bessidess a bug?" Preed ventured.

Gratifyingly, the human essayed a half smile. "I didn't say that."

An excellent beginning, Preed decided. This human, an important member of the local diplomatic staff, was already predisposed toward the AAnn and against his hosts. With more such benign developments, much might be accomplished in the coming days.

"May I carry your baggage, Envoy?" The human extended a helpful hand. To Preed, it looked as if the straps on his case would cut right through the soft, unprotected flesh. "By the way, my name is Jorge Sertoa."

"Yess. I wass informed it would be you who would be meeting me. No thank you, truly, Jorge. I prefer to carry my own gear. The exercisse iss a good thing for me."

Outside the little terminal, the all-pervasive green of the plateau forest made him wince slightly. He longed for fa-miliar earth tones: for yellows and reds, burnished orange and fiery vermilion. Such hues were not to be found any-where on Hivehom, and certainly not here in the place of the humans' choosing. Gasping as the chill air entered his lungs, he bundled his weather suit tighter around his neck, clasped his hands together, and paced the escorting human to the impressive little high-speed transport. Within moments, they were racing northward through the towering woods.

"This transport cabin is equipped with an individual climate control." The human was at pains to be accommodating. "Would you like me to turn up the heat?"

Diplomacy be strangled, Preed decided. "I would like that very much, truly. My thankingss, Jorge."

Within minutes the temperature inside the cabin had risen to nearly thirty-three degrees. Though the human was starting to look uncomfortable, he did not ask to reduce the temperature, and Preed gladly took advantage of the other's obliging nature.

They bantered inconsequentialities all the way to the outpost. There, Preed was assigned quarters that had been hastily adapted for his arrival. There were chairs with slots in the back for his tail. The high bed had been replaced with a basin filled with sand, complete with a crude, hastily adapted, but functionally adequate warmer. As with the cabin aboard the high-speed transport, the room's temperature could be individually regulated to suit its occupant. Preed immediately pushed it to maximum without bothering to try to translate the digits on the readout and without worrying about the possible consequences to the room's contents.

He spent the rest of the day relaxing as best he could amid the alien surroundings and renewing his acquaintance with his recordings of human facial expressions, which AAnn xenopsychs had discovered early on in the course of formal exchanges were a vital key in understanding the mammals. Oftentimes they would say one thing while their countenances would convey something entirely different. The fact that the thranx were not yet very good at this business of interpreting facial muscle positioning only inspired Preed's people to try to master it. No one could claim that ability yet, but among those assigned to diplomatic posts especially, great progress had been made.

For example, his host, the human male Sertoa, had been politely neutral in his greeting and conversation. But the sub-

cutaneous flexing of his facial muscles had suggested a
warmer predisposition toward his AAnn guest. As time
passed, if his interpretation was further confirmed, Preed
could play on that. Much good could be done here. He reminded himself of that repeatedly, by way of compensating
himself for having to endure the frigid conditions atop the
plateau. At least the local humidity, while higher than any AAnn
would choose, was tolerable, as opposed to the simmering soup
of an atmosphere that prevailed in the bug-infested lowlands
below.

"We have sso much more in common," he hissed to his
host the following day, as Sertoa toured the visiting diplomat
through the facility. "Physsically, we are infinitely more alike
than either of our resspective sspeciess are to the bugss." By
way of demonstration, he reached out and put a four-fingered
hand, polished claws and all, on the human's shoulder. The
flesh was soft beneath the thin garment, but Preed had expected and prepared for that.

"You ssee? We are on average nearly the ssame height,
though your kind runss to more extremess than mine. We are
both bipedal, though you lack the counterbalance of a tail. Internally, we are both bissymmetrical. Your earss are rather
prominently external, but our eyess are identically possitioned,
though your pupilss are round and ourss vertical. Your facess
are pusshed in—excusse my terminology, are flat—but when
you look me in the eye and I look back, I see a being that iss
not sso very different from mysself." He gestured southward,
toward the teeming lowlands. "When I look at a thranx, I ssee
ssomething that iss truly alien."

"The thranx are as intelligent as you or I, and as deserving
of respect," the human responded.

"Truly." Had he overstepped his bounds? Preed wondered
furiously. After all, the humans were on this planet by the
grace of their insectoid hosts. Had he misread this mammal
so badly? "I wass ssimply pointing out ssome interessting
and unavoidable ssimilarities. I did not mean any dissresspect
to thosse who, after all, are hosstss here to uss both." Disrespect, he mused silently, could come later.

"I understand." The human directed his guest down a footpath paved with round stepping-stones. Preed's sandals clicked softly on the artificial rock, his feet swathed in protective cold-resistant gear. Meanwhile, the human strolled about virtually naked in the chill air of afternoon.

"We musst all get along in thiss tiny corner of a vasst galaxy. You know that the emperor hass petitioned your government for the ssame ssettlement and ssharing rightss that are pressently enjoyed by thesse thranx?"

Sertoa's face revealed his surprise. "No, I didn't know that. In what way?"

The AAnn diplomat explained. "As the thranx have esstablished ssmall hivess in your Amazon and Congo Bassinss, and are conssidering another in your Ssepik River region, my government hass requessted that we be allowed to consstruct a tesst community in either the center of your Ssahara Desert or an alternate region called the Ssonoran."

"That's exciting news." Sertoa led the way into one of the complex's sealed structures. The air inside was slightly warmer than without, for which Preed was inordinately grateful. "I hope it comes to pass."

"You do?" Preed kept his tone subdued.

"Why, of course. I've always admired the accomplishments of the AAnn. At least, what we know of them. No one looks forward to closer relations between our two peoples more than I."

Breakthrough. Though his scale-covered snout and face were far less flexible than those of any human, they were still capable of movement. Lest the humans be studying the expressions of the AAnn as intensely as his kind were scrutinizing theirs, Preed struggled to hide the quiet exultation he felt at the human's response. This diplomat was not only friendly toward his kind: If his words could be believed, he was positively enthusiastic.

There were a number of ways of checking.

"If you are interessted, I might perhapss be able to arrange a reciprocal vissit to the Imperial capital at Blassussar, or at leasst to one of the principal Imperial worldss."

Sertoa's expression brightened. "That would be wonderful! I'd enjoy that very much."

Confirmation of a quickly formed opinion, however casual, was always welcome. Here, on the thranx homeworld, was a sympathetic if not openly biased human diplomat. This was in itself enough to justify the discomfort of his trip, and he had only just arrived.

"I have a surprise for you." A grin, an expression that Preed recalled indicated a combination of personal satisfaction and amusement, dominated the human's face. "I think you'll like it."

They entered a substantial edifice where Preed was startled to encounter humans in various states of undress. If anything their naked bodies were, while of scientific interest, more disconcerting than their clothed forms. Leading the way deeper into the complex, Sertoa guided his guest to a windowless chamber. The pair of humans there hurried their dressing when they discerned the nature of the alien visitor.

"If you would kindly disrobe, sir. I know that your people do not suffer from any nudity phobias." As he ventured the suggestion, Sertoa had already begun the process of removing his own clothing.

"That iss true, but I am not ssure thiss iss in accordance with proper diplomatic procedure, my friend." The AAnn eyed the human uncertainly.

"Trust me, Baron Preed." By this time the human diplomat was nearly naked.

We must all make sacrifices for the Empire, Preed told himself. He began to remove his decorative official garments.

When both were unclad, Sertoa led his guest to a smaller chamber. Preed did his best to avoid gawking at the jiggling, pulpy body of his host. Sertoa opened a door and stepped inside. Preed followed, only to find himself in—if not the fabled nirvanic sands of Ss'ra'oun, at least a place where he could feel comfortable. The small chamber was suffused, bathed, washed in perfectly dry heat. It was almost, but not quite, a slice of home.

"Tanning room." Sertoa sat down on a convenient bench.

"To make sure we get our proper bimonthly dose of the right kind of sunlight. I thought you'd be more comfortable conversing here than anywhere else in the settlement."

Embracing the arid, humidityless heat, Preed almost unbent. "I am more grateful than I can ssay. Ssuch courtessy doess you proud, Jorge Ssertoa."

The human shrugged off the compliment. "Just doing my job." At his touch, a concealed wall alcove disgorged a thin-walled metal container containing a mix of both liquid and frozen water. Preed eyed it askance, hoping he would not be asked to partake of the frigid concoction. When he found out he could request uniced, room-temperature water, he relaxed once more.

"Now then." Sertoa smiled at his reptilian guest. "If you're reasonably at ease, what would you like to talk about? What exactly is the purpose of your visit here? Why aren't you at the AAnn diplomatic mission in Daret?"

By shifting his tail to one side, Preed found he could repose quite comfortably on the bench fashioned of native wooden slats. "There are a number of issuess involving the relationsship between your people and the thranx that intimately affect my kind. Given the natural biological ssimilaritiess between AAnn and human, my ssuperiorss felt that thiss outposst of yourss might be an appropriate place to broach them. Truly. Of coursse, we are alsso curiouss to ssee how you have progressed and what you have accomplisshed here. Though but recently arrived, I am already much impressed."

"I'm listening. Go on." Sertoa took a long swig of his water and Preed cringed internally as he heard cubes of frozen water actually clink against the human's teeth.

"My government feelss sstrongly that you are devoting far too many ressourcess to developing relationss with these bugss, when ssimilarr overturess between alike ssentientss ssuch as humankind and AAnn could be of infinitely greater benefit to both."

Sertoa nodded, an easy gesture to recognize and interpret. "First let me say that I couldn't agree with you more. I think trying to develop anything beyond standard diplomatic relations between humans and thranx, given the obvious profound differences between our respective species, is a waste of time and money. And I think the neglect of relations between your people and mine has been shameful. The thranx, of course, feel otherwise."

"That iss undersstandable." Preed started to gesture, then remembered to dip his head in the simple human nod. "As you may know, from the time of firsst contact, relationss between my people and the thranx have been . . . awkward. No amount of perssuassion and imploring on the part of my government hass ssucceeded in altering their beliefss." Luxuriating in the dry heat that saturated the chamber, he leaned forward. Not too far, aware that proximity to sharp, curved AAnn teeth had been known to unsettle an unwary human.

"Thiss need not affect in any way developing relationss between our resspective sspeciess. It iss good to have come all thiss way and know that we have at leasst one friend and ssympathizer among thosse of your kind empowered to make the decissions affecting thosse relationss."

Leaning back against the wall, his eyes half closed against the overhead tanning lights, Sertoa replied quietly. "There are others. Some feel even more strongly about this matter than I."

Preed considered. It was silent in the chamber for several moments before he made the decision to take a step that as recently as yesterday he had not believed would be possible. "How sstrongly, my friend?"

The human turned toward him. "More strongly than I am at liberty to say."

"That iss mosst encouraging. Truly. Perhapss before I depart I might be able to meet ssome of thesse like thinkerss?"

"Perhaps," Sertoa replied noncommittally. While willing to be obliging, Preed noted, the human remained cautious. "Meanwhile, I consider this a promising vein for further discussion, which I hope we may enlarge upon during the rest of your visit." He waved a hand, and Preed marveled at the sheer slackness of the gesture. "When we happen to find ourselves in appropriate surroundings, of course."

"Truly," Preed agreed. "Allow me, if you will, to detail

ssome of the sspecific ssuggestionss I am authorized to make, and to elaborate upon how they might be implemented to our mutual advantage."

"I would enjoy hearing them." Smiling encouragingly, Sertoa turned fully toward his reptilian guest, admiring the play of the tanning lights on the AAnn's gleaming, iridescent scales.

When in the course of the next morning's casual conversation an acquaintance happened to mention that Jorge Sertoa had spent the entire previous morning and well on into the afternoon in the company of a visiting, high-ranking AAnn envoy, Fanielle Anjou began a frantic search of the compound for the pair. She was more than a little exhausted and out of breath when she was eventually directed to the diplomatic compound's gymnasium and health complex. At first thought, it seemed an unlikely venue in which to pursue diplomacy between differing species. It did have the virtue of comparative privacy, however. That in itself conjured unwelcome possibilities she tried but was unable to put out of her mind.

She thought about mentioning it to Toroni, but without anything more to go on than suspicions of suspicions, she could hardly go barging into his office with eyebrows raised and arms flailing. She would have to bring something more to such a confrontational meeting than a personal dislike of the reptilian bipeds.

It was midafternoon when she found herself peeling off her clothes as she strode determinedly through the changing room. A few users she knew spoke to her. She returned their hellos and greetings as amiably as she could, even though her mind was elsewhere.

It was almost worth forcing the encounter just to see the look on Sertoa's face when, as naked as anyone else in that end of the complex, she pushed her way into the otherwise deserted tanning room to confront him and the AAnn envoy. Ignoring her open-mouthed colleague, she directed her attention to the alien, whose shimmering, leathery scales served to frame an otherwise interesting if unremarkable anatomy.

"Fanielle . . ." More than a little nonplussed, the unabashedly uncomfortable Sertoa struggled to keep his eyes on her face. Though she paid little attention to him, his efforts to appear resolutely uninterested amused her. She was far more interested in the AAnn. Seated on one of the long wooden benches, his tail switching from floor to wall, the envoy regarded her with curiosity. That his slitted eyes roved freely over her nude form unsettled her not a bit. Being utterly nonhuman, there was nothing in his gaze to affect her.

Bypassing Sertoa, she approached the alien and extended a hand. Not as her colleague had done, but with fingers upraised, crooked at both joints and parted, nails pointing forward. The AAnn did not rise, but gracefully met her gesture with his left hand. Their fingers interlocked, her soft ones separating his tough, leathery digits. She felt the strength of the highly evolved carnivore held in reserve. Then he released his grip. The not-unpleasant sensation reminded her of letting go of the strap of a particularly well made leather handbag. As he leaned back against the molded wall, she introduced herself. Nearby, Sertoa was stammering something as he tried to regain control of the situation. AAnn and female ignored him. For a brief moment, he was unsure which of the two was the more alien.

"I am Fanielle Anjou, second assistant undersecretary for thranx affairs on Hivehom."

Slitted, reptilian eyes met her own. Neither pair fell; neither pair wavered. "I am Baron Preed NNXV, sspecial envoy at large for his Imperial Majessty Hezenezzk V. I greet you as an equal, and wissh you all the natural warmth that doess not exisst in thiss place." One clawed hand gestured second-degree irony. "Except in thiss peculiar but mosst welcome inner chamber. While my quarterss are ssatissfactory, if the facilitiess would allow it, I would gladly sspend the remainder of my sstay right here." Before Anjou could respond, he added, "Does not thiss sstrong light burn your pale, unprotected sskin?"

"If one spends much time in here, yes, it does," she admitted.

Double eyelids blinked. "But you come in here to do thiss voluntarily."

"I already told you; it's necessary for our health," an increasingly impatient Sertoa reminded his guest.

"Most remarkable." The AAnn's gaze traveled unapologetically up and down Anjou's nude form. Not only did it not trouble her, she found it instructive to reciprocate the action. "I was enjoying a usseful chat with your good friend and colleague here concerning the lamentable sstate of human-AAnn relationss, and how it would be agreeable if more attention could be devoted to improving the nasscent relationsship that pressently exisstss between our two peopless. But it sseemss that certain of your associatess feel ssuch time iss better sspent attempting to win over the affection of thesse reeking, sswarming bugss."

"The government of Earth and its colonies manages the development of all interspecies relationships with equal care and attention. I'm sorry if the AAnn feel neglected." Off to one side, Sertoa was looking unhappy.

Preed's jaws parted, showing very sharp theropod-like teeth. "It iss not that we feel neglected. Intersstellar, inter-sspeciess conssanguinity cannot be fasshioned overnight. It iss merely that ssome of uss feel your people are devoting overmuch in the way of diplomatic energiess to attempting to create ssome kind of association with thesse hard-sshelled creaturess that goess beyond the ussual diplomatic formali-tiess. As you musst know, the Empire hass had ssome ssmall differencess with the bugss in the passt. Therefore, it iss only natural that we would pay sspecial attention to anything that would ssuggesst the bugss are attempting to misslead another, powerful sspeciess ssuch as yoursselves as to the true nature of our hisstorical relations."

"I can assure you that is not the case." Perspiration was beginning to pour in tiny rivulets down her body: her cheeks, her shoulders and breasts, down her belly and thighs and back. She ignored the damp stickiness. "My government respects all sentients, and treats equally with all. As to any quarrels you and the thranx may have had in the past, that is none of our business and does not affect our relations with them or with you."

Preed's hands wove patterns in the superheated air, indicating contentment and—something else she could not interpret. "It iss alwayss reassuring to hear ssuch words, particularly from ssomeone sso clearly versssed in the realitiess of intersstellar diplomacy as yoursself, Ms. Anjou. While I have time left here, I would look forward to converssing with you at greater length on ssuch interessting matterss."

"So would I." She blinked sweat from one eye. "Unfortunately, I have to travel to Daret tomorrow."

Sertoa frowned. "I don't recall your being scheduled for a visit to the capital this week."

"You can't know everything, Jorge. You know how these things come up. I'm not happy about it myself." She returned her attention to the AAnn diplomat. "I regret that I will not be able to talk with you further, noble Preed."

He gestured his disappointment. "We musst each of uss follow our directivess. My own sschedule iss ssimilarly inflexible. I wissh you a ssafe journey. I undersstand there wass a ssorrowfully fatal accident recently in your local transsport ssytem that affected you perssonally."

She stiffened slightly. "Yes, it did."

He tilted his head to one side as he gestured balletically with his left hand. "I would disslike hearing that a ssimilar fate had befallen one sso charming and knowledgeable as yoursself."

"I'll be careful," she assured him evenly. "As for you, have a care with your room's climate control. It can sometimes get quite chilly up here at night. And chilly for us could mean forced enervation for you." Somewhat against her better judgment, she allowed herself a small smile. "I would dislike hearing that your stiffened form had to be shipped back to Blassussar in a crate because you forgot to check your room's temperature settings."

Again the AAnn's head and hands danced in concert. This time she could not tell what, if anything, he was gesturing. "I will remember your cautioning with thankss."

Turning, she exited purposefully from the tanning chamber.

Sertoa watched her for longer than he intended before resuming his interrupted dialogue with the AAnn.

"I fear that where human-thranx versus human-AAnn relations are concerned, my colleague is of a different mind than you or I. She has developed not only a working relationship with the bugs, but something suspiciously like affection. I'm afraid she's allowed her admiration for the local culture to cloud her professional judgment." He resumed his seat on the wooden bench. "She and I often find ourselves on opposite sides of discussions. It's all very polite and professional, of course, but each of us knows where the other stands."

Swinging his long tail around, Preed used the tip to scratch under his left leg. "It iss of no import. My government understsands that opinion among your kind iss sstrongly divided over how to proceed with human-thranx relationss. It iss my tassk, and that of my compeerss operating on other worldss, to enssure that human-AAnn relationss are not overlooked in thiss headlong russh that iss being advocated by ssome of your people to erect an unnecessarily intimate association with the bugss. In the coursse of normal negotationss it would be unreassonable to expect that everyone in your diplomatic sservice would believe as ssenssibly as yoursself. But that iss all right; that iss acceptable. We musst ssimply work harder to convince Ms. Anjou of the right way of thinking."

Sertoa let out a derisive laugh. "You've only just met Fanielle. You might as well try to move the local star to another system as change her mind."

Preed gestured, expanding to soak up the wonderful parching heat of the chamber. "My people were engaged in the bussiness of intersstellar diplomacy long before your kind took itss firsst tentative sstepss into deep sspace. We have made it, if not a sscience, at leasst a very well honed tool. With great experience and patience, many thingss originally thought impossible have come to pass. Perhapss thesse achievementss might even extend to recruiting your redoubtable Ms. Anjou to our way of thinking." Lowering his spread arms and upraised tail, he settled himself as best he could on the bench opposite the human.

"Now let uss sspeak of comely thingss, of what pleasses you and what pleasses me, and for a while at leasst, talk no more of diplomacy and matterss portentouss."

But while Sertoa nattered on, a portion of the noble's thoughts were devoted to the female human who had so recently departed. She was bright, that one, and determined. An unhealthy combination. Despite what he had told Sertoa about the experience and expertise of the AAnn diplomatic service, and the skill of its operatives, she would be difficult to convince of the right way of seeing things. Procedures lined up in his mind like spikes in an advanced game of *jyss-ul-nacch*.

If she could not be convinced, she would have to be persuaded.

11

As the most populous of the thranx colonies and the first to be settled from Hivehom, the prideful inhabitants of Willow-Wane had worked to conceive and erect an exceptionally interesting pavilion for the fair on Dawn. Situated in the northern section of the grounds, on a slight rise, it offered much to interest both human and thranx visitors alike. Incidental to its design, its builders had created a place where members of both species could relax in one another's company in ways only the most dedicated adherents of closer ties could have envisioned years earlier.

The pavilion's purpose was entirely nonpolitical. Its exhibits were intended to entertain, amuse, and delight, not proselytize. That they had unintended effects on their audiences, both mammalian and insectoid, might have been predicted but was not considered. Certainly those families, groups, and individuals who found themselves wandering among the displays were not conscious of being bombarded with preconceived propaganda. Nevertheless, a number of innocuous messages managed to manifest themselves amid the more immediate.

We can enjoy one another's company, the several eating and drinking facilities declared wordlessly. *We can appreciate each other's art,* multiple slash sculptures and background music insisted. *We can band together to accomplish that which we cannot do by ourselves,* the build-and-climb exhibit demonstrated.

That there were differences could not be denied. For example, the pavilion contained no playground for children, because thranx larvae existed in a state of limbless attention.

Their amusements were wholly nonphysical. As a result, there were dozens of visual and aural displays entirely controlled by voice. Larvae could speak, but were otherwise completely dependent on the resources of the modern nursery.

This realization and the accompanying demonstrations had an unintended effect: They generated immediate sympathy on the part of visiting human children for their temporal thranx counterparts. Those larvae who had been chosen to participate in the exhibition found themselves the recipients of sympathetic attention from sad-eyed young bipeds who were already fully capable of movement. Many of the subsequent discourses between the young of both species were recorded for later study and proved highly revealing in the understanding of future developments.

As for the incipient as well as the fully mature adults of both species, they were enthralled by the excellence of the elaborate displays. One of the more popular involved demonstrations of human martial arts and their thranx equivalents. Both species had evolved from warlike ancestors. Humans who were embarrassed by a past now seen to be irrational if inevitable were startled and often overcome by the history display that showed entire hives of ancestral thranx engaging in endless primitive warfare.

As for the martial artists, humans were larger and heavier, and faster over a short distance. But thranx had more endurance and eight limbs to utilize in fighting instead of four, although the delicate truhands were not of much use in hand-to-hand combat and were usually kept folded close to the body and out of the way. Still, clever and well-trained thranx could often hold their own against combative humans. Built closer to the ground, they were harder to get off their feet. A judo leg sweep was not of much use against an opponent who could stand on six legs, and the bodies of the chitinous insectoids offered few soft spots to attack.

Such demonstrations were carefully choreographed and all in good fun. At other exhibits, the individual inclinations of humans contrasted sharply with the thranx tendency to perform tasks through cooperation. Human gymnasts tended to flip and fly by themselves, while their thranx counterparts built astonishingly stable pyramids consisting of dozens of individuals interlocking their hands and feet. These latter edifices were judged not only by their size and by the number of thranx involved in each structure, but by the aesthetics of the completed design.

But it was at the food stations where inhibitions really dropped away, as thranx discovered numerous human foods they could consume and humans luxuriated in the literally hundreds of new juices and soups concocted by thranx food preparators. Great scientific discoveries interest people, as do entertaining new works of art or exceptional demonstrations of physical skill, or ways to improve an individual lifestyle. But nothing enthralls quite so homogeneously as a new flavor.

Briann and Twikanrozex wandered through the pavilion, drawing fewer and briefer stares than they had elsewhere. Everyone was too intent on the exhibits, or on trying new foods and drinks, or on laughing at the wandering thranx sniggle poets, to pay special attention to one roving human-thranx pair. As for the two padres, they did not comment on the obvious lack of attention being paid them. They were too used to each other's company.

But they did observe, with pleasure, the unconscious ease with which their respective species had begun to relax in one another's presence. Seduced by the exotic surroundings of the pavilion, by its engaging food and drink, marvelous exhibits, unusual demonstrations, and the multitude of singular diversions set before them, few visitors had any time left in which to remark unfavorably on the mere physical differences between them.

"Observe," Twikanrozex remarked, "how the essence of shapeism vanishes when everyone involved is having a good time."

Briann nodded. "It's hard to hate when one is laughing too hard. Barring a very few isolated incidents, everything I've seen so far at this fair bodes well for better relations between our species. Amid such good feelings, the Church should prosper."

Twikanrozex indicated second-degree concurrence. "*Criill,* we need to nurture these good feelings, and to be available to succor and assist those whose inner emotions are conflicted. There is still an enormous amount of work to be done."

They rounded a slowly rotating disc on which thranx body-poets were arranging themselves in ever-more-complex patterns. Ancient traditions that had once been employed in the service of constructing impressive underground chambers had been transformed into a wondrously intricate kind of performance art human acrobats could only hope to emulate, but never duplicate.

"Myself," Briann declared, "I'll know we've achieved our goals when I see a human outside the Church consent to be ministered to by a thranx."

With delicate movements of head and antennae as well as hands, Twikanrozex insinuated a fusion of understanding and general bemusement. "It is a puzzle to me how sentient beings can feel more relaxed in the presence of a hostile but similar shape than in the company of a sympathetic but differently constructed intelligence."

Using their rigid exoskeletons like pieces of sculpture, the body-poets had erected a complex geometric structure that reached almost to the polarized roof of the pavilion. A mixed audience of complimentary thranx and perspiring humans stridulated and cheered in unison. As always, the reaction of the human children was particularly heartening. To them—to those children whose minds had not yet been poisoned by prejudiced or chary parents, Briann reminded himself—the thranx were a beautiful mystery, aromatic and alien, like oversized toys that could talk back. As Twikanrozex had pointed out, there was much work to be done.

The Church intended to be in the forefront of such work. There was no place in its self-deprecating structure or formal hierarchy for shapeism or any other kind of species bigotry—

only for souls. And as far as anyone had yet been able to determine, scientifically or theologically, all souls had the same shape. Exactly what the "soul" consisted of was a question both humans and thranx had been dealing with for thousands of years. Despite enormous advances in the technology of quantification, it remained an abstract, something that still could not yet be measured or weighed. The taxonomy of metaphysics was still in its infancy. In that sense it was akin to the never-ending search for the ultimate building blocks of matter, which every fifty years or so seemed to shrink a little farther in the direction of infinite smallness.

Briann did not worry overmuch about such matters. Or nonmatters, depending on one's point of view. He had joined the Church to help people, no matter their shape. Thus far he had encountered nothing to make him second-guess his decision. His family remained puzzled, but supportive. Interestingly, Twikanrozex had encountered even more difficulty with his choice. Thranx society was not as fluid as that of the humans. Radical changes in lifestyle and direction were not as freely countenanced. Twikanrozex had been compelled to hoe a harder row than his human companion.

Still, even though both considered themselves more sophisticated in matters of interspecies relations and had prepared themselves for this occasion with much serious study and preparation, the fair had already shown itself capable of delivering an endless round of surprises. Presently, they were passing a lively display devoted to illustrating the history of agriculture on Willow-Wane. Virtual thranx drove virtual machines to the accompaniment of narration in both Low Thranx and Terranglo. Appropriate odors suffused the area immediately around the exhibition. Generating the story via tridee transducers allowed the thranx producers to incorporate huge mechanicals and hundreds of workers without overwhelming the individual display.

Passing by, a larger than usual human family paused briefly to gaze at the roof-high exhibit, whereupon the smallest child in the group raised a hand and pointed, yelling gleefully.

"Look, look—an ant farm!"

Briann felt his face flush slightly as he and Twikanrozex ambled on past the thoroughly enchanted family. His reaction was not in response to the child's comment, but because Twikanrozex, overhearing, requested an explanation of the term. When a slightly flustered Briann had finished eluci- dating, as diplomatically as he was able, the thranx gestured reassurance.

"There's no need to be embarrassed, my friend. Your native arthropods are not my ancestors. Actually, I find the concept rather endearing." Swiveling his head to look directly back over his shoulder at the gawking family, he gestured with both truhands. "Certainly it has proven useful, as the larvae in question show no fear of my kind. Perhaps a general distribu- tion of the educational toys to which the youngest referred might be considered by the Church."

"There are other concerns," Briann endeavored to explain. "Although I have never owned such a bio-apparatus myself, I believe that the resourceful little arthropods in question have a tendency to escape their controlled environment, to the an- noyance of any resident adults. I think the Church is better to stick with those visual aids that can provide instruction without the possibility of accompanying infestation."

Twikanrozex's antennae drew together, showing that he was deep in thought. Finally he responded. "Perhaps, *se!licc,* you are right. I don't think self-contained habitats holding miniature humans would be welcome in the private chambers of many hives, either." He glanced at his friend. "Assuming such a contrivance could be constructed."

"A people farm?" Briann pondered the notion. "I don't think so. Although if you offer humans enough monetary compen- sation, they'll do just about anything. In that respect, the thranx are more virtuous than my kind."

"Not at all," Twikanrozex demurred. "It is only that we are most of the time too busy to be corrupted. When time exists for contemplation of possibilities, we too can be persuaded to make fools of ourselves."

"Another vinculum between our peoples." Reassured by his friend's reiteration of the existence of mutual foolishness,

Briann led the way out of the pavilion. All the walking, not to mention all the talking, was making him hungry.

He shared the state of his stomach with his companion, who allowed as how he, too, could stand some sustenance.

"What would you like?" Briann inquired. "We can go back inside, where the climate is more to your liking, or continue wandering until we come across something that appeals to both of us."

"Let us wander." Twikanrozex was enjoying himself hugely. "The air is a little dry today, but not entirely intolerable."

Briann hitched his sweat-dampened shirt higher on his shoulders and chose a pedestrian walkway at random. There was no need to consult a fair directory. The Church would guide them.

It did indeed, as they soon found themselves resting comfortably in an outdoor venue that was raised slightly above ground level, giving the patrons a pleasant view of the busy fairgrounds that stretched to the lake and the green-clad hills beyond. Not for the first time, Briann reflected on what an excellent choice Dawn had been for such an enterprise. The semitropical nature of the climate was bearable to the thranx while not unduly uncomfortable for humans. Locating the fair next to a large lake had the effect of injecting additional humidity into the local atmosphere, thus pleasing the insectoids even further.

At the moment, one of those aliens was finding exceptional pleasure in a mango-starfruit-guanabana crush, the terrestrial fruit juice drink being not only acceptable to his system, but avidly welcomed. The only difference between that and a similar beverage being enjoyed by Briann was that the thranx had ordered it made with tepid water instead of pulverized ice, a request that had left the perspiring human attendant shaking his head in silent disbelief. To the thranx, the notion of a "cold drink" was an oxymoron.

Twikanrozex admired the flexibility of his friend's prehensile lips as Briann sipped easily at his own libation. With four opposing mandibles, the thranx could make quicker work of solid food than any human, but liquids gave them problems.

Fluids had to be poured directly into the open mouth, or inhaled via often elaborately swirled and decorated, narrow-spouted drinking utensils. Only by inserting the tip of such a siphon partway down the insectoid throat could a thranx generate enough esophageal vacuum to draw liquid from a container. In contrast, the malleability of human flesh allowed someone like Briann to form an airtight seal around the edge of an open container and pull fluids up and in. There were advantages to having a ductile epidermis.

Of course, Twikanrozex mused, such abilities were more than offset by the inherent aesthetic handicaps all humans suffered from. The thranx would not have exchanged his burnished, gleaming, blue-green exoskeleton for all the fluid-vacuuming abilities in the Arm. Slipping the drinking tip of his siphon-cup between his parted mandibles, he luxuriated in the slippery, sugary taste and feel of the exotic terrestrial refreshment as it coursed down his throat.

"Ah, there you are!"

Briann looked up from his chair to see two men advancing toward him. Both were older, one considerably so. Their eyes were intense, but not baleful. They were neatly dressed. Excessively so, given the ambient temperature and humidity within the pavilion.

"May we join you?" the younger of the two asked politely. "We've been searching for you two ever since we came across your display."

"We like to move around." Briann set his drink aside. "You know: meet folks, see the fair, try new experiences."

"Well, you two are certainly a new experience for us. We've read about you, and seen bits and pieces about your organization on the tridee. I am Father Joseph." He indicated the distinguished, white-haired senior who had settled into the chair alongside him. "This is Father Jenakis. I am Twelfth Baptist, and he is Orthodox Episcolic."

Briann explained to his watchful companion. "Traditional human churches."

Twikanrozex gestured welcome to the two men of the cloth. "I'm pleased to meet a pair of fellow theologians."

Joseph accepted the proffered chitinous hand tentatively. Making no move to emulate the gesture, Father Jenakis maintained a respectful distance to go with his thoughtful silence.

"We hadn't expected you to be so fluent in our language."

Twikanrozex dipped his antennae forward, keeping one truhand wrapped around his drinking utensil. "I am conversant in several languages, including one that involves only the use of gestures. If one has information to impart, one cannot expect the audience to go to the trouble of learning the imparter's tongue."

Briann smiled pleasantly. "Twikanrozex doesn't have a tongue, of course. The thranx modulate sounds deep within their throats, by means of mechanisms that would choke a human. That it comes out sounding so similar to us is as remarkable as it is advantageous. I am Padre Briann and this is Padre Twikanrozex."

Father Jenakis snorted curtly. His younger associate winced ever so slightly before resuming the conversation. "As you may know, a number of the established Terran religions are having some trouble with this United Church of yours."

"It's yours, too," Twikanrozex observed, managing to unsettle the earnest Father Joseph in as few words as possible.

"No, not mine, I'm afraid. Some of my colleagues and I are concerned. At first, no one paid much attention to your efforts."

"No one paid *any* attention to our efforts," Briann corrected him, still smiling.

Joseph had the grace to smile back. "But now your message, peculiar and unconventional as it is, appears to be having some small effect. In particular, you are making inroads among the young who dominate the upper intelligence percentiles. This is not only disturbing, it is unprecedented."

"Yes, we know." Briann sat back in his chair. Around them, crowd sounds rose and fell: laughter and squeals of delight and shouts of surprise. "Usually it's the other way around. It's those in the lower percentiles who tend to be persuaded first."

"Dangerous nonsense!" the older man huffed, deigning to speak for the first time.

"Not a bit of it." Briann had heard it all before, though not usually from official representatives of terrestrial churches. "We don't proselytize. We don't try to convert anyone. We just put our creed out where it can be examined by anyone who might be interested. We don't push it. It's a free society we live in, in these days of open communications and galactic colonization. Anyone is free to join any organization they wish, provided the tenets of that fraternity do not impinge on the rights of others." He spread his hands wide. "We don't even ask anyone who joins the UC to give up their previous religion, if they have one, or stop going to that particular church, if they wish to continue to do so."

"So how can we be dangerous?" Twikanrozex finished for his friend.

"Your doctrine is seductive," the older man growled, his true sentiments clearly held in check by the admonitions of his own. "Worse than seductive, it mocks all other religions. You worship nothing but irrelevancy!"

Twikanrozex motioned for understanding. "We don't worship irrelevancy: We simply recognize it. We *are* irrelevant. All of us. I, my colleague Briann, you, everyone in this pavilion, everyone on this planet. Our presence justifies nothing, and signifies only the accidental evolution of some exceptionally active amino acids. The results are admirable, even praiseworthy. But they are not relevant to the evolvement of the universe. One of the core beliefs of the United Church is that every sentient being should come to understand its place in the scheme of things."

"And what is that place?" Father Joseph ignored his senior's look of disapproval.

"A little to the left, we think." Briann's smile widened. "I'm sorry if that sounds too irrelevant. You see, we are a dogma that is founded on full comprehension of our own individual and collective insignificance. Having accepted that, we can mature in comfort. I am quite content with who I am and with my place in the cosmos. Likewise, Twikanrozex is content with his."

"What about eternal damnation and salvation?" Father Jenakis looked as if he wanted to thunder the question but, mindful of the many others seated nearby, restrained himself.

"Questions we can't answer," Briann replied. "If they exist, we can't do anything about them. And if they don't, why, we'd be wasting an awful lot of otherwise productive lifetime agonizing over them." He met the older man's gaze unflinchingly. "There are plenty of others willing to do the agonizing already, and we have no desire to intrude on their territory."

Joseph turned apologetic. "You know that there are proposals being put forth to limit your activities."

"Among my people, as well," Twikanrozex felt compelled to point out.

Briann shrugged. "We don't spill time worrying about that. It's a matter for the legal logisticians. Twikanrozex and I, we're just two among many who have chosen to help spread the message." He sat forward. "Having been by our display, you know that everything about the Church is available for the asking. Why don't you try reading the first forty maxims or so and their antecedents?"

Joseph replied with the confidence of the convicted. "I already have plenty to read, both religious and otherwise."

Briann sighed resignedly. "Too bad. They'd give you a couple of good laughs. What is it you want from us? If it's simply to discuss theology and the economics of organized religion, we're happy to oblige you. If there's something more . . ."

Father Jenakis looked as if he were about to rise from his seat. "We want you to shut down that infernal display of yours and stop trying to convert people! Especially young people."

"But we have told you." Twikanrozex responded with a four-handed gesture of some directness. "We are not trying to convert anyone—much less anyone of a particular age. I must add that in this respect I have already encountered such a request. The fanciful situation to which you allude arouses even greater passions among my people, since our children are incapable of moving about on their own. There is much unreasoning talk of what you call, I believe, 'captive audiences.' "

"Our display stays." Though still conventionally courteous, Briann's tone hardened slightly. "We have the permit, and as much right to exhibit as any other authorized vendor at this fair."

"Vendor!" Father Jenakis shook his head slowly. "If you are willing to denigrate your own beliefs so freely, how can you expect others to take them seriously?"

"We don't," Briann informed him. "That is, we don't expect others to do anything, except read what is on offer. And since we don't expect others to take us seriously, why should you? If we're going to, as you put it, denigrate our own beliefs, why should you take the trouble to do so when we're doing it for you?"

"We told you," Joseph declared softly. "Because it's that very irreverence that appeals to intelligent youngsters. It intrigues them."

"It also makes them laugh," Briann could not keep from pointing out. "Nothing like a lack of seriousness, of preaching, and of regulations to puzzle a clever kid. Where is it writ that a religious organization can't consecrate fun?" He shook his head. "I won't tell you from what particular theology I came to the United Church, but suffice to say I never could understand how making you continually feel bad was supposed to ultimately make you feel good." He folded his arms and radiated quiet contentment. "We have the same eventual end in mind as do you. We've simply chosen to follow a path that cuts out all that conflicting, confusing first step. We proceed directly to making people feel good."

"You will be stopped." Father Jenakis was quite convinced. "Laws will be passed to prevent you from doing any more harm. Furthermore, people will soon begin to see through the insubstantialities of your clever but childish polemics. You are a fad, gentlemen. Nothing more. I feel sorry for you, and will pray for your souls."

Briann maintained his maddening air of self-assurance.

"As to the possibility of restrictive laws being used against us, Father, only time will tell. I can tell you that we have very good lawyers. As to people seeing through what the Church propounds, we intend that they do so. That's why we abjure complex dogma, and try to keep things simple. When they see through our maxims, we hope that on the other side they will find truth. That is all that we seek: truth and happiness. The former to gratify the mind, the latter to satisfy the soul. And we thank you for your offer to pray for us. We of the Church would never turn down such a benevolent offer. 'In a Universe vast with uncertainties, never turn down an offer of expiation, no matter what the source.' Maxim number sixty-eight, part four."

The older man rose precipitously. "You people are impudent and shameless!"

"I know," Briann admitted, "but it keeps us smiling."

Jenakis looked like a man ready to begin a sermon. Thinking better of it, he reached down and put a hand on his younger associate's shoulder. "Come, Father Joseph. We can do nothing more here. One cannot reason with harlequins."

His expression rueful, the younger man rose. "I'm sorry. We can't help you if you won't let us. I will pray for you, too."

"That's very kind of you." Leaning forward, Briann whispered conspiratorially, "Remember—all our literature is easily mollyed right from our display tower!" As the younger man turned to depart in the wake of his senior, Briann placed a thumb in each ear, raised his hands, and wagged his fingers at the retreating figures while simultaneously sticking out his tongue.

Twikanrozex eyed him with interest. "That is a gesture I do not recognize from the Church canons."

Looking content, Briann dropped his hands. "It's decidedly nontheological in origin. Among my people, an ancient and traditional folkloric form of farewell."

"Very kinetic. Can you teach it to me?"

Briann considered. "You have no ears to stick thumbs into, but your ability to make use of an extra pair of hands more than compensates. I think you'll do well with it—but you have to pick the operative situations carefully."

"I know that you will instruct me properly." Twikanrozex shifted his lower abdomen on the padded straddle bench, eager to learn.

Padre Briann proceeded to enlighten him.

12

A breathless Therese Holoness led Cullen Karasi and Pilwondepat out of camp and down the walking track that led to
the primary excavation. Along the way they passed the location of several other smaller digs begun in the hopes of
finding something interred in the hard-packed earth of the escarpment. Every one of these was deserted; tools powered
down, water bottles set aside, laser grids shining unimpeded
in the morning sun. When Pilwondepat remarked on the absence of workers, Holoness pointed ahead.

"They're all down at the main site. Everyone's gathering
there." She hopped over a narrow ravine. Cullen followed
easily, while Pilwondepat had to pick his way. He did not fall
behind, but neither did he hop. Thranx were not very good
jumpers.

The truth of her words became clear as they neared the site.
A large crowd had assembled. As they drew nearer, Cullen
saw that not only the exoarcheological crew but a goodly portion of the camp's nonscientific staff was also congregating
around the open pit. As he approached, he was recognized,
and murmuring onlookers moved aside to make room for him
and Holoness. A few less-than-friendly looks greeted the
presence of the thranx in their midst, but he was granted passage, as well, and no one said anything. At least, nothing that
could be overheard.

A number of Cullen's people were clustered around something at the bottom of the excavation, blocking it with their
assembled bodies. Pilwondepat was inordinately displeased
to see Riimadu among them. The AAnn was standing slightly

to one side, tail switching back and forth in as transparent an indication of excitement as if he had been hissing wildly and throwing his arms in the air. Holoness led the way to the earthen staircase and then downward into the depths. Around the rim of the hole in the ground, the crowd continued to enlarge until it seemed to Pilwondepat that every worker on the site was present.

Descending the steps cut into the hard-packed earth more slowly than his human companions, he waited for the cluster of diggers to part. He thought Riimadu might have glared once in his direction, but he could not be sure. In any event, it didn't matter, since he was soon as dumbstruck as everyone else by what the excavators had uncovered.

It was a vitreous dark brown surface with a meter-wide dimple in the center. That in itself was not especially striking, nor was the fact that they had certainly uncovered an artifact. What was of far greater import was the realization that the object was not made of stone, like the grand statues that dominated the far side of the valley opposite the escarpment.

"It's not metal." Holoness started talking before anyone asked. "Or plastic. As best we've been able to determine without knocking off a chunk for analysis, it's some kind of bonded ceramic." Crouching over the depression, she used one palm to brush at the sensuous alien curve. "See how it shines?"

Stepping forward, both Pilwondepat and Cullen made their own cursory examination of the phenomenon. The thranx did not have to bend to do so. The unusual material was slick to the touch and unexpectedly warm. He would have expected something that had been buried at the top of the escarpment for untold eons to be much colder, the temperature of the ground notwithstanding.

"Any ideas as to its function?" Straightening, Cullen kept his eyes on the article of all their fascination.

Holoness shook her head. "It's plenty solid, sir. Chenowitz took the liberty of tapping gently on it with a rock, then harder. It's not hollow."

"Well, whatever it is, it's different from anything anybody's found on Comagrave to date. We'll be able to get a better idea of its intended purpose when we've dug it out."

That was the signal for the diggers to go back to work. Pilwondepat waited and watched their laboring until the afternoon light began to wane. While the falling temperature had no effect on the much more heat-tolerant humans and the single AAnn in their midst, it soon drove him back to his quarters. There he performed his regular evening ablutions while waiting for the excited call that never came. Surely Cullen would not be so indifferent as to forget to notify him when they finally freed the object from its stony matrix.

He was right. It was still there when he emerged the following morning, after the sun was well up in the sky and the surrounding high desert had heated up enough to accommodate him without danger of hypothermic paralysis.

His fixed compound eyes could not widen, the multiple lenses could not expand, but his antennae stood straight up and his abdominal gaster contracted, letting out an involuntary stridulation of surprise, when next he cast his gaze down into the pit.

It had grown. Apparently, the humans had been sufficiently intrigued—or perhaps *astounded* was the better description—to work on the site all through the night. Holoness confirmed his supposition when he confronted her on the now rapidly expanding rim.

"We thought we'd have it out, even if it was pretty big, by dinnertime last night." She was perfectly polite, but he noticed she consciously avoided contact with him. As always, he let the implied slight pass without comment. "But the more dirt and rock we cut away, the bigger it got." She gestured into the hole. "As far as anyone can tell, we're still nowhere near reaching its limits."

The excavation was now some twenty meters on a side and still expanding. Every piece of heavy exhuming equipment in the camp had been brought into play within the depths of the widening cavity. As laser drills sliced rock into manageable chunks and sonic blasters shattered the larger boulders into powder that could be easily vacuumed, the exoarcheological staff employed finer tools around the edge of the artifact. Additional dimples had been revealed in the lustrous, gently undulating surface. More significantly still, the succession of concavities had given way on the eastern flank of the relic to a perfectly flat surface devoid of indentations or any other blemish. A team of workers was laboring relentlessly to extend this platform, or landing, or whatever it was, in Pilwondepat and Holoness's direction.

"If they don't come to the end of it soon," the female told him, "we're going to have to start thinking about moving camp."

He gestured understanding, then remembered to add the easily mimicked human head nod. "Has any further progress been made, *sir!ilp,* in identifying the material of which it is made?"

"Actually, yes. Mr. Karasi gave permission last night for a sample to be taken for analysis. It resisted like mad, until we finally got a laser tuned enough to cut away a tiny piece. It's a bonded ceramic, all right. Incredibly tough stuff. The internal crystal lattice is unique, and the molecular structure designed, if that's the right word, to last pretty close to forever. It has a beryllium base, and then it starts to get crazy with introduced metallic salts. Or so the chemistry people tell me. You can't get them to stop talking about it."

Pilwondepat did not inquire about the artifact's purpose. That was unlikely to be ascertained until they had all of it exposed. "One presumes it's of Sauun manufacture, but without proof . . ."

"Mr. Karasi thinks he has that." The admiration in her voice for the abilities of the project's leader bordered, Pilwondepat thought, on reverence. "There's a temple on the Coruumat Plain that has a couple of interior walls bearing the same alternating dome-and-depression pattern. The concavities are even the same size. But those on the plain are of stone." She gestured down into the excavation. "No one working on Comagrave has encountered anything like this material before now."

Pilwondepat watched the humans at work: energetic, capable, able to labor efficiently in a climate so dry the thranx's lungs would have shriveled to half their size after less than a couple of days of exposure to such a desiccating atmosphere. But they were not as precise in their movements as his kind. Still, they were not excavating a pin-sized structure. There was margin for error with hand pick or drill.

"What," he wondered aloud, "if there *is* no end to this expanding flat surface?"

"I don't follow you." She looked over at him curiously. "There has to be an end."

"Does there?" Seeking signs of an edge, a rim, to the steadily broadening artifact, he saw none. "What if this object, whatever it is, has been built on an order of magnitude comparable to the icons across the valley? What if it is even larger?"

It took her only a moment to formulate a reply. "Why then, it will take a long time to get there, but it will still have an end."

"I wonder. Perhaps instead of trying to expose it all, we should be trying to penetrate it."

Now she laughed. "A lot of good that will do, if it's as solid as a statue."

"I am not saying that it is. Only that in light of its size, seeking an interior or an underside is another option that should at least be considered."

She suppressed her amusement. "Talk to Supervisor Karasi. He would be the one to make that determination. If you'll excuse me?" In the brusque manner of humans, she started down into the pit without waiting to learn if he would.

Pilwondepat stood staring down into the rapidly expanding pit. Riimadu was there, as usual: chatting with individual humans, gesturing suggestions, frequently pausing to consult his communicator. Pilwondepat envied the AAnn researcher his easy camaraderie with the mammals. Not only was their stature similar; so were their movements. Upright bipeds, albeit one tailless, they shared physical commonalties he could not hope, despite his best efforts, to emulate. Certainly the reptiloids enjoyed advantages in establishing relations with the humans that immediately put any hopeful thranx at a disadvantage.

It frightened him. It was bad enough that no human could follow the threatening sequence of calamity that was being subtly propagated by the AAnn. That they should become friends with the very people who sought their ultimate ouster from Comagrave was worse than sinister: It was downright infuriating. He wanted to grab Cullen or someone of equal authority with all four hands and shake them until they began to molt. He did not only because he knew that they would react defensively, and with even less interest in what he had to say than before.

At least Cullen had promised to convey Pilwondepat's findings to the central colonial administration. Another few days, and he could rest a little easier knowing that his findings had been passed on to, hopefully, more perceptive authorities. Until then, and until a reply was forthcoming, he could only continue with his own research, while incidentally keeping a close watch on Riimadu. That the AAnn appeared wholly engrossed in his fieldwork might deceive the humans. It would never be so with a thranx. The two species knew each other too well.

Cullen gave up on the horizontal dig two days later. By that time, the excavation crew had exposed an area of glistening brown ceramic more than a hundred meters square, lying an average depth of twelve meters. Nowhere could the diggers discern an edge or a break in the material. Nor could they locate a single seam, joint, nail, bolt, clip, or path. The mysterious material appeared to have been poured whole and entire into a huge mold, like lava into a bowl. Of dimples and ripples, of small protuberances and extensive flat surfaces, there were plenty. Of indication as to dimensions, function, or age, there was none.

Brard Johannsen, the expedition's chief geologist, chipped in with a report stating that the location of the site, almost proximate to the rim of the escarpment, exposed it to howling winds heavily laden with particulate matter. As a consequence, erosion was considerably more active near the campsite than it was farther inland. Preliminary dating of the rock and the packed earth layer overlying the artifact suggested that it had originally been buried far deeper beneath the surface, which had been worn down and carried away by untold millennia of strong winds.

"There's no question that it's a significant relic, and not just because of its fascinating composition." Cullen had invited Pilwondepat to join him for midday meal. They were seated away from the now quiescent excavation, on a little ridge that provided a fine view over the great valley beyond. The human gnawed on a stratified pulpy compaction called a sandwich, while Pilwondepat chewed *jheru*-flavored food pellets and sipped from his turbinate juice bottle.

"That was suspected from the very beginning." In the absence of teeth or horn-covered maxilla, Pilwondepat's four opposing mandibles worked against one another to masticate his food. Since he breathed through the spicules on his thorax, he did not suffer from a fear of choking on his food, as humans were frequently wont to do. In a thranx, air and food took separate internal paths.

Raising a hand, Cullen pointed across the valley. There was no wind today, and the air was absolutely still. The vast wild panorama possessed an absolute clarity that stunned the eyes.

"It gains in significance every day. There's nothing of importance behind the Mountain of the Mourners. Similarly, only very minor discoveries have been made to its north and south. Yet here, we find this boundless brown ceramic enigma—right where the Mourners are staring."

"As Riimadu originally pointed out." Pilwondepat was surprised he could say it without stridulating. "But what can it be?"

Cullen shook his head and took another bite of his sandwich. Pilwondepat would have had no trouble digesting the human food, but the smell was not to his liking. Anyway, the supervisor had not offered.

"Nobody has any idea yet. I suppose you've heard that

we're due to get the results of the combined surveys back some time this evening?"

The thranx's antennae twitched with agitation. "No, I had not."

Rising, Cullen mashed the wrapping that had contained and warmed his sandwich into a compact ball. Drawing back his arm, he flung it forward in a smooth, arcing motion no thranx could duplicate. The ball sailed out over the edge of the escarpment. By nightfall its transiently bonded organic components would have disintegrated.

"Come by the presentation tent. I'd be interested in your opinion."

"I would not miss it." Tucking his drinking bottle neatly into his thorax pack, Pilwondepat followed the human back toward the camp.

The double survey Cullen had authorized was intended to furnish some dimensions for the object the team had unearthed. Any additional information gleaned in the course of the survey would provide a welcome bonus. Riding in the camp's two aircars, separate teams had utilized a pair of sonic scanners to probe beneath the barren Comagravian surface. Reflected back to the scanners' receivers, measured and recorded, these sonic echoes could be instantly analyzed by onboard instruments to give a detailed picture of any buried artifact.

But not, it seemed, this one.

The inability of any of the scanners' sensors to penetrate the ceramic material was revealing in its inadequacy. It proved that the brown stratum was far thicker, and denser, than anyone had previously imagined. Whatever lay beneath the ceramic layer, it could not be perceived by the scanners. What the survey teams *were* able to do was to come up with an estimate of the layer's horizontal dimensions. These were sufficiently mind-boggling that both teams were compelled to return to base to have their equipment rechecked, and then checked again. Assured that everything was working properly, the team members returned to their task. By nightfall this had not yet been concluded. Even so, the occupants of both aircars voted to return to camp to present what findings they had managed to accumulate.

At the same time, a third team dropped over the edge of the escarpment and proceeded to perform a vertical scan, hovering above the valley floor while traveling slowly back and forth along the sheer rock wall. With their sensors aimed not down, but sideways, they hoped to obtain clues as to how deep the ceramic layer ran. Information they gathered in abundance: They simply refused to believe it.

Meanwhile, at Cullen's request, the orbit of a mapping and climate-monitoring satellite had been shifted slightly so it could take several high-resolution vits of the dig site and the region immediately surrounding it. These proved to be of little beyond aesthetic value. No underlying pattern of construction could be distinguished from overhead. Geology had not masked from above what lay hidden beneath the ground.

Following the informative presentation, Pilwondepat sought out Cullen. As soon as they saw the thranx approaching, the human couple who had been conversing with the supervisor found reasons to be elsewhere. Ordinarily, Pilwondepat might have been mildly miffed at the slight. Tonight, he did not care.

"Hello, Pilwondepat." A subdued Cullen peered down at the thranx. "What did you think of the presentation?" Around them, site workers and scientists were taking their flustered conversations and often wild suppositions out into the swiftly cooling night. Pilwondepat knew he was in danger of freezing on the way back to his chamber, but he didn't care.

"*Cwissk*—we're sitting atop a seamless layer of radical ceramic material that is, according to the reports handed in by the survey teams, hundreds if not thousands of square kilometers in area. One that also, according to the other team, is at least as high as the escarpment itself. It is surely the single largest artificial structure found to date on this world, easily dwarfing even the icons comprising the Mountain of the Mourners."

The human nodded. "Yet we're no nearer to knowing its function than we were when Verwoerd and Olsen exposed the first depression. If it is solid, then it is certainly the biggest enigma we've yet uncovered here. If it's hollow ... If it's hollow, there's no telling what it might contain."

"Perhaps only dead air," Pilwondepat ventured.

Cullen responded with an emphatic denial. "Nobody, no sentient species, builds a box of these dimensions, if that is indeed what it is, to hold nothing."

"It could be that it was intended to accommodate certain contents that never arrived prior to the emptying of this world. It might also be designed not to store something, but to hide it. To seal it up."

The biped gazed back into enigmatic compound eyes. "Are all thranx as cheerfully optimistic and reassuring as you, Pilwondepat?"

"Most of the time we tend to be ..." Examining the human's expressive face, the thranx researcher terminated his intended reply. "Oh, I see. You are being sarcastic. We regard ourselves as more than a little adept at the behavior ourselves, you know." He gestured repeatedly and eloquently with his truhands.

"I have been proposing for days that instead of expending time and resources in trying to seek out an external boundary, your people make an effort to search out an entrance to the hypothesized interior."

Cullen let out a derisive grunt. "There are no seams, no doorjambs, no rills or surface inclusions. Where do you propose that we start?"

Pilwondepat had prepared for the question. "At the bottom of one of the innumerable concavities that dot the otherwise smooth surface. With cutting lasers and other devices. Dampened shaped charges, if necessary."

"What if the material is combustible? The use of either lasers or charges could cause the entire structure to oxidize." He chuckled humorlessly. "That would make a fine headline in the *Journal of Interstellar Archeology*. 'Comagrave Dig Supervisor Discovers Greatest Single Artifact in North Arm. Promptly Burns It to a Crisp.' "

"You are being theatrical. Good material for ire-poetry; not for science. One sample of the ceramic has already been subjected to thorough analysis. Others can be taken from elsewhere and checked to ensure that such an explosive reaction will not take place."

"It's going to take time," Cullen warned him. "The stuff is incredibly tough."

"But not impenetrable," Pilwondepat reminded him.

"No," the supervisor was forced to concede. "Probably not impenetrable. The question remains, is there anything down there to penetrate?" Wearied from work and worry, he reached up to rub the base of his neck. "If it's an ancient floor, we're going to waste an awful lot of time digging our way through it just to find more rock on the underside."

"The alien ceramic protects the greatest treasure in the Arm," the thranx exoarcheologist countered. "All the knowledge and riches and wealth of the Sauun, just waiting for someone to uncover it."

Cullen's gaze narrowed, a peculiar ability of humans. The AAnn could not do it, Pilwondepat knew. "What evidence do you have to support such a claim?"

The thranx gestured elaborately. Sarcasm, indeed. "None whatsoever. But it is an inspirational notion, is it not? And what are your alternatives? To keep surveying and measuring, forever expanding the size of the mystery without ever making an effort to solve it." Stepping forward, he placed his left tru- and foothand on the human's lower arm.

"I know that your kind shares the same distinguishing characteristic of intense curiosity as those of us who have been born to the Great Hive. You want to know what lies beneath this outer layer of rigid matter as badly as do I."

"Probably more layers of rigid matter," Cullen muttered. "You're right, of course. We'll get started tomorrow. I'll authorize the necessary heavy equipment—and attitude."

"One more thing." Pilwondepat spoke as the human had turned to depart. "It would be salutary to keep the AAnn away from any discoveries that may appear. Can't you send him away somewhere while the penetration attempt is taking place? To confer with his own legation in Comabraeth, perhaps, or on some superficially significant field trip?"

Looking back, Cullen eyed the thranx pityingly. "You know I can't order him to do anything, unless it can be proven he has broken some colonial law, or flouted scientific convention in the course of his work, or otherwise made his presence here intolerable." A small smile creased the supervisor's face. "I'm afraid your enduring dislike of him doesn't qualify."

"Then at least set a watch on him while the work is being carried out," Pilwondepat begged with his four-fingered hands as well as with his words. "If something of real significance should be unearthed, he will report it to the AAnn delegation immediately." He hesitated, wondering how best to balance fact and supposition.

"Sorry, Pilwondepat. This is yet another occasion on which I can't indulge your personal paranoias. I have more pressing concerns—like whether I'm about to preside over the opening, or the destruction, of something of real importance." Turning on his sandaled foot, he exited from the large, seamless tent.

Pilwondepat stood, watching the human depart. Against his thorax, the backpack humidifier hummed softly as it extracted moisture from the arid atmosphere and supplied it to his lungs. Cullen Karasi, who had previously demonstrated at least mild interest in the thranx exoarcheologist's conclusions, was now consumed by the need to comprehend what might prove to be the most important find in the brief history of human exploration on Comagrave. He had no time to devote to the fears of a double-antennaed, eight-limbed alien, however insistent.

If humans knew the AAnn better, Pilwondepat brooded in frustration, he would not be having this problem. He forced himself to stay calm. What mattered now was that the supervisor convey Pilwondepat's findings to the human authorities at the capital. Would Cullen be too preoccupied with the unfolding discovery to do so? Worse, would he postpone the journey altogether, perhaps assigning it to an underling with no understanding of or interest in the succession of inimical coincidences Pilwondepat had so painstakingly compiled?

He had no choice but to exercise patience. It was already apparent that if he tried to force the issue, the human would react defensively and the vital information would never reach the appropriate colonial authorities. Therefore Pilwondepat would have to keep silent on the matter, at least until it was time for the supervisor to make his excursion to the capital. Pilwondepat could corner him then and remind him of the matter as forcefully as discretion allowed.

Resigned but not content, he ambled out of the tent. He was as interested as anyone else on the project to see what tomorrow's digging might reveal. If only he could bury his fears as easily as the ancient Sauun had inurned their marvelous, enigmatic, sinuous layer of impermeable ceramic.

Asking for volunteers to run a night shift, Cullen had been overwhelmed with offers. Quickly setting up lights, workers and machines continued to probe the site all through the chill desert night and on into morning, when fresh laborers took over. By the time Pilwondepat emerged from his sealed environment to check on their progress, the sun was already high.

When next he strolled to the edge of the pit, he was astonished at the progress that had been made while he slept. Utilizing every bit of the precision cutting equipment at their disposal, the adrenaline-pumped staff had cut a circular shaft into the cinnamon-hued ceramic to a depth of nearly ten meters. If the extraordinary material was a foundation for a vanished building of some kind, the thranx exoarcheologist reflected, it must have been a mighty structure indeed. But why pour such a formidable base for so easily erodable an upper edifice? As the shaft continued to deepen, the likelihood of Cullen's comment about the tough ceramic forming some kind of ancient floor seemed less and less probable.

Then someone working in the depths of the excavation screamed, and Pilwondepat felt himself running forward and down as fast as all six legs could carry him.

Cullen was not there. Nor, thankfully, was Riimadu. The senior overseer on the site bridled slightly at Pilwondepat's arrival but did not try to prevent the thranx from advancing to the very edge of the excavation. Hearing the scream, every member of the staff within earshot had clustered around the rim of the opening. Anxious, sweaty humans pushed and shoved for the best view, unlike an equivalent group of thranx who would have assembled in an orderly manner.

Simple ladders made of artificial fiber with sturdy plastic steps dangled over the edge of the hole. Designed to accommodate human hands and feet as well as the upright human form, Pilwondepat could not have mounted any of them had he tried. To descend to the bottom of the shaft, he would have to use the single power lift that had been hastily attached to the far side. As he peered over and down, he had no fear of falling. Carrying the bulk of their bodies parallel to the earth and with six strong legs to grip the ground, he was in less likelihood of falling than any of the humans clustering around him.

Down at the bottom of the pit, two humans in shorts and shirts were beginning to rise from their crouching positions. Pilwondepat's interest, like those of the others gathered around him, was not on the extraordinary flexibility of the two men but on the figure they were slowly pulling upward. Ashen-faced, the young woman had apparently fallen into a smaller hole that had been started at the bottom of the main shaft.

As soon as they had the distraught woman safely clear, the site supervisor looked up. Studying the faces arranged around the rim of the excavation, she settled on the one Pilwondepat would have least expected: himself. Given that she had been noticeably cool to him during their previous encounters, the thranx was therefore surprised when Therese Holoness beckoned for him to come down.

A number of the assembled workers watched in surprise as he hurried to the power lift and descended to the bottom of the excavation. By this time the shaken young woman had been helped to the side of the dig. With her back against the smooth, gleaming ceramic, she sipped cold sweetened tea from a dispenser cradled in shaky hands.

"What happened?" Though she was addressing the three

workers, Holoness's gaze was fixed on the central cavity that dominated the center of the main dig.

Looking up over her tea, the younger woman responded carefully. "I was working the drill over the center of the next start hole when I heard a funny cracking sound. It was different from the stuttering splits you get when you cut into the ceramic. Then the surface collapsed under my feet, and I felt myself falling." She struggled to bring the rim of the container to her lips. Her hands were shaking so badly that tea was flying out of the container. "I'm afraid I lost the laser."

"Never mind that." Holoness glanced at the larger of the two men. "You caught her."

His expression drawn, the man nodded slowly. "Just barely. When I heard Miranda scream, I was working a scooper. I dumped that and made a dive in the direction of the center hole. Caught her right arm and held on tight."

The other, smaller worker chimed in. "I managed to grab her left wrist. Together, we pulled her out."

The woman looked up again. "I don't know how deep the fissure is. My feet never touched bottom."

Holoness considered, then glanced over at Pilwondepat. "Like to have a look? Understand, I don't particularly like you, or your kind, but I think it's vital when something like this happens to have the advantage of a completely different point of view."

Without commenting on her opinion of him, Pilwondepat gestured acknowledgment. As the two men wrestled a pair of powerful lights toward the cavity, he walked gingerly toward the dark aperture. To put as little pressure on the now unpredictable surface as possible, Holoness approached from the other side.

The lights were gradually positioned until they were hanging directly over the opening, with their beams aimed straight down. Remembering that he was a guest, Pilwondepat gestured courteously in Holoness's direction. "You first, if you like," he said.

Nodding, she dropped to all fours and crept to the edge of the dark cavity. Pilwondepat was quietly amused at this human effort to imitate the more stable thranx stance. Peering into the darkness, she gazed downward. She stared for a long time, in fact, saying nothing. After several minutes of this Pilwondepat felt he would not be breaching either personal or professional etiquette if he joined her. Moving to the gap, secure in his six-footed stance, he tilted his head forward.

A constant breeze was pouring out of the opening. It was cold with the echo of ages past. Dipping his antennae into the hole, he tried to identify the strange smell that rose upward on the steady wind. It reminded him of something familiar. He pushed the thought aside. The eccentric efflux could be dealt with later. Of much more immediate importance was the identification of what they could not see, and why. Powerful as they were, the deeply penetrating survey lights that were shining directly down into the black void revealed nothing.

Not because there was necessarily nothing to reveal, but because despite the fact that their operators had them pushed to maximum, the powerful beams could not reach bottom.

13

It was not to be an official excursion. Mindful of what had happened to her late fiancé, and acutely conscious of the continued presence of the AAnn envoy Preed NNXV at Azerick, her trip back to Daret was officially listed as a "vacation." She had ample off-time coming to her, and while some might have remarked on her unusual choice of a destination at which to relax, there was nothing illicit about it.

Had Toroni or anyone else known the real purpose of her visit, they would at the least have been seriously upset. Technically, what she was about to do constituted a clear case of ignoring the diplomatic chain of command, if not directly undermining local authority. This was a risk she was prepared to take. Issues of far greater import were at stake.

Diplomats, too, could belong to secret organizations.

She was especially careful to avoid the inquisitive Sertoa as she slipped out of the settlement in the early hours of the morning. Always ready to disparage the thranx in conference, he had been positively enamored of the AAnn envoy ever since Preed had arrived at the settlement. She had no fear of her colleague, whom she regarded as too irresolute to cause real trouble. The AAnn, however, was another matter.

Acquiring a transfer from Chitteranx to Daret was no problem, but the comings and goings of every human from Azerick and its vicinity was carefully monitored by the settlement's transportation staff. Therefore she made no advance reservation, but instead appeared at the terminal hoping to secure a vacancy on the next air shuttle. There were usually a number of empty seats, and this morning was no exception. Unaccountably nervous during the tube journey from the settlement to the shuttleport, she did not relax until the aircraft was airborne and heading south toward the Hysingrausen Wall.

She was no longer surprised by how comfortable she felt in Daret. From the shuttleport, one of eight enormous facilities that surrounded and served the thranx capital, to the low-ceilinged transport shells that carried travelers deep into the sprawling underground metropolis, to the tens of thousands of crowded corridors packed with locals, she was utterly relaxed. There was crime in Daret, for no civilized species seemed to have completely solved the problem of how to wholly eliminate or integrate an antisocial underclass, but it was far less than what one might expect to encounter in a human conurbation of similar size and density. And as a human, she was virtually immune from such limited threats as did exist. Not only would assaulting her possibly result in an interstellar incident, she carried nothing the average thranx castoff would want to steal.

Since she was not in the capital on official business, there was no reason for her to revisit the burrow where the diplomatic service chambers were located. Instead, she took lodging in one of the two establishments within the city that specialized in catering to offworld travelers. Not only were individual quarters equipped with instrumentation for adjusting the proportion of nitrogen, oxygen, and trace gases within the sealed rooms, there were even provisions and facilities for methane breathers, and for those two sentient species who extracted their oxygen directly from liquid water. Light, temperature, and to a certain extent gravity could also be tailored to suit individual requirements.

Best of all, more than half the rooms were located above ground, with views of the domesticated jungle that grew atop the subterranean megalopolis like wild green hair on a multi-leveled head. Her fluency in Low Thranx helped her to secure lodgings on the top floor, with a superb view to the west. Native avians and other rain forest dwellers occasionally appeared before her window, indifferent to the presence just below the surface of some thirty-five million industrious thranx.

She spent the first day of her holiday enjoying the room and the services provided by the hotel, luxuriating in doing absolutely nothing, improving her language skills by monitoring the local tridee equivalent, and indulging in a positively hedonistic massage at the hands, or rather the tendrils, of an exceptionally cosmopolitan Nevonian masseur. Employing six sensitive tentacles, it somehow achieved the seemingly impossible task of relieving her of six months of accumulated tension. She'd heard stories of the legendary Nevonian nerve and muscle therapists, beings dedicated to mitigating the accrued stress of chaotic civilized galactic life, but this was the first time she had been able to experience their talents. Suffice to say that had she been a person of means, she would have hired the quasi-cephalopodian away from the hotel so it could attend to her on a daily basis.

It was thus relaxed in body if not entirely in mind that, by sheer designed coincidence, while strolling through the rooftop garden and observation deck the following morning, she encountered none other than Haflunormet. After exchanging greetings that would have piqued the interest of no one—and were intended to do precisely that—she agreed to accompany him to a place of exceptional natural beauty located on the northern outskirts of the urban dominion.

On the way there they intentionally confined their conversation to small talk; Anjou avowing as how she was doing as well as could be expected considering the unexpected passing of her fiancé, Haflunormet responding with the mundane details of the daily life of a minor thranx diplomat. She let him rest a truhand on her belly, which was only just beginning to show. This prompted him to observe that while the effort of passing objects through a pair of ovipositors was a strain on the thranx female, at least eggs did not move on the way out.

When they arrived at the preserve, they took a circuitous path to the destination Haflunormet had chosen. Despite her anxieties, Anjou could not help but be enchanted by the silvered streams of the twin waterfalls that spilled into a turquoise pool below, like rivers of mercury gushing from a gigantic stone bottle. Built up over the millennia by the accumulation of red- and yellow-tinted limestone, the rills that dammed the turquoise pool sparkled with pockets of embedded calcite and selenite crystals.

Swooping and diving at the twin cascades, the pools, and the small river these begat, hundreds of *pecrikks*, looking like faceless chameleons sporting the most marvelously stained butterfly wings, filled the heavy, humid air above the glistening water. A few other visitors, thranx all, lounged among the striking surroundings, boldly taking their ease above ground, away from the immense city whose farthest reaches extended even beneath the wholly natural preserve. It was doubtful that any of them had chosen to visit the place of exceptional beauty because the splash and crash of the twin cataracts conveniently combined to do an excellent job of masking their conversation.

"Has he arrived?" Calm and at ease as she was, Anjou could restrain herself no longer.

"Not yet." With multiple lenses, Haflunormet studied every tree and bush, every lounging thranx and proximate creature. Espying nothing unnatural or out of place, he continued. "His ship is due to arrive tomorrow, or possibly the following day. I cannot check too often without incurring suspicion, or at least questions I would rather not have to answer."

Nodding, she bent slightly to study something like an animated ruby necklace that was munching on a spatulate leaf. "I'm eager to hear the latest news. It's too bad we have to rely on couriers, but when you work for the government there's no such thing as a private space-minus communication."

He gestured agreement mixed with understanding. "It's always better to receive vital information in person, and far easier than trying to carry on a conversation between star systems. Not to mention infinitely less expensive."

"Do you anticipate any difficulty in arranging our meeting?"

Haflunormet's antennae had not stopped moving since they had arrived at the pool. No thranx went too close to the

water, of course. While they could admire its beauty, they
elected to keep well clear of its dangers. Had Anjou felt like a
swim, she would have had the warm, crystalline lagoon all to
herself, and would invariably have drawn an audience. Not
only were the thranx prone to drowning because of the location of their breathing orifices, they swam like bricks.

"Everything is already in place. I will notify you with an
invitation to attend a musical performance that will give both
time and place. You are familiar with the applicable code. I
also have, of course, the necessary means for contacting your
personal communicator directly, via closed transmission. If
there are any changes, rest assured you will be informed of
them the instant they are confirmed." He touched one antenna
to the skin of her right arm, bare below the short sleeve of her
blouse. "At this point, I foresee no problems." Executing the
thranx gesture indicative of wry amusement, he simultaneously whistled softly through his spicules. "After all, we are
all three of us 'on vacation.' "

They wandered along the discreet path that bordered the
turquoise pool, chatting for a while about personal matters,
before retracing their steps to halt close by the base of the
twin falls. Up close, the coupled cataracts were even more
beautiful than they were from a distance. Their thundering roar
would also serve to prevent anyone monitoring their stroll who
happened to be equipped with sophisticated eavesdropping
apparatus from picking up the threads of their conversation.

"Events are clearly moving toward a climax, though one
whose eventual outcome none can foresee." With his superb
natural peripheral vision, the thranx was able to keep a sweeping watch on their surroundings. "I can tell you that there is
pressure within the Grand Council to do something definitive
soon."

Anjou kicked at the colored pebbles that lined the pathway.
Though her specially designed tropical clothing was not bur-
densome, she wanted to strip off every hi-tech stitch and run
splashing into the cool, inviting, pale blue pool. She wanted
to sink beneath the surface and let the pristine waters wash
over her, obscuring the alien world above and all the appre-

hension, strain, and tension that seemed to control every one of her waking thoughts these days. But she could not, of course.

As far as the pressure was concerned, she had no one to blame but herself. She could have, she reflected, chosen a less stressful profession to enter. In fairness, when she had decided to enter the diplomatic service, she had never expected to find herself at the center of galactic politics, much less at a flash point where the profound interests of not one but three burgeoning civilizations were colliding. She had anticipated long days of shuffling information, attending dull meetings, and filling out boring forms. Certainly she had not foreseen her eventual membership on an "advisory" committee that was semilegal at best. If her participation was discovered, she would be searching for a new career soon enough. Haflunormet's situation was no less ticklish than her own.

"What *is* happening with the council?" she finally asked.

"Reactionary elements are working to abrogate many details of existing treaties, and to prevent consideration of new ones. They are pushing to formalize a much more conventional relationship between my people and yours. No more reciprocal settlements. A limiting of cultural exchanges. A ban on the informal contacts that are being instituted between individual organizations." He looked up at her. "There is talk of trying to halt any further expansion of Azerick, and the placing of a permanent ban on any more human outposts on any of the thranx worlds. All contact to be between formal diplomatic missions only, *seelliik.*"

Her lips tightened. "That's pretty much what the retrogressive fanatics among my kind are up to. Their first order of business is to shut down the hives in the Reserva Amazonia and the Congo." She allowed herself a small smile. "The success of both settlements, particularly the way in which they are successfully integrating themselves into the local culture and economies, is driving some of these regressives a little crazy. It's a beautiful thing to see—or at least, to hear about on the tridee." Reaching out with cupped hands, she caught water from a warbling rivulet and brought it to her lips. A taste of thranx homeworld, she mused, quietly astonished at how rapidly she had come to feel at home in the hothouse, alien civilization of Hivehom.

"They're still in the minority," she continued, "but like all radical minorities they're very vocal. They make irresistible media copy, especially on slow news days, so their message is extensively disseminated and widely seen. They have powerful friends whom members of our organization keep watch on, and more sympathy in the Terran Congress than actual votes." Splashing water on her face, she blinked and shook droplets from her fingers as she turned back to Haflunormet.

"The Pitarian War did more to mute their influence than all the logical and reasoned argument that had gone before it. But good feelings fade, memories slip into the past, and there is always a new generation of ignorant innocents determined to overturn the carefully considered judgments of their wiser elders."

Haflunormet gestured a mix of sympathy and understanding. "So it is among any sentients with typical life spans." He edged closer to her, mandibles in motion, unafraid of the water so long as there was solid ground underfoot. "There are rumors of great resolutions astirring. I have not been able to verify their nature. Presumably, they are among the details that our mutual friend is coming to speak to us about."

She nodded absently. "I hope so. I could use some good news." Glancing down at her belly, she wondered how much longer she would be able to devote her full attention to such matters.

Four blue-green, chitinous fingers, each roughly a third shorter than their human counterparts, rested lightly on her left forearm. Eyes composed of multiple golden mirrors stared up into her own.

"Be of good hearts, Fanielle. Not for such as you and I the contentment of a quiet burrow. We each of us do as we must, because we serve a higher cause."

Reaching down, she placed the soft fingers of her right hand over his sleek, harder ones. "Who would have thought that the forging of friendship among sentients of like mind would entail so much personal anxiety?"

Feathery antennae waved at her. "Not all are of like mind," he reminded her somberly. "In our mutual racial immaturity, there still exist those who seemingly employ no mind at all."

They were quiet for a while then, each lost in thought, contemplating a future neither of them could have anticipated when they were young. Around them, a few other individuals and couples strolled, enjoying the peace and tranquility of the park, the additional moisture diffused into the already saturated air by the twin falls, and the free-roaming native fauna. Below their feet, an immense, vibrant metropolis pulsed and surged with the activities of tens of millions of intelligent beings, very few of whom were aware of the issues of great import that were being decided by a comparatively small number of their own kind and a comparable group of soft-skinned, fleshy, flexible-skinned mammalian bipeds from a planet whose modest star was but one of thousands visible in the night sky.

"I am most concerned of all," Haflunormet finally murmured after the long silence, "about the possibility of violence."

Anjou sighed heavily. "I also. I don't know much about your radicals, but among my kind, both on Earth and at least two of her major colonies, there are known groups of hotheads who'll do anything to prevent a deeper, more singular relationship from developing between a 'blinded' humankind and a race of 'bugs.' We both know the specific incidents that have already occurred." Kneeling, she ran a hand through turquoise water, stirring memories of motherworld sky. "It's the groups we don't know about and therefore cannot keep track of that have me worried."

"It's easier for us." He crouched to join her, bending all four trulegs beneath him. "We are more organized than you, and so it is harder for splinter organizations to form. Nonconformist individuals, however, are another matter."

"If only they were all like Ryozenzuzex, or Desvendapur."

He whistled soft laughter. "You speak of exceptional thranx. I could as soon cite the intervention of noteworthy humans.

Strange, is it not, how history imprints itself so similarly on different minds?"

She put a comforting arm around his b-thorax. They stared at the rippling waters together. " 'Intelligence and sentience share the same shape, and ignorance is its own reward.' "

His head swiveled to regard her thoughtfully. "I had not heard it put quite that way before."

She shrugged. "I'm quoting one of the wild new religious orders. This particular one is fond of propounding a lot of irreverent maxims. You know the type: They try to explain life and the meaning of everything in one sentence or less. It's almost frivolous, yet oddly engaging." She straightened. "An intellectual diversion. A friend back at Azerick passed the information on to me. This lot seems to be the spiritual flavor-of-the-moment."

"They seem to be well scribed. I would not mind skimming a little more of their oratory myself. I could use some fresh entertainment. Do you think it will last?"

"What, this 'United Church' bunch?" She replied with confidence and the knowledge that history was on her side. "They never do."

It was dark by the time she returned to her lodgings. Sealing the door behind her, she walked to the window and gazed out at the surrounding jungle. Transported directly to such a room without first transiting the city, no traveler eying the verdant panorama could imagine that a nonhuman megalopolis of tens of millions toiled and thrived beneath the surface. Like all other thranx hives, Daret never slept. Accustomed to and comfortable with life beneath the ground, day and night were discretional terms dictated only by classical thranx custom. As such, their internal biological clocks were far more flexible than those of humans, being unaffected by the presence or absence of daylight.

Fanielle was not thranx, however. Tired as she was, she was tempted to go down with the sun. Contemplating the view, she considered opening the window to let in fresh air and the night sounds of the alien rain forest. As that would have

meant trading the delightfully cool, drier atmosphere maintained by the room for the hot, muggy air outside, she decided against it.

A bath, then, followed by perusal of her private notes, and
a good night's rest. The meeting with Haflunormet had gone
well. If their mutual friend arrived in good order and on time
tomorrow, she would have accomplished all she had come
for. Then she could embark sincerely upon the aboveboard
portion of her vacation.

"Sso very green, thiss world. *Jississt,* I do find it sso."

She did not scream because her lungs were too busy
sucking in her breath. By the time she had whirled and focused on her unexpected visitor, that instinctive urge had left
her. Given her quarters' special soundproofing attributes,
characteristic of every individual room in the establishment,
it was moot whether anyone would have heard her anyway.

Baron Preed NNXV made no attempt to conceal himself.
He had been standing by the entrance to the hygienic facilities. Engrossed in the view beyond the plasticine transparency, she had walked right past him.

"I am ssorry." He took a stride toward her. "Did I sstartle
you?"

She took an equivalent step back, acutely aware that if the
tentative dance were to continue, she would be the one to
eventually run out of maneuvering room. The AAnn was not
between her and the door, nor did he give any indication of attempting to block her exit. But the reptiloids could move very
fast. She decided to save the proverbial mad dash to safety for
a last resort.

His tone, if not his presence, was apologetic. As apologetic
as an AAnn could manage, she decided.

"What the hell are you doing here? How did you get into
my room?"

She tracked him warily as he sidled slowly to his left—and
sat down on the bed. The juxtaposition was openly ludicrous:
Had he been a human male, her anxiety level would have
gone up. The end of his tail flicked against one of the two pil-
lows, which she then and there irrationally determined not to

use for sleeping. The AAnn might be a pugnacious species, even as treacherous as Haflunormet and his hive mates claimed, but they were exceedingly clean in their personal habits.

"I have been unable to esscape the feeling that our previouss encounter went badly, and ever ssince have ssought a meanss by which I might redress any lingering awkwardnesses." Reaching up, he scratched at an exfoliating neck scale with the index claw of his right hand. "When I went looking for you to requesst a ssecond meeting, I learned that you had departed the compound at Azerick."

"Not through the usual channels, you didn't." Willing herself to relax, she found that her muscles remained tight. Her specialist training proved unequal to the task of countering the atavistic urge to retreat in the face of subdued lighting, sharp teeth, and long claws—even though the latter belonged to an educated, multilingual member of another species' diplomatic corps.

"Truly." The acknowledgment was accompanied by a second-degree indication of recognition tempered with irony. The subtleties of the gesture were lost on Fanielle. "It wass not difficult to learn where you had gone." He indicated her lodgings, a hand movement sufficiently obvious that it needed no translation.

"Or to bribe or force your way into my private quarters, evidently." Along with the fear, some of her initial fury was beginning to fade. That did not lead her to unbend, or to relax her vigilance for a moment. She could not see a weapon or other threatening device, but their visual absence was hardly conclusive. The diplomat wore a standard-issue vest replete with pockets over the usual loose-fitting swirls of feathery opaque material, sandals, and muted tail makeup. Small pockets could conceal large surprises.

"Tsstt," he admonished her. "I did no more than bend a few housse ruless, not break them." There was nothing reassuring in the diplomat's expression. "That iss no more than the nature of our profession, iss it not?"

She strove to establish some sort of command of the situa-

tion. "Good old Jorge. I knew that he favored the AAnn above
the thranx, but I never dreamed—"

"Do not be too hard on your colleague." The smile widened.
Sophisticated and educated or not, the envoy's teeth were very
pointed, and very sharp. "He iss compossed of lesser material
than yourrself, and iss ssubject to flattery and manipulation."

"Don't think you're going to escape the consequences of
this break-in with flattery," she warned him.

"I have already apologized." Preed hesitated and gestured
simultaneously for emphasis. "For intruding upon your 'vacation.' " The gesticulation that accompanied his pronuncia-
tion of the last word was as sharp as it was unmistakable. "A
relaxing few dayss in the ssuccoring ressort city of Daret.
From what I know of your kind, thiss sstrikess me as a mosst
peculiar choice of desstinationss for taking one'ss easse."

"I'm a peculiar sort of human," she shot back.

He indicated comprehension. "Peculiaritiess can have
their virtuess. I admired your professional and intellectual
qualitiess during our previouss meeting. I ssit in praisse of
them now. They are why I have gone to ssome painss to meet
with you in thiss fasshion."

She considered. The route to the door remained unbarred,
and the envoy was seated with his legs facing in the opposite
direction, watching her over his left shoulder. How high
could a middle-aged AAnn leap? How fast? She took a
couple of casual steps in the direction of the doorway. Preed
did not move.

"All right. I won't call for Security—yet. You certainly have
gone to a lot of trouble. Not to mention exposing yourself to
possible prosecution, diplomatic immunity notwithstanding.
Say what you have to say."

The AAnn responded with a gesture of unsurpassing elegance. "That iss very politic of you. As I ssaid, I have admired
your sskillss from the sstart. It hass therefore been thrice dis-
stressing to me that our earlier encounter ended sso poorly.
Even sso, it wass clear to me at the time that you are perhapss
immoderately fond of thesse thranx, and thuss inclined to
take their sside in all matterss, be they large or small. I would

be grateful of the opportunity to assk that you do no more than keep an open mind on the subject where my kind are concerned. Someone of your sself-evident erudition musst perforce be aware that a certain amount of hisstory exisstss between the bugss and my people, and that not all of it iss pleassant. Thiss undersstandably colorss their ssentimentss toward uss."

Haflunormet was right, she reflected. An accomplished AAnn could make gravel taste like butter. Preed was by far the suavest emissary she had ever encountered, either in person or via tridee.

"Alsso," he added while she mulled his words, "regardless of your perssonal feelingss toward my kind, or toward me, you should resst assured that I intend you no perssonal harm. Had that been my intention, I could have torn your unprotected flesshy form to sshredss while you sstood unawaress, contemplating the sstinking forest outsside."

"Or maybe not," she countered. "In tests comparing the respective physical abilities of different sentient species, humans consistently surpass AAnn in strength."

His gesture she could not interpret. His words were quietly chilling. "Truly, that iss sso. But the sscales comprissing your epidermal layer are ineffectual in combat, your clawss are frail even when not overly trimmed, and your teeth are dessigned for grinding and biting, not sshearing." He had the grace, she noted, not to smile when he said this.

"But why sspeak of unpleassantnesses that will not happen? Will you at leasst, in the sspirit of fairness, impart ssome value to my wordss?"

She ought to order him out, she knew—if only to test the veracity of his promise. She ought to make a break for the door, or shout aloud the personal lodging code she had been given at check-in. The room's sensors would pick it up, relay it to the appropriate station, and Security would arrive on the run. That she did not do this spoke more for an innate sense of tolerance than for any feeling that this emissary or any other could convince her to change her opinion of the thranx or the AAnn.

"All right. In the interests of impartiality, I promise to consider what you've said. And as long as you're here uninvited, why don't you tell me what else the emperor's manifold cheerful subjects want from me?"

Either Preed did not detect her sarcasm, or else he tactfully chose to ignore it. With an AAnn, it was always difficult to tell. She really did not expect the envoy to reply at length, much less to provide specifics.

"All the People of the Ssand wissh from humankind and itss coloniess iss a certain degree of resspect."

Professional interest was beginning to supplement, although it could not entirely replace, her initial fear. "You enjoy full diplomatic relations with us. The Empire is treated on an equal basis with the two other major interstellar powers we know: the thranx and the Quillp."

"Truly." Preed gestured acknowledgment. "Yet sstill we feel our petitioningss diminisshed in the ssight of the bugss. We are concerned, and have been from the time of firsst contactss, that your government continuess to favor them above uss."

For that complaint she had a ready rejoinder. "First of all, you're wrong. My government, and the average citizen of Earth and its colonies, does not prefer the thranx to the AAnn. Indeed, among many of my kind, the reverse is true. This despite the invaluable aid the thranx rendered to us in the Pitarian War." Slitted eyes blinked back at her, the double lids adding an oddly feminine fluttering to the action. "You are accorded equal treatment, both formally and otherwise."

One clawed hand described an intricate succession of curves in the air. She noted that the envoy was wearing no special supplemental attire. The air-conditioning that kept the muggy Hivehom night at bay must be chilling him to the bone. This realization did not upset her. Though she could have done so, she made no move to adjust the temperature.

"Why then have our propossalss to esstablissh reciprocal ssettlementss in your Ssonoran and Ssaharan desertss been refussed? You grant thiss intimate privilege to the thranx but deny it to uss."

"Truly," she told him, utilizing the soft AAnn word, "I don't know. Personally, it strikes me as unfair, and contrary to the spirit of the treaties that exist between our two peoples. But that is only my opinion. As a minor diplomat assigned to this world, I have no voice in the making of policy."

"But you would perssonally ssupport ssuch an exchange?" For a moment, his interest struck her as going beyond the professional. Here was a matter in which the AAnn envoy took a specific interest.

"Of course," she lied facilely. "Why not? The regions you refer to are to this day little utilized or visited. Why *shouldn't* the AAnn have the same rights of reciprocal settlement as the thranx?"

His tail switched from side to side. "It sshortenss my journey to hear you ssay that." Had he believed her? She couldn't tell. "Truly, if only your people would recognize what to uss is sso blatantly obviouss. That we have far more in common with one another, both in sshape and attitude, than your kind ever could with thesse pesstilential bugss. That we sshare sso very many ultimate aimss and interessts. That a closser alliance between our peopless would permit the resultant political force to permanently dominate this one modesst portion of the cossmoss, to our mutual benefit. Perhapss, with time, thiss may come to pass."

"Perhaps," she responded noncommittally. It was not a lie. Who knew what the future would bring? No one could predict the course of interstellar relations. The way contact between humankind and the thranx had developed—accidentally, unpredictably, and in defiance of careful diplomatic procedures—had already proven as much. That she intended to do everything in her power to prevent the scenario Preed had just laid before her from ever coming to fruition was something she kept wholly to herself.

His unannounced nocturnal visit only served to confirm everything she already knew or had ever heard about the AAnn. They were sly and cunning, skilled sycophants, adept students of other cultures. All of which made perfect sense.

One did not have to be a professional diplomat to realize that if one species wished to dominate another, learning everything there was to know about one's quarry was a prerequisite for ultimate success.

The AAnn were devoted scholars of other cultures. She had no doubt that Preed was well versed in the fragmented, frequently unseemly history of humankind. Like others of his kind, he would employ that learning to exploit any discernible divisions within human government and society to the eventual benefit of the People of the Sand. She did not condemn him for this. It was his job as well as his nature. Feint and retreat, test and examine: That was how Haflunormet and the other thranx diplomats she had spent time with had told her the AAnn operated. That was the AAnn way. Avoid far-reaching, open confrontation. Poke and probe and wait for the victim to bleed to death.

That was not going to happen to humankind, she knew. Any chance of that, any naïveté on the scale of interstellar relations, had vanished in the macabre upheaval of the Pitarian War. What might have happened had her kind first encountered the subtle, duplicitous AAnn and not the Pitar, she did not know. The most dangerous, the most ominous explosives did not always produce large, easily visible fireballs in space.

He was playing to her, ever the urbane and accomplished diplomat despite his rather fearsome appearance. Gazing back at him, she did indeed see a being much closer to her in appearance than any thranx. Only when one looked deeper did one begin to discern the insidious nature and intent that lurked beneath every AAnn and that, insofar as she had been able to discover, was absent among the thranx. What was it the ancient writer Melville had written? "Better to sleep with a sober cannibal than a drunken Christian." In the context of future relations, of humankind's ultimate destiny, she had become convinced some time ago that the interests of her kind would be far better served by lying down with oversized, aromatic insectoids than upright, sharp-toothed reptiloids. If there was one lesson her people should have learned since

venturing into deep space and making contact with other intelligent species, it was that physical appearance counted for
nothing.

But all too many of her kith and kin had not yet mastered
that lesson. Hence the continued need for diplomats, for sub-
terfuges, and for the kinds of lies she was all too often forced
to live.

"I wonder," he murmured, interrupting her thoughts. "I
wonder truly how much of what you have jusst told me you
believe, and how much you have sscribed for my benefit.
Equivocation and invention iss, after all, your vocation."

"As it is yours—truly." She met his stare unwaveringly. Let
him accuse her of lying if he wished. He could prove nothing.
Her only real fear was that, having tracked her down with
such apparent ease, he might somehow also have become
aware of the meeting she was due to have tomorrow with
Haflunormet and their arriving friend. Though he had given
no indication of cognizance, she knew the possibility would
trouble her until the meeting was concluded.

Concentrate on the moment, she told herself. One small
galactic step at a time. For right now, it would be enough to
get him out of her room.

"We undersstand one another, then." Gesticulating gracefully with both hands, he tilted his head down and slightly to
one side. "As before, I sstand in admiration of your sskillss,
and can only hope that all you have told me arisses from the
inner depthss of your true sself." Straightening, he approached
until he was standing closer to her than formal diplomatic
protocol required. She held her ground. Easier to do in the
room than elsewhere, she reflected nervously, since there was
a wall not far behind her and she could not retreat anyway.

His bright yellow eyes with their vertical pupils peered
down into her own. He was of average height and build for an
AAnn, slightly taller than she but not proportionally as massive as a comparable human male. But there were those teeth,
bequeathed from a wholly carnivorous ancestry, and those
hooked, knifelike claws.

Reaching up, he let the sharp, pointed tip of one talon

graze her right cheek. His hissing voice was a singular whisper. "Sso profoundly, abssurdly pliant. It is a curiossity to uss how your sspeciess ssurvived ssuch fragile integumentss long enough to develop intelligence. Truly, the universse iss full of wonderss." To her considerable relief, he let the clawed hand drop, holding it in front of his chest parallel to the other in the familiar resting position of his kind.

"I hope we can meet and talk like thiss again. I have already sspoken of you to otherss of like mind. Their interesst matchess mine."

"I have no objection to meeting with or talking to anyone," she admitted truthfully. "Provided that next time, certain minimal courtesies are observed."

He acknowledged her outrage without argument as he backed toward the door. "Truly. Until then, I wissh you, Fanielle Anjou of Earth and not of Hivehom, ssafe sstriding and ssmooth ssurfacess under your feet." As the door responded to the shrouded covert electronics that had gained him entrance, he added, "And may your pending offsspring emerge into the world sslick of sscale and free of blemissh."

He was out the door and gone before she could ask him how he knew of her pregnancy. But of course, she realized when he had left, he could have found that out from the garrulous Sertoa, or many others at Azerick Station. One hand dropped unconsciously to her upper belly as she saw the door shut. She resecured it as best she could. To her surprise, she found that her heart was racing and her lungs were pounding against her chest. All the tension, all the pent-up anxiety engendered by the AAnn's unexpected appearance, now raced to the fore.

Stumbling into the bathroom, she rummaged through her gear until she found the bottle she wanted. One—no, two— of the pills accompanied by hastily gulped water slid down her throat. Leaning back against the glassy wall, she wondered if she ought to change rooms. That would not be easy to do. Not in the middle of the night, on a thranx world, in an establishment dedicated to providing adequate accommodation not only to visiting humans but to representatives of many other species who frequently had very different lodging requirements. Besides, if Preed could gain entry to one room, there was no reason to assume entering another would present him with any insurmountable obstacles.

In the end she settled for the bath that had been her initial goal. After a while she managed to stop glancing in the direction of the outer room and the doorway beyond. She needed to be rested and alert for the meeting tomorrow. Haflunormet would want to know all about the intrusion, of course. Steps could be taken to prevent a recurrence.

Raising a hand, she touched her cheek where the diplomat's claw had lightly depressed the flesh. *Did rather well at that moment,* she complimented herself. *No shuddering, no trembling.* Toroni and the rest of her colleagues would have been proud of her, standing up to a carnivorous AAnn like that, alone and unarmed. She smiled hesitantly, relishing once more the memory of the small triumph.

Then it all hit her at once, and she finally began to shake.

14

"Don't tell me—it is not possible." The short, dark human was gazing at the two padres with eyes that were a little too wide and muscles that were taut to the point of twitching. His chest had begun to heave. "It is not bad enough to see untainted humans congregating in this place and mixing together with filthy bugs and dirty bug activities: Now you are trying to get people to worship with them! What will come next? Bugs teaching human children? Preparing our food? Sleeping in the same rooms with us?"

Briann listened in silence to the angry tirade, forbearing from interruption or reply. Twikanrozex did his best to memorize it all, down to the last sputtering slur. Neither man nor thranx was especially offended. They had heard it all before, though usually couched in flaccid overtones of false civility. Unusually, this human was unabashedly vociferous in his bigotry, not caring if anyone overheard. It was possible, Briann mooted, that he wanted to be overheard. Certainly those strollers within easy hearing distance, human and thranx alike, turned to stare in the direction of the diatribe. To their credit, most appeared embarrassed by the outburst of undisguised vitriol.

Her dark green hair cropped fashionably short, the ranter's taller female companion made an effort to calm her comrade. He would have none of it, disdaining her murmured words and twice shaking her hand off his shoulder. When neither of the targets of his interminable vehemence showed any signs of reacting, either to his tone or to his words, he began to advance in their direction.

"That's close enough." Briann's tone was decidedly sharp, sufficiently so to bring the man to a surprised halt. His countenance twisted into a perfect sneer.

"Why, Padre, or whatever it is you degenerates choose to call yourselves, that's hardly a spiritual attitude."

"You're wrong, visitor. The spirit takes many forms. Hallowed also is the spirit of defiance."

Looking decidedly uneasy, the woman continued to badger her companion from behind. "That's enough, Nevisrighne. We'll be late for our . . . appointment."

The man gestured in her direction, evidently enjoying himself. "No, no, Pierrot. We have time. Time enough to instruct the degraded." His attention shifted back to the quietly watching Briann. "Why, I do believe, Padre, that if I were to intrude too much on your personal space, you would physically push me away."

"I might." Briann's tone had not changed.

"You might even take a swing at me."

"In a universe of infinite possibilities, all things are possible," Briann admitted piously.

"In which case I would be forced to defend myself. While it is true that we stand equal here in the number of witnesses, mine is human, whereas yours is only a lowly bug."

"Enough of this. Come away from here, Nevisrighne!" The woman was not distraught, Briann noted, so much as she was enraged.

"Shut up, Pierrot." The dark man's sneer slipped smileward. "Just a quick lesson. In possibilities." His right hand slipped toward the inside of his open shirt—and froze before the first finger could edge inside. His rage vanished, subsumed by a look of total surprise. It was focused not on Briann, but behind him.

Twikanrozex held a gun in each gleaming, chitinous hand. All four of them. Faced with this entirely unexpected and formidable quadruple arsenal, the swarthy fanatic slowly drew his one hand away from his chest and let it fall back to his side. So shocked was he that it took him a moment to find his voice.

"Very spiritual," he finally muttered uneasily to Briann without taking his eyes off the unexpectedly heavily armed thranx. "Not only have you become personally debased, who-ever you are: Your so-called holy organization is founded on hypocrisy."

"Wrong again. This must be your day to wallow in wrong-ness, my friend." Briann did not have to look behind him to know what Twikanrozex had done. The thranx's actions were reflected in the shorter man's reaction as clearly as if in a mirror. "We who serve the United Church believe very strongly in always maintaining a sound defense against any who would do us harm. It is one of the fundamental tenets of our belief."

"What about turning the other cheek?" The ranter had for-gotten whatever lay hidden against his left armpit. And wisely so.

"We are always willing to do that. Twikanrozex, turn the other cheek for this man." Behind him, the thranx obediently turned his head to the right. His astonishing peripheral vision still allowed him to keep that now subdued individual in view. At the same time, the muzzles of the four pistols did not waver.

"An unsurpassed model of sarcastic religious miscegena-tion." Retreating, the speaker rejoined his plainly exasperated companion. "If the Fates so decree it, we may meet again some day, Padre. I would enjoy having the chance to resume your education."

"And I yours, my friend. Enjoy the fair."

"Indeed, I will. More than you can imagine." With that he turned and stomped off, making no effort to disguise his enduring furor, brushing aside the arm of his annoyed companion.

Briann followed the curious pair until they passed out of sight behind a cluster of bobbing, transparent spheres that pe-riodically paused to engulf unsuspecting passersby in an as-sortment of cleverly preprogrammed advertisements.

"That was unpleasant," he observed.

"Yes." Twikanrozex had slipped his quartet of weapons

back into their respective pouches. "I'm convinced that if I had not intervened, he might have tried to do you an injury. A disappointing first for us."

"Maybe more than that." Briann's thoughts were churning. "Unless you have a specific destination or prospect in mind, I think I'd like to follow those two for a while."

Twikanrozex moved forward to join his friend. "Follow them? To what end?"

"I don't know." The human half of the team rubbed the damp back of his neck. "That one was more than xenophobic. There was something in his gaze. Just a little wildness, maybe. Or perhaps a little something more."

"You are suggesting he is even more volatile than he appears?"

"I'm thinking that, at least when he was looking at you, he bordered on the homicidal. I may be imagining things, but it wasn't just him, either. The woman he was with? The longer he rambled on, the more agitated she became. And it wasn't the kind of nervousness that someone exhibits when their companion is making a fool of himself. It struck me as more profound than that."

Reaching up, Twikanrozex touched his friend's bare arm with a truhand. "Like you, I have no agenda for the remainder of this day other than to wander, to observe, to converse, and to learn."

"Then let's track those two for a while. If nothing else, it ought to be educational." He grinned over at his colleague. "While we're at it, you can still realize three out of four."

It was not difficult to do. Outside the fairgrounds, their pairing would have made them conspicuous. Strolling along the shore of the great lake would have seen them stand out against the flat, unsparing surface. But lost among the bustling crowds that had begun to swarm the exhibition in ever-increasing numbers, they were able to blend in without being noticed. Acolytes of the Church received training in how to be inconspicuous as well as obvious.

Though they spent some time wandering among the exhibits and made a show of feigning interest in several, it was

evident to the pair of trailing Church representatives that neither the slim woman nor her excitable male companion were
much interested in the components of the fair. They spent a
lot of time looking around while expending a considerable
effort not to be seen looking around. Once, they disappeared
into a public rest room and did not reemerge for nearly thirty
minutes, a visitation that suggested they were responding to a
call that came from someone other than Nature. Not once did
they pause to eat, drink, shop for souvenirs, ask questions, try
out hands-on displays, participate in a virtual, or otherwise
indicate that they were somewhere besides an ordinary city
street.

"I can't figure them out." His face blocked by a large cerise
blob of calorie-free sugared air puff, Briann watched the peculiar pair pause in front of an exhibit on the undersea life of
Cachalot. They managed to look bored and apprehensive at
the same time. "If these are your standard-issue xenophobes,
then why are they spending any time at all in the thranx-built
zones of the fair? We've followed them through three already.
Are they just eccentric, or is there something to them we're
not seeing?"

Twikanrozex idly groomed an antenna, bending it forward
and down with a foothand until he could slide the plumed
prominence between his mandibles. Unlike Briann, he did
not try to conceal his presence from the couple they were following. There was no need. Except at the diplomatic and gov-
ernmental level, contact between humans and thranx was
sufficiently infrequent that the majority of humans were convinced that all thranx looked alike.

"I feel that I have spent enough time in the company of humans to know that the behavior of this pair is most unusual,
crr!ll. Their actions do not strike me as those of a mated
couple, yet that is the appearance they clearly are striving
to convey. We have already observed several instances of interaction suggesting they do not especially even like one
another."

Briann inhaled a portion of his air puff. "Among humans,
that does not necessarily signify the absence of ceremonial

union. But in this case, I happen to agree with you. None of their actions seem normal. Still, while interesting from an anthropological point of view, it's not grounds for alerting the authorities." He glanced surreptitiously in the couple's direction. They were arguing again.

"Let's give this another ten minutes or so. Then I suppose we should get back to the tower and check its condition."

Twikanrozex gestured agreement. Five minutes into Briann's proposed ten, something so extraordinary happened that all thoughts of abandoning the unobtrusive stalk were forgotten.

Both padres saw the approaching thranx. One was especially large, with prominent wing cases and a deep blue sheen to his exoskeleton. Except for a possible passing glance of disgust from the humans, there was no reason to suppose the two pairs would even acknowledge each other's presence. Absolutely the last thing Briann expected was for them to swerve toward one another. No, that was not quite right, he corrected himself. That was the second last thing. The first last thing occurred when they met in the middle of the busy pavilion walkway, pointedly inspected their immediate surroundings, and then fell into what could only be described even at a distance as casual conversation.

Not only was the rabid antithranx human male palavering with representatives of the species he had a little while earlier professed to loathe, he was doing so without any sign of distaste. His taller female companion likewise participated in the conversation enthusiastically.

"These are not strangers talking." Twikanrozex was as spellbound by the unexpected tableau as was his soft-skinned friend. "They know one another."

"Or of one another." Shielding his face as best he could, Briann watched the four-way conversation. "I am of the feeling that more than the preposterous domesticity of our couple is on view here. But what, I can't begin to imagine."

"Nor I." Twikanrozex inclined his antennae forward, but the voices of the nattering quartet were drowned out by the shifting, swirling babble of the crowd. "What can they possibly be talking about?"

"Whatever it is, they've finished." Briann pointed. "The party is breaking up."

As they looked on, the humans and thranx parted company. As if to cap the unreality of the encounter, they exchanged formal farewells before heading off in opposite directions. Twikanrozex started forward immediately.

"You want to keep following them?" Briann trailed his friend for a moment.

"Not them. It may be that we have, *kuiit,* learned all we can from the odd human pairing. I think we should follow these new thranx that they met for a while." He glanced over at his brother-in-the-Church. "For reasons too convoluted to explain in a short time, and because of regrettable omissions in your cultural education, I must tell you that the two representatives of my kind are acting in a manner as strange as the humans'. This bespeaks eccentricities that go beyond individual iconoclastics. I should very much like to be enlightened."

Of like mind even though he could not be sure of his colleague's analysis of the encounter they had just witnessed, Briann nodded and followed.

Since any meeting between a group of apprehensive humans and an equally large clutch of edgy thranx was bound to attract the attention of curious fair-goers, Skettle arranged to have only Martine accompany him to the final pre-Armageddon rendezvous. Having been guided to the place chosen for the final meeting by Skettle's followers Nevisrighne and Pierrot, Beskodnebwyl met them attended by, as agreed upon, one other single representative of his kind. On this, the fifth day of the fair, the two humans and two thranx drew hardly a glance as they convened in the farthest reaches of the joint human-thranx forestry pavilion.

Giant *tceri!xx* from Willow-Wane grew side by side with tall kauri from Earth. Twisted kokerbooms shared the magnified heat of the day with lush *gotulba* from Hivehom. There were sequoias and *serypta*, *volmats* and ginkgo, diterocarps and the famous flowering *eryouou* from Long Tunnel that grew only in perfect circles from a common root.

In nature, none of these formidable growths grew together in the same ecozone, and many of them came from different planets. As representative examples of their kind, they had been selected for individual elegance and overall appearance. Only through the application of advanced hydroponics could they share the same ground. Each had been carefully sterilized prior to transport to ensure that no unwanted fellow travelers accompanied them on their mission of education. Each had been rendered incapable of reproduction to make certain no seed or cone, no spore or shoot could take root in the untainted alien soil of Dawn.

Into this impossible artificial forest, Beskodnebwyl and his companion wandered. Near the back, in the farthest reaches of the soaring pavilion with its transparent divisions, they found Elkannah Skettle sharing a hot drink with his collaborator Martine. Thranx and humans greeted one another formally. While the two leaders conversed, Martine and her thranx counterpart took up positions between them and the pathway. Deep in apparent discourse, they were paying as little attention to each other as possible while keeping their eyes on the pavilion's transient visitors. Though expecting neither trouble nor interruption, they were fully prepared to deal with either.

"Interesting, isn't it?" Skettle ventured conversationally. "That in this time of instantaneous local and rapid interstellar communication we still find the best way to assure a private conversation is to meet in person?"

Beskodnebwyl gestured agreement mixed with contempt, confident his human counterpart was incompetent to detect the latter. It amused him to so denigrate the unwitting biped. "Electronics are too easily intercepted, and voices imitated. Better to meet face-to-face."

"Even if you don't have one." Skettle smiled thinly. He was wonderfully content, secure in the knowledge that by this same time tomorrow chaos would have paid its long-planned visit to the fair, leaving death, destruction, and ravening hatred for the thranx in its wake. No doubt this odoriferous pest with whom he had agreed to temporarily cooperate felt similarly.

"At least I know my face." Antennae and truhands waved in Skettle's direction. "It was thus when I was young, it will be the same tomorrow, and except for a darkening of color will be unchanged when I am old. Whereas yours will shrink and crumple like a fruit left too long in the sun, until it threatens to disintegrate from its own rotting loathsomeness."

Skettle's smile slipped away. "I'm certain this happy little tryst is as disagreeable to you as it is to me. Therefore let us do our business so we can both be spared any unnecessary additional contact." Glancing back the way he had come, he proceeded only when Martine acknowledged his wordless inquiry with a slight wave of one hand.

Clicking a button on his handheld, he projected into the air between himself and a nearby tree a perfect miniature replication of the fairgrounds. There was no one else around to see, the nearest tourists being some distance away from the two alert scouts. As Skettle manipulated the elementary controls on the handheld, portions of the projection lit up accordingly.

"My people will set to work where you see the red highlights." As his fingers moved, so did the responsive lights. "We'll be starting fires in the most vulnerable places. Each of my people has undergone extensive training and is dedicated to the cause. In the event of unforeseen interruption or capture, they are prepared to operate independently of one another. Their assignments are overlapping, so that if one or more are intercepted or otherwise detained, any other can strike their missed targets for them." Using the controls, he rotated the projection and expanded individual sections, finally settling on one bordering the lake.

"I myself will be seeing to the interfair communications facilities, and then sabotaging the relevant backup installation so that my original work will not be detected." His voice had taken on a biblical tone that was lost on the thranx.

"Deprived of a central command, the fair security personnel will be unable to properly coordinate any reaction with one another. Separated and assailed on all sides by both my people and yours, they will either flee in confusion or be cut down should they attempt to interfere with us. Long before reinforcements can be brought from Aurora, we will have completed our cycle of destruction." He offered the handheld to Beskodnebwyl, who took it in a truhand. Having paid careful attention to the human's hand movements, the thranx had no difficulty operating the straightforward device.

"My followers will spread out from this central point." Another bright light appeared in the air before the conversants. "Each will be carrying a small arsenal of compact high explosives as well as hand weapons with which to ward off the curious security personnel to whom you have already referred. As you have pointed out, by the time adequately armed forces can arrive from the city, my people will also have finished their work. Weapons and any other incriminating evidence will have been abandoned at preselected points, and my clan mates will have rejoined the pitiful surviving remnants of the panicked crowd. Any visiting thranx who happen to observe us at work will be killed. I am not worried about surviving humans identifying us, since it is well known the casual mammalian observer cannot tell individual thranx apart. In any event, the turmoil and disorder should be enough to blind even the most heedful of your kind."

Skettle was nodding appreciatively. "Once their work is done, my people will embark on a similar course of action, whereupon among the resulting turmoil and confusion we can all go our separate ways, having accomplished far more together than we ever could have hoped to working separately." Except, he added to himself, I'm going to try and kill you myself while Martine and Botha and Pierrot and the others dismember the rest of your revolting entourage. And if you and your disgusting fellows are entertaining similar thoughts in regard to us, you'll see why we humans didn't really need your help at Pitar.

"Then all is in readiness." Glistening compound eyes stared up at the tall human. "This time tomorrow will see us putting a glorious end to any thoughts of closer human-thranx contact while consigning them forever to the wholly conventional level where they belong."

Skettle voiced his agreement. He did not offer to shake hands with his many-limbed fellow terrorist, and Beskodnebwyl was careful to keep his delicate antennae as far from the foul-smelling human as possible. As soon as they had rejoined their respective lookouts, the four parted company, striding purposefully out of the pavilion.

Behind, they left only silent, imported trees to bear witness to the appalling plan of mass murder they had agreed upon. Trees, and as unlikely a pair of bystanders as were to be found promenading the fairgrounds.

As Briann helped his companion climb down out of the baobab, the padres considered what they had just seen. Not even Twikanrozex, with his sensitive antennae, could overhear conversation at such a distance. But he had been able to follow the complementing hand gestures of his fellow thranx, while Briann was an accomplished lip reader. Intervening vegetation and the need to avoid the attentions of the two lookouts had conspired to interfere with their observations, but they had seen and read enough to realize that something monstrous had been planned for the following day.

"It is so sad." Twikanrozex's antennae were weaving alternately back and forth. "To see humans and thranx working in concert together, only to discover that they are doing so for all the wrong reasons."

Briann let out a despondent sigh of resignation. "And to think I was worried that the humans we followed for a while might go so far as to insult someone else, or that the two thranx might be involved in creating an incident."

"And so they are." Truhands wove patterns in the air as the two padres exited the pavilion. "An incident that beggars the imagination."

"I wish we had been able to learn all the details of their plan."

A truhand reached up to touch his shoulder. "We did well enough, Brother, and a good thing we did, too, else thousands might have died."

"Some might yet." Briann raised his gaze. Around him music and gaiety, laughter and contented clicking filled the bright blue of afternoon like birdwing butterflies dancing above a tropical pool. "We don't know where they're staying, or what the rest of them look like."

"Steps can be taken. There may be some small disruption."

Briann lengthened his stride, trying not to look at the children or the young unmolted thranx among whom he and his friend were walking. "There will have to be. The authorities can't shut down the fair. If they do that, it will only help to frighten these people offworld, human and thranx alike. Based on our descriptions they might stop the four we saw at the shuttleport. Regardless, their associates will be alerted and take care to slip quietly offworld. The next time they strike, society might not be so fortunate. We have to catch them all, every one of them, here and now."

Twikanrozex whistled affirmation. "You're right, Brother. To accomplish everything, some risk will have to be taken. Some innocents may be hurt."

His friend nodded. "Fortunately, the Church understands the necessity of proportional sacrifice to achieve a greater goal. I hope the local authorities will see it that way."

"If not," Twikanrozex observed as they turned a corner, heading for the tasteful, sweeping structure that housed Fair Administration, "then we will have to convince them."

"It must be done the right way," Briann concurred, "though it will not be easy. The Church does not yet command immediate respect from secular authorities. It will fall upon you and me as individuals rather than as Church representatives to make the case for an immediate and discriminating response to this threat. We will have to be direct and convincing. In this the Maxims are not likely to be of much help to us. When it comes to matters of philosophical discourse, police are notoriously indifferent."

15

Due to the thickness and strength of the ceramic strata, it took several days to enlarge the opening through which the unfortunate digger had almost fallen to where it was wide enough to admit a small aircar. In that time, a laser range-finder had been lowered into the fissure to measure the distance from the opening to the first surfaces below. The distances were not as great as first supposed. Still, had anyone fallen through the gap, they would have suffered a fatal plunge of several hundred feet into the lightless depths.

The laser and other scanning devices revealed the presence of nothing but empty space. The brown ceramic appeared to form a roof above an artificial void. No one in the camp accepted this conclusion. It would be a truly eccentric species indeed that would go to so much trouble and expense to seal such a vast volume of apparent nothingness away from the world. There had to be something more. Given the extent of the disclosed subterranean space, an aircar equipped with powerful lights and calibrating lasers would be the simplest, safest, and quickest means of exploring the mysterious alien emptiness. Hand weapons were also issued all around. On closer inspection, seemingly secure large underground spaces often were not as hermetically sealed as initially supposed. Local fauna might well have made use of so much protected, enclosed living space and needed to be guarded against accordingly.

Cullen and Pilwondepat were accompanied by Holoness and an aircar operator named Dik. To Pilwondepat's barely concealed delight and in spite of energetic protestations,

Cullen insisted that Riimadu remain behind on the surface. The thranx made an effort not to gloat over this decision.

Their vehicle was the smallest available to the exploration team, one intended to be used for quick jaunts to outlying sites of interest. As Dik maneuvered it over the edge of the much enlarged and thoroughly shored excavation, a crowd of students and workers gathered to see the voyagers off. Pilwondepat forced himself not to search among the gathering for the scaled face of the frustrated AAnn representative.

Eager but restrained, Cullen was musing aloud as the craft began to descend slowly into the pit. "Usually, archeologists crawl into ancient monuments and mausoleums, or if they are lucky, walk. In all my experience I don't know of any expedition that uncovered an artifact large enough to fly into."

"Personally," Pilwondepat replied reflectively, "I happen to like crawling."

"If I had six legs, so might I." Cullen went quiet as the softly thrumming aircar approached the augmented cavity.

Their driver maneuvered the compact craft into the opening, fixed for vertical hover, and then dropped them through the cleft ceramic layer and down into the alien void itself. "Lights," an unintimidated Cullen snapped briskly. Instantly, their immediate surroundings were illuminated by the spray of high-intensity search beams that had been hastily attached to the vehicle. Recorders mounted within the body of the craft switched on. Around them, all was blackness save where the powerful beams penetrated.

Holoness activated the scanning laser. Utilizing its far greater throw range, she played it across the western wall, a task for which it was not designed. Beyond that bulwark of dark ceramic lay an unbroken rampart of metamorphic rock and eventually, the outer wall of the escarpment.

"Turn." Cullen was standing next to the driver. Everyone was too excited and nervous to make use of the aircar's available seats. Even had he wished to lie down, the design of the seats rendered them useless to Pilwondepat. "Let's have a look at the opposite wall." Dik complied, and the craft pivoted neatly on its axis. As they came about, Holoness kept the ranging laser aimed parallel to the vehicle's keel. The bright beam revealed—nothing. The opposite wall was so distant that even the laser's tuned coherent beam could not illuminate it.

There was, however, a floor. Dropping down, the driver tentatively tested its solidity. It appeared to be composed of the same cryptic ceramic material as the ceiling. Against all reason, the vast chamber, of still unknown dimensions, appeared to have been built to hold nothing but ancient air.

"This doesn't make any sense." So far apart were the walls that Cullen's voice produced no echo. The emptiness swallowed his emphasis. "There has to be something more to it than this. No species goes to this much trouble just to build an enormous empty box."

"Who can quantify alien intentions?" In the dim glow of the aircar's subdued internal lights, the multiple lenses of Pilwondepat's compound eyes sparkled like mirrors tinted gold. "There are still many things humans do that strike my people as having no basis in reason."

"Many humans would agree with you on that." Opening one of the two personnel hatches in the transparent cab, Holoness started down the integrated steps molded into the hull and put a tentative foot on the floor. It supported her weight easily. "It's solid enough."

"As solid as the ceiling?" Tilting back his head, Cullen was able to make out the narrow shaft of sunlight that marked the hole the digging team had drilled in the rugged material. "All right: We're in a big box with no visible internal landmarks. Where do we go from here?"

"Over there, perhaps?" Pilwondepat was pointing with all four hands. "*Creellt*—I think I see something."

Dik swung a search beam in the indicated direction. Sure enough, the glossy bulge of a small dome marred the otherwise perfect flatness of the floor. It was about four meters in diameter and completely isolated. "Looks a lot like all those decorative bulges we found on the outside of this roof." He grunted.

"So it does." Holoness was staring, shining her own hand

beam in the direction of the unassuming protrusion. "But why only one?"

"Get back aboard and we'll go have a look," Cullen told her.

Smacking the ceramic underfoot with her heel, she shook him off. "It's solid as a rock here. I'm going to walk."

With the aircar paralleling her, she strolled over to the swelling protuberance. It was a dark brown, the exact color as the rest of the ceramic material. Its central apex rose no higher than her waist. Reaching down, she tapped it with her light beam. The muted plasticene-on-ceramic clacking that resulted was not nearly loud enough to produce an echo in the enormous chamber.

"Likewise solid." She straightened. "Maybe these isolated domes have some ceremonial significance. Let's see if we can find some more." She started to walk around the wide, low protrusion.

When she was halfway around, something hissed imperceptibly, and the entire dome began to slide in her direction.

Stumbling backward, she nearly fell as the massive convexity slid silently toward her. The blast of incredibly frigid air that erupted from the opening the dome had been covering might reasonably have been expected. The pale light that accompanied it could not.

"Therese, get back in here!" Cullen was shouting at her through the open hatch.

His anxious urging was superfluous. She all but flew back aboard. As soon as she was safely back inside, the exoarcheologist shut the hatch behind her. The icy atmospheric swirl that accompanied her retreat did little more than briefly chill the humans, but it threatened to freeze the moisture in Pilwondepat's less tolerant and unprotected lungs. Fortunately, the craft's heater quickly brought the internal temperature back up to human normal and thranx tolerable.

"What the hell happened there?" Cullen found himself gazing out through the transparent cowl at a perfectly circular opening in the ceramic floor. The dome that had blocked it lay to one side, apparently disinclined to move any farther.

"Maybe her walking on the floor has annoyed the gods."

Dik kept his hands on the aircar's controls, ready to boost
ceilingward and take them out of the murky chamber at an instant's notice.

"Very funny." As her breathing steadied, Holoness moved
next to the cowl to stare out at the aperture. It was perfectly
round, with walls as sleek as the floor beneath them. "Cold air
I can understand—though maybe not *that* cold. But not light.
Where can it be coming from, down here?"

"I expect," Cullen responded, "we'd better go and see. Dik?
Take it slow."

The pilot nodded as he edged them toward the opening.
The glow emerging from the passage Holoness had inadvertently brought to light was not intense. It dissipated long before reaching the ceiling of the vast, empty chamber. Gingerly,
Dik eased the aircar forward, positioned it carefully over the
opening, and then commenced a controlled descent.

The gap in the floor was wide enough to admit the craft,
but with little margin for error on any side. They descended
five meters, ten, thirty, with no sign of the walls surrounding
them either opening up or contracting. As near as Cullen
could tell, the perfectly vertical shaft had been formed to tolerances of less than a millimeter. Then, as abruptly as they
had entered, they found themselves floating free in another
open chamber. According to the console instrumentation, the
temperature outside the aircar's canopy was well below freezing. No one paid much attention to the external temperature
readout, or for that matter, any of the others. They were too
entranced by the light.

Tinted a pale green, it seemed to emanate from the floor
overhead that had now become another ceiling. Below, revealed by the ethereal yet extensive illumination, was . . .

Pilwondepat uttered something in High Thranx that was
incomprehensible to his human companions. Dik cursed under
his breath. Holoness just stared. Cullen, their leader, mouthed
the inaudible human equivalent of Pilwondepat's whistling
and clicking.

They were in another room. Except that *room* was so inadequate a designation to describe their surroundings that it did

not bear audiblizing. Below them, rank on rank, tier on tier, row on row, were thousands upon thousands of teardrop-shaped cylinders. These stretched as far as the eye could see to north, to south, and to the east. Only to the west could the possibility of a boundary be faintly discerned. In that direction, Pilwondepat realized, lay the outside wall of the escarpment.

Below the hovering aircar, the endless tiers of cylinders dropped away to infinity. Searching for an end, for the bottom, brought only tears to the eyes of straining observers, and no closure. Lying between each level of cylinders were strips of gleaming metal and of plastic, and conduits of the ever-present ceramic. Only here, the latter was present in a veritable rainbow array of hues. The tiers were wrapped, criss-crossed, enveloped, in a web of lines and connectors and ducts that looked to have been spun by the mad mother of all spiders.

Gently swathing each cylinder, seemingly supported only by their flimsy, deceptively fragile selves, were halos of filaments and fibers that pulsed with a soft golden glow like the breath of babies become glass. So delicate were they that they might have been spun instead of wired. A narrow strip of some transparent substance ran the length of each cylinder, which themselves appeared to be fashioned from some dark purple metallic substructure.

"What can they be?" Holoness was standing as close to the canopy as possible, her nose pressed against the transparent plexalloy. "There must be *millions* of them." She waved a benumbed hand in the pilot's direction. "Dik, you've got to let them know about this up top!"

Emerging from the same daydream into which all of them had been plunged, the pilot nodded. After a couple of tries, he looked up and shook his head. "No can do. Something in this ceramic sucks up even long-wave transmissions like a sponge. I've lost the outpost's carrier wave, too."

Cullen swallowed hard, aware he was in the presence of something as exalted as it was alien. "Can you get us any closer? We can't go outside here without environment suits."

"No kidding." The pilot manipulated controls. "At these temperatures I'm surprised there's no frost on anything."

"No moisture." Everyone turned to look in Pilwondepat's direction. "Hot desert above, cold desert below. No moisture. This place must be absolutely dry." He gesticulated irony seasoned with aversion even though he knew that his companions would not be able to properly interpret the entire gesture. "Temperature excepted, Riimadu would probably like it down here."

Under Dik's circumspect guidance, the aircar drifted over to the nearest rank of cylinders. In the process, it passed above a narrow strip of metal, one of uncounted thousands that crisscrossed the chamber like steel silk. They might be walkways, Cullen reflected. If so, they had been designed for beings with far more slender builds than humans or thranx. Beings who were also utterly unafraid of heights. Despite omnipresent drops that could only be measured in the hundreds of meters, there were no railings.

With practiced hands, Dik drew the skimmer closer to the uppermost row of cylinders than Pilwondepat would have thought possible. While the pilot remained in his seat and at the controls, everyone else moved to stand next to the portside. From there they could look out and down at the first cylinder in the row. It lay directly below the edge of their vehicle's hull. The vitreous band that ran down the center of the artifact was perfectly clear. Gazing through it, they could see the cylinder's contents clearly. These immediately and unexpectedly supplied the answer to the main question that had plagued exoarcheologists ever since they had first begun to explore the wilds of Comagrave.

What had happened to the Sauun?

They had not expired of loneliness due to a failure to achieve space travel. They had not perished of racial melancholia. They had not obliterated one another in some undetected, undeclared war for which no evidence had yet been found.

They were still here.

Cullen remembered to breathe. "Next cylinder," he ordered Dik. "We have to confirm similitude."

"Okay, but this isn't easy going. We're in pretty tight quarters here." As he adjusted the controls and the aircar began to move again, he indicated the pulsating nimbus that seemed to float just above each cylinder. "There's a hell of a lot of energy fluxing here, and I'd just as soon we don't make contact with any of these filaments, or whatever they are. Nonconductive hull notwithstanding."

"We just need to be able to look into a few more," Cullen assured him. "Then I think we can safely begin to hazard some preliminary extrapolations."

Each cylinder, or pod, held a single Sauun. They were instantly recognizable as such because their features were intimately familiar to the three awestruck exoarcheologists—familiar from the graven faces of the Mourners, visible to anyone who cared to gaze from the escarpment across the great valley. Here were their living likenesses, held immobile in some kind of deepsleep. The same narrowness of features, the same sorrowful countenance, the familiar long faces that had been cut out of an entire mountainside—all were replicated in multiples of individual detail within the cylindrical pods. Millions upon millions of pods.

Pilwondepat had tried to count, multiply, and estimate, and had quickly given up. Without knowing the dimensions of the chamber, any guess would invariably fall short of the far more majestic reality. How many of the Sauun had sought slumber in this place? A quarter of the planetary population? Half? All of it?

"This explains why they never expanded into space." Holoness was staring down at the dignified, composed alien visage sealed behind the transparency below. "They were too busy expanding into this plateau. It must have taken the combined energy and output of their entire civilization. But why?"

"Some kind of gel." Cullen seemed not to hear her. "Probably heavily oxygenated, temperature and greatly reduced nutrient level sustained by all this machinery, which in turn has to be able to maintain itself." He shook his head slowly. "Incredible, just incredible." Blinking, he summoned up a delayed reaction to her question. "Why indeed? Perhaps they retreated here to escape some incurable plague that was ravaging the surface. Or maybe this was once a much wetter world. A long-term planetwide climate change could have threatened famine." He gestured at the row upon row of pods and their dreaming occupants. "Put everyone in stasis, program appropriate instrumentation to awaken everyone when the rains return, and sleep until the planet is receptive to large-scale agriculture again."

"No."

Cullen frowned as he turned to regard the thranx. "No? Why 'no'?"

Pilwondepat's head swiveled to meet the human's stare. "The technology we see here exceeds the difficulties you hypothesize." He gestured with both his right truhand and foothand. "Any civilization capable of constructing a sleeping sepulcher on this scale could surely have solved the problem of climate change and potential famine. Or of a devastating pandemic. The time and physical resources expended just do not resonate with your theorized causations."

Had not Cullen Karasi's skills as a scientist exceeded the demands of his ego, he would never have been given charge of an expedition on a plum outpost like Comagrave. "Granted, for the moment, your reasoning: What would you propose as a motive?"

"Some external threat. Something they could not have anticipated, and therefore not prepared for. Perhaps the spread and sweep of an interstellar conflict they wished to avoid. Not the AAnn. I am willing to venture that neither the AAnn nor for that matter the hives or your people had achieved even rudimentary space travel by the time this place was finished and sealed." He glanced upward. "The chamber above us may be an airspace, intended to provide insulation—or a decoy area, to distract any curiosity seekers. Or probers with less altruistic motives."

"You sound like a paranoid Quillp." Moving away from the canopy, Holoness turned her attention to the endless corridor that extended eastward into the unfathomable distance. "Still, any and all theories are open to investigation. What can't be denied is the reality of this place, and the extraordinary effort that went into its construction."

"Certainly," Cullen agreed, "something drove them to this. I find it hard to imagine that all this—" He gestured with one hand at the immense enclosed universe outside their craft. "—came about as the result of casual choice, or boredom, or a desire simply to pass a few eons without dying."

"Fear," Pilwondepat observed quietly, "can drive people to greater heights than aspiration."

"Easy enough to find out." Holoness turned to the senior scientist. "All we have to do is wake one of them up and put the question to it." She made no attempt to mask her eagerness.

"In good time, that is precisely what we will try to do." Cullen's tone was carefully neutral. "But killing a few of the Sauun would not be a good way to endear ourselves to the rest of the survivors. We must be sure of what we're doing before we commence. That means study, plenty of preliminary work." His voice softened as he moved closer to her. Not for the first time, Pilwondepat thought there might be something more to their relationship than supervisor to subordinate.

"There's work here for a thousand researchers for a dozen lifetimes. Much as I'd like to know the answers to all the big questions, this is still a traditional dig, and we have to proceed in accordance with traditional procedure. That means measure and record, record and measure. Extrapolation with models will follow. Only when we're sure we know what we're doing, or as sure as anyone can ever be when something like this is encountered, will we advance to more dramatic steps." He pondered a new thought.

"If Pilwondepat is right, or even half right, and these people withdrew to this place to escape some unknown threat, there might be more overt defenses in place to deal with intruders than simply an empty decoy of a room. Maybe we should count ourselves not only fortunate in making this discovery, but lucky that no such devices have taken an interest in us—yet." He turned back to the pilot.

"Dik, let's take a look around. Keep it straight and simple. We don't want to get lost down here."

Nodding, the pilot manipulated controls. Gingerly, he backed the craft away from the row of pods they had been examining, pivoted the aircar on its axis, and accelerated slowly, heading east and down. Pilwondepat stopped counting levels at four hundred. No one tried to count the number of pods. The actual figure was beyond casual estimation. Cullen had used the word *millions* when they had first dropped into the deepsleep chamber. As they dove ever deeper into the dreaming vastness, that began to seem a quaint underassessment.

"I'd like to know where the power to sustain all this comes from." Away from the rows of closely ranked tiers, Dik had time for musings of his own. The open corridors between banks of pods were far more expansive than the narrow walkways that linked them would have suggested. Support vehicles larger than their aircar would have required access to every row, to each individual pod. "Sure as hell there's more than one central support facility. Wouldn't make sense to concentrate everything in one place. Me, I'd disperse backup capacity throughout the project."

Cullen was in agreement. "There are some clues in the abandoned Sauun cities on the surface. That's one of the reasons why nobody thus far has been able to explain their failure to achieve space travel. They appeared to have all the necessary technological capability. They simply chose not to develop it."

"Maybe Pilwondepat's right." Holoness glanced over at the awestruck thranx. "Maybe they didn't have a choice."

"What would impel an entire species to burrow underground and place themselves in deepsleep, at the mercy of machines, to awaken at some far future time to unfamiliar surroundings and an unpredictable fate?" Pilwondepat gestured with both antennae. "With time to examine and reflect, we may find the answer." He looked back at her, his mandibles working. "Perhaps we may even be able to do so without having to wake the Sauun." Walking on only his four trulegs, he ambled over to stand alongside Dik. The vacant seat next to the pilot was useless to him. "We spoke earlier of defenses. Now I think there may be none."

"Why not?" Unlike some humans, the pilot did not shy away from proximity to the thranx.

"Any danger sufficiently profound to force the Sauun to resort to racial deepsleep as a means of avoiding it would likely not be discouraged or deflected by what weapons their technology suggests they were capable of constructing."

"Certainly wouldn't be of any use against plague or famine." Cullen refused to surrender so quickly his initial theses. "Take us back up, Dik. Everett, Bajji, and the others will be in an agony of impatience wondering what's happened to us. Besides—" He smiled. "—I think we've accomplished quite enough for one afternoon."

Obediently, the pilot pirouetted the craft and began to retrace their course. Endless rows of shimmering purple pods sped past on either side, rising to imposing heights above and majestic depths below. Millions upon millions of sentient beings, suspended in silence, each of them heir to a great and tantalizing secret, silently tracked their progress. And across the great valley, the statues of the Mourners stood gazing eternally in this direction, the reason for their melancholy expressions now perfectly clear.

Did the Sauun raise this immense mausoleum first and then surround it with masquerading stone, Pilwondepat wondered, or did they burrow into an already existing plateau? If the former, it would explain why the edge of the escarpment was so near to the entrance they had found. He tried to envision an entire race striving mightily to prepare a vault of almost incalculable proportions, to receive every one of them before something happened. Instead of choosing to fight whatever it was that threatened them, they had elected to go into hiding. Whatever that something might be, the Sauun had decided they could neither confront it, nor negotiate with it, nor appease it. They had fled into deepsleep, hoping to awaken to find that the threat, whatever it was, had gone, had passed them by.

Plague, Cullen had suggested. Famine. To Pilwondepat such explanations seemed wholly inadequate to the Sauun's response. Even his own hypothesis, that some as-yet-undocumented interstellar conflict had threatened them, was already beginning to sound incommensurate. Whatever had driven an accomplished, intelligent species to hide itself away like an estivating *hrulg* grub surely was of greater consequence than that.

While his human associates chattered around him, he tilted back his head to gaze up and out through the skimmer's transparent roof. Two hundred levels surpassed, two hundred more to go. He found himself suddenly longing to be out of that boundless, brooding place, away from those millions and millions of living corpses. Checking the ascending craft's chronometer, he saw that less time had passed since they'd left the surface than he thought. They would emerge into daylight. That meant he would not have to look up at the grim immensity of the night sky and wonder at what might lie in hiding behind the stars.

16

When she awoke the next morning, Fanielle saw that she had overslept. The last thing she wanted, after the menacing encounter of the night before, was to be late for the rendezvous with Haflunormet and their mutual friend. As she dressed, she found herself looking sharply in directions and at places that would never have previously engaged her attention. With each mercifully unrequited glance, she relaxed a little more. The Baron Preed NNXV was, as he might have put it, truly gone. From her lodgings, if not from her thoughts.

She waited for Haflunormet at an eating establishment he favored, resting her bifurcated behind on a padded bench designed for thranx to straddle. As the only human in the underground insectoid bistro, her presence drew stares and remarks. The looks were less direct than the comments, given the thranx mastery of peripheral vision. Other patrons were quite capable of staring *at* her without actually turning in her direction. After a while, the novelty of her silent presence wore off, and they returned to their own conversations. The air around her was filled with a harmonious cacophony of clicks, whistles, and words.

She was sucking on a domestic fruit juice blend that was more than palatable to her digestive system when Haflunormet arrived. A prearranged glance and gesture told her all she needed to know for the moment. "He's here." One of the few humans on Hivehom with access to local methods of reimbursement, she paid for her half-finished drink and followed the diplomat out into the bustling corridor.

Roof over a New New York street to a height of ten meters

or so and you would have a good analog for the principal burrows of Daret. Still, it was not a place for the claustrophobic, or for those who were uncomfortable in crowds.

From the burrow, they took public transport to an outer suburb. Yet again, Fanielle was grateful for her petite frame. It allowed her to ride thranx transportation without having to bend uncomfortably at the waist. Twenty minutes later they exited the transport system and took a lift to the surface, where Haflunormet had a private vehicle waiting. Following a preprogrammed course, the small aircar rose and headed westward, flying above untouched savanna and low-lying jungle. Several hours later it slowed as it approached a clearing at the base of rolling, verdure-covered hills. Not far from this easily visible landing site, enormous bulk carriers wound in procession past triple loaders, grinding their ponderous way along the base of the nearest hill with cargoes of recently extracted ore.

"*Sat!wi!t* rare metals." Haflunormet took manual control of the aircar and directed it toward a covered parking area. "The mine's owners are sympathetic to our cause." Multiple-lensed eyes looked over at her. "A more difficult place to eavesdrop on a conversation I could not find. I was determined to arrange one where after the unfortunate encounter in your room you would feel comfortable about speaking freely."

She gestured understanding and thanks, her two hands having to do the work of four. That they would be rendezvousing in a mine did not trouble her. Its interior could be no more confining than the side streets of Daret.

After securing the aircar, Haflunormet led the way past busy workers and administrators. Fanielle drew more direct stares here than she had in the cosmopolitan capital. Not all of them bespoke affection. She might well, she reflected as she ignored some of the less-friendly gestures, be the first human to visit this place, the first one many of the miners had ever seen in the flesh.

At the entrance Haflunormet made contact with Security.

Conversations were exchanged via communicator, subsequent to which the two visitors were allowed to enter. From time to time Haflunormet would pause to check directions on his recorder. Unlike in the city, internal transportation here operated on an irregular schedule. Twice, they had to wait for an automated conveyance to arrive. A tall human, Fanielle reflected as they zoomed along one subterranean track deep within the mountain, might easily have lost his head in such a place. Within the tunnels and shafts there was very little overhead clearance.

From time to time they passed a bore or passageway where active mining was in progress. Here was another justification for closer commercial, if not political, contact, Fanielle saw. No human miner could compete with an equally well-trained thranx, who was not only more comfortable beneath the surface than above it, but enjoyed a greater tolerance for the heat that often turned mine tunnels into sweltering saunas. A crew of these highly trained workers could find top-salaried gainful employment at any tunneling mine on Earth or any of its colonies.

The transport they were riding began to slow. As it did so, the narrow corridor opened up to reveal a spacious underground rest area. Here miners could relax in comfort, waiting for assignment to the far-flung reaches of the diggings. There was illumination, and refreshment, and vit-style entertainment.

Haflunormet led her to a distant corner, where a single middle-aged thranx was engrossed in the concealed readout of a personal recorder. Antennae rose in their direction as they approached. As Haflunormet made the introduction, the other thranx slid off the bench he had been straddling and dipped both antennae forward. Fanielle brushed the feathery extremities with her fingertips, a gesture that in the past couple of years had become more familiar to her than the shaking of hands.

"I am Lyrkenparmew. Before we begin, I would like to wish you painless deposition of your egg."

Taking a seat on an empty bench, Fanielle glanced wryly in

Haflunormet's direction. "Does everyone on this planet know that I'm pregnant?"

Where a human might have responded with something like "Good news travels fast," her fellow diplomat did not comment verbally. In place of words, Haflunormet gestured ambiguousness leavened with gentle humor.

"Thank you," she replied dryly. "However, I still feel compelled to point out that we are not here to discuss my maternal condition." By now used to thranx benches that were devoid of back support, she found herself leaning forward automatically as she addressed the new arrival. "Haflunormet has apprised you of my recent difficulties here, and in Azerick?"

Lyrkenparmew gestured acknowledgment. "I've been briefed. I am sorry for the many inconveniences you have suffered. I myself lost a close clan member three years ago to the gentle ministrations of the AAnn." He added a series of rapid clicks that were shocking in their manifest obscenity. Fanielle decided she liked him right away.

"What results can you report from your recent informal sojourn on Earth?" Haflunormet's antennae were aquiver with eagerness. "Deliberation still burrows faithfully?"

"More than faithfully. Beneath the surface turmoil there is a newly dug tunnel that runs straight to the light, with walls that have been burnished to an unfolding glow by truth." He paused to check his own recorder, which at present was set not to record but to scan for others who might be recording. Assured that their conversation was being monitored neither in person nor electronically, he continued.

"It has been proposed, and preparations are being made to announce, a formal union between our two governments. The resulting Grand Hive is to be known as the Humanx Commonwealth. There is to be full integration of all administrative functions, first on the interstellar level, later on the local. This is not an alliance; it burrows far deeper." Having delivered himself of this extraordinary pronouncement, he took a sip of the sugary liquid that half filled the translucent green container standing by his side. "Nothing else like it exists in this part of the Arm. Once integration is complete, other species will be invited to join. An official Commission of Interest to the Quillp has already been drafted, though it is considered unlikely the ornithorps will wish to confederate. Nevertheless, it will be extended out of courtesy."

Haflunormet and Fanielle hardly knew how to react. Desiring to hear that relations between their respective species were on the upswing, Lyrkenparmew had unloaded on them the culmination of hopes that heretofore both diplomats had only dared to dream about. Until now, neither of them had ever heard of a proposed "Humanx Commonwealth." Haflunormet said as much.

Lyrkenparmew gestured apologies. "As you know, the friends of the committee have had to function on multiple levels in order to escape potentially injurious scrutiny on all those worlds where we are active. I assure you, this is not some wild rambling on the part of our mutual friends. It's quite real. The details have been carefully worked out, debated, refined, and prepared for general dissemination on all thranx- and human-occupied worlds. A small band of especially adept agents have been working on the minutiae ever since we entered the Pitarian War on the human side."

"I hardly know what to say." Haflunormet's antennae were waving about as if in a dream. "This is more than I, than any of us here on Hivehom, dared to hope for."

Fanielle scrutinized their surroundings. A few miners were staring in their direction. In her direction, she corrected herself. But they appeared to be no more than what they were, and after a while they departed aboard a battered transport. She was determined not to let paranoia get the best of her. Not now, after receiving news of such import.

"How is this proposal going to be presented to the public?" she finally managed to ask their guest.

Lyrkenparmew employed all four hands for emphasis. "If the proponents did not do it themselves, it would never be brought up for consideration by our respective dominions. The intention is to spring it on both governments simultaneously, and bring it to a vote in yours and to a mass closing in ours as quickly as possible, thereby catching our xenophobic opponents by surprise. Continued secrecy is obviously there-fore of utmost importance."

Haflunormet whistled for attention. "Presentation before council is one thing; adoption something else entirely. Does this astounding concept have any real chance of being affirmed?"

Now it was the otherwise academically inclined Lyrken-parmew's turn to manifest excitement. "In all seriousness, three cycles ago I would have laughed at such a notion. Two cycles and I would have responded to you with an unequiv-ocal no. This last cycle past I might not have replied at all, foundering deep in contemplation of the previously unthink-able. Tomorrow . . ." He finished with an unexpectedly em-phatic gesture and a particularly piercing click of his two vertical mandibles.

"There has been a recent and unexpected upsurge of sup-port on both sides from a number of previously disinterested clans. Coupled with those important individuals who have already previously espoused these sentiments—influential politicians of Earth and tri-eints and others here on Hivehom—it is believed that there may exist on both capital worlds suffi-cient votes to just barely pass the proposal. I am also assured that we can count in council on the voting bloc that dislikes humans but desperately wishes for such an alliance."

Fanielle frowned. "Isn't that a contradiction?"

Lyrkenparmew gestured ironic amusement. "Indeed—a very useful one. Among the military, there are those who will agree to anything if it will secure the promise of human inter-vention against the AAnn. These high-ranking eints have a positive affection for humans as—what is your colorful term?—*cannon fodder*. They seek allies who can be placed between the hive worlds and the Empire. If humans desire to occupy such a position voluntarily, why, there are many semixenophobes among my kind who are ready to welcome them."

"Strange," Haflunormet mused aloud. "To think that those who may support this proposed Commonwealth the most en-thusiastically may also intensely dislike the people to whom they are about to surrender a portion of their sovereignty."

"It's not important." Fanielle was confident in her reply. "All that matters is the final, irrevocable cementing of relations and melding of our two societies. In the service of that end, we'll take what help we can get."

"So we shall," Lyrkenparmew agreed readily. "Once it becomes clear that ratification is not only possible but probable, I have been assured that others who would like to declare for a Commonwealth but who for reasons of provincial politics or hive affiliation have not yet been able to do so will announce their support." He gesticulated urgency. "But the proposal must pass on the first inclusive stridulating. After that, our opponents will be able to muster their objections and quite likely defeat any reconsideration."

"This is grand news." Haflunormet was struggling to find something to do with all his hands. "When you return to Earth, you may inform our mutual acquaintances that their friends here in the capital will be ready to move the instant their support is required."

"I can't vouch for what will happen in the Terran Congress," Fanielle added, "but as you know, I am not alone in my sympathies at Azerick Outpost. We'll be ready to offer what help we can from here."

"As will your counterparts on your homeworld, in the Reserva Amazonia, and elsewhere." Having delivered himself of the most critical news, the envoy finally began to relax. His trulegs were no longer clasped tensely against the padded flanks of the bench he was straddling, and his antennae inclined forward in a more natural resting position instead of being held vertically by the muscles in his forehead.

"Everything—hopes, dreams, and much effort—is building to a peak. The timing has been very carefully worked out. The sometimes bumpy relations between our species are about to crest at a high point. There are at present no major disagreements in dispute. The controversy over exploration rights on Comagrave has been settled in return for reciprocal rights on Drax Four. Ongoing commercial disputes of note have at last found a home in the binary-staffed commission that has been designated to review and settle such matters.

The intercultural fair on the human colony world of Dawn is, by all accounts, performing to large crowds and great acclaim among those of both our peoples who have attended. Unless some unforeseen catastrophe of major proportions occurs within the next several weeks, the relevant edicts should be presented and the appropriate votes called for." He took a long, throaty swig of his remaining drink.

"This is a most momentous time in the history of our respective species. It will go down as such in the history scrolls—or else be memorialized as one of the great lost opportunities in this sentient part of the galaxy. Though you and I are but insignificant players in the sublime drama, we must each of us strive at the moment of truth to maximize our whistling."

It was a fine sentiment, Fanielle felt. There was a nobility to it that calmed her anxieties. Very rarely are individuals actually aware of balancing on the crux of history. She hoped she would live long enough to see come to pass all that the glittering-eyed Lyrkenparmew had described. For that matter, painfully recalling what had happened to Jeremy, she hoped she would just live long enough to see the actual voting on the proposal take place.

Lyrkenparmew had set his drinking utensil aside. His manner had grown more somber. "There are other threats besides the declared intention of our opponents on both councils to vote no on any such proposition. While our people have been hard at work behind the scenes, lobbying human politicians and thranx eints alike, the AAnn have not rested. They are ever active, making mischief." He glanced in Fanielle's direction. "As I have been informed you know from more than merely speculative experience."

She nodded slowly, a gesture both thranx would recognize. "As you know, I lost . . . I lost the father of my child." She swallowed hard. Though she had been down this road many times since Jeremy's death, remembering was still agonizing. Only her work, into which she had thrown herself with more intensity than ever, kept her from seeing his face in familiar places and from crying uncontrollably.

Something hard and unyielding brushed softly against her right side. Eight of Haflunormet's fingers grazed her ribs in a particular ellipsoidal motion, a soothing motion designed to show sympathy for both egg-layer and prospective offspring. She sniffed only once as she returned his touch with a smile. Surrounded though she was at residence and on the job by fellow humans, it took a bug's caress to put her at ease.

"Surely," she observed, collecting herself, "the AAnn can't hope to match this flowering joint effort with one of their own?" Around them, clusters of miners came and went, toiling at flexible shifts. Whenever a new group lay down on benches nearby, the diplomats' conversation shifted to innocuous, generalized topics until the diggers departed. The information being discussed at the small table in the back was too sensitive for general dissemination. It would have to remain so until the grand proposition had been announced to the public.

Lyrkenparmew indicated mild distress. "They've been very busy, the scale-skinned ones. In the area of commercial treaty making they have been especially active. The accumulation of individual wealth occupies greater status among the AAnn and humankind than it does among my people. This similar outlook affords a kind of instant rapport among certain of your kind and many of the AAnn." His truhands were in constant motion, making it difficult for Fanielle to follow every subtle overtone of the conversation.

"Many covenants have been proposed between AAnn and human, and several adopted, but nothing like the Commonwealth. The AAnn would never contemplate such an intimate union with anyone." He let out a series of shrill clicks. "They are too enamored of their own imagined destiny as rulers of this part of the galaxy to ever surrender any real control to another species. But beyond that, they are quite willing to consider all manner of agreements."

"The problem," Haflunormet continued, "is that too many humans are easily blinded by promises of the riches to be gained from trade with the scaled ones, who are not above bribing your people to secure support, special treatment, and whatever other perks they believe they can so acquire."

Fanielle was embarrassed for people she did not know and would never meet. "My kind have come a long way from the time when we used to beat one another's heads in for the most insignificant reasons. But there still exist those who crawl through life as ethical hemophiliacs."

"What they don't realize," Lyrkenparmew went on solemnly, "is that opportunism is ingrained in the AAnn social structure. They will treat fairly when it best suits their needs, and break legs when it does not. The grief arises from their skill. They have made a science of duplicity. I am not saying that humans are naïve, but there is no sentient in the known universe as crafty, sly, and cunning as a mature, experienced AAnn." He gestured mild apology of oversight. "But then, there is no need for me to tell you this. You have already met one such."

She nodded. "The emissary in question could charm a *sifla* out of its *morgewout*. When not tearing out your throat."

Haflunormet whistle-clicked concurrence. "His reputation spreads wider than does his water."

"I know he charmed a colleague of mine back at the compound." She looked straight at Haflunormet. "Mind the name 'Jorge Sertoa.' He's a very clever fellow, but a bit of cold plasma. Has dark matter in place of a backbone." At the dual gestures of bemusement from her companions, she hurried to modify the simile. "Sorry—in place of his predominate dorsal chitin." At this clarification, they gesticulated knowingly.

"And he's not alone in his sympathies for the AAnn. There are others at the settlement who feel similarly, though I'm happy to say they're in the minority. When the proposal is announced, I think you'll be able to count on the support of the majority of the staff, diplomatic and support personnel alike, at Azerick." Her expression hardened. "I'll arrange to keep an eye on Jorge and the others so they don't cause any trouble."

Lyrkenparmew indicated understanding. "Everything is suddenly starting to move very rapidly. There is a sense of great events having been set inexorably in motion. I hardly need tell either of you that if this proposal goes down to defeat, it could be fifty or a hundred cycles before anyone dares to bring it up again. Failure carries with it the concurrent risk that the opponents of unification, alarmed by the boldness of the proposition, will unite in even more formidable leagues to oppose any reconsideration." His voice lowered as his clicking subsided to the intensity of pins landing on a metal sheet.

"I'm not trying to alarm you, but this is the way the gist is seen. Our first chance may very well prove to be our best chance, if not necessarily our last."

"I wonder if it's too soon." Fanielle almost leaned back on her bench before she remembered that it had no back. "I wonder if we're pushing too much too fast."

The genial twisting of Lyrkenparmew's truhands insinuated inevitability. "Those in charge of making such decisions feel they have no choice but to press for the establishment of the complete Commonwealth. Now that the concept has been brokered, it has gained a momentum all its own. It is like entering into a burrow that has been slimed. Once you've started downward, there's no stopping until you reach the bottom."

Haflunormet drained the last of his drink. It was nearing time to leave, lest they become too conspicuous. "This will be the cycle that the progeny of our clans will venerate forever."

"*If* our designs are fulfilled." Lyrkenparmew slipped sideways off his bench while Fanielle straightened and stretched. Her back was stiff from sitting so long in one place without any support.

"I suppose I'll be heading back to the plateau in a few days." She checked her comm unit. "They won't be expecting me so early, but no one will question the timing of my return." She smiled wryly. "After all, what right-minded human could stand more than a couple of days of vacation in a place like Daret?"

"We are all of us hoping," Lyrkenparmew commented quietly as they left the table behind and headed for the transport platform, "that it is individuals like yourself who are the right-minded humans."

Reaching out, she momentarily rested the flat of her hand against the back of the envoy's abdomen, feeling his upper set of wing cases vibrate against her palm. "I'm not alone in liking your kind, Lyrkenparmew, and not just for the ever-amazing variety of wonderful fragrances you emit, or for your aid in the Pitarian War. There are plenty of us who are fond of thranx culture, and philosophy, and your way of looking at the universe. It's minds we seek in common, not shapes."

"How fortunate." The widely spaced nerve endings in Lyrkenparmew's exoskeleton conveyed to him the warmth of the barely insulated mammalian flesh. Such a strange sensation it was, to be accompanied by a creature that was little more than a loose sack of fluids wrapped around a barely balanced upright bony framework held together by fragile bonds of stretched protein. That this female's often erratic kind might be the ones to at last put an end to centuries of AAnn depredations was scarce to be believed. Many thranx, in fact, would not believe it.

They would have to be convinced.

17

Conversation in the room was subdued. Skettle let them talk. It helped to relieve the tension. As Nevisrighne and Botha, Pierrot and Davies and the others chatted quietly, the old man looked on with pride. In a stern, paternal fashion he was as proud of them as if they were his real children. Very soon now they would join gloriously together, patriarch and progeny, to sow destruction in order to prevent an onslaught of racial commingling of a kind their virtuous ancestors could never in their wildest dreams have imagined.

Walking over to where Botha was seated poring one last time over his beloved charts, he put a hand on the other man's shoulder. "The special explosives are ready?"

The other man adjusted his multifunction lenses and nodded. "It's a shame we couldn't disguise them the way we did the smaller stuff and just bring them in with us. I'd feel better knowing the full provenance of the ingredients."

"I know. But even a couple of small tanks of highly sensitive reactant would have set off alarms in customs. How fortunate that you and our other equally brilliant technical people have been able to devise a liquid explosive that can be produced from widely available materials."

Botha allowed himself a rare grin. "Catalyzed right here in their own city, too. Anyone reviewing the purchases would think one group was going to mix up some lacquer to paint a house, and the other a few crates of home brew."

"Home brew it is," Skettle replied, "only this blend is not for drinking." He raised his gaze to the far corner of the hotel's reserved and shielded conference room. The pair of trivarium tanks standing upright on the floor near the window—through which they could be hastily chucked in the event of a lightning raid by the authorities—were small, light, exceptionally strong, resistant to the caustic liquids they were originally designed to hold, and of a familiar commercial design that would spark no alarms in the minds of anyone who happened to see them. For all anyone espying them might know, they could easily contain cold-drink concentrate destined for delivery to one of the fair's numerous food concessions.

Skettle would take charge of one, Martine the other, in the unlikely event either of them should be stopped and questioned. The volatile contents of one tank should be more than sufficient to blow the bulk of the fair's central communications facility halfway across City Lake. As a further security precaution, they would take separate routes to the complex. Meeting there, they would then make their way into the facility by a prearranged, rehearsed route. Any security or communications personnel unlucky enough to encounter and query them would be dealt with as necessary.

Once the explosives had been placed and set, the two would join their companions in creating general havoc. Skettle was a tower of tranquility among his associates, some of whom for the first time since they had arrived on Dawn were beginning to exhibit the first understandable symptoms of agitation. Even the righteous, he reflected calmly, could grow nervous on the eve of retribution.

He had boundless confidence in all of them. All of them, men and women alike, had dedicated themselves to the cause of the Preservers. They were here to buy time, to allow humankind to reflect upon the mad course of action a few species traitors were hell-bent on pursuing. By tomorrow evening, the festering pace of human-thranx relations would have come to a crashing halt. By the day after, he and his companions would be safely on their way home, on separate KK-drive ships, able to relax and reflect on the good work they had done.

Yes, some innocent humans would have to die. It was quite possible some of his own people would also perish, although every precaution had been taken to ensure their quiet and successful escape from the zone of carnage they intended to enkindle. These unwitting tourists and visitors would go down as martyrs to the cause of species purity. It would take time, but when humankind finally came to its senses and realized the absurdity as well as the danger of trying to merge with another species, the names of the dead would be remembered gratefully by many millions more than the few relatives who would grieve over their loss next week and next month.

When he raised his hands for quiet, the low buzz of conversation ceased. All eyes—some anxious, some expectant, others alive with the anticipation of the work to come—were on him.

"My friends, my good companions: We stand at the threshold of the greatest calamity mankind has ever experienced. The uneducated and ill-informed gather in mindless herds, ready to be pushed into oblivion by the traitorous politicians and philosophers among them. Shall we who have taken the name Preservers allow this to happen?"

The multitude of murmured "no"s that rose in response to his query were no less bone-chilling for the restraint with which they were ululated.

Skettle's jaws tightened. "Then let us go forth, comrades mine, and once and for all put a stop to this murderous collision course on which the betrayers of our own kind have set us." He smiled at them, and though he was quite unaware of it, it was a smile that would have set young children to running. "And while we are doing so, let us be sure to kill as many worthy people as possible while taking care to spare the visiting bugs."

This last bit of carefully concocted perfidy would serve to further heighten the suspicions of those humans who would rush to investigate the tragedy. There was delicious irony in the knowledge that the ones the Preservers most wanted to kill would, by surviving, serve to impair the cause of their own conciliators. Beskodnebwyl's coworkers would not be so lucky. Skettle had given his colleagues free rein to shoot down as many of them as they could as they made their way clear of the pandemonium. It was the ordinary, bewildered thranx they planned to spare—to suffer the suspicions and outrage of the surviving humans.

As his people began to file out of the room, individually and in pairs so as not to draw the attention of the hotel staff or anyone else to their departure, Skettle paused to glance out the window. Across the great lake, shimmering like a sheet of blue metal in the pellucid morning sunshine, the swooping, soaring structure of the fairgrounds could just be seen in the distance. By this evening, all of it would be in flames, cleansed and deserted, its name become tragedy spread by space-minus communications throughout the civilized portions of the Arm. Walking to the window, he picked up one of the two inauspicious-looking tanks of liquid explosive. Martine had already left with hers.

As the last one out of the conference room, he was careful to close the door behind him. He would make his own separate way to the fair. There he would pause for coffee and a quick meal, his attention on his own synchronized chronometer.

At exactly half past one, it would be time to start killing.

Nordelmatcen, one of the most able among the Bwyl, sidled up next to his clan leader and touched the latter's right antenna with one of his own. Beskodnebwyl turned immediately.

"I don't trust my own chronometer. How long until we induce permanent collapse into this vile burrow?"

Around them, blissfully ignorant humans and thranx alike promenaded to and fro throughout the fairgrounds. They had no reason to glance in the direction of the three thranx who were quietly scrutinizing an exhibition of art especially prepared for the fair by creative talents of both species working in tandem. Nordelmatcen had taken one look at the prancing abominations and dismissed them as obscene. Beskodnebwyl was too indifferent to be similarly enticed.

Had any curious passersby paused to stare in their direction, they might have wondered at the extra layers of external sheathing that enclosed the trio of insectoid males. Given the subtropical climate of the region in which Aurora had been founded, these wrappings might have struck even another thranx as excessive. Closer inspection, had it been allowed, would have revealed that the innermost layer of covering consisted not of finely machined fabric from Drax IV or special lightweight abdominal insulation from the *sythmills* of Amropolus, but of self-propelled explosives and kindred virulent mechanisms.

"Patience," Beskodnebwyl lectured his companions. "The time for dispensing annihilation will come soon enough."

Deimovjenbir whistled his displeasure. "I would have preferred that we proceed with our intended business on our own, without having to rely on, of all things, a group of contemptible if like-minded humans."

Beskodnebwyl gestured to emphasize lofty thoughts. "But it is the fact that they are like-minded that compels us to restrain ourselves. If we can make use of some of the soft ones to triple the amount of chaos we can create, should we not do so?"

"I did not say that." With a series of deep clicks, Deimovjenbir mimicked a disapproving human grumble.

"The humans of Skettle—I have still not been able to decide if that is properly a family or clan designation—are convinced they are making use of us. We feel the opposite is true. None of which matters. What is important is the result. It doesn't matter if the humans blame the thranx or the thranx blame the humans. What is meaningful is that blame is ascribed." He gestured with a truhand. "Are you ready to kill some artists?"

"I am ready to kill anything that thinks it controls the destiny of my hive. Artist, worker, prognosticator, musician, scientist—occupation is unimportant. What matters is that we stop this unclean mixing before it has a chance to fuse." Reaching back with a foothand, he caressed a brace of the self-propelled explosives that were bound to his abdomen. "I am anxious to spread the flowers of destruction."

"Soon." Beskodnebwyl checked his own chronometer. "Within the current major time-part." Slipping a foothand into a thorax pouch, he removed a communicator. Holding it in all four fingers, he used a truhand to activate the compact device. "Time to make certain everyone else is in position." Addressing the pickup softly, he called to the team of Vedburankex and Hynwupletmer.

There was no answer.

He tried again, with the same result. Nordelmatcen's attention was still concentrated on the swirling, cheerful crowd. "Trouble with their units. Perhaps they are in a location that restricts short-range, closed-beam communications. Try Yiwespembor and Cuwenarfot."

Beskodnebwyl did so, to another nonresponse. "Possibly there is something wrong with my unit." He extended a truhand. "Let me have yours."

Nordelmatcen obediently passed over his own communicator. Beskodnebwyl first tried Vedburankex and Hynwupletmur again, only to be rewarded with the same pensive electronic silence. It was the same for Yiwespembor and Cuwenarfot, who were supposed to be milling about among the largest of the eating pavilions that had been built out into the shallows of the lake. If they were in position, as they ought to already have been for several time-parts, there should be nothing around to interfere with the receptiveness of their communicators.

Growing increasingly concerned, Beskodnebwyl proceeded to try to contact every one of the widely scattered armed teams. It quickly became apparent that the rest of the Bwyl either could not or would not respond. As for the possibility that Nordelmatcen's as well as his own communicator was defective, that was a likelihood so unreasonable as to be beneath consideration. Designed to take a lot of mistreatment, field communicators simply did not fail. The thought that two could falter in such close proximity to one another was not to be believed. Beskodnebwyl did not even bother to try Deimovjenbir's unit.

They were standing on a raised platform that wound its way through the interspecies exhibition of art. While it was conceivable that some of the larger sculptures might block communication to and from the east, there was nothing to divert beams being broadcast in the other three directions. Searching for an explanation, Beskodnebwyl could conceive of none.

Then Nordelmatcen was striving to suppress an instinctive stridulation as he tapped his mentor on the thorax and pointed sharply.

Beskodnebwyl recognized the strike team that was walking rapidly toward the art exhibit. They had just appeared inside one of the entrances on the far side of the pavilion. Sujbirwencex and Waspulnatun were looking around more than was necessary, and their antennae were positively dancing. There appeared to be nothing wrong with them, either physically or mentally. For the first time since he had started scanning, Beskodnebwyl received an acknowledgment in response to his query signal.

He was about to ask if the recently arrived team members were having similar difficulties contacting other members of the group when Sujbirwencex and Waspulnatun were abruptly swarmed by a collapsing ring of humans and thranx. Shocked by the swiftness of the maneuver, Beskodnebwyl could only stare, one finger still on the *send* contact of his communicator. It was as if a portion of the milling crowd had collapsed on top of the stunned pair. Neither had a chance to fire a shot in their own defense, or even unlimber one of the many weapons they carried. One time-part fraction they had been making straight for Beskodnebwyl and Nordelmatcen; the next, both were in custody and in the process of being disarmed.

Deimovjenbir benefited from a slightly different perspective on the calamity. "Sujbirwencex and Waspulnatun have both been immobilized. Whether by fume, shock, or other means I cannot say, but both are now lying on their sides and offering no resistance."

Beskodnebwyl's colleague was not quite right. As the three dismayed thranx looked on, Sujbirwencex managed to wrest free a small hand weapon not yet confiscated by her attackers. She was immediately swarmed, but not before she succeeded in getting off at least one shot. A few nearby wanderers looked on in shock as the explosive shell blew one human patroller in half. In response, the downed Sujbirwencex received half a dozen blasts of varying intensity from at least three different kinds of weapons. The ferocious counterattack left little behind suitable for future identification.

From the brief but lethal confrontation nary a sound was heard.

"Silencing sphere," Nordelmatcen clicked unnecessarily. Whoever had ambushed the two Bwyl carried equipment to ensure that whatever else resulted from any confrontations and challenges, crowd panic would not be among them. The throng of sightseers had been effectively and efficiently shielded from the unsettling sounds of violent verbal and physical combat. One human and one Bwyl lay dead on the pavilion floor, but only those visitors who had been close enough to observe the challenge directly had any inkling that anything untoward had taken place in their midst. It was all very slick and masterful. The actions of the ambushers smacked of extensive training and ample rehearsal.

They suggested, inescapably, the participation of skilled professionals.

Deimovjenbir moved to discard his unnecessary outer garb, the better to access his firepower. "We have been betrayed! The burrow where we have stored our secrets has been breached!"

"No." Though he disagreed with his clan mate's appraisal of the situation, Beskodnebwyl was also scrambling to unlimber his weapons. "The Skettle folk would not do that. Revealing us would gain them nothing, since the first Bwyl to be captured would immediately expose them in turn."

Deimovjenbir almost had the streamlined launcher free and ready to lock in position on Nordelmatcen's back, where it could be clipped firmly to the other thranx's wing cases to provide an excellent mobile firing platform.

"But someone *has* delivered us up to the Dawn authorities. I cannot envision who. Somehow, somewhere, there must have been a fault in our planning. We will locate it, however."

"*Srrillp!* Yes we will!" Nordelmatcen avowed. He was fully

alert now, alive with anticipation as he prepared to join his honored mentor in blowing the adulterated physical arts pavilion to splinters. "There is no reason to wait any longer to begin what we came for."

"No, *crr!!t*!" Deimovjenbir slipped a compressed charge into the launcher now resting securely on his colleague's back.

He was preparing to activate the firing sequence when a pair of very small shells composed almost entirely of radioactively neutral depleted uranium passed through his head, entering via the left compound eye and exiting at the back of the skull. Barely slowed by the organic contact, they continued onward to pierce the wall of the pavilion and eventually fall harmlessly into the lake. Slowly, the four trulegs of the Bwyl gave way in response to an absence of instructions from their controlling cerebrum, and the gleaming blue-green body slumped to the floor. The extended truhand never came closer than half a meter to the firing mechanism of the launcher fixed to Nordelmatcen's back.

Emitting the sharpest, most piercing whistle of which he was capable, Nordelmatcen sprang forward on all four trulegs, firing a pair of hand weapons as he leaped. Undeadened by a silencing sphere, the racket his firearms made was as loud as the death of his friend and colleague had been comparatively silent. Humans scattered and let out satisfying screams. Less prone to panic, adult and adolescent thranx nonetheless broke out in alarmed clicks and stridulations, adding to the general confusion. Meanwhile, Beskodnebwyl used the diversion to force his way in the opposite direction, finding a path through the forest of sculptures. Human, thranx, and jointly conceived alike, the towering works of art seemed to be leering down at him. Or worse, laughing.

The ensuing uproar lasted less than a couple of minutes. Firing madly, Nordelmatcen brought down one human and one thranx patroller before he was obliterated in a hail of gunfire as lethal as it was diverse. Alert for any surprises, such as booby-trapped internal organs, plainclothes police surrounded the shattered remnants of the insectoid terrorist. One kicked at the badly burned head, which had been separated from the rest of the body.

"Stupid bug—pardon, thranx—bastard. What are they trying to accomplish with all this?"

His female companion made a disgusted sound in her throat, behind her face shield. "We'll know when the psychs get to the live ones and their human cronies who've already been taken into custody." Raising her gaze, she stared hard at the raised walkway from which the dead thranx had leaped. "There's another dead one up there. I thought I saw three."

Her comrade pushed at the back of his slightly too-tight helmet. "Dunno. Must've just been the two. We've been mostly picking 'em up in twos."

"I guess you're right." It was her turn to nudge the black-streaked insectoid head with a booted foot. "Funny how the color drains out of the eyes when they die. Their equivalent of a human closing her lids, I guess."

Her fellow officer shrugged. "Dead is dead. Me, I leave the dirty details to the biologists." He brightened slightly. "Hey, you ought to join me and Vermenyarkex one night."

"Why? Is there such a thing as a thranx strip club?" she replied dryly.

"I wouldn't know." Her partner looked hurt. "He said something about sharing some special hi-ups that work equally well on both our metabolisms."

"Oh, that's different, then." Holstering her pistol in its hidden compartment inside her casual tropical blouse, she turned to rejoin the rest of the covert patrol. "Let's make sure we've got the rest of this mess cleaned up, first."

Lawlor and Rabukanu were getting nervous. Everything had gone according to plan: their arrival at the fair, the gradual dispersal of the group, the casual stroll to their assigned position. No one had contested their entrance or challenged their presence. Uniformed security personnel had ignored them, treating them like any other visitors. They had followed a memorized, circuitous route to the Pavilion of Cooperative Science and remained there, wandering through and about the exhibits until they were as sick of each and every one as they were of the unrestrained fraternizing of thranx and human tourists. Still, they waited. And waited.

They continued to wait, but with a growing sense of unease long months of training could no longer dispel. Around them, the crowds thickened. There was no indication anything was amiss at the fair.

Then Rabukanu frowned and pointed. "Isn't that Botha and Marion?"

Lawlor strained to see past a drifting tactile holo that was entertaining a clutch of delighted, laughing children. A pair of adolescent thranx, their blue-green exoskeletons jewel-like with the freshness of recent emergence from pupahood, looked on in silence, striving to puzzle out the attraction the yellow-and-pink electronic apparition held for their human counterparts.

A well-dressed—indeed, overdressed—middle-aged couple had just entered the far side of this quadrant of the extensive pavilion. Their constant glancing to right and left betrayed no ulterior motives: Striving to see everything at once was a common affliction among fairgoers. Then Marion happened to meet Lawlor's distant glance. Despite the range, she stared fixedly in his direction, as if trying to impart a question through sheer force of expression.

"It's them, for sure." Lawlor blinked. "What are they doing in here? They're supposed to be working the health and gengineering displays."

"She looks confused." At a distance, Rabukanu's eyesight was slightly sharper than that of his companion. "Maybe you were right when you wondered a few minutes ago if something's gone wrong."

"What about Botha?" After Skettle, the engineer was the most admired member of the group.

Rabukanu fought to see through the noisy, milling throng. "Hard to say. He never looks confused."

"Well, something must be up for them to vacate their position." Lawlor checked his timer. "Elkannah's late."

The other man did not bother to corroborate. "There's still

plenty of time. More accurate to say that he's not early. Maybe he and Martine had to take a more roundabout route to the communications center. Maybe they were delayed. It's plenty early. Relax."

"Yar, surely I'll relax." Beneath his lightweight tropical jacket, strips of explosive material vied for room with a brace of exceedingly stylized pistols. The pockets of his pants held handfuls of tacnites. He forbore from sarcastically pointing out to his companion that neither of them had come dressed for leisure. "What are they doing?"

"Still coming this way." The more laid-back Rabukanu shrugged. "Maybe they just want to kill a few minutes." He wore the unpleasant, sadistic smile of a schoolteacher who enjoys humiliating his students. "As opposed to bugs. Or maybe something's rendered their assigned position untenable. You know that if that happens we're supposed to join up and share locations. A number of possible developments might have forced them to make a move."

Lawlor scanned the eddying herd of sightseers. "Yar, you're right." He could not repress another quick glance at his timer. "I just wish Elkannah would do the communications facilities so we can get to work."

"Itchy to lay down a little arson?" Rabukanu's smile vanished. "Me, too. Know what a fried bug smells like?"

Lawlor did not reply. Rabukanu had an irritating tendency to repeat himself. It was an old joke among the group, and he didn't need any distractions right now. Instead, he focused on their approaching collaborators, still wondering what had driven them to abandon their assigned location. Rabukanu's appraisal of the situation had been reassuring, but a lingering concern continued to nag at him.

It all happened so fast he hardly had time to react. One minute, their compatriots were strolling toward them; the next, they had been smothered by more than a dozen tourists. Men, women, even a couple of teenage girls. Except they were not tourists. Coagulating restraints glued Marion's fingers together and her hands to her sides, rendering her immediately helpless. Botha managed to retreat a couple of steps before a shaped shot of soporific mist splashed his wide-eyed face. One sniff, and he collapsed like a broken doll. Moving with far more athletic grace and digital dexterity than any dozen tourists could muster, the party of plainclothes agents wrapped up the two terrorists as efficiently as a swarm of communal arachnids enwebbing a trapped moth.

Lawlor stood frozen where he had been standing. "How did they know? *How did they know?*"

Once more it was left to the sharp-eyed Rabukanu to explain what was happening. "Weapons sensors. I think I can see the bulge of one under one woman's jacket." He smiled faintly. "I thought she was awfully well equipped, but I had no clue. Funny—if we were all carrying nothing but the components of the explosives, the sensor probably wouldn't pick anything up. Elkannah erred on that one."

Lawlor found himself disagreeing as he reached inside his shirt and brought out the three-thirds of an explosive whole. "We can't wait for him and Martine anymore. We can't wait for anyone." His eyes were blazing in advance of the fires he was preparing to set.

His companion looked at him in alarm. "Hey, we can't start anything on our own! You know the rules. In the event of a general breakdown in planning, we're supposed to dispose of our materials and make our way out of here and offworld, so we can strike again later somewhere else."

"Distractions of evil. Suck bug blood!" Lawlor was backing away from his colleague. "I didn't spend a year busting my brain and my butt in training just to walk away from this." Pressing the three sections of the explosive components together, he slapped the resultant compaction against a nearby pillar and doused it with catalytic fluid. The three-centimeter square instantly began emitting smoke. Reaching inside his jacket, he used one hand to draw a pistol while the other fumbled frantically for more squares. While his words had been frenzied, his expression fully reflected his inner zealotry. Catching sight of the pistol, nearby visitors screamed and ducked or ran for cover.

With a curse, Rabukanu saw that several of the agents who

had taken Botha and Marion down were now looking in his direction, pointing and jabbering excitedly. They'd probably already recorded his image, he thought helplessly. For better or worse, the decision to *act* had been made. He hoped Skettle would not be too upset. Maybe it would turn out to be a good thing. Time *was* running.

As the wild-eyed Lawlor stumbled away from him, Rabukanu started digging for his own carefully stored essentials. If they could just set off one or more detonations, they might have a chance to slip away unscathed in the ensuing turmoil. Already, there were indications of general panic among those tourists who were close enough to see what was happening.

The catalyst would take several minutes to fully bind the tripartite ingredients into an explosive whole. The delay was intended to allow those planting the devices enough time to escape the blast zone, but not enough for possible searchers to find the weapon.

If only, Rabukanu thought as he prepared a second explosive patch, Skettle could take out the central communications facilities, the general chaos and destruction they had come to Dawn to wreak would manifest itself fully, to the greater glory and preservation of an unadulterated humankind. Fired with the devotion that had led him to give his life to Elkannah Skettle and to the Preservers, he prepared to apply the explosive patch to an exterior wall of the pavilion. Around him, humans and a few thranx continued to scatter. Their screams and stridulations melted together into a dull ache at the back of his mind.

As if from far away, he heard Lawlor alternately howling defiance at the onrushing agents and spewing frantic warnings into his communicator. Probably trying to alert the others, Rabukanu knew. The crisp electric *spang* of the other man's pistol going off penetrated the general tumult like a sore-throated trumpet criticizing a balm of violins. Then he smelled something sweet as chocolate and stifling as a pillow. Reaching for a single tacnite, he managed to drag a stiffening thumb down the short length of the electronic trigger.

The powerful little grenade was still clutched firmly in his fingers when it went off.

As Lawlor's crazed, bloodthirsty alert was received by those of his fellow Preservers who were still at large, they quickly came to the shocked realization that their purpose and presence had somehow been exposed to the authorities. One couple was taken into custody even as they were preoccupied with listening to the broadcast. Another pair were debating whether to try to flee the grounds or proceed with their assignment when they were enveloped by a sphere of silence and a strong dose of the same immobilizing gas that had toppled their comrade Rabukanu.

Several, however, were able to set in motion fire and destruction, albeit on a greatly degraded scale. Having heavily infiltrated the fairgrounds in response to the padres' advance warning, well-prepared local police equipped with sensitive weapons sensors were able to pounce on the perpetrators even before they could reveal themselves. Those few disturbances that did occur were localized, explosive appliqués that were neutralized before they could go off, and there was no widespread panic among the fair-goers. In the midst of rounding up the last of the terrorists and their even more baffled thranx counterparts the Bwyl, fair business proceeded as usual.

Beskodnebwyl's two companions had reacted sharply to the approach of the human and thranx agents. In the ensuing firefight, both had been slain before they could make use of the heavy explosives they were carrying. The consequent confusion had opened an almost imperceptible escape route for Beskodnebwyl, who had seized upon it the instant it had revealed itself.

Now he found himself staggering through a service corridor, surrounded by the portentous hum of machinery, bleeding green from one side. Both his left truarm and foothand had been shot off, and he had only barely been able to slap a brace of traumagulents over the gushing injuries, followed by strips of self-adhering surgical chitin. Much more running threatened to reopen the life-threatening wounds. If he was not to bleed to death, he needed to seek medical attention soon.

Not a problem, he told himself sardonically as he skittered along down the dark, conduit-strewn tunnel. He found comfort in its shadowy confines, a reminder of more congenial burrows back home. All he had to do was present himself at the nearest medical facility in Dawn, and they would fix him up. Him, a thranx, obviously damaged by weaponry, on a day when the most important public activity on the planet had been rent by a fusillade of gunfire. Not a problem at all.

It was over, all over. Everything he and the rest of the Bwyl had worked so long and hard to achieve. Finished. When the mostly human authorities had begun taking his compeers into custody, he had at first been bewildered, then frustrated. That had long since given way to anger. Though the Bwyl's human counterparts were also being killed or captured, it was clear that somehow, the local authorities had been alerted to their mutual presence and intent. Who would do such a thing, and why? Not one of the Bwyl. There were no traitors among his dedicated, adoptive clan.

No, *crr!!k*, it had to be someone with a thorough knowledge of the overall strategy, someone who had access to both the Preservers and the Protectors as well as the authorities. Someone who could be sure of a favorable, even laudatory reception among the species traitors on both sides. Who? Who had not yet been slain, or captured? Who had the wherewithal to call forth such a general alert, and to possibly profit from it?

Skettle.

His now-deceased companions had been right to challenge his initial disbelief. Weakened but resolved, Beskodnebwyl of the Bwyl knew he had one last duty to carry out before he could begin to devote any time to the admittedly increasingly remote possibility of preserving his own life.

18

In the short time people had spent on Comagrave, much progress had been made in deciphering the elegant, elaborately ideographic Sauun script, though much remained to be done before complex thoughts could be translated in detail. The discovery of the gigantic mausoleum offered up thousands of new inscriptions for study. Meanwhile, researchers utilizing the camp's two smallest aircars undertook to carry out a preliminary census of the silent sleepers. Preparing a simple mathematical model based on dimensions and density observed within one sizable portion of the crypt, they came up with an initial figure of between two and five billions. If not the entire planetary population at the time of final suspension, it was certainly a substantial portion of the total. And over every new discovery, over each new revelation, hung one single foreboding, dominating question.

Why?

Though he had been nominated to lead the expedition and oversee the excavation because of his organizational and leadership skills, Cullen Karasi was also a formidable analyst. Poring over raw data, dissecting and repositioning with the aid of several exoarcheoanalytical programs he had helped develop himself, he felt the key to the mystery of the mass Sauun deepsleep was not nearly as problematic as initially believed. Given sufficient time in which to work, he was confident he would have solved it already. But the need to supervise everyone else's labor slowed his own efforts significantly. He felt like a sprinter forced to muddle along in the middle of the pack during an especially dull marathon.

Even so, he was close to the answer. He knew it.

So when Riimadu volunteered the unpaid assistance of a professional, well-trained crew of excavators, Cullen jumped at the offer. Though some of his own people expressed hesitation at allowing the AAnn an intimate look at the work in progress, Riimadu assured them that the crew would operate entirely under human supervision and would strictly follow camp regulations. Furthermore, they would do no work on their own or without first obtaining human authorization. Besides which, there were only four of them. Eager to make as much progress as possible as quickly as possible, the humans' initial uncertainty quickly vanished when they had the chance to observe the AAnn team in operation.

As for Pilwondepat's vociferous objections to the presence of still more AAnn at the site, these were dismissed as without foundation. "I'd be just as happy to have four, or forty, trained thranx assisting here, if they were made available and were willing to work under the same guidelines," Cullen told him. Needless to say, the thranx exoarcheologist was less than delighted with this response, but there was nothing more he could do.

With the aid of the skilled AAnn, exploration proceeded apace. Results were passed along on a regular schedule to planetary administrative headquarters. There they were compiled for forwarding to the specific Terran institutions that were supporting the dig. Everything was going so smoothly that when Cullen's people began to fall sick around him, coughing and breaking out in red blotches on their faces and upper bodies, he was particularly anguished. The more everyone else's work suffered, the more it slowed his own.

Bhasiram, the camp physician, diagnosed the rapidly spreading contagion as an upper respiratory disease caused by exceedingly fine spores arising from the excavation. Dust masks were of no use. Nothing in her arsenal of antibiotics had any effect on the condition, which one camp wag christened "Sauunusitus." While not fatal, it was exceedingly debilitating and beyond the frustrated Bhasiram's ability to cure. Hospitalization was required to restore the strength of the afflicted. Pilwon-depat and the AAnn were not affected.

It was clear that work at the dig could not go on until a cure, or at least a suitable prophylactic, was found for the spores. Working in sealed masks and breathing canned air was a possibility, but the necessary equipment was not available on Comagrave and would have to be imported. Neither solution was satisfactory. It was therefore proposed that the AAnn, who were by now familiar with the site, would remain to maintain it without in any way advancing the work until their human supervisors could safely return. Though they ex-pressed sorrow at the need for the humans to temporarily leave the dig, the AAnn agreed to care for it in their transitory absence. Riimadu CRRYNN would stay behind to oversee. In the absence of any immediate availability of human vehi-cles, the AAnn also thoughtfully offered to bring in several of their largest cargo carriers to ferry the afflicted and their as-yet-uninfected companions on the long journey back to Comabraeth.

As soon as he got wind of the proposal, Pilwondepat stormed into Cullen's quarters. It required a considerable effort on the thranx's part not to stridulate wildly as he entered. Even so, with antennae waving and mandibles clacking, he still pre-sented a highly agitated figure. An insectophobe would have been intimidated. The head of the excavation team was not.

"Something I can do for you, Pilwondepat?" Cullen in-quired pleasantly. Though he had not yet succumbed to the insidious spores, the noticeable splotch of scarlet that marred his left cheek was not a blush.

"Do for me? Do for me! *Crllhht!*" The need to speak in Ter-ranglo forced the insectoid exoarcheologist to keep his thoughts as well as his words under control. "I can't believe you are going to turn this unprecedented scientific discovery over to the AAnn!"

"We are not turning over anything to the AAnn." Having previously experienced the thranx's ire, Cullen was not dis-turbed by Pilwondepat's latest outburst. The supervisor knew it was merely the latest in a long series of attempts to freeze

Riimadu out of the ongoing research. "Since arriving to assist us, they have conducted themselves in an exemplary manner. They've done exactly as they were told, and no more. Would that I had another dozen humans on staff who took instructions as well."

"That is precisely my point." Antennae whipped forward. "Don't you remember any of our discussions? Have you forgotten all that I've told you about AAnn methodology and technique? They rely foremost on cunning, and deception." Both antennae straightened. "It's patent they have certainly deceived you."

Cullen's civility gave way to annoyance. "Until and unless they act in a nonprofessional manner, neither I nor any of my people have any quarrel with them." He continued packing away his personal effects. These would remain behind until he returned from Comabraeth, properly equipped to work among the drifting spores. "Other than academically, I'm not interested in the personal animosities that endure between your people and Riimadu's. You're both of you here thanks to the magnanimity of the local government." Setting aside a container of clothing, he added pointedly, "That permission can be withdrawn at any time."

Pilwondepat brushed off the quiet threat. "Would you say that infecting you and every member of your team with imported bacteria designed to drive you away from the site constituted acting in a nonprofessional manner?"

Cullen gaped. "You're joking, aren't you?"

"Do I sound like I am jesting? Do I look like I am jesting?"

"I wouldn't know, not being versed in the more subtle overtones of thranx enunciation and gesture. You can't be serious, Pilwondepat."

The thranx exoarcheologist raised all four of his vestigial wing cases. Another thranx would have recognized the action as expressive of the absolute utmost seriousness. To Cullen, it was unfortunately only interesting from a morphological point of view.

"Do you really think I would joke about such a thing? What has happened here, to this expedition, fits with all that I have been telling you for many time-parts. The AAnn want your kind off this world. To accomplish that they are willing to do anything and everything to obstruct, inhibit, and damage your efforts here. Even, should it prove necessary, to kill. These incidents are disguised, with typical AAnn cunning and thoroughness, as accidents. When they occur, the AAnn are always right there ready to assist in any way they can." He paused, clicking all four mandibles for effect.

"Consider, Cullen: You make a great discovery here. Word of what you have found begins to leak out. Following the breakthrough and initial follow-up, your crew begins to come down with a previously undetected ailment. Only nonhumans are resistant. How convenient for the AAnn."

"We're not abandoning the site," the human reminded his visitor. "Our departure is only temporary, until suitable protection can be secured against the vector of infection." He continued with his packing, wishing the thranx would leave but unwilling to order him out. Let him rant, the exoarcheologist mused. Soon enough he'll run down and depart of his own accord.

" 'Temporary,' *z!!lnn!* While you are absent from this place, the AAnn will go through it with an intensity they have so far barely managed to hold in check. Anything of significance that they find, they will keep to themselves. Most likely they have prepared other surprises, to keep you away from specific areas below or even from the surface itself, until they have accomplished all that they wish. Leave now, and your absence from the site will be as 'temporary' as the AAnn desire."

Unable to stand it any longer, Cullen put his packing aside and turned to confront the agitated thranx. "Look, you've been bugging me"—the choice of verb was inadvertent on the exoarcheologist's part—"with your AAnn conspiracy theories for weeks now. I said I would convey your concerns and your 'findings' to the proper authorities for further study, and that I'll do. But as for myself, I'm sick and tired of it, understand? From now on, you keep your suspicions and your racial enmity to yourself." He grunted testily. "As if I didn't have enough to worry about."

"They'll drive you off the planet." Pilwondepat gestured desperately with all four hands. "This is only one more in a long succession of incidents cleverly designed by them with that end in mind. You must resist! And you must not give them free and unsupervised access to this site. It is simply too significant."

"And you are simply too paranoid." Fed up, Cullen turned his back on the distraught alien. Among the thranx, he knew, the gesture was even more final a form of dismissal than it was among humans.

Remarkably, Pilwondepat persisted. "Then you will not order an end to the evacuation, or at least assign a few of your healthiest people to remain until the rest can return?"

"Absolutely not." Resuming his packing, Cullen did not look back at the thranx. "I won't trifle with the health of my staff, and I have confidence in Riimadu. You forget that I've worked with him even longer than I have worked with you."

"Very well. I understand your position. I will trouble you about this matter no more."

When he finally looked around, Cullen saw that the thranx had left. It was sad, he reflected, that two such admirable species as the thranx and the AAnn could not settle such long-standing differences. That could not be allowed to affect either human-thranx or human-AAnn relations, he knew. " 'Drive humans off the planet.' " The exoarcheologist might not be politically sophisticated, but he could recognize blatant propaganda when he heard it. He also knew what the insectoid's most recent visit was really all about.

Pilwondepat was afraid to remain behind in the company of five AAnn. That fear, at least, was one that Cullen could accept. The thranx was welcome to join the humans in their evacuation to Comabraeth. It would give the insectoid exoarcheologist time to collate his own research.

All the rest of that day and into the night, Pilwondepat agonized over how to proceed. The AAnn and their transports would arrive tomorrow morning. What, after all, could he do to affect things in the limited time that remained? He was but one of the family Won set down among many humans and AAnn. If the leader of the humans would not listen to him, it did not matter if anyone else did. He could envision Riimadu, grinning contentedly, his sharp carnivore's teeth glinting in the bright light of his quarters as he finalized strategy with his quartet of "well-trained" colleagues. Who among them had brought along and introduced the carefully cultivated spores into the excavation, there to fester and multiply and spread until the unsuspecting mammals were infected? What vital, important secrets had Riimadu inventoried that were to be accrued to the AAnn alone as soon as the overseeing humans had been evacuated? Isolated in his quarters, Pilwondepat sensed threat and smelled danger.

Very well—he was alone. Like a solitary male of ancient days, soaring high on his single glorious but brief mating flight, he would have to act. If he did not, others would, and his flight would be wasted. In response to a muted mandibular click, a chronometer appeared briefly before him in the hot, humid air of the room. He considered his options.

There was still time.

Along with everyone else in the camp except the seriously ailing, he was up early the following morning. Despite a lack of sleep due to undertaking the task he had set himself, he was alert and observant. He would sleep later, he knew. Sleep soundly.

Activity was picking up throughout the site as the evacuation gathered steam. Those too ill to walk were being assembled beneath a temporary field canopy that had been erected to protect them from the wind and the sun. Nonmedical personnel not assisting with the infirm were stacking individual baggage next to the landing area's service shed. These were minimal, since everyone fully expected to return to work as soon as an appropriate treatment for the mysterious ailment was devised. No one would bother personal effects left in the camp. Not out in the middle of a place that ranked as nowhere even for a world as sparsely populated as Comagrave.

Pilwondepat took in all the activity, occasionally pausing to converse briefly with members of the staff he knew. He tried not to envision the dig where he and everyone else had worked so hard to make the great discovery overrun with gimlet-eyed AAnn.

He found Cullen Karasi in his quarters, packing a small travel bag with the trivialities that humans seemed to deem necessary for even short-term travel. Idly, he wasted a couple of moments attempting to identify the unfamiliar. The function of many of the devices was known to him by now. His time spent among the mammals had expanded his education.

"I came to ask you one last time to change your mind, *cirraat*."

The supervisor glanced back and down at the hovering thranx. "Listen, I'm sorry about the tone I used with you yesterday, Pilwondepat. I was tired, and frustrated, and yes, angry. But not at you. At having to leave this place just when I feel I'm on the verge of answering the biggest question of them all."

"Why the Sauun sealed themselves away the way they did."

Cullen nodded. "I'll lay out my hypothesis for you when we're back in Comabraeth. I think you'll find it interesting." His thoughts wandered to distant visions of academic glory and professional acclaim. "I promise that everyone will find it interesting. But there's no time now. According to Riimadu, the AAnn transports will be here any minute."

" 'According to Riimadu.' I'm not going back to Comabraeth, Cullen."

Curious, the senior exoarchaeologist frowned at his visitor. "You're not? I know that, to all intents and purposes and everything the medical people have been able to determine, your kind is immune to this infection. And I can understand your not wanting to leave your work if you don't have to. But I don't see you being very comfortable staying here among Riimadu and the rest of the AAnn conservation staff."

"You're correct. I would not be comfortable. But neither

am I going to the settlement." Without hurry, he reached back into the pouch slung against his abdomen. "Nor are you."

Cullen Karasi was not a man easily startled. He had spent too much time on other worlds, working and surviving in alien environments, to be surprised by much of anything. The gun that had appeared in the thranx exoarcheologist's right truhand surprised him. No, he corrected himself. It astonished him.

He was too dumbfounded to be frightened. "So that is what happens when a thranx loses its mind. Very interesting. My first observation is that your people go about slipping into the pool of insanity more peacefully than do mine."

"I am not psychotic. I was awake all last night, and though tired, I assure you I am in complete command of my mental and physical faculties. Would, *sevvakk*, that it were otherwise."

Placing his hands on his hips and tilting his head slightly to one side, the unruffled scientist regarded his weapon-wielding caller. "What do you intend to do with that firearm? It is a firearm, I presume, and not an ingredient in some eccentric thranx ritual of which I am unaware?"

A steady thrumming noise was now audible off to the east. It grew steadily louder, heralding its approach with a deep, mechanical hum. Gazing past his deranged visitant, Cullen tried to see out the partially open doorway to the distant landing site.

"That's our transportation arriving. Go or stay, I don't care, but make up your mind. And put down that silly gun. I know everyone carries something when they travel outside camp boundaries to protect themselves in the unlikely but possible event of attack by one of the local inimical life-forms, but it hardly becomes your academic standing."

"I'm staying." Mandibles closed, and a soft whistle emerged from between flinty insectoid jaws. "So are you. Everyone is staying."

Cullen inhaled deeply. "You realize that after this, there's no way I can in good conscience recommend extending your permit to work here?"

"Of course I understand. If our situations were reversed, I should act in exactly the same fashion." The thrum of heavy transports now permeated the walls and floor of the prefabricated structure. "The point is, as you humans are fond of saying, moot." He repeated the word, savoring it. "Moot." With a small *c!k* on the end, it could almost be a word in Low Thranx. "It is moot because of the pending AAnn attack on your camp here."

Cullen's pitying aloofness quickly gave ground to sudden anxiety. "What kind of nonsense are you talking? What AAnn attack? The AAnn are here to help us travel to Comabraeth. Why on Earth or any other world of your choosing would they want to attack an inoffensive, nonstrategic scientific site?"

Pilwondepat waved the gun with disarming indifference as to his surroundings. "Why indeed? I am certain that very question is going to puzzle many who will try to rationalize what is going to happen here. It would be interesting to be able to examine some of the explanations. Unfortunately, that will in all likelihood not be possible."

The senior exoarcheologist's gaze narrowed sharply. "What do you mean, 'what *is* going to happen here'? What do you know?" Dawning realization began to transform his expression. Color drained from his face. "Good God, Pilwondepat—*what have you done?*"

The thranx gestured a first-degree expression of regret. It was heartfelt, and very lissomely executed. "I believe too strongly in the importance of this discovery to allow it to be turned over to the AAnn. I am convinced, without having to hear your nascent theory, that something on this world holds the key to matters of very great consequence. Too consequential to leave to the discretion of the scaled ones. Casting about for a means with which to ensure the continuation of the human presence on Comagrave and the possible expulsion of the AAnn, I find myself caught in a noteworthy irony: To secure both, I must make use of the techniques of the latter."

The explosion that punctuated the thranx scientist's somewhat cryptic explanation caused the shelter to shudder on its foundation. Cullen had to catch himself on a nearby cabinet to keep from stumbling as the earth heaved beneath him. Standing firm and foursquare on his quartet of trulegs, Pilwondepat experienced no such unsteadiness.

"That was satisfyingly loud," he murmured softly. "More substantial than I had hoped."

"What? What are you jabbering about?"

"The first AAnn cargo carrier attempting to set down at the camp's landing site has been fired upon by the site's occupants. A shocking and unprovoked attack. The AAnn will react instinctively. Among the AAnn, this takes the form not of query or discussion, but of returning fire immediately. Having been attacked in turn, your people will struggle as best they can to defend themselves. They will fail, of course." He spoke so casually, so diffidently, that he might have been relating a minor point of relic dating taken from a recent learned journal.

"The AAnn are used to and expect conflict. Your staff here is drawn from scholars and students, not soldiers. They will all be killed. The only chance the AAnn will have to explain away the frightful misadventure depends on there being no human survivors to contradict whatever feeble story they will strive to contrive." He gestured again with the gun, making Cullen flinch. "It doesn't matter. Whatever fiction they fabricate will not be believed by your people."

"How . . . ?" Cullen was struggling desperately to understand what was happening around him. The first explosion had been followed by a second of lesser magnitude, then a third. Shouts and screams in abundance could be heard echoing throughout the camp. "How can you be so sure of that? If we all die . . ."

"I programmed my own communications unit to transmit an alert via the camp's automatic relay. It contains a full explanation of the treacherous assault by the AAnn, which they have carried out under cover of evacuating innocent personnel to Comabraeth."

"What if they intercept it?" By now Cullen was too dazed to question anything but the abject reality he was experiencing.

"They can't intercept. The alert was programmed to send as soon as the AAnn transports were detected approaching. It has already gone out."

"Those explosions—can they really be firing on us?" Once more, the exoarcheologist tried to see out the door. Cries of confusion and despair filled the air outside with a general disharmony of desperation.

Pilwondepat's sensitive antennae had twisted about to focus directly behind him. "Not at first. They are now. I told you I did not sleep last night. The last two detonations you heard were simple excavation charges, creatively positioned and designed to go off subsequent to the first. That one required a good deal more effort to get right. Shaped disinterring charges are not intended to be retrofitted with proximity programming. It took several time-parts to modify the instrumentation to where I was reasonably certain it would operate properly.

"The first vehicle attempting to set down at the landing site activated the sensor attached to the charge. Though not as suitable as military munitions, I suspect that the ensuing blast destroyed or damaged the alighting AAnn cargo carrier and killed or seriously injured many if not all of its occupants. *Triillc,* I certainly hope so."

Wide-eyed now, but no longer with disbelief, Cullen started to push past his former colleague. "You *are* insane. You'd have everyone murdered, people you've come to know, people who have learned to trust and even like you, just because you want the AAnn off this world!"

"And humans to remain on it. Yes, that's the intention. There are matters of significance at stake here, Cullen."

"Well, it won't work." The furious supervisor was almost to the doorway. "There's still time to put a stop to this madness. I'm going to find Riimadu. Together, we'll get on the camp communicator and issue a statement on all frequencies explaining what has happened. With Riimadu translating, I'm sure we can make the rest of the AAnn understand."

"No, you won't." The muzzle of the gun in Pilwondepat's truhand shifted slightly to the right.

Cullen glared pityingly back at the ludicrous insectoid. "What are you going to do, Pilwondepat? Shoot me in the back?" He turned to exit the shelter.

"I could not do that. It goes against everything my hive stands for," the sorrowful scientist confessed. "But an AAnn would."

The very tiny shell made a very loud noise and a very large hole in the middle of the stunned supervisor's dorsal side, blowing a majority of his internal organs out through his flaring ribs. Pilwondepat did not have the opportunity to appraise the exoarcheologist's final expression because the biped toppled forward onto his front, facedown on the packed earth. No doubt his countenance was as fully convulsed as the wonderfully expressive human face could manage.

"Primitive things, explosives." Pilwondepat ambled past the wide splotch of spreading redness as he exited the shelter. "They have the useful virtue of being entirely non–species specific. As long as no identifying residue is left behind, it is credible that any idiot intelligence can assume responsibility for them going boom." In Low Thranx, this concluding sentiment emerged as a long, drawn-out whistle marked by a single intermediary sharp click.

"The AAnn are not the only sentients capable of cunning, Cullen. I did like you. Very much. You forgot that for my kind, the safety and security of the hive comes first. Even if it is not our hive, but one that is of potential importance to us. Say for example, *sr!iik,* the human hive." Dolefully, he ululated a final, forlorn whistle of farewell. "You might be willing to relinquish Comagrave to the care of the AAnn. We will not, I will not, the Great Hive will not let you. Not even at the cost of all our lives." Clutching the tiny but lethal firearm in both truhands, he inclined forward to place his foothands on the ground. Supported now by all six lower limbs, he exited the edifice and surveyed the rising panic outside. He did not look back at the body lying on the ground behind him. Unfortunately, the proper expiration formalities could not be observed on behalf of his late colleague. There was simply no time for lengthy lamentations. He regretted that, but knew he had no choice.

Not when there was an efficacious chaos in need of stoking.

For once, he was hardly noticed. Flames and smoke rose from the direction of the landing site. In crashing, the AAnn cargo carrier had evidently sparked fires among the assembled baggage and modest temporary buildings. Intended to advance the cause of science, the explosives he had spent the night modifying and setting into position had apparently performed better than expected in the service of conspiracy.

Nearby, the crashed and burning transport's two sister craft hovered ten meters off the ground. A few desultory bursts of gunfire issued from one, while the other was quiet. That would not do. Firing his weapon, he raced through the encampment yelling at the top of his voice. It was weak compared to the deeper intonations of humans. Clicks and whistles and stridulating would have reached much farther, but were incomprehensible to the bewildered mammals stumbling all around him.

"Defend yourselves! Shoot back—don't let them kill you all!" All the long hours practicing the difficult vowel sounds, the endless evenings spent listening to human conversation, now paid off in what ironically was likely to prove to be an elaborate and unrecognized epitaph. He could even manage the correct inflections, as was shown by the alacrity with which the humans he encountered responded to his shouts of alarm.

A number of those emerging from the camp's shelters were doing as he hoped without having to be prompted. As more and more small arms were brought into play, their combined firepower began to inflict real damage on the nearer of the two AAnn transports. Fired upon for what must have seemed to them to be no reason, the AAnn finally responded in traditional fashion. One after another, every camp structure was obliterated, though without the usual reptilian efficiency. They were still confused.

Then someone aboard one of the surviving transports,

probably a senior military advisor, realized that the abrupt and unanticipated confrontation had passed a political point of no return. Humans had been slain, in numbers too large to explain away as the result of an accident. Having plunged too deeply into slaughter, the visitors now had no choice, as Pilwondepat had surmised, but to eliminate any possibility of contradiction in the hopes that a suitable postmortem explanation could be concocted by their military psych specialists.

The much-vaunted AAnn martial methodology was applied to the scientific camp. Moving off in different directions both to make a more difficult target for the humans below and to enhance their operative efficiency, the two transports positioned themselves to flank the camp and trap the remaining humans between their combined fire. Pilwondepat agonized as he watched one dazed but defiant human after another go down beneath the heavier firepower of the two cargo carriers. It was doubly hard for him to look on knowing that those who were sacrificing themselves for a greater cause had no inkling that they were doing so.

He continued to take cover where possible and fire his own weapon. The handgun could not bring down a vehicle as substantial as a cargo carrier, but with luck he might penetrate its lateral edge and kill an AAnn or two. Sprinting on all six legs from a large rounded boulder toward the still-standing communal eating building, he found himself suddenly face-to-face with one figure that was neither trying to flee nor fighting back. He slowed.

Slitted eyes flicked sideways in his direction, and the silky voice that had been hissing harshly into a handheld communicator turned on him. "You. *Fssst!* You have ssomething to do with thiss, thiss outrageouss happening. Thiss iss no accident, inssect!"

"We are all of us accidents in the sight of the cosmos, scaled one," Pilwondepat declared humbly as he raised his gun and shot the surprised AAnn exoarcheologist square between his glaring, accusing eyes. Peaceable soul that he was, the action gave Pilwondepat more satisfaction than anything else he had done that day. He did not wait for the body to hit the ground, but instead rushed toward the still-standing structure to further incite those inside.

Battles that begin in confusion often end the same way. So it was with the massacre at the camp. Without knowing exactly what had happened, the AAnn found themselves presiding over a scene of complete devastation. One of their own craft had been destroyed, and many of its crew killed or seriously injured. A second transport was severely damaged but still capable of flight, albeit at a greatly reduced speed. The deceitful humans had perished to the last, males and females alike. So had the Empire's sole representative in the camp, who had he survived might have been able to shed some light on what was becoming an increasingly disturbing and impenetrable conundrum. There was also one dead bug, to whom the AAnn paid no attention.

Precisely why this had all taken place, in the space of less than an hour, no one on the surviving AAnn craft could say. Hasty tight-beam communications were exchanged with the AAnn consulate in Comabraeth. A frantic exchange of appalled questions and choleric recriminations followed. Presented with a horrific fait accompli, the ranking AAnn determined to contrive an elaborate explanation for the tragedy that had devastated the human scientific outpost. This involved the rapidly spreading disease to which many of the humans had previously succumbed, consequent nervous disorders, a few cases of isolated madness and paranoia, followed by something akin to mass hysteria.

Intruding with the best of intentions onto this psychochaos, the neighborly AAnn had found many humans already dead at the hands of their fellows. Coming under relentless and inexplicable attack, they had been forced to defend themselves with no more than a minimal amount of firepower. Meanwhile, the crazed humans had continued to go on about killing one another, much to the anguish of the observing AAnn, who were powerless to stop the disease-induced madness.

An improbable story, it was the best the AAnn tacticians

could devise while operating under the press of time. It was not, however, inconceivable. Lending support to the elaborate fabrication was the self-evident fact that there was no reason, no reason whatsoever, for the AAnn to attack and annihilate a peaceful, harmless scientific campsite. In the absence of motive, it was hard to see how the humans could accuse the AAnn of anything more than a serious but not malevolent lapse in judgment.

Therefore, Vaarbayel CCVT, senior consul for the Empire on Comagrave, was feeling hopeful if not completely confident as she was admitted to the office of Malor Narzaltan. The old human was disgustingly wrinkled and shamelessly exhibited an unrepentant mane of white keratin that spilled down the back of his head and neck. His eyes were small, sharp, blue, and seemed to take in tiny bits of airborne debris the way a magnet attracts iron filings. Vaarbayel tried to look at him without staring. Her tail switched lazily back and forth behind her, a sign of patience.

"You requessted that I appear before you. I assume thiss iss not an informal vissit."

"It never is with your kind, is it?" Narzaltan was standing, not sitting, behind his desk. It was a simple artifact, as were the remainder of the complementary furnishings that filled the office. As an outpost world, Comagrave made do with the hand-me-downs and leftovers of government.

She chose to ignore the query, which insofar as she could judge carried with it some small suspicion of sarcasm. "Then everything will be recorded by mysself as well, sso that there can be in the future no missundersstandings as to what wass ssaid or disscussed."

"No," the human administrator agreed quietly, "we certainly wouldn't want there to be any misunderstandings. Not like the one that led to yesterday's tragedy near the Mountain of the Mourners." Aged though they were, those tiny blue eyes seemed lit from within. "I was hoping you could shed some light on the matter."

"Having recently been given the opportunity to fully perusse the official report on the distressing and tragic incident,

I assure you I can do precisely that." She proceeded to give the AAnn version of the "grim misadventure," concluding that the eventual devastation was the result of terrible conditions on the ground and consequent grave miscommunication between the humans at the site and the AAnn who had been sent to ferry them back to the capital. This was followed by a formal apology—even though, given the circumstances, one was technically not required—and a conjoined offer to pay reparations. Within reason, of course.

She concluded by adding her personal, as opposed to official, condolences, taking care to remind the furrow-faced old human with both word and gesture that more than a few of her own kind had perished in the course of the incident. Despite this, the AAnn took no offense. Such calamities were bound to occur in the course of exploring unknown alien worlds. But among those who understood such things, who were mature explorers of a threatening and oftentimes bewildering firmament, they need not impair relations.

She felt she had done as best she could given the material the psychticians had prepared for her. Now she stood in silence, only her tail moving metronomically from side to side, waiting for the shriveled mammal to respond. After a long pause he finally did, in language that was somewhat less than tastefully diplomatic.

"You're a liar."

She blanched as much as an AAnn could. Anger rose in her throat. "You are insulting."

"The truth is never insulting. You're a big-mouthed, carrion-eating, earless, bloodthirsty liar who probably shits where she eats. I'm starting to think that's true of all your kind. Like the rest of my people, I've been inclined to usually give you the benefit of the doubt here on Comagrave, even if you persist in your communications in referring to it as Vussussica. A recently viewed vit changed my mind. It's changed a lot of minds here. I expect that after it receives wider dissemination, its mind-altering potential will expand exponentially. Would you care to see it?"

Stunned beyond outrage, the AAnn representative could

barely choke out a terse affirmative. "I sshould like to ssee what hass prompted thiss unprecedented outbursst of sslander, truly."

Without replying, Narzaltan waved a hand over a proximity control. A holo image appeared above his plain, unadorned desk. Vaarbayel recognized the restraining boundaries of a satellite scan. Without input from the human, the view plunged surfaceward until the slightly flickering but otherwise quite viewable image froze at a high magnification.

She had only read the hastily compiled formal report and seen the follow-up. Looked down on from above, the carnage took on a detached yet oddly individualistic horror. There were the two surviving AAnn transports, systematically sweeping the blazing encampment, the AAnn aboard utilizing their aerial platforms to methodically shoot down every last remaining human. Afterward, landing parties examined the camp, going through those structures that were still standing—making sure of possible survivors. There were too many details of the sweeping vit, too many peculiarly bloody episodes, that could not be faked. She could not question what she was seeing.

The image evaporated like a bad dream in a sandstorm. "I do not know how to properly resspond other than as I already have," she finally hissed. "I wass not there. I can only reference what I wass told, and explicate from thosse materialss that I have been given."

Narzaltan was nodding, a typically unsophisticated human gesture she readily recognized. "I understand that. In retrospect, if not now, maybe you will understand my bitterness. Not that I really care if you do. We're both vessels, you and I. Vessels and vassals, administrators and diplomats. We're supposed to transmit and forward, not think or feel. Right now I'm afraid I and everyone on my staff is failing that mandate.

"You're probably wondering how we came by that satellite imagery. Turns out the local thranx consulate here in Comabraeth received a request to run a high-magnification check on the campsite just as your people arrived. Standard procedure. Our technicians complied. When they saw what was happening in real time, they locked the satellite's orbit to keep the high-def scanners on location." He gestured at the empty air above his desk. "You just saw the result. If that particular request hadn't arrived when it did, I might, just might, have been willing to withhold judgment on your official story." He smiled, and although a human could not begin to match an AAnn for expanse of exposed teeth, it was threatening enough. "Now you've gone and contradicted that stinking small slice of reality. There will be consequences."

The thranx! Vaarbayel thought ferociously. Whenever something untoward happened, the *gssrsst* bugs seemed always to be found at the bottom of the contaminated dune. "I am ssure that upon further reflection, the incidentss ssurrounding thiss regrettable missundersstanding can be explained."

Once more the human administrator responded with little more than that terse and by now infuriating nod. "Until further notice, all AAnn on Comagrave are to consider themselves under detention. No vehicles or other craft are to travel beyond Comabraeth without permission from this office. Stellar proximity to the Empire notwithstanding, this is an officially recognized colony of Earth. Your people remain on this world on sufferance of my government and its colonies."

"This is outrageouss. I musst regisster an official protesst."

"You do that. You relay everything to Blassussar. I've already been in contact with Earth via the space-minus bore. My actions have been cleared, and I've been granted authority to augment however I see fit—short of shooting people. Further communications between your government and mine are in the process of being formulated." He crossed his slim but wiry arms in front of his unimpressive chest. As a gesture of dismissal and finality, it was oddly convincing.

"One last thing. If I were you, I'd start packing."

19

Like everyone else in the vast underground burrow that contained the diplomatic division serving the Great Hive, Haflunormet encountered the report from the human outpost world of Comagrave in advance of the general populace. That he was not the only one to respond with an involuntary stridulation of shock was shown by the number of abrasive chirrups that echoed in close succession through the various individual workstations. Staff rose from their positions to engage in intense informal discussions of the report's potential impact.

Haflunormet did not join them. While he was as stunned by the details as the rest of his colleagues, they did not sit quite right in either of his guts. Perhaps it was due to the increasing amount of contact he had been having with humans themselves, and with one individual in particular. Whatever the reason, he found himself impelled to dig deeper into the body of general information contained in the horrific account.

These personal preoccupations in no way mitigated his sympathy for the doomed humans of Comagrave or his outrage at the manner of their death. One could expect no less from the deceitful AAnn. Here at last was proof of their persistent perfidy so overwhelming that even those humans most favorably disposed toward them could not ignore it. That the incident would give at least a temporary, and perhaps a permanent, boost to the furthering of thranx-human relations could not be denied. In the Pitarian War the collected hives had shown themselves to be reliable allies. Now the AAnn had revealed the true nature of their innate treachery. Among those members of the diplomatic staff who had labored long and hard, suffering criticism and cynicism in tandem for their efforts to bring the two species closer together, there was quiet jubilation. The cautious and the outright dissenters were reduced to skritching their mandibles in quiet frustration.

And yet—and yet ... certain facts, assuming they had been correctly recorded, continued to nag at him like the aggravating *sqik* parasites that could infect an ungroomed adult's exfoliating integuments.

The deeper he probed, the more convinced he became that he was on the track of uncomfortable truths. His colleagues in the section appeared to accept the report and its attendant conclusions without question. A perfectly normal reaction— but not for one who had spent time among humans. A little of their tendency to question everything seemed to have rubbed off on him. Of course, they also tended to suspect the obvious and the self-evident. This led to a widespread wasting of time the thranx could not stomach. Somewhere in between the two extremes, Haflunormet suspected, might lie the eventual path to a new way of looking at the universe.

His present interests, however, were not half so exalted. Details, details—so much of diplomacy was often in the details. When he finally stumbled over the one he was looking for, self-congratulation escaped him. He was too shocked.

It was plain enough for anyone who knew the ways of the hive to see—if one had the desire and determination to look for it. The contradictions lay in the timing. How had this scientist managed to send a warning that the human exoarcheological site was under attack several time-parts before the surveying satellite provided the first confirmation that an attack was actually under way? Haflunormet checked and rechecked the relevant chronologs. There was no mistake.

The warning had arrived *before* the attack.

Then there were the many protests, all ignored, that had been raised by the AAnn. That they had journeyed to the site with the declared intent of rescuing, not exterminating, its occupants. That upon preparing to touch down, one of their transports had been fired upon without warning and for no apparent reason. That its destruction had been followed by an outbreak of small-arms fire from the encampment, where-upon they had then, and only then, responded in kind. This last assertion had been met with the contempt it deserved. By no method of accounting could a defensive reaction "in kind" justify the complete annihilation of all the camp's inhabitants.

Delving ever deeper, Haflunormet noted that the initial blast that had crippled the AAnn transport could not be explained in light of the encampment's professed lack of heavy weapons. If the humans on Comagrave were lying and the occupants of the scientific camp *had* possessed such devices, why did they not use them on the other two AAnn transports? Someone in the report had hypothesized about the possibility of unstable explosives used for purposes of excavation having been stored at the landing site. This conjecture was quickly dismissed. Scientific teams did not make use of the risky or unstable. And why would humans fire on supposedly friendly AAnn if they did not feel directly threatened?

Haflunormet focused every one of his lenses on the series of high-res satellite images. Easy enough to see the AAnn transport crashing at the landing pad, vomiting flames. Then the flare-up of small-arms fire. How ultimately detailed was the imagery? He enhanced, zoomed, and enhanced again. At the maximum augmented magnification possible, a single figure could be observed firing at the incoming AAnn craft. A number of humans could be seen running, a couple cowering together behind a temporary shelter, but none of them shooting at the AAnn. Not yet. Haflunormet's wing cases quivered.

There had been exactly one thranx working on the site at the time of the tragedy. It was a thranx who had transmitted the very possibly premature report of the AAnn attack. Now, in imagery freshly augmented, it was a thranx who could be seen firing on the AAnn in advance of anyone else. Taken together, the evidence seemed to point to more than mere reaction, more than just coincidence.

It was entirely possible, a stunned Haflunormet realized,

that the respected thranx exoarcheologist in question, a certain Pilwondepat, had not been reacting to an AAnn attack, but had been working to provoke one.

The potential ramifications were explosive. Throughout the human sphere of influence, outrage against the AAnn over the atrocity that had occurred on Comagrave was spreading like an unstoppable contagion. If it was disclosed that on this one exceptional occasion the AAnn were actually innocent, and that the massacre had in fact been initiated by a thranx, the shift in human public opinion could be devastating. What had possessed a respected scientist of the hive to do such a thing Haflunormet could not begin to imagine. Certainly the initial consequences were salutary, but the risk . . . !

He lay unmoving at his position, sprawled on his bench, until a neighboring coworker thought to inquire after his health. Responding positively, and as calmly as he could, Haflunormet realized that his long moments of contemplation had led him to a decision. Whatever justification might have been claimed by the perpetrator for provoking such a heinous incident had already been subsumed in matters of far greater import. Though every particle of his being screamed at Haflunormet to reveal the truth, he knew that he could not. To do so would be to set thranx-human relations back to a point where even formal diplomatic relations might be placed in jeopardy. As for any thought of forging stronger, deeper bonds between the two species, they would evaporate like dripping water on a hot rock.

But he could not keep the secret to himself. Others needed to know, deserved to know, so that in the event someone besides himself happened to chance upon the same conclusions, beings of like mind could be ready and prepared to deal with the potentially damaging revelation.

First, he erased every trace of his activity. What he could not erase because it had already been entered into general storage he buried as deeply and innocuously as he could. Satisfied at last that someone would have to be either very determined or very lucky to retrace his work, or to find the paths of inquiry he had taken, he steeled himself to confide his findings in the one other person he felt he could trust with so virulent a discovery.

But first he would have to find out where the human Fanielle Anjou was spending the remainder of her actual vacation.

The thranx liked mountains, but only from the inside. Mountains tended to be cold, or at least cool, dry places. Neither characteristic appealed to the heat- and humidity-loving insectoids. So the resting place where Fanielle had chosen to spend the remainder of her time away from Azerick lay at the upper limit of the thranx comfort zone.

Overlooking the undulating jungle-carpeted plains, beneath which lay the outermost suburbs of the city, the exclusive Retreat of Xer!kex featured individual burrows with spectacular vistas. The contradiction inherent in spending most of one's leisure time ignoring the view outside in favor of activities occurring deep within the mountainside was not lost on Fanielle. On the contrary, she was delighted by this wholly thranxish choice. It left her free to dawdle in the peculiar low-lying thranx version of a hammock, swinging outside above an exposed slope, sipping chilled fruit juice while gazing sleepily at the vast green panorama spread out before her.

Cool enough in its hillside location so that she felt comfortable in long pants and long-sleeved shirt, her communal refuge received occasional visits from other occupants of the retreat. They would click and whistle and chatter, pointing out this or that distant landmark, before retiring to their assigned burrows and away from the, to them, mountainside chill.

In the distance, the sporadic howl of a shuttle climbing heavenward rolled across the plains. Not even the distant Xer!kex could entirely escape the industrial-strength rumble and roar of the capital's major shuttleports. Relaxed and at ease, Fanielle viewed these isolated auditory interruptions with tolerant indifference. So content was she with the amenities of the retreat that neither shuttle yowls nor choruses of curious clicking could trouble her.

Among all the auditory distractions, the last thing she expected to hear was a familiar voice.

"Found you at last, *shleeck!* With only a handful of humans authorized to be in Daret, one would think it would not have taken so long."

Startled, she started to sit up, forgot where she was, and nearly ended as tightly wrapped up in the exotic hammock as a fly in a spider's shroud. Clearly ill at ease so close to an exposed cliff face, Haflunormet was nonetheless unabashedly pleased to see her.

"What are you doing here?" Carefully extracting herself from the hammocklike contrivance lest it try to ambush her dignity again, Fanielle sat on the edge of the low retaining wall that separated the scenic overlook from the jungle directly below. "I thought we had concluded all the necessary business between ourselves and our mutual friend."

Twisting an antenna around to make sure no one was standing behind him and listening, Haflunormet explained. "I came across a recent incident that in the course of further investigation has given birth to some disquieting conclusions." He indicated their surroundings. "You've been out of touch, and I presume you do not watch the local equivalent of your tridee broadcasts."

"No," she confessed. "I came up here looking for peace and quiet."

"I am sorry to intrude, but this matter cannot wait. I must tell someone I can trust, or I feel I will break into a premature molt. You've heard of Comagrave?"

She frowned, then brightened slightly. "Distant outpost world. Class X, I think. I remember reading something about a long-extinct but quite advanced native race. It's close, in galactic terms, to the AAnn Empire. What about it?"

Haflunormet proceeded to enlighten her as to the recent tragic developments on that world. When he had finished, she sat very still, digesting the scope of the disaster—and its diplomatic import.

"This will make the AAnn look bad. Very bad. A terrible thing to have happen—but perversely, it serves our ends."

Haflunormet gestured second-degree concurrence displaced by distress. "All true—except for my disquieting conclusions. They involve a respected exoarcheologist of the hive Pat, clan De. In the course of my investigation I researched this individual's background thoroughly. There is nothing in it to suggest a tendency to madness."

"I don't follow you, Haflunormet."

"This Pilwondepat filed a thick report detailing a list of incidents on Comagrave that he felt pointed to a methodical attempt on the part of the AAnn to drive your people off the planet, despite the official recognition of your suzerainty by the Empire. This report was filed the night before the event I have alluded to previously." He stridulated softly to emphasize his words. "That shocking incident would seem to provide final proof of his thesis, except for certain ambiguities that I have subsequently discovered." He proceeded to detail them for his friend.

She waited quietly until he was finished. "That's monstrous!" She hardly knew what to say to the quiet, expectant diplomat standing before her. "You're telling me that in order to back up his claims, this scientist provoked the AAnn into attacking and slaughtering everyone at the archeological site where he had been working?"

"Not sparing himself," Haflunormet reminded her solemnly.

"If word of this got out to the media . . ." Her voice trailed away, lost in hurried thought. "It would have exactly the opposite effect from what its perpetrator intended." She stared hard into those golden compound eyes. "You're *certain* of your findings?"

He gestured elaborately. "I wish it were otherwise. There are simply too many coincidences that cannot be rationalized away. And there is sufficient visual documentation to back up my conclusions, for any who happen to look in the right places. As far as I know, I am the only one to have done so." Both antennae had been pointing in her direction for some minutes now. The diplomat did not want to risk missing any critical nuances. "What do you think we should do?"

She started to reply. Before she could do so, they were interrupted by the sudden appearance from the mouth of the access passageway of three thranx: two males, and one female with particularly tightly coiled ovipositors. The younger male and female deferred noticeably to the older male in their midst.

"You don't have to decide." Though not especially elderly in thranx terms, the senior favored a noticeably gimpy right front truleg. "We will make the decision on your behalf."

Taken by surprise, Haflunormet whirled to confront the newcomers. Still seated on the stone retaining wall, Fanielle tensed. "You were listening to us," the thranx diplomat asserted accusingly.

"Most certainly we were." From a thorax pouch, the female removed a compact weapon. She held it casually in a truhand, not aiming it in any particular direction. Fanielle looked past the trio. In spreading out, they effectively blocked the way back to the tunnel. She and Haflunormet were alone on the outlook with the confrontational strangers. The female's tone, insofar as Fanielle could follow the stream of Low Thranx, was laced with contempt. "We have been listening in on you for a long time while following your deviant attempts to force thranx and humans obscenely closer together. To strive so hard to achieve secretiveness and to fail so miserably gains you little merit."

The elder in the middle spoke up, directing his words to Haflunormet. "The solution to your dilemma is simple, diplomat of the hive. You are going to tell the truth, difficult as that may be for one of your ilk. So . . . the AAnn are not responsible for what happened on Comagrave. It was the work of a brave and resourceful thranx determined to eliminate as many humans as possible. That, at least, will be how our organization will tell it."

Haflunormet's valentine-shaped blue-green head swiveled to appraise each of the intruders in turn. A sweeping gesture performed by both truhands underlined his pithy response. "You three are crazier than the suicidal exoarcheologist was."

"Who are you?" Handicapped by a lack of the requisite number of limbs, Fanielle tried her best to underline her queries with the appropriate hand gestures. "Why have you been following and listening to us?"

"We belong to a noble hiveless clan called the Bwyl," the oldest one told her. "We call ourselves the Protectors, and we work to preserve the purity of the Great Hive, to keep it free from outside corruption and defilement."

"Never heard of you." Haflunormet's words were cold, the verbal equivalent of blocking off a burrow to visitors.

"You will," the female assured him, waving her weapon around with blatant disregard for everyone's safety, including her own. "Very soon. Within a few time-parts." She whistled a terse tune of ironic humor. "A major element of our group is even as we speak working hard to pull down this false bridge of unwelcome conviviality that has been erected between the Great Hive and the filthy soft-bodied bipeds." Fanielle tensed, but said nothing.

"You are going to release your findings and all the evidence necessary to support your clever and correct deductions as to the truth of what happened on Comagrave." The elder spoke with the confidence of one who is convinced of his righteousness. "Both thranx and humans must know what happened on that world, and why. It is knowledge that will serve to drive a most satisfactory wedge between those misguided representatives of both species who seek a deeper and unnatural degree of harmonization." A soft whistle indicated a different kind of humor.

"Imagine it, diplomat. A chance to tell the truth of a matter instead of having to invent clever lies. Think of it as a novelty." His younger companions whistled and clicked approvingly.

"You can't do this," Haflunormet protested. "It will set back the course of thranx-human relations for an untold number of birth cycles."

"At the very least, one hopes," the speaker declared with satisfaction. "We don't need you to do this, *wirri!t*. Though we don't have access to your materials, they can be tracked down and recovered readily enough. We could make the announcement ourselves, but it will carry more weight if it comes from a representative of the diplomatic section." The confident male performed a hand gesture Fanielle did not recognize, but it was sufficient to cause Haflunormet to draw back slightly.

"If you refuse, you will be caught smothering the truth with the lie of omission. Your career will be ruined, and you will be consigned to simple information gathering and processing. Your family and clan will lose merit, and your disgrace will be substantial. We are offering you the opportunity to avoid all that. Indeed, by allowing you to reveal your discovery we give to you the chance to enhance your reputation."

"At the expense of seriously damaging thranx-human relations," Haflunormet responded.

Gesturing indifference, the younger male spoke for the first time. "We waste burrow-time here. Get the apostate to commit, or to decline. I am anxious to know of the success of Beskodnebwyl's enterprise."

"As are we all," the elder agreed, by his gestures counseling patience. "Beskodnebwyl works what he must, and we work what we do. No living chamber of significance is completed in a single birth cycle." He returned his attention to Haflunormet. "In keeping with the great traditions, we give you this choice. Make it now. By either means, the truth will become known."

Feeling completely left out, Fanielle sat stiffly on the barrier as she struggled to follow the conversation between the four thranx. The finely worked black schist was warm against her legs and backside. Haflunormet could not agree, of course. At the same time, how could he not? In her entire professional life, she had never felt so helpless, so completely at a loss for options. She was still agonizing over possibilities when Haflunormet stepped forward and extended both foothands.

"Very well, *sriippk*. I disagree with you completely, but it is better to dig through soft earth in the wrong direction than to break one's digits against solid rock in another." Reaching out, he took the senior Bwyl's foothands in his own. "Let this grasping of work digits serve to emphasize the new bond between us."

The elder gestured gratification. "I am not surprised by your decision. Most diplomats act in a sensible fashion when presented with clearly defined parameters." He grasped Haflunormet's eight digits in his own.

Whereupon the diplomat bent and twisted with unexpected speed. The thranx equivalent of jujitsu, involving as it did a maximum possible eight limbs, was something to behold. The surprised Bwyl flew up and over Haflunormet's abdomen, past a shocked Fanielle—and over the retaining wall.

The dull *thump* humans make when they take a hard fall was in startling contrast to the loud *crack* of the thranx's exoskeleton shattering as it struck the rocks below.

Before the elder's stunned companions could react, Haflunormet was on top of and locked in a seemingly inextricable clinch with the younger male. Superior knowledge and experience was matched against greater strength. The former was, tragically, of no use whatsoever against even a very small gun.

Discharged by the female, it replaced the struggling diplomat's left eye with a large hole. Haflunormet's limbs went limp, his antennae collapsed atop his head, and the bright golden sheen of life began to fade almost immediately from his remaining oculus. As the surviving male strove to shove the now slack body away from his own, the female swung the deadly little weapon in Fanielle's direction.

There is a time for diplomacy, and then there is a time for reverting to the doctrines that have always preceded hopeless confrontations. Bringing her knees up toward her chest, Fanielle spun on her tail end; swung her legs wide, high, and wild to her right; and dropped over the outside of the overlook's stone wall. Faced with the gun, her reaction had been entirely instinctive. Several thoughts collided for attention as she fell, with one uppermost in her mind.

Dear God, please—not my baby.

She landed in untouched jungle some five meters below, the thick undergrowth helping to cushion her fall. Pain shot up her right leg, lingered for a terrifying moment, and then began to diminish as rapidly as it had arrived. Her hand went immediately to her slightly protruding belly. Everything felt normal, unchanged. Healthy. Immensely relieved that her body had handled the drop so well, she straightened, her mind taking inventory of her condition before she had time to feel fear: She was not crippled; nothing was broken, maybe a slight sprain. She could still walk, but could she run? Could she run for two? She had no choice but to try.

As she started to push herself erect, her hand slipped against something thick and wet. Less than a meter from her eyes, the broken face of the elder Bwyl stared lifelessly back into her own. The stiff-limbed, stiff-bodied thranx had not taken the fall half as well as the more flexible human.

Something burned the foliage to her left, and she immediately stumbled off in the opposite direction, wiping her bloodstained hand against a leg of her pants. Surely the surviving Bwyl could not see her, concealed as she was by the thick rain forest vegetation. They were firing blindly, hoping to hit her. She had no doubt that they would pursue. With her witness to them having killed Haflunormet, they now had no choice. Despite their six legs, the thranx were not good leapers. They would have to find another way down. That would buy her some time.

She fought to remember everything she knew of thranx physiology. Over a short sprint, a human's longer legs would quickly outdistance them. But they had great endurance. If she couldn't lose them quickly in the forest, they would eventually run her to ground. If only there were a river to cross, or a lake to swim, she would be safe from them. But the steep hillside did not allow for the deep pooling of water. There was something else, something more useful still . . .

It flashed hot and bright in her mind. In addition to being weak jumpers, the thranx were poor climbers. They would expect a fugitive to go downward in any case. Angling more to her right, she struck off parallel to the slope. When she felt she had traveled far enough to be beyond the farthest extent of the retreat, she turned sharply and started upslope.

The grade was steep and the permanently damp ground underfoot slippery and uncertain. She had been wearing air sandals while relaxing in the pseudohammock—hardly the most appropriate gear for rain forest hiking. Their feet naturally shod in tough chitin, the thranx needed no footwear. Nor would the precipitous incline slow them down.

She found what she was looking for a short while later. The cliff face was dizzying, but fractured with plenty of handholds. Taking care to avoid a slip on the moist surface, a determined human would have no difficulty ascending. But the vertical rock face would stop a thranx cold. The exposed granite extended as far as she could see to right and left. With luck, her pursuers would give up the chase, or at least lose track of her at the base of the moderate precipice. At the very least, it would give her a chance to put some serious space between herself and her pursuers.

Once, she lost her grip and nearly fell. Though in good physical shape and something of an amateur athlete, she was no mountaineer. But by choosing her route of ascent carefully and taking her time, she found herself sitting at the top well before evening. That was important. Having evolved in a subterranean civilization, the thranx possessed far better night vision than the average human. It behooved her to find sanctuary, in one form or another, before nightfall, when she would be at a disadvantage.

Which way to go? The unspoiled rain forest was still home to dangerous as well as engaging creatures, the majority of which she had never encountered and knew absolutely nothing about—another reason for avoiding any nocturnal rambling. If the Bwyl were still on her trail, she might do well to try to circle back to the retreat. Once back inside, she felt sure she could rely on the well-trained staff to protect her until her pursuers gave up and departed.

Another, less acute slope lay before her. She would scale

this final, foliage-choked obstacle and then try to descend down to the retreat without being observed. The last step up proving to be a bit of a reach for her, she sought support from a nearby tree, taking a firm grip on the blue-barked bole with her right hand. One strong pull, and she was up, gazing through an opening in the bushes and trees that promised a few moments of easier hiking before she had to start looking for a sheltered route across and down.

A quick glance behind showed no signs of pursuit. Either she had lost them, or the Bwyl were struggling to find a way around the bluff she had surmounted. She was breathing hard, but she was not exhausted. The knowledge that she had no more climbing ahead of her gave strength to tired leg muscles and invigorated her spirits. Thus renewed, and a little more confident of her chances, she started down the irregular path through the trees.

The gun that appeared in front of her face was held tightly in the grasp of not two, but four hands. Sixteen digits covered every possible switch and button, slide and trigger. Downy antennae and bulging eyes swung immediately in her direction as the muzzle of the rifle started to come around.

Of course. Her thoughts were oddly peaceful, and she found she was no longer tired. How stupid of me. Naïve and stupid. Forward thinkers like the Bwyl would be likely to bring backup along to any potential confrontation. The rifle and its handler both looked very efficient.

None of the armed patrollers who had been called out by the alarmed operators of the retreat to search for the missing human had ever encountered one in person, though they were familiar with the bipeds' appearance from the numerous visual displays that had played regularly ever since early contact. As to the murderous intruders, the surviving pair had already been apprehended. The patroller who encountered the human had, upon doing so, turned promptly to reassure her.

So, even though many aspects of human behavior were reputed to be strange and incomprehensible, he was still taken aback when the hunted one's single-lensed eyes appeared to perform the astonishing feat of rolling back inside her skull; her long, fleshy legs gave way; and without a word or gesture in his direction she crumpled unconscious to the damp earth.

20

Monitoring his tracker while listening to the reports filtering in from the other plainclothes police who had spread out to cover the fairgrounds, the supervising officer managed to spare a moment or two to contemplate the pair of peculiar padres chatting nearby. Though the purpose of the fair was to expose humans to thranx culture and, to a lesser degree, thranx to human culture, this association was sufficiently unusual to pique his normally pedestrian curiosity. That they had also saved hundreds, perhaps thousands of lives rendered them that much more interesting.

Representatives of something they called "the United Church," they were. Lieutenant Romero had never heard of it. His openly professed ignorance had sparked a quiet but eager interest on their part to resolve it, to a degree that had involved him in their disquisition despite his usual disdain for matters theological.

Time enough for that later, after this unpleasant business of die-hard terrorists had been concluded. Given the number of infiltrators, the police had been unable to round them all up in time. A few small fires were burning around the fairgrounds, but nothing, he had been assured by the relevant authorities, that the on-grounds facilities could not handle. The most stubborn blazes were already succumbing to flows of suppressant being pumped from the fair's central fire-control facility. Following a few anxious moments when the intruders' strength was still uncertain, everything was now under control. It was merely a matter of picking up those few remnant infiltrators who were still at large.

And best of all, he knew, it had not been necessary to close down or evacuate the fair. The majority of attendees would never know how close they had come to perishing in an orgy of deliberate, preconceived destruction.

For that, he, his department, and the people of Dawn had this oddly matched pair of proselytizers to thank. Looking up from his tracker, he was reminded to do so. It was the tenth or maybe the twelfth time he had given voice to his gratitude.

Briann was not counting, but he was embarrassed. Incapable of blushing, Twikanrozex was reduced to gesturing his discomfiture. "You have already thanked us enough, Lieutenant." As always, Romero was amazed at the thranx's fluency in Terranglo. There were a few words he did not recognize that the human padre had identified as belonging to a new class of informal communication street folk were calling symbospeech, but his unfamiliarity did not hinder his understanding.

"I've already been told by the Auroran city council that you two are to have the run of the city as well as the fair. Anything you want will be provided."

Briann smiled graciously. "Our needs are simple. We ask only to be allowed to continue in our work." He glanced in the direction of his companion, presently standing tall on four trulegs. "Our intentions in coming here were to operate only during the fair, but since your superiors have extended so gracious a welcome, it would be churlish of us to leave early."

"We only did what anyone would have done," Twikanrozex added.

Romero grunted softly. "Followed heavily armed outsiders to learn what they were up to? I don't think so." A voice yammered in his cochlear implant, bringing a taut look of satisfaction to his deeply tanned face. "Two more picked up. Thranx this time. They don't seem to be coordinating very well, these rogue antisocial elements of respective species."

Twikanrozex gestured with all four arms. While Romero had not a clue as to the meaning of the complex hand movements, they were fascinating to watch. Graceful creatures, these thranx, he thought. Wonder why I hadn't noticed that before?

A different voice in his ear caused him to glance once again at his companions. "They've located another weapons source." He nodded to his right. "Not far from here. Would you like to witness the arrest? Unless more of these fools are still outside waiting to enter the fair, we're running out of targets to pick up. My people will wait for us before moving in to make the seizure."

Briann responded for the both of them. "We might as well. If possible, Twikanrozex and I would like to question one or two of the arraigned. There are moral ambiguities in question we would like to establish, and perhaps help to correct."

Romero was firm in his reply. "That's not up to me. The invaluable aid you've rendered aside, you're not law enforcement or legal. Your official status is as ambiguous as those morals you'd like to investigate. But I'll see what I can do." Following the directions displayed on his tracker, he led them in the general direction of the lake. A red light blinked on the small readout, indicating the location of an unauthorized weapon.

As the officer led the way, the two padres conversed energetically in his wake. He wished he could make sense of what they were saying. What, for example, did immortality have to do with the story of the baker's wife and the two dwarves?

A most peculiar theology, indeed.

Elkannah Skettle was beyond apoplexy. The pressure of trying to keep calm and inconspicuous while running from the law threatened to burst a blood vessel in his forehead. Slipping out from behind one of several brightly colored pylons supporting a children's play area, he walked as rapidly as he dared toward the pavilion exit. Would he be more or less vulnerable to detection outside than within? Even that fragment of knowledge was denied him.

What had gone wrong? How had the authorities learned of the presence and plans of the Preservers and their thranx comrades, the Bwyl? Every few moments for the past hour, his communicator had informed him of the arrest of another one or two of his people. Attempts to contact the thranx had been met with streams of abuse in the coarse alien language, interspersed with a few crude bursts of Terranglo that were enough to tell him that his insectoid counterparts were also suffering the remorseless attentions of the authorities.

A year's planning, a year of dreaming and working and rehearsing, was falling apart all around him. A few fires had been set, a few bombs had been detonated, shots had been fired, but for the most part, the fair continued to function as smoothly and impassively as if Preserver and Bwyl had never set foot within its expansive boundaries. Some of his best people, dedicated individuals he had worked with for years and knew intimately, were dead or in custody. Botha and Lawlor, gone. Nevisrighne and Stephens, gone. The damage to the movement was so severe that it would take years to recover. Years during which, if something was not done, the unclean bond between human and bug might be cemented beyond sundering.

That could not be allowed to happen. Whatever happened to him now, or to any of his followers, paled into insignificance. Those few explosions that his fellows had succeeded in setting off held the key. If he could only follow through on destroying the fair's central communications facility, the consequences might be sufficiently distracting and damaging to allow him and his surviving collaborators to carry out at least a portion of what they had planned to do.

No one intercepted him as he strolled briskly, eyes darting constantly from left to right, across the fake Dawnic turf toward the fair maintenance facilities. Once, a child caught his eye, and he had to remind himself that police authorities rarely employed children of such a tender age. Still, he was relieved when the child's parents finally hauled it from view.

Behind the gaily decorated fencing lay support facilities for much of the fair. Food service, water, hygienics machinery, power distribution, communications—much of it specially modified to serve thranx as well as human needs. He did not need to check his communicator for the location of the com-

munications center, having memorized the entire layout of
the fairgrounds several months earlier.

Unusually, there was a live guard at the entrance. Short and
burly, he looked ineffably bored. As Skettle approached, the
man barely bothered to look up. The warm sun of Dawn was
in his face, and he had to blink.

"Morning, visitor. Can I help you?"

"Yes, you can. Here is my identification." Reaching into a
pocket, Skettle drew the compact pistol lying holstered and
shoved it roughly against the other man's neck. With his free
hand, he spun the startled attendant around. "I require admit-
tance to the maintenance area."

Give the fellow credit; he tried. "You—you're not authorized, whoever you are. What is this?"

Skettle's voice was strained, but as controlled as ever.
"Epiphany, my friend. Let us in, or I swear by every unconta-
minated gene in your body, I'll blow your head right off its
shoulders."

With the muzzle of the pistol dimpling his neck, the guard
hastened to comply. "You won't get away with this, you
know."

"Get away with what?" Skettle smiled humorlessly. "You
have no idea what I'm doing here. Maybe I just need to use a
bathroom."

The gate hummed to itself as it drew back. A second barrier lay beyond, which the guard also activated. Standing
among muted machinery and functional buildings, unpol-
luted blue sky still visible overhead, Skettle felt he was at last
approaching a small part of the triumph he sought.

"Thank you for your help," he told the guard as he fired.
Contrary to his threat, the shot did not blow the unfortunate
man's head off his shoulders. Skettle disliked a mess that
could be difficult to conceal. Gripping the body by its sandaled feet, he dragged it behind a large pulsating tank and
covered it with one of several sheets of green patching fabric
he found there. A quick check to ensure that his actions had
not been observed, and he resumed his advance. With no one
to witness his progress, he broke into a run.

Minutes later he found himself standing across a walkway from the central communications facility. There were no guards here, deep within the restricted area. It would be assumed that anyone present inside the fenced perimeter had a reason to be where they were. Should he encounter any active personnel, he would be able to rely on that assumption.

The tall double doors that led into the building were unlocked. Inside, automated electronics and photonic circuitry filled the modest edifice with a compact network of switching and transmission instrumentation. Loud humming indicated that the facility was operating on a level higher than standby. That was hardly surprising, given the volume of communications that were doubtless flying not only at the fair but between the fairgrounds and the city.

With the internal schematic of the facility imprinted deeply on his memory, he hurried down several passageways until he found himself standing before the nexus he sought. Instrumentation mounted on a panel monitored the operational status of this small but critical portion of the complex. In a pants pocket lay the special key Botha had programmed to allow him to access the protected, lightly armored panel. All he had to do was pop the seal, affix the cylinder snugged against his chest to the internal components, activate the timer, and get clear.

He envisioned the consequences: confident police unable to contact one another; hasty attempts to relay all communications through distant city facilities; fair workers incapable of coordinating fire-fighting efforts; medics cut off in the process of receiving diagnostic and treatment information. Communicationswise, the entire fair should be shut down for a minimum of several hours—long enough for his surviving acolytes to wreak at least a portion of the havoc they had planned. He wished he could be there to see it, but knew he would have to wait to view the resultant catastrophe on the tridee. Human terrorists! the media would scream. No, thranx saboteurs! another would cry. He smiled to himself. Let the media apportion the responsibility however they wished. The resulting death and destruction would give pause to anyone inclined to think that the two species could enjoy closer relations than they did at present.

From his pocket he withdrew the key, then slapped the flexible circle of integrated circuitry over the sealed lock. He was preparing to activate the device and pop the covering panel when a voice commanded him to halt what he was doing, put his hands over his head, and lie down on the floor. It did not, he sensed despairingly, sound like the voice of a maintenance attendant, bored or otherwise.

With the two padres looking on, Romero nodded to his people. Holding a brace of body seals, one patroller advanced on the stunned Skettle while his two flanking companions kept the muzzles of their handguns aimed unwaveringly at the Preserver's torso. There was nothing Skettle could do, not a thing. Even if he disobeyed the command and activated Botha's key, it would only open the panel. The prospect that he would then have enough time to remove the key, detach the still-concealed cylinder of explosive, affix it to the instrumentation, and activate the trigger was nonexistent. It was all over. The traitors had won. The contamination of human society by the intrusive, alien bugs would continue unimpeded.

Something loud, threatening, and unseen resounded through the still air of the facility. The sonic burst struck the nearest patroller in the back of his head. Briann saw the man topple, the back of his skull caved in by the concussion. His comrades tried to react, but they were caught out in the open while their unknown assailants were firing from cover. Both Romero and the female officer went down in quick succession. The lieutenant managed to get off one shot before he, too, was felled. Whoever the attackers might be, Briann reflected tensely, they were excellent shots. As a consequence, he kept his hands out in plain sight, where they could be seen from a distance.

Both he and Twikanrozex were more than a little surprised when only a single injured thranx hobbled out from behind a dividing wall. Unwilling to grant that the assassin had acted by himself, Briann searched the shadows for others of his kind.

"You are alone," Twikanrozex declared in Low Thranx.

"It was not always so." The wounded sharpshooter stood halfway between the two padres and the perplexed Skettle. "I have been isolated by conspiracies, by failings, and by circumstance."

Skettle finally recognized the intruder. "Beskodnebwyl! Then not all of you bugs have been taken by the authorities."

"No," the leader of the Bwyl replied in Terranglo. "Not all of us bugs."

The Preserver promptly turned back to his work. As the key popped the seal on the panel, he reached inside his shirt and pulled out the cylinder of volatile solution. "We can still accomplish much of what we came for. Shoot these two and come and help me."

Twikanrozex performed a half bow in concert with a series of hand movements too rapid for Briann to follow. "We are spiritual advisors. We carry no weapons."

"That is unfortunate for you," Beskodnebwyl declared, "since it prevents you from defending yourselves." The muzzle of his sonic projector came up. Briann tensed.

"Come on; come on!" Skettle was struggling to affix the cylinder to the now open, blinking interior. "Let's do this and get out of here." On the floor nearby, the injured female officer moaned as she struggled to crawl toward the exit. He ignored her.

Beskodnebwyl turned slowly. The great golden eyes were as expressionless as ever, but the clipped thranx voice was not. "Are you giving me orders, you sickening sack of slack slush?"

Skettle barely looked over from his efforts. "Not now, bug. We can discuss species primacy another time. Come and help me."

"*Crr!!k,* I will help you." Whereupon he proceeded to shoot the leader of the Preservers in his left thigh. The blast of highly focused sound waves smashed into the thick quadriceps muscle and broke the bone within. Letting out a cry of anguish, Skettle collapsed to the floor clutching at his crushed leg.

Advancing with deliberation, the Bwyl approached him. As the thranx changed his focus, Briann considered reaching into his shirt's inner pocket. A glance in Twikanrozex's direction showed that his companion felt this would be, at least for the moment, a bad idea. Taking into consideration the Bwyl's phenomenal marksmanship with his frightening weapon, together with the usual exceptional thranx peripheral vision, Briann kept his hands out in front of him. Alert but cautious, the two padres waited to see what the other thranx would do.

"You cretinous insect!" Wincing in pain, Skettle was clutching his smashed leg. "What did you do that for?" Indicating the cylinder of liquid explosive, which was now securely fastened to the sensitive instrumentation and needed only to be activated to disrupt communications throughout the fair, the Preserver tried to pull himself back to the open panel, dragging his unusable leg behind him.

Beskodnebwyl calmly shot him in the other leg—the calf, this time.

Elkannah Skettle had been toughened, by work in the field and by philosophy both, but this time he screamed. Very little blood leaked from his ruined limbs, since the condensed burst of sound had compressed veins and arteries without cutting them. Designed to shatter the resistive chitinous material that comprised the thranx exoskeleton, the gun's output passed comparatively harmlessly through soft, spongy human flesh but was highly effective at breaking human bones.

As the two padres looked on, the leader of the hiveless clan Bwyl stood staring down at his whimpering human counterpart. "This is all your fault. If you people had not come here, all would have gone as planned. Everything would have transpired as set down in the burrow layout."

"You're out of your deranged bug mind!" Skettle tried to stand on his broken right leg, only to have it collapse beneath him.

"You betrayed us." Beskodnebwyl was quietly implacable. "Your clumsiness revealed our presence to the local authorities."

"Us!" Unable to walk or even to rise, Skettle was reduced to glaring murderously at his tormentor. "Our security was airtight! My people were, to an individual, highly trained and motivated. There were no breaches of security on our part. Somehow, someone from outside must have learned of our presence here. I am not accusing your kind directly, but—" He broke off unexpectedly.

An impatient Beskodnebwyl prodded the severely injured human with a foothand. "What now, *srrlkpp?* Finish your thought before I kill you."

Skettle said nothing, but instead continued to stare. He was looking not at his antagonist, but past him. Following his gaze—a simpler matter with humans than with thranx, Beskodnebwyl reflected—the Bwyl turned his head in the same direction to find himself gazing at the two beings who were still standing, hands held inoffensively in front of them. At the two padres. Theologians, by their dress and demeanor. Upholders of misplaced virtue and the wrong right. That by itself was not enough to condemn them.

Their presence among the dead and wounded police, however, was rather more suggestive.

"Yes, I will kill them," the Bwyl finally declared. "It may be that they are not responsible for this failure. But I am no longer willing to take chances, and what compassion remained within my upper gut has died along with my friends and companions."

Skettle spoke through pain-clenched teeth. "About time you came to your senses. We can still activate the explosive, still reduce this squalid convocation to pandemonium. Still accomplish many if not all of our goals here." He extended a hand upward. "Help me to finish this."

"I surely will do that," Beskodnebwyl agreed. Raising the muzzle of his pistol, he placed it against the top of the injured human's skull. Briann flinched inwardly, having already seen what the weapon could do to solid bone.

Screaming at the top of her lungs, Martine burst from the corridor behind the two padres, rushed past them, and brought the cylinder of explosive she had been carrying down with great force. The police trackers had never singled her out since she was carrying only the cylinder and not a weapon. Espying her charge without having to turn, Beskodnebwyl calmly fired in the wildly onrushing biped's direction.

The sonic burst struck the curved cylinder and glanced off, causing her to stumble but not to slow her mad charge. Before the startled Bwyl could get off a second shot, she brought the cylinder down on his V-shaped head as hard as she could. There was a loud, sickening sound as the insectoid skull was split. Blood and internal fluids gushed forth in a green fountain as the open circulatory system was ruptured. Falling sideways, Beskodnebwyl fired one last time. Too close to dodge, the woman caught the burst square in her chest. Fragments of shattered sternum were blown into her lungs and heart.

Briann immediately started to reach for his own concealed handgun, only to find himself restrained by his companion. Turning, he saw that Twikanrozex was pointing with both truhands.

Using both arms, a determined Skettle had levered himself into position to reach for and activate the cylinder of explosive. Neither padre knew what the slim bottle contained, but if it was worth this many lives to attach it to the appropriate instrumentation, then its contents would surely do the crowds of unsuspecting visitors who were presently thronging the fair no good.

Nor was there time to call in a warning. As Twikanrozex let go of his friend's arm and rushed forward, Briann was right behind him. The biped's greater speed over a short distance enabled the human to reach Skettle and the open panel at exactly the same time as his multilimbed companion.

Cursing defiance, Skettle mustered one last supreme effort. Pulling his useless lower body upright, he threw himself forward. Both hands latched onto the cylinder, one gripping it for support while the other stabbed at the softly blinking contact that would activate its contents. At almost the same instant, the leaping, stridulating Twikanrozex struck the larger biped with all six feet, knocking him away from the exposed instrumentation. Briann launched himself at the cylinder, grabbed hold, and twisted, throwing his whole body into the maneuver. The tough sealant that had been incorporated by the deceased engineer Botha to hold the cylinder against the panel's interior snapped beneath the padre's weight an instant after the desperate Skettle succeeded in activating it.

There was supposed to be a delay of several minutes between activation and detonation to allow the bearer enough time to escape the blast perimeter. Perspicacious terrorist that he was, however, the recently demised Botha had assumed that once the cylinders of liquid explosive were emplaced, the only individuals interested in removing them would be representatives of the unwelcome authorities. He had therefore rigged the cylinders' triggers to bypass the programmed time lapse in the event of early dislodging.

A frantic Skettle was in the process of trying to deliver himself of this explanation when the cylinder Briann and Twikanrozex were conveying as rapidly as possible toward the exit supplied its own clarification.

Explosively.

21

It was a locality Lyrkenparmew never expected to have to visit. It was not necessary that he do so now. Through the highly covert channels that were open to him, he could have requested that the individual in question return to meet with him, instead of him going to see her. But upon learning the details of what had happened, and knowing the suffering she had already endured on behalf of their mutual interests, he felt it was incumbent upon him to repay the honors.

Which was why he found himself, bundled and shivering beneath an overcast sky, walking slowly through an open, neatly tended garden asprout with vegetables so alien in shape and coloring he felt he might have fallen into the proverbial pupae land of psychedelic metamorphosis. At the moment, there was only one biped tending to the fantastic, exotic growths. She did so for purposes of therapy, he had been informed. What benefit there was to be gained from attending to an excrescence the shade and shape of a *gorn!eyak* he could not imagine. Just looking at it threatened to upset both his stomachs.

Fanielle glanced up at his approach. Rising, she wiped sweat from her forehead and dirt from her gloved hands. It was a pleasant, cool day, but the thranx envoy was obviously uncomfortable.

"No, *yrr!kk,*" he replied when she suggested they go inside. "It is cold out here, but private. Let your friends think we are discussing the merits of rehabilitative agriculture." He searched her face, trying to apply what knowledge he had acquired of the multiple meanings conveyable by the wonderfully flexible human countenance. Insofar as he could tell, he detected there neither fear nor permanent damage. "I have seen the official report dealing with your unfortunate encounter. While vacationing outside Daret you were accosted by fanatical adherents of a xenophobically antihuman sect called the Bwyl. You fled, were chased, and were rescued by local peace patrollers called by the staff of the retreat, whereupon you lapsed into unconsciousness." His tone was candidly solicitous. "You suffered no permanent scarring, physical or psychological?"

She managed a thin smile. "I retain my fondness for your people, if that's what you mean. Physically, I'm fine." Her expression shifted as unpredictably as the low clouds overhead. A captivated Lyrkenparmew looked closer.

"Fascinating. There appears to be saline fluid leaking from the sockets in which your optics reside."

Reaching up, she wiped at her eyes with the back of one hand. The gesture rubbed a few grains of Hivehom soil into one eye, which resulted in an increased flow of the liquid to which her visitor referred. While the agent looked on, she fought to regain control of her emotions.

"It's an involuntary expression of remorse," she explained, seeking refuge in biology. "Analogous to certain of your sorrowing gestures. We call it *crying*. I'm crying for Haflunormet."

"A credit to his hive, his clan, and his family." Lyrkenparmew gestured appropriate melancholy. "Much merit did he bring to them."

"You have no idea." Putting down the nitrogen fixer, she settled herself into a sitting position alongside the cucumbers. They thrived in the clean air and fine soil of the Mediterranea Plateau, hundreds of parsecs from home. Responding to her action, Lyrkenparmew folded his legs beneath him and settled on the ventral side of his abdomen. She gazed evenly at her visitor.

"What do you know about a human outpost world called Comagrave?"

The agent gestured emphatically. "Until just recently, *viyyrp*, very little. A small outpost world undergoing explo-

ration by your kind. Apparently, some serious unpleasant-
ness occurred there recently that resulted in the expulsion
of all transient AAnn on the planet." His next gesture probably should not have been translated, but Fanielle recognized
it anyway. "I can't say that I, or anyone else in my section, is
disappointed by the news. There was talk of a massacre
perpetrated by the AAnn at a scientific site of considerable
importance."

She nodded slowly, enveloped by the atavistic, loamy musk
of freshly turned earth. Something black and slinky slithered
through the dirt by her legs. Convergent evolution in earth-
worms, she thought as she watched its oily progress: refuge
for a mind overwhelmed by clashes on a galactic scale. Ne-
matodes crawling near her toes.

I'm getting silly, she told herself firmly, and this visit is
serious.

"There's more to it than that. Much more." A glance
showed that they were alone, and the device she was wearing
beneath her gardening dress would ensure their privacy from
any stray electronic pickups. "Haflunormet found out about
it. In a way, that information contributed to his death. He had
just finished telling me the details when we were attacked."

Lyrkenparmew gestured second-degree empathy swirled
with intense curiosity. "Details of the incident were even then
common knowledge. What about it was there that could
prompt a violent assault on your persons, even by extreme
xenophobes?"

She considered how best to tell him. "Insofar as Haflunormet was able to determine from the available records, the
AAnn on Comagrave had no intention of attacking the archeological dig. Haflunormet became convinced they were provoked into doing so."

Unlike humans, Lyrkenparmew could not frown. But at the
moment, he wished he could. It was so much more econom-
ical than waving one's limbs about. "Provoked? By whom?"

"By a resident thranx exoarcheologist named Pilwondepat."
At the agent's gesture of disbelief, she added, "Haflunormet
found proof. Enough to convince the skeptical. I don't know

where it is now, or how he stored it, but without the requisite commands I'm sure it would be extremely difficult to recover." She put her fixer aside and pushed back the brim of her shade hat. "However, from the details he gave me, I'm sure that *I* could reconstruct the necessary evidence."

Lyrkenparmew was silent for a while, trying to comprehend the magnitude of what the human female had told him. If true in all details, it was an exceedingly dangerous bundle of knowledge. He eyed the biped closely. He liked a majority of humans, and this one more than most. Besides, she was *Bryn'ji!*. All of which, notwithstanding, did not prevent him from contemplating how best he might execute her and still slip away from the human outpost unnoticed.

No, that would not be necessary, he told himself. If she had intended to release the information, she would already have done so. And, she certainly wouldn't be sitting there in the dirt, relating it to someone she knew was likely to kill her to prevent its release. It was sufficient to reaffirm what he already knew: They were of different body, but like mind.

"If the substance of Haflunormet's report was to achieve general dissemination, it would rejuvenate human-AAnn relations while severely impacting those between your kind and mine." Feathery antennae waved gently. "I need not tell you that those are presently entering a most sensitive stage."

"No, you need not." Idly, she contemplated an incipient radish. "We want the same thing, Lyrkenparmew. You, I, poor Haflunormet, everyone who has worked so hard and for so long to achieve our final goal." Picking up a handful of alien earth, she let it trickle out between her dirt-smudged fingers. "But we might not have any choice. We may have to release the information and try to spin it as best we can."

"Why in the name of the Eight Original Great Hives would we want to do that?" Lyrkenparmew's disbelief was plain to see in his flowing gestures.

She swallowed hard. "Because others besides myself know the truth of what happened on Comagrave. Those xenophobes who attacked me and Haflunormet, who call themselves the hiveless clan Bwyl, are still in custody. I know—I've checked.

But they have been allowed outside communication. I don't think there's any question but that they've passed the general thrust of Haflunormet's story, which they overheard that day on the lookout at the retreat, along to others of their kind." Her expression was stricken. "It's too late, Lyrkenparmew. Too late. By now the Bwyl have spread it to all their branches, possibly even off Hivehom. So you see, we can't bury it. All we can do is try to preempt their disclosure."

Lyrkenparmew considered a moment before gesturing with both right hands. "Is that what is worrying you so? Let them disclose all they want. Their story will not be believed."

"You don't understand." Full of regret for the consequences she knew would ensue the instant the story reached the unrestricted media, she looked at him intently. "Details can be researched, traced, unearthed. The truth can be reconstructed. Slowly, perhaps, but when the Bwyl release their version of what happened on Comagrave, some dedicated pundit oblivious to the consequences will find it intriguing enough to pursue."

"*Girritt,* that might have been the case a month or two ago, but no longer." The four delicate manipulative digits of a truhand reached out to brush against her forearm. "You haven't heard about what happened yesterday on Dawn?"

"Dawn?" Her expression twisted. "What has that colony got to do with what happened on Comagrave?"

"Directly, nothing. Coincidentally, perhaps quite a good deal." He gestured meaningful apology. "The details will not arrive through regular diplomatic channels until tomorrow morning, but I could not be certain of what you knew and what you did not without asking." He gestured meaningfully. "Our mutual confidants have their own sources. Because of what happened on Dawn, the Bwyl can now spew any tales they like. Whatever their superficial veracity, they will not be believed. Dawn has destroyed their credibility as a responsible clan. Anything they choose to say from now on will be regarded as a fabrication."

Fanielle mined her memory. "I remember reading something about Dawn recently. The usual mundane fodder that those of us in the diplomatic service are expected to assimilate. Wasn't some kind of elaborate seminar or multispecies conclave going to be held there?"

"You are scurrying down the right burrow, but to the wrong destination," he corrected her with utmost finesse. "The term you are seeking in Low Thranx is *drim!!ata*."

"Oh, that's right." She remembered now. "A fair. Something to promote interspecies harmony and understanding while hopefully making a little money on the side. It was to be quite a production, I recall now. The locals were putting everything they could muster into the effort, hoping it would raise their profile on the colonial scene. Planetary promotion, investment opportunities, tourism—that sort of thing."

Lyrkenparmew gesticulated sharp irony. "If it was attention they were seeking, they more than achieved their objective. But not for the reasons you might think." Emphasizing the importance of what he was about to say, he switched seamlessly to speaking in High Thranx. "Fan'l Anju, this has been an eventful succession of correlative time-parts. It seems that elements of the very same renegade clan that attacked you and Haflunormet at the Retreat of Xer!kex planned to disrupt this fair, setting off bombs and shooting visitors indiscriminately. By coincidence, the identical notion appears to have appealed to a group of similarly xenophobic humans who call themselves *the Preservers*." He gestured confusion. "I am always astonished at the organizations and individuals formed to promote destruction who identify themselves with names like *Preserver*, or *Savior*, or *Rescuer*, and the like.

"Unaware at first of each other's existence and aims, these two groups apparently learned of their parallel intentions and presence sometime before attempting to carry them out. The scheme propounded by the human group was particularly insidious." He leaned toward her, bowing slightly from his thorax.

"That both of these antisocial organizations were found out and reported just in time for the domestic patrollers to prevent widespread disaster was due to the good work and intervention of a pair of theologians, or padres as they call themselves, who notified the local authorities. As a consequence, many hundreds of lives were saved and a diplomatic disaster was averted." Lyrkenparmew executed a gesture involving his entire upper body that Fanielle recognized as indicative of extreme regret. "Unfortunately, both of these heroic ecclesiastics perished in the course of the operation."

"That's too bad," she remarked sincerely.

"For them, yes. And personally, I would prefer they had survived." He straightened. "But since they did not, their unintentional sacrifice, combined with the debacle on Comagrave that has been ascribed to the AAnn, presents us with an exceptional opportunity."

She rested her hands in her lap. "I don't follow you, Lyrkenparmew."

Compound eyes glittered in the sun as the envoy drew his protective warming garments tighter around him. "One of these ill-starred padres was thranx. His companion was human. Don't you see? Thranx and human give their lives to save humans and thranx." He gestured first-degree significance. "The cause of unification has, inadvertently, acquired its first martyrs."

She considered the possibilities. They were striking. "Did they intend to become martyrs, these two?"

"Most probably not, but it will not matter to the general media that serve both our kind. Among humans, they will be remembered as having given their lives to save babies and innocents. Among my people, they will be thought of as two brave soldiers who sacrificed their bodies to seal a critical opening into a vulnerable burrow. It comes to the same thing. A report filed by two human patrollers who barely survived the final encounter corroborates the details of the matter." He gestured diffidently.

"The fringe belief system to which this pair belonged calls itself the United Church. A grandiose appellation, *crrk!k,* for so modest an organization—though I am told it is gaining adherents at a surprisingly rapid rate. Despite the fact that the sacrifice of their two disciples on Dawn will bring them a considerable amount of beneficial publicity, the leaders of this religious order interestingly want nothing to do with the promoting of it. They are sorry for the death of two of their own, but their doctrine apparently does not believe in or sanction the concept of martyrdom. They say there is no future in it.

"As long as they don't directly oppose our efforts to promote or make use of this sacrifice, be it intentional or otherwise, their indifference won't affect the results." Much intrigued by everything Lyrkenparmew had told her, Fanielle's active brain was starting to rev with possibilities. "And with the Bwyl utterly discredited, as you point out, by their actions, Haflunormet's investigation of the events on Comagrave becomes just one more apocryphal rant against closer cooperation." For the first time in many days, a smile began to spread across her suntanned countenance.

"This is wonderful!"

"Yes, *ri!t,* wonderful it is, Fan'l." Moving closer, he extended his b-thorax in order to be able to reach and caress her forehead with both antennae. The touch was so light as to be nearly imperceptible. "I have been in frantic consultation with our supporters inside the Great Hive. They agree that now is the time to make an all-out push for amalgamation. Our supporters on Earth concur. A formal recommendation based on our earlier proposals is to be made in your government sometime during the Second Season of Gathering, when the publicity from the incidents on Dawn and Comagrave is predicted to have achieved maximum visibility. Both political efforts will be closely coordinated."

She was nodding understandingly, her face lit by rising excitement. "I'll do everything I can to help from my circumscribed position, of course."

"It may not be so circumscribed as you think. You are to be elevated in status. Raised to a higher level of significance within your profession."

She eyed the insectoid uncertainly. "I've heard nothing about a promotion."

"Sources," the thranx explained with admirable tact. "Do

not reject the advancement. It will be useful to our mutual interests."

"Of course," she told him. Reaching over, she plucked a carrot from a row of green sprouts and showed it to the agent. "You can digest some of our food just as we can eat some of yours, so long as it's plant-derived. Have you ever had a carrot? Fresh grown. From my own little patch here." She extended the vegetable.

Taking it in his truhands, Lyrkenparmew inspected the yellow spike uncertainly. "How does one eat it?"

"Raw or cooked. Your mandibles will have no trouble with it. Go on," she urged him. "Try it. I know its composition lies well within the tolerances of your internal chemistry. I wouldn't offer it to you otherwise. Break off the root first and eat it from the bottom."

Hesitantly, the agent followed her instructions. Placing the end of the carrot between his mandibles, he bit down with all four, snapping off a piece between them. Having nothing to chew with, he had to wait for it to make the journey to his upper, grinding gut. The release of exotic, alien juices followed.

"That is . . . delightful," he finally was able to tell her. "A c'rt, you called it?"

"Carrot," she corrected him. If she could learn the two principal thranx dialects, then the agent could master Terranglo. Although *c'rt* had a nice, succinct ring to it. Perhaps the word could be compromised. Another addition to that strange multispecies patois its adherents were calling symbospeech, she decided absently.

"Whether it wants to or not, this United Church is going to gain a number of new followers as a result of all the fanfare. I suppose I'm going to have to study up on it further in case I'm asked to comment." She let out a resigned sigh. "These faddish creeds come and go, especially in an era of galactic exploration."

"Yes," Lyrkenparmew agreed. "Such caprices are common among the thranx as well. The great majority are inevitably defined by their transitory nature. I'm sure that when the incident on Dawn becomes part of the public memory as opposed

to an item of current interest, the same fate will befall this
sect as well."

She nodded as she fondly surveyed the rest of the garden.
"It certainly sounds like an eccentric little philosophy. Maybe
there will at least be a laugh or two to be had from looking
into it."

"Hopefully," Lyrkenparmew added. "For professional reasons only, of course."

"Of course," she agreed. "What else?"

From above, the benign sun of Hivehom shone down on
their friendship, on the little garden in the diplomat compound, on the rest of the human settlement called Azerick,
and on the dawning of a great many unknown but exhila-
rating possibilities that were fraught with promise.

22

Lord Naasab IV was brooding in the gallery when Eiipul II approached him. Below, the magnificent Great Hall of the People, the center of Blassussar and the locus of the Empire, was clearing out, the crowd of notables apportioning a babble of hissing conversation in their wake. The emperor himself had long since departed, leaving his constituents in the form of their representative nobles to debate and discuss any remaining business. It was the business that was not resolved, that could not be resolved, that troubled Naasab and left him pensive and ill at ease in mind and belly.

A gesture of greeting from Eiipul indicated that his fellow peer felt similarly. As if to further confirm his visitor's mindset, one pair of eyelids remained half closed as he spoke.

"I fear, *rssst*, that regarding a certain matter too many of our colleaguess refusse to pull their headss out of the ssand."

Naasab was glad to see that, if nothing else, he was not alone in his concern. "We sspeak of the ssame certain matter, I am ssure."

Eiipul gestured second-degree concurrence. "Many feel there iss nothing more we can do, yet we cannot jusst ssprawl idly asside and concede to the inexorable. My family did not reach itss pinnacle of prominence by ssquatting alongsside the water hollowss and watching otherss catch the swimmerss."

His counterpart gestured almost impertinently. Eiipul forgave the discourtesy because he understood Naasab's distress. It was no less than his own.

"Let the otherss vacillate and fight with wordss if that iss all they can do. The emperor iss no fool. If we can proposse a

311

coursse of action, he will ssee that it iss implemented. What ideass have you?"

Eiipul slapped his stomach with the tip of his tail, a sharp, smacking sound that did not travel far in the enormous, gold-toned gathering chamber. "Nothing sspecific, *gtssk*. As you know, I am on the committee that iss trying to undersstand what happened on Vussissica. We have yet to ressolve the many contradicting reportss. Thuss far the one point that everyone can agree upon iss that it hass been a complete and utter diplomatic dissaster. Chasstissement sshould already have been meted out, but no one can agree on who iss ressponssible for what. In every asspect, a truly unssettling epissode."

Naasab gestured agreement, rapidly blinking both sets of double eyelids. "My concern liess more with our notable failure on the disstant human world they call Dawn. A continuing run of bad luck. If not for the intervention of the two sstupid sspiritualisstss, all might have gone as planned. Now, that enterprisse alsso liess in ruinss." In his anger, he parted his jaws to show his tongue as well as all his teeth. "The combined effect of thesse two recent dissasters hass been to bring the bugss and the ssoftsskinss much closser together insstead of driving them apart, as we dessired."

Moving to the edge of the overlook, Eiipul gazed down at the now nearly empty gathering chamber. Glorious episodes from the history of the AAnn—from the race's humble beginnings as barely organized bands fighting for control of herds in the plains of Blassussar, to the wars of unification eventually won by Keisscha the First, to the rapid rise of technology and the eventual expansion of the Empire to other worlds—lined the walls in the form of mosaics fashioned from gemstones and rare metals. Strong light illuminated every corner of the impressive hall, and the sand that formed the floor was fashioned of specially ground synthetic corundum that gave it the appearance of a single multifaceted jewel. The dais where the emperor sat was as empty as the rows of individual reporting stations, and no informative holos floated free in the dry, heated air.

"Doess a closser union of the two lesser sspeciess really

pose ssuch a threat? Are we perhapss not overreacting, my friend, and thosse of our compeerss who have jusst departed are the oness in the right?"

Naasab gcsturcd his unhappiness. Was he about to lose his strongest ally among the members of the Imperial Gathering? "No one sshould forget what happened to the Pitar."

"That sspeciess received what they desserved. I wass never comfortable conssidering them as alliess. An unsstable race."

"Agreed. And now they are no more—thankss to the effortss of humanss and thranx fighting together. My greatesst fear, my friend, iss that thesse two sspeciess cojoined may ressult in ssomething far more powerful than the ssum of their individual partss."

"I, too, am concerned, as you know. But it may be that this proposed union of theirss, thiss Commonwealth, will be like a human mating: the living together more contentiouss than the courtsship."

Naasab gestured admiration for his counterpart's knowledge. He would not have suspected that the quiet Eiipul might be the master of arcane alien erudition. It was often the quiet ones, he reflected, who hid in the sand to spring on the unwary from behind. Henceforth, he would measure his comments with more care lest he reveal something that in the future might prove personally damaging. Eiipul would do no less, he knew. By such means did the ever-competitive AAnn acquire status and gain advancement. For the moment, however, the truce relationship between them was sound. As lords of the Empire, they could advance no farther—at least until the emperor began to show signs of mental or physical weakness.

"What of our dissappointing ssupporterss among the humanss?" Eiipul was asking.

Naasab hissed resignedly. "Many dead or captured on thiss Dawn world. Not all, I am told, but enough to prevent them from attempting anything ssimilar in the immediate future. I have taken sstepss to ssee to it that their organization continuess to receive the necessary funds to susstain them. They will go to ground until the furor over the incident on Dawn hass died down, then attempt to ressume their activitiess on our behalf. As for their thranx equivalentss, you know that we have no influence among them. No bug will accept assisstance from an AAnn. That doess not mean they will not be usseful to uss in the future; only that we will, as alwayss, have no control over their actionss."

Eiipul gestured understanding. Though he had much work to do, he continued to linger. Naasab always had interesting information to impart, and it was always good to know what so resourceful a rival was up to. Besides which, they shared many similar interests.

"If thiss union comess about, we will ssimply have to deal with it. It doess not pressage the end of our expanssion. Nothing can prevent that."

"Truly," Naasab agreed, adding a gesture of first-degree assent. "But it could make eassy thingss difficult, and ssimple undertakingss complex. Better to avoid complication where possible. It certainly would make harder bringing the obsstinate bugss to heel."

"You will ssee." Eiipul wished to depart on a positive note. "The bugss and the humanss will not get along. They are too different, far more sso than the humanss and oursselvess. Even if it should come to pass, this Commonwealth will collapsse of itss own inherent contradictionss. I am confident in that."

Wellness for you, Naasab thought. He wondered if he would live long enough to see Eiipul's prediction come to pass. He hoped so, because he sincerely feared the consequences for the Empire if it did not.

Truly, *fsssst* . . .

There was so much to do. Integrating colonies was one thing. Merging two entirely different political and social systems developed over thousands of years by two very different species reduced the complexities of the former task to insignificance.

Ordinary folk on both sides would notice no change for some time. Average citizens did not travel between worlds, did not participate in interstellar commerce or politics, and cared little for anything beyond the realm of their daily lives that did not impact on them directly. Politicians would be affected, and business folk, and of course the military. The latter would have perhaps the easiest time of it. Not only did warriors of different species possess an innate understanding of a profession whose basic tenets did not vary widely because of mere shape, but they had already cooperated closely with one another during the Pitarian War.

Changes would first manifest themselves in the largest, most cosmicpolitan cities. Humans would be able to move freely through the teeming thranx burrows, while their eight-limbed counterparts would no longer be restricted to a few specific locations on Earth and a couple of its more populous colonies. Without endless inspections and dozens of restrictions, trade would expand exponentially. Cultural exchanges of the kind that had taken place on the world of Dawn could proceed without reams of government paperwork, on scales both larger and more intimate. Integration did not happen overnight, but happen it would.

The announcement of the impending unification was greeted, except by those who had opposed it for so long, with a mixture of excitement, anticipation, and uncertainty. Since nothing like it had ever been tried before, no one was quite sure how it was going to work, or what would happen from day to day. But both sides went at it with a will.

The Terran government proceeded to orchestrate a number of grandiose celebrations, with the largest taking place in or near the most impressive cities; more modest festivities were contrived for smaller conurbations, and local demonstrations occupied the time and attention of towns and country. Among the thranx, the occasion was marked by congratulations on a much more individual and personal level, following which everyone went back to work. Above it all hovered a feeling of general satisfaction: The thranx had gotten what they wanted, and the humans what they needed.

After weeks of speeches, parades, demonstrations, fireworks, feasts, gatherings in stellar locations both astonishing and ordinary by the starships of both civilizations, hours of

reciprocal programming by the media of both species, end-
lessly repetitive programs of the Why This Is Good For You
kind, debates both tumultuous and politic, and a good deal of
soul-searching among ordinary citizens, the public at large of
both species discovered something else they had in common:
the ability to rapidly get fed up with self-appointed experts
and so-called specialists and zealous politicians who were
determined to tell them what they should be doing and why.
So when the time arrived to actually formalize the unification
instead of simply praise or weigh it, the actual event came as
something of a blissful anticlimax that was ignored by most
folk, who were busy getting on with their lives.

The site chosen for the signing of the Articles of Amalgamation was as grand as the canyon after which it was named.
Not far from the small amphitheater chosen for the official
ceremony, moving walkways suspended from spidery sup-
ports carried a steady stream of tourists from the rim and its
spectacular perspective to the surging, ice-cold river at the
bottom. Most were intent on the scenery and took no notice
of the cluster of diplomats and media reporters milling about
nearby. A few thranx, Fanielle noted with satisfaction, were
among the continuous stream of gawkers descending into the
ancient depths carved by the river. In the heat of midafternoon they needed no supplemental attire, though each wore a
compact humidifier over their breathing spicules. Of such in-
cremental developments as mutual enjoyment of time's won-
ders were unbreakable bonds forged.

Stuck near the back of the gathering, but fortunate to have
acquired an invitation at that, she listened with interest to the
speeches whose brevity belied their significance. One by one,
the various human and thranx dignitaries mounted the temporary dais, their physiques if not their words much reduced
in perspective by the immense red rock panorama that filled
the horizon behind them. The ritual could as well have taken
place on Hivehom, she knew, or some neutral world, but the
thranx had deferred to the wishes of their new human conso-
ciates. Though equally as fond of pomp and ritual as the bipeds,
albeit on a much reduced scale, they were understanding when

their mammalian counterparts asked if the first signing could be held on Earth. A second, equivalent ceremony would take place later in the high ceremonial burrows of Hivehom.

That kind of understanding, she reflected, was not only what was going to go a long way toward making the new union work, it was something the pysch techs insisted humankind had lacked, and had been looking for, ever since the species had first come down from the trees millennia ago.

Eventually the speech making, with its simultaneous translation, lurched to an end. Formal documents were signed, and initialed, and signed again, until there was no more room on paper or plastic for markings of the duly appointed representatives of either species. As each was completed, holos of the actual documents appeared in the air before the audience. These were broadcast to watchers whose distance from the site could sometimes be measured in kilometers and sometimes in parsecs. As each instrument was completed, it was simultaneously rendered in blocks of polished marble and sheets of anodized titanium that would more readily memorialize the gravity of the occasion.

When it was over, there was much gratified shaking of hands and touching of antennae. Fanielle was particularly struck by the moment when the current head of the United Church, the Fourth Last Resort David Malkezinski, grasped a truhand of the venerable Tri-eint Arlenduva while her antennae dipped forward to make contact with his forehead. Far from vanishing as she had once imagined it would, the still-evolving creed founded by a human minister and his thranx counterpart had continued to expand, swiftly gaining new adherents among human and thranx alike. If anything, its overall influence with the public at large had expanded even faster.

Counted among its followers was the diplomat Fanielle Anjou, recently promoted to assistant councilor for human affairs on Hivehom. It was about as significant a post as there was to be had in the rapidly reorganizing and consolidating governments.

As she stood chatting with friends and associates, doing

her best to avoid the media, a small hand tugged at her arm. Eric Haf-Lyr Anjou looked up at her out of alert, anxious eyes that were largely indifferent to the import of the ceremony that had just concluded.

"Mom, Mom—Barehtezen and Jacque want to hike down to Indian Gardens. Can I go? Can I? Hey, did you know she smells like apple blossoms?"

She smiled down at him. "Of course you can go, Eric. Just make sure you and Jacque keep a close eye on Bar. There are plenty of fountains along the trail, and she'll adore the fact that it gets hotter the deeper you descend, but you know how quickly thranx can parch in this climate." She indicated the high, dry mountain country where they were standing.

"Aw, she'll be all right. She's wearing her humidifier, and she promised to use all six legs at all times, even on the easy parts."

"Make sure she keeps hydrated. Have a good time, and be back up here before six." She checked her chronometer. "We have to get up early tomorrow to catch the transit to the shuttleport."

He nodded, his words lost in the crowd as he yelled back at her while racing off in the opposite direction. "I know. I can't wait to get back to the burrow!"

Kids, she thought. Progeny. Offspring, with the emphasis on *spring*. Waking up to a new universe every day. Only tomorrow, it would be more than an aphorism. It would be for real. She wondered how it would all work out: the amalgamating of two radically different species, an unprecedented fusion of arthropod and anthropoid. Nothing like it had ever been attempted in the portion of the galaxy humankind had come to know. Just how close, how intimate could it become? Would the old adage "Don't let the bedbugs bite" come to take on an entirely new meaning? Or would it lead to, if not a golden age for humankind, at least a more settled and confident one?

She was wandering, she knew, and when she let her mind wander, her thoughts inevitably degenerated into flippancy. She wished she could live another couple of hundred years or so, long enough for any lasting doubts to be resolved. That was not possible. She let out a regretful sigh. We're too transitory, she mused. We don't live long enough to really learn anything. I need another five centuries.

It was not to be. Flesh is not so accommodating, and we all of us die just when we've acquired the minimum necessary wisdom to graduate the first grade. The universe belonged to her son now. To him, and to his new friends, even if they did have two extra sets of limbs, bulging eyes, and feathery stalks growing out of their foreheads.

To the universe of the Commonwealth.

Read on for a sneak peek at the next exciting novel
by Alan Dean Foster,

Drowning World

Available in hardcover from Del Rey Books.

Jemunu-jah didn't want to have to take the time to rescue
the human. If it was foolish enough to go off into the Viisiiviisii all by itself, then it deserved whatever happened to it.
Kenkeru-jah had argued that it was their *mula* to try to save
the visitor, even if it was not spawned of the Sakuntala. As he
was ranking chief of the local Nuy clan, his opinion was listened to and respected.

Jemunu-jah suspected that the much-admired High Chief
Naneci-tok would also have argued vociferously against the
decision to send him, but she was still in transit from an important meeting of fellow Hatas and was not present to
countermand the directive. As for the war chief Aniolo-jat,
he did not seem to care one way or the other where Jemunu-
jah was sent. Not that the cunning Hata-yuiqueru felt anything for the missing human, either. All the war chief wanted,
as usual, was to conserve clan energies for killing Deyzara.

Perhaps it was Jemunu-jah's cheerless expression that
caused the two Deyzara passing him on the walkway to edge
as far away as they could without tumbling right over the
flexible railing. The speaking/breathing trunk that protruded
from the top of their ovoidal hairless skulls recoiled back
against the edges of their flat-brimmed rain hats, and the
secondary eating trunks that hung from the underside, or
chin region, of their heads twitched nervously. Their large,
protuberant, close-set eyes nervously tracked him from behind their visors. Another time, Jemunu-jah might have found
their excessive caution amusing. Not today.

He supposed Kenkeru-jah was right. Chiefs usually were.

But for the life of him, he could not understand how the death of a missing human, and a self-demonstrably reckless one at that, could affect the clan's *mula*. But the chief had made a decision. As a result, he now found himself directed to present himself to the female in charge of the human community on Fluva. Since Lauren Matthias's status was equivalent to that of a senior Hata, or High Chief of the Sakuntala, Jemunu-jah would be obliged to put his own feelings aside while showing her proper respect. He smoothed his long stride. Actually, he ought to be proud. He had been selected as a representative of his people, the best that Taulau Town had to offer. But if given a choice, he would gladly have declined the honor.

At slightly under two meters tall and a wiry eighty kilos, he was of average height and weight for a mature male Sakuntala. Though smaller than those of a Deyzara, his eyes provided vision that was substantially more acute. From the sides of his head the base of his flexible pointed ears extended out sideways for several centimeters before curving sharply upward to end in tufted points. The outer timpanic membrane that kept rain from entering his right ear was in the process of renewing itself, slowly being replaced by a new one growing in behind it. As a result, the hearing on his right side was at present slightly diminished. It would stay that way for another day or two, he knew, until the old membrane had completely disintegrated and the new one had asserted itself.

His short, soft fur was light gray with splotches of black and umber. The pattern identified an individual Sakuntala as sharply and distinctly as any of the artificial identity devices the humans carried around with them. In that respect he felt sorry for the humans. Despite some slight differences in skin color, it was often very difficult to tell one from another.

His cheek sacs bulged, one with the coiled, whiplike tongue that was almost as long as his body, the other with a gobbet of khopo sap he alternately chewed and sucked. Today's helping was flavored with gesagine and apple, the latter a flavor introduced by the humans that had found much favor among the Sakuntala. He wore old-style strappings around his waist to shield his privates, while the bands of dark blue synthetics that crisscrossed his chest were of off-world manufacture. Attached to both sets of straps were a variety of items both traditional and modern, the latter purchased from the town shops with credit he had earned from providing services to various human and Deyzara enterprises.

Now it seemed that despite his reluctance he was about to provide one more such service. Despite the prospect of acquiring *mula* as well as credit, he would just as soon have seen the task given to another. But Kenkeru-jah had been adamant. He was as stuck with the assignment as a kroun that had been crammed into the crook of a drowning sabel-bap tree.

Raindrops slid off his transparent eyelids as he glanced upward. Not much precipitation today: barely a digit's worth. Of course, it had rained very heavily yesterday. Clouds, like individuals, needed time to replenish themselves. The fact that it rained every day on most of Fluva seemed to be a source of some amusement to newly arrived humans. Once they had been stuck on Fluva for about a season, however, Jemunu-jah had observed, the weather rapidly ceased to be a source of humor for the bald visitors.

Well, not entirely bald, he corrected himself. A fair number of humans owned at least a little fur. In that respect they were better than the Deyzara, who were truly and completely hairless.

With an easy jump, he crossed from one suspended walkway to another, saving time as he made his way through town. A few humans could duplicate such acrobatic feats but preferred not to. One spill into the water below, arms and legs flailing wildly, was usually enough to prevent them from trying to imitate the inherent agility of the tall, long-armed Sakuntala. No Deyzara would think of attempting the comparatively undemanding jump. Human children could not be prevented from trying it, though. This was allowed, since the waters beneath the town limits were netted to keep out p'forana, m'ainiki, and other predators who would delight in making a meal of any child unlucky enough to tumble into unprotected waters. That went for Sakuntala children as well as human and Deyzara, he knew. But when *they* jumped, Sakuntala youngsters only rarely missed.

The rain intensified, falling steadily, if not forcefully. Making his way through the continuous shower, he passed more Deyzara. Like the humans, the two-trunks wore an assortment of specialized outer attire intended to keep the rain from making contact with their skin. To Jemunu-jah this seemed the height of folly. For a Sakuntala, it was as natural to be wet as dry. As visitors who came and went from Fluva the humans could be excused for their reticence to move about naked beneath the rain. But the Deyzara, who had been living and working on the world of the Big Wet for hundreds of years, should have adapted better by now. For all the many generations that had passed, they still displayed a marked aversion to the unrelenting precipitation, though they had otherwise adapted well to the climate. The one month out of the year that it did not rain was their period of celebration and joy. In contrast, it was during such times that the Sakuntala tended to stay inside their houses, showering daily and striving to keep moist.

It all seemed very backward to Jemunu-jah, even though he had viewed numerous vits that showed many worlds where it rained only intermittently and some where water fell from the sky not at all. If forced to live on such a world, he knew he would shrivel up and die like a gulou nut in the cooking fire or in one of those marvelous portable cooking devices that could be bought from the humans or the Deyzara. Rain was life. There would be no flooded forest, or varzea, as the humans called it, without the rain that fell continuously for 90 percent of the year.

With the water from the many merged rivers of the varzea swirling ten meters below the suspended walkway and the surface of the land itself drowned twenty to thirty meters below that, he lifted himself up onto another crossway. This strilk-braced major avenue was strong enough to support multiple paths and was hectic with pedestrians. Humans mixed freely with Sakuntala and Deyzara, everyone intent on the business of the day. Nearby, a spinner team was busy repairing a damaged walkway, extruding the strilk that kept the town's buildings and paths suspended safely above the water. The silvery artificial fiber was attached to huge gray composite pylons that had been driven deep into the bedrock that lay far below the turbid waters and saturated soil. On the outskirts of the sprawling community a carnival of lesser structures whose owners were unable to afford pylons hung from the largest, strongest trees.

The single-story building in front of him was the administrative headquarters of the Commonwealth presence on Fluva. Jemunu-jah had been there a few times before, on official business for the greater A'Jah clan. That particular business being of lesser importance, it had not given him the opportunity to meet Lauren Matthias. He had heard that she was very good at her work, not unlike Naneci-tok, and could speak fluent S'aku. Matthias would not have to strain her larynx in his presence. His command of terranglo, he had been told, was excellent.

A single human stood guard outside the building. He looked bored, tired, and, despite his protective military attire, very, very wet. Visible beneath a flipped-up visor, his face was frozen in that faraway expression many humans acquired after they had spent a year or more on Fluva. He was nearly as tall as a Sakuntala. Drawing himself up to his full height, Jemunu-jah announced himself.

The guard seemed to respond to his presence only with great difficulty. Water ran down the human's face. It was not rainwater, as both of them were standing under the wide lip of the roof overhang that ran completely around the front and sides of the administration building. Jemunu-jah recognized the facial moisture as a phenomenon humans called perspiration. It was a condition unknown to the Sakuntala, although the Deyzara suffered from it as well.

"Limalu di," the guard mumbled apathetically. Jemunu-jah was not so far removed from the culture of his kind, nor so educated, that he did not gaze covetously at the long gun that dangled loosely from the human's left hand. A single swift snatch and he could have it, he knew. Then, a quick leap over the side of the deck into the water below, and he would be gone before the sluggish human barely knew it was missing.

With a sigh, Jemunu-jah shifted his gaze away from the highly desirable weapon, away from the ancient calling of his ancestors. He was here on clan business. He was civilized now. "I am called Jemunu-jah. I have appointment with Administrator Matthias," he responded in terranglo.

Reaching up to wipe away sweat and grime, the guard blinked uncertainly. "Appointment?"

"Appointment," the lanky gray-furred visitor repeated.

Eyeing the Sakuntala with slightly more interest, the guard tilted his head slightly to his left and spoke toward the pickup suspended there. "There's a Saki here to see Matthias. Says he has an appointment." Jemunu-jah waited patiently while the human listened to the voice that whispered from the tiny pickup clipped to his left ear.

A moment later the guard bobbed his head, a gesture Jemunu-jah knew signified acceptance among humans. Parting his lips and showing sharp teeth, he stepped past and through the momentarily deactivated electronic barrier that was designed to keep out intruders both large and small. Another door, Jemunu-jah reflected as he entered the building. Humans and Deyzara alike were very fond of doors. The Sakuntala had no use for them.

Behind him, the guard had resumed his lethargic pose, leaning back against the wall, his expression having once more gone blank as a part of him dreamed of other worlds and of the long-forgotten state of being dry. Rain fell steadily beyond the brown composite decking and overhang. A few streaks of olive green *walus* were visible on part of the porch railing. It had taken only a hundred years for several of the millions of varieties of fungus and mold that thrived on Fluva to learn how to survive on the supposedly inedible specially treated composite.

Chief Administrator Lauren Matthias had red hair, green eyes, a short and solid (but solidly attractive) build that was growing stouter with every passing year, a temper to match her contentious official position, and a desk full of worries. She had been chief Commonwealth representative and administrator on Fluva for just over a year now, ever since Charlie Sandravoe had gone nuts and been granted a hasty medical discharge. Like everyone else, she remembered the day when the well-liked Sandravoe had finally lost it, tearing off his electrostatically charged rain cape and the clothes underneath before flinging himself out the window and off the deck outside the office she now occupied. He'd fallen nearly twenty meters to the water below. Several members of the cultural staff, whose offices were in the building below Administration, had seen him plunge past the window of their workplace, arms at his sides, legs together. Maria Chen-ha had had the best look. To this day, she insisted that the face of the ex-administrator had been oddly calm.

They'd found him floating below, miraculously alive, having just missed cracking his skull on a number of intervening branches. A couple of Deyzara had fished him out of the water and brought him up. Diagnosis had been swift: mental breakdown brought on by too much time on Fluva. Sandravoe had extended his tour of duty several times, receiving a bonus for each extension. His offers had been reluctantly accepted because it was hard to find qualified personnel willing to remain on Fluva for any length of time. Besides having to adjudicate the never-ending turmoil between the Deyzara and the Sakuntala, there was also the often hostile and unpredictable flora and fauna, the interesting new diseases, the voracious molds and fungi, and of course the small and slightly disturbing fact that it rained 90 percent of the year. And the absence of dry land.

There *was* permanent dry land, Matthias knew. Up in the western mountains that ran the length of Fluva's single substantial landmass. The mountains caught the flow of moisture from the western ocean and turned it into rain. The rain fed thousands upon thousands of rivers that, for most of the year, overflowed their banks and drowned the immense tropical woodland that the moisture supported. The result was varzea, where the land lay thirty meters or so below the surface of the merged rivers. It was a morass, it was a mess, and the combination had a disconcerting tendency to drive visiting humans insane.

Not the Deyzara. Imported from Tharce IV a couple of hundred years ago, the Deyzara were well adapted to working in Fluva's sodden conditions. They thrived in its climate, working the plantations that produced dozens of highly valued botanicals and other products. Preoccupied with fighting among themselves, the native Sakuntala had accepted the Deyzara's presence from the beginning. Unfortunately, the Deyzara bred rather faster than the locals, with the result that there were now nearly as many Deyzara as long-arms. Now, a highly vocal and influential faction among the Sakuntala wanted all Deyzara off the planet.

Yet these Deyzara knew nothing of Tharce IV. Some were fourth- and even fifth-generation Fluva-born. The consequent conundrum constituted a mess and morass of a different kind. One that fell squarely in the lap of the resident administrator. Her lap. As if that weren't enough, she also had to deal with the plants and animals that were constantly evolving in their attempts to penetrate the perimeter of Taulau Town and the other tentative Commonwealth outposts that were scattered around the planet. Not to mention the problems she had with Jack and Andrea. Her husband, a plant physiologist with the Commonwealth's research and taxonomy division, seemed reasonably content lately. On the other hand, Andrea had decided last month, on the occasion of her twelfth birthday and for no discernible reason (at least, none that an adult could discern), that from then on her given name would be Fitzwinkle.

And then there was the unnerving problem of Sethwyn Case. "Sethwyn Case—always on the chase," the other women posted to Administration were fond of murmuring and sometimes of giggling. One of many independent contractors who had come to seek their fortune on Fluva, Bioprospector

Sethwyn was tall, handsome, bold, with a grin that induced uncommon tremors in parts of her that she had long thought tectonically stable. He would be gone for weeks at a time, always returning with this or that fascinating new specimen or information or, hopefully, profitable discovery.

Once he had checked in, he would always report dutifully in person to Administration. It was not necessary for him to see her to render his report, but he always did so. At such times he would grin and joke and make light of the dangers he had faced. Once or twice, he had brushed up against her. Accidentally, she chose to believe. But there was nothing accidental about that grin or what she felt she saw in his eyes. As if she didn't have enough to worry about.

And now this fool—what was his name?—she checked the hard copy. Shadrach Hasselemoga. This Hasselemoga person, another freelance bioprospector not six months arrived on Fluva, had gone and gotten himself lost in the depths of the Viisiiviisii. One more irritation to add to a list that was already far too big. It was her job, as administrator, to send someone to try to find him. Apparently, and remarkably, the man's emergency beacon had been completely destroyed or, at the least, damaged beyond repair.

She would have sent Case, but he was out somewhere in the foothills of the Varaku mountains. Jillis Noufoetan was on leave at the orbiting station, and Nicolo Manatinga had been laid up with a fever and an infection that mutated as fast as the doctors tried to isolate it. All of which meant she would have to send out a search team consisting entirely of locals. It had been done before, successfully. Staff had presented her with several possibilities, from whom she had selected a couple on intuition and recommendation of past service.

Outside, the downpour was becoming heavier, sealing off the view across the town and into the dense Viisiiviisii beyond. With a sigh and conflicting thoughts of Jack and a certain free-ranging explorer in her mind, she turned and resumed her seat behind the curving desk. Like everything else in the administration building, it was fashioned of resolutely nonbiodegradable materials.

Everything else, that is, except the people.